MW01132121

Emma Scott x

the
BOOKWORM
box

Helping the community, one book at a time

A FIVE-MINUTE LIFE

Emma Scott

A Five-Minute Life
©2019 Emma Scott Books, LLC

Cover art by Lori Jackson Design
Interior Formatting by That Formatting Lady,
https://thatformattinglady.com
Proofreading by Proofingstyle.com
Editing by Suanne Laqueur, Meanest Editor Ever™

PLAYLIST

Trampoline by SHAED (*opening credits*)
Sweet Child O' Mine by Guns N' Roses
bury a friend by Billie Eilish
Bad Romance by Lady Gaga
Black by Pearl Jam
I Will Follow You Into the Dark by Death Cab for Cutie
Dreamer by LP
Tidal Wave by Portugal. The Man
We Are Young by Fun. (feat. Janelle Monáe)
BOOM by X Ambassadors
Good Riddance (Time of Your Life) by Green Day
Beloved by Mumford & Sons
Times Like These by the Foo Fighters (*closing credits*)

DEDICATION

For Melissa. You mean more to me than I can say because you are
everything to Izzy too...

And to

My precious Talia. You light up the darkest of rooms…

A FIVE-MINUTE LIFE

PART 1

PROLOGUE

Thea
Richmond, Virginia, two years ago

My sister's voice echoed up the stairs from the foyer.

"Thea, let's *go*."

"Coming," I shouted back from my old bedroom in my parents' house.

I'd turned it into a temporary art studio while I stayed for the summer, with a tarp on the floor and an oversized canvas on an easel by the window. Delia bitched I'd only been home for three days and could I not make a mess of myself for her graduation? But not painting for three days was like asking me not to eat or breathe.

Behind me, I had Netflix running through episodes of *The Office*, the World's Best TV Show. I'd seen every one a hundred times. Mom said I was probably obsessed with it because it was like me: funny and honest and prone to cringe-worthy jokes at the worst times. Guilty as charged.

I brushed a lock of blond hair out of my eyes and wiped my hands on my linen smock. Purple and orange smears joined streaks of yellow and midnight blue. I used my fingers as well as brushes to manipulate the paint. Dad liked to tease I began finger painting as a toddler and never grew out of it.

The tarp shuffled under my bare feet as I stepped back to study the canvas. An Egyptian pyramid cast a dark shadow across gold desert sand as the sun set in swathes of twilight color.

My gaze jumped to the photo I'd taken of the real deal on our family trip to Giza last summer. I didn't know what it was about those damn pyramids—or all of Egyptian history for that matter—that fascinated me so much, but I couldn't leave the subject alone. Tombs that huge were mind-boggling to me. The Egyptians packed the pyramid's inner chambers with all the things the dead pharaoh would need for the next life.

As if they weren't dead forever but just going away for a little while.

"Like on a trip," I murmured.

"Althea, get down here *right now*," Delia shouted. "We're going to be *late*."

"It's not possible to be late if you insist we leave three hours early!" I shouted back.

I cocked my head at my work and a slow smile spread over my lips. I always let the painting decide when it was finished, and this one was done. Its colors and shapes evoked the majesty of the pyramid, the beauty of the desert, and the vastness of the sky above, exactly the way I wanted.

I took off my smock. Beneath it, I wore a silky pink dress that swirled around my knees. A quick inspection showed only a few spatters of paint at the hem.

Delia's voice whipped up at me again. "I know my graduation doesn't mean anything to you—"

"Thea, dear," my mother called up, smoothly interjecting. "Please come down now."

I gave my painting a final glance and grinned. "Not too shabby, Hughes," I murmured.

"Thea, I swear to God…"

"I'm *coming*," I said. I shut off the TV and bounded down the stairs. "By all means, let's hurry, or else we won't be able to sit around and wait for hours."

My parents—Sandra and Linden—were smartly dressed, waiting

with Delia, who was in her navy-blue graduation gown that she wore like a uniform. She smoothed an errant strand of her shoulder-length dark hair and gave me the stink-eye as I forced my feet into the low-heeled pumps she urged me to wear for the occasion.

"It's my graduation and I say when we leave," Delia said. "And what are you *wearing*?"

"Heels," I said. "But only because you're forcing me."

"I meant your dress. There's paint all over it."

"It's only a few drops. Gives it character."

Delia rolled her eyes. "You're a mess. As usual. I'm surprised you brushed your hair."

"It's a Saturday, isn't it?" I shot my dad a wink.

He winked back. "Let's go, my dears. It's an hour drive, and if we leave now, we'll be..." He pretended to check his watch. "Yes, quite early."

Delia sucked in a breath, switching on her infamous Business Mode.

"I know you think I'm crazy, but you'll thank me when we don't have to hunt for parking. It's going to be crowded and I get anxious if we run late."

"You? Anxious?" I said. "Get out of town."

"God, can you take anything seriously for once in your life?" Delia said, rounding on me. "Stop with the jokes. And when the ceremony starts, you are not to cause a scene and embarrass me."

I blinked my eyes innocently. "Whatever do you mean?"

She gave me a Delia Death Glare. "You know exactly what I mean. Nothing inappropriate."

"You're no fun."

"You're enough *fun* for the both of us."

"Truth."

My big sister was the most by-the-book gal you could hope to meet whereas I lived for the moment. Dad liked to joke that he had to take Mom's word that we were blood-related.

"We have time for a few photos," Mom said, readying her cell phone. "Squish together, girls. You too, Linden."

"You gotta get in here, Mom," I said. "Use my phone. It has a timer."

I bounced forward, opened the timer app in my phone and set it on the ledge across from our stairway. Then I bunched up with my favorite people in the world.

"We have ten seconds," I said through a smile. "Say cheese doodles."

The phone made a clicking sound. Mom took it off the shelf and checked the image.

"Perfect. You both look beautiful." Her eyes filled as she turned the camera to our dad. "Don't they look beautiful?"

Dad nodded. He hugged Delia around the shoulders. "We're so proud of you, sweetheart." He looked to me and shot me a wink. "You too, sweet pea."

Twenty-one years old and he was still calling me sweet pea. I hoped he'd never stop.

I slung an arm around Delia. "I'm proud of you too, sis. University of Virginia's salutatorian. You're kind of a big deal."

"Thank you, Thea," Delia said with the warm smile she saved for special occasions. Then she cleared her throat. Business Mode. "Can we please go *now*?"

"Yes, yes." Dad took his car keys off the hook on the wall and opened the front door with a flourish. "Ladies."

We shuffled toward the door, my feet already pinched in those silly shoes. A phone chimed in someone's bag or pocket.

"Mine," Delia said, rummaging in her purse. She read a text and clenched her teeth. "Roger's parents flaked on him. Again. He needs a ride to graduation."

"They're not going to his graduation?" I asked. "God, they are the *worst*."

The Nyes lived a few blocks down, in a house like ours, on a street as nice as ours, and yet they may as well have lived on the moon, they were so different from Mom and Dad. My parents' unfailing love and support for Delia and me made it impossible to understand how the Nyes consistently treated their son like an afterthought.

"No problem," Dad said. "We can swing by and pick him up."

Delia took her car keys off the hook now. "No, I'll drive him. You guys go."

"Honey, we have time to get him."

She shook her head. "You know how Roger is. He'll be embarrassed. It's better if I drive him."

She caught us exchanging curious glances as we always did when

4

she brought up Roger. They swore they were only friends, but they'd been inseparable since kindergarten. Only a Roger-in-need could throw my sister off her rigid schedule. Their friendship was one of the few things that brought out her softer side.

"Look," she said. "Driving with us will only make Roger feel even shittier. He'll have to watch Mom and Dad be perfect together minutes after his parents let him down again."

"If you say so," Dad said.

"I say so." Delia kissed his cheek, gave Mom a hug and patted me on my head. "Be good," she said. "I'll meet you there. Drive safe, but don't dawdle."

She gave a final, stern look, then swept past us, out into the warmth of the late May afternoon. Her sharply pressed robes snapped crisply around her smart, low-heeled pumps that clopped on the pavement like a snare drum. *Get. Out. Of. My. Way.*

"Awesome," I said. "Now we can stop for pizza."

Mom gave her blond-going-silver curls a pat. "I think one of the best graduation gifts we can give your sister is to be in our seats when she arrives."

"Hold up." I slipped off the heels and took my yellow sandals from the shoe rack at the door.

"Thea," Mom said. "You promised."

"Hey, I promised this boring dress. Delia-approved footwear was not in the contract. She won't know until it's too late."

We climbed into Dad's silver Cadillac. Mom rode shotgun while I sat in the back behind her, and we hit the road, heading out of Richmond toward Charlottesville, Virginia. The views were stunning—rolling green hills and trees under a cloudless blue sky. I loved my home state, but I had no plans to stay in it. After graduating from VCU School of the Arts next year, I was hauling my ass directly to New York City.

"How about some music, Pops?" I said from the back seat.

"Eight seconds of silence," Dad said. "A new record."

"Music is life," I said, laughing. "Right after painting. And *The Office*. And pizza."

"No pizza." Dad fiddled with the knob until he found my favorite station, and "Bad Romance" filled the car. "Good?"

"Can't go wrong with Lady Gaga."

Dad smirked. "I'll take your word for it."

I grooved to the song as best I could within the confines of my seatbelt until Mom turned down the volume.

"Poor Roger," she said. "What are his parents thinking?"

"I wonder what *Delia* is thinking," Dad said. He peered at me through the rearview. "You have any sisterly intel on the two of them? Are they an item?"

"No idea," I said. "You know how Delia is. Wound up tight. She never tells me anything."

Mom craned around to peer at me. "And how about you? No date for the occasion?"

"This is a family thing," I said. "And none of the guys I've dated lately are worthy. They think I'm 'fun' and don't want anything serious with me. Or maybe I don't want anything serious with them. Maybe I'm not capable of serious."

"I'm sure that's not true, honey," Mom said.

"Delia would beg to differ."

"I love your sister to pieces, but a monastery isn't serious enough for her."

"Honestly, I can't wait to fall in love, but I guess you can't force these things. It'll happen when it happens. I'll meet That Guy. The one I can't stop thinking about. And when what I feel about him starts to spill over into my art, I'll know he's the one."

"A wise philosophy," Dad said.

"Speaking of art," Mom said, "how is your latest project coming along?"

"It's done. I finished just as Delia was about to blow a gasket."

"Wonderful, I can't wait to see it." Mom knocked my knee with the back of her hand. "You and your pyramids."

"Right?" I laughed. "If I ever get famous, Egypt will be my thing. Like Kahlo's self-portraits or O'Keeffe's vagina flowers."

"Thea." Dad chuckled.

"I'm not saying I'm a Frida or a Georgia—"

"You *wouldn't* say that because you're too modest," Mom said. "But as your mother, I'm allowed to brag that you're right up there with the greats."

"As my mother, you're *contractually obligated* to say that," I said.

"But thanks, Mama. You're the best. I—"

"Dear God," my father cried out.

Mom started to turn. "What...?"

A flash of pale blue and blinding chrome.

A bang as loud as the universe. I felt it in my bones. In my teeth. It echoed through the hood, through the windshield.

It kept coming and coming and coming, tearing through us until there was nothing.

CHAPTER 1

Jim

The red-and-white For Rent sign caught my eye through my helmet's face shield. I slowed my Harley FX, parked it at the curb and lifted the visor.

Behind a rickety fence was a tiny house, probably no more than nine hundred square feet, squatting on a patch of dried grass. The cement path leading up to the door was cracked. A crooked step on the stoop. Peeling white paint on the siding.

Small, plain, and cheap.

Perfect.

I took off my helmet fished my cell phone out of my black leather jacket and called the faded number on the sign.

It's just a damn phone call, I thought, inhaling deep. *Keep your shit together.*

A man answered. "Yeah."

Inhale. Exhale.

"I'm calling about the house for rent in Boones Mill?"

No stutter. Not even on the *m* in Mill. A minor victory.

"Okay," the guy said. "Six-fifty per month. Utilities included but not water. No pets. Wanna see it? I can be down there in five."

"I have a job interview at the Blue Ridge Sanitarium," I said. "If I get the job, I'll be back in a few hours. I could see it then."

The guy sighed. "So why call me now?"

"I don't want anyone to take it."

He chuckled over the distinct sound of an exhale of a cigarette—half cough, half laugh.

"Son, you're the first to call in a month. I think you're safe." A drag off his smoke. "You going to work up at Blue Ridge? With all the head cases and whackos?"

I gripped the phone tighter. *Asshole.* "Just don't rent the house, okay?"

"Sure, sure. I'll put a courtesy hold on it, just for you."

"Thanks," I muttered. I hung up and my hand dropped to my jeans-clad thigh.

The guy was right—no one wanted his crappy little house but me. The phone call was a dry run for my job interview at the sanitarium. I'd been driving since six this morning from Richmond and didn't want my interviewer to be the first person I talked to.

My ex-foster mother's sneering tone filled my head.

Like it matters, you big dummy. You're going to stutter your way through that job interview and you know it.

"Shut up, Doris," I muttered.

Of all the foster homes I'd been bounced around since birth, I'd been in her care, if you could call it that, from the time I was ten until I turned eighteen. At twenty-four, her taunting voice still wouldn't leave me the fuck alone. I didn't stutter through every sentence anymore, but it still lurked under my tongue and came out to play when I was pissed off. Or nervous.

Like job-interview-nervous.

When I was twelve, doctors labeled my stutter a psychological disfluency: a reaction to a traumatic event, rather than physiological issues in my brain.

"A reaction?" Doris had said with a sneer in the doctor's office. "You saying he can't talk right, but it's all in his head? Pfft. He's a big dummy, is all. This just proves it."

The doctor stiffened. "Has there been a traumatic incident recently?"

"Of course not," Doris snapped, while I wanted to scream across my tied-up tongue that yes, something had happened. Just the week before Grandpa Jack died.

Technically, Doris' father wasn't my real grandfather, but he was nicer than anyone had ever been to me as I was kicked around the South Carolina foster system. He took me to Lake Murray to fish. He bought me ice cream and snuck hard candies into my hand after dinner.

"Don't tell your mother," he always said.

Mother. Doris took in foster kids for the money, not out of kindness. She sure as shit wasn't any kind of mother. How a man like Jack had a daughter like Doris, I'd never know. He was kind. He ruffled my hair instead of pinching me and he never called me stupid. When he died, he took with him the only sliver of happiness I'd had in my twelve miserable years.

Standing next to Doris at the funeral home, staring down into his casket, I started to cry. Doris dragged me into a side room, her fingers digging like claws into my skin. She gave me a rough shake.

"You don't cry about him, you hear me? He wasn't your family."

"He... he was Grandpa J-Jack," I said, my sobs breaking the words apart.

"Not your grandpa." Doris' dark eyes bored into mine as if she were putting some kind of goddamn spell on me. "You don't talk about him like he's yours ever again. He was *my* father. *My* kin. You ain't my kin. You're nothing but a check in the mail every month, so stop crying."

I did.

I sucked it all in, pressed it all down. Everything I'd wanted to say to Grandpa Jack got stuck somewhere behind my teeth. The grief crowded my brain and stiffened my jaw, settling into a stutter that promised years of torment from school bullies and worse abuse from the woman who was supposed to take care of me.

Doris never took me for speech therapy or treatment of any kind. It wasn't until seventh grade that I got any help. My teacher, Mrs. Marren, felt sorry for me and looked up some stuff on stuttering. She wasn't a specialist, but she found some breathing techniques that helped me get through a sentence.

Inhale the thought, exhale the words. Nice and easy, James.
Inhale. Exhale.

A FIVE-MINUTE LIFE

Try singing. Sometimes music can help get the words out.

I inhaled out of the South Carolina memories and exhaled into present-day Boones Hill, Virginia. All my hopes set on a crappy little house and a job interview.

I put my helmet back on, gunned my bike and hit the road. In fifteen minutes, I was in Southern Hills, just outside Roanoke. To the southwest, the Blue Ridge Mountains slumbered under a clear blue summer sky. I followed a winding, two-lane path up the rolling hills, surrounded by vibrant green ferns and tall trees. An antique-looking sign in old wood and ornate calligraphy came up on my left.

"Blue Ridge Sanitarium, est. 1891"

A newer sign with brighter paint was stuck into the soil below.

"Specializing in long-term brain injury treatment, memory care, and rehabilitation."

"Whackos and head cases," the rental guy had said. I gave him a mental middle finger. We were all whackos and head cases to a certain degree. Some were just better at hiding it. For some of us, hiding it was our life's mission.

I headed up the path until I came to a tall stone wall that stretched far on either side and disappeared in the woods. The wall was broken by a wide metal gate with a guard in a small outpost. I rolled up.

"Jim Whelan," I said. "Got a job interview."

A man in a light gray uniform with a security badge ironed on the front checked his clipboard.

"Whelan... Yep. You'll see Alonzo Waters. Ground floor. They'll tell you where at reception. Visitor parking on the left."

"Thanks."

The gate retracted with a lot of metal scraping on metal and I rode up the paved road. In another hundred yards, I arrived at the Blue Ridge Sanitarium.

The tall house looked like a plantation manor, which was probably what it had been until 1891. A solid, three-story mansion in red brick with white trim, fronted by four white pillars.

I veered toward the empty visitor lot and parked the Harley. The grounds were quiet but for insects buzzing in the humidity. No one was strolling the paths or sitting on any of the stone benches that lined them.

At the black-painted front door, a speaker box looked out of place on the old wood. I pressed the red button.

A woman's voice came through. "Can I help you?"

"Jim Whelan, here to see Mr. Waters."

The door buzzed and clicked. I turned the knob and pushed into the sanitarium's cool confines. Hardwood floors led to the reception area. The scent of cleaning products hung over the that of the old wood. An air-conditioning unit shared wall space with an oil painting of a bowl of fruit. The sanitarium seemed caught between being a plantation house and a healthcare facility. Maybe that was the point—to give the patients a sense of being at a home, rather than in a hospital.

A middle-aged woman with a dark ponytail waved me over. She wore the same security uniform as the guy out in the booth. Her nametag said Jules and her eyes grazed me up and down unapologetically.

"Well, hello handsome. Who are you here to see?"

"Alonzo Waters."

Her eyes widened. "You're here for the orderly position?"

I nodded.

"Huh. If you say so. You don't look like an orderly to me. Hot doctor from one of them TV shows, maybe."

I didn't return her smile but waited until she was done being obnoxious, arms crossed, my boots planted to the floor.

"Strong, silent type," Jules said with a small laugh, her gaze still roving. "Well, I sincerely hope you get the job. You're a sight for sore eyes. Plus, we're short a few orderlies since the last two moved out of town."

Good. If the sanitarium was short-handed, they'd be eager to hire and start me as soon as possible.

"No chitchat?" Jules heaved a dramatic sigh. "Okay, okay. Alonzo will be in the dining hall now, straight back through the double doors. Can't miss it."

"Thanks," I said and strode where she pointed.

"Ah, he speaks! Good luck, handsome."

I felt Jules' gaze follow me and shrugged it off.

The dining hall had white floors and walls, with tall windows letting in the June sunlight. A dozen square tables, each set for four. A man with a visible dent in his head the size of a coaster sat with a nurse at one table by the window, slowly eating soup. He gave me a hard, sharp look as I came in.

I looked him in the eye and gave him a respectful nod. His eyebrows shot up, then he pursed his lips with a grunt and went back to his soup.

A plump lady in a white chef's coat stood behind a small case of pastries and salads. Coffee brewed behind her in tall silver canisters. She was talking to an older black man, who looked to be in his sixties, his hair gone gray. He wore a white, short-sleeved shirt tucked into white trousers. Black belt, black boots. A huge ring of keys jingled on his waist.

I drew closer and the lunch lady jerked her chin at me. "Can I help you?"

The man turned around. "You must be Jim Whelan," he said.

I nodded and offered my hand.

"Alonzo Waters," he said, sizing me up. "Want to be an orderly, do you?"

"Yes, sir."

"Got a résumé?"

I pulled two pieces of paper folded into fours from my jacket pocket. "Yes, sir."

"Sir," Alonzo said with a chuckle. "You hear that, Margery?"

She rolled her eyes. "Don't let it go to your head."

"Come on, let's sit and talk." Alonzo led me to an empty table for four and sat across from me. "Coffee?"

"No, thanks."

"Trying to cut down, myself." Alonzo perused my résumé. "Twenty-four years old. Graduated from Webster High, South Carolina. Straight to work at the Richmond Rehab Clinic for… six years?"

"Yes, sir."

"Why'd you quit? Or did you get fired?"

"It shut down." I cleared my throat and indicated my résumé. "There's a letter of recommendation on the back, there."

"Oh yes, here it is." Alonzo leaned back and read the letter from my former supervisor. "Wow. Says here you were an 'exemplary employee' and that he wishes he'd had ten just like you." He folded his hands on his stomach and looked at me. "Not bad, not bad. RRC was for drug addicts. How'd that go for you?"

"Good."

"Care to elaborate?"

Don't fuck this up. Just talk.

"I showed up on time," I said. "Never missed a day."

I let out a breath. No stutter on a sentence that had three of my worst consonants. *D, n, m, s,* and *f* were my nemeses, but *d* was the King Dick of them all. My stuttering over Doris' name drove her batshit crazy, so she'd smack me on the back of my head. "*Spit it out, you big d-d-dummy.*"

"What about patient interaction?"

"Not much," I said. "I did my job."

"You ever deal with brain injury cases?"

I shook my head.

"I worked in all kinds of facilities, myself," he said. "Drug rehab too. And I can tell you these brain injuries are a whole different ball of wax. Drug addicts, for one thing, are still themselves. That ain't always the case here. We have twenty-seven residents at Blue Ridge and some of them ain't all there anymore." He tapped his forehead. "You have to learn their case histories. How to talk to them properly. The slightest wrong words could set them off or confuse them. Can you handle that?"

"I think so."

I hardly had to speak at all at RRC, which was why I liked the job. But the idea of participating in the patients' care at Blue Ridge tried to reawaken a distant dream of mine—to help kids like me with speech impairments. Kids who felt stupid and frustrated every damn minute of their life. It was a dream born of my stutter but that died with it too.

Who wanted their stuttering kid to be treated by a stuttering therapist?

No one, that's who, you big dummy, Doris offered.

"Contrary to local rumor," Alonzo was saying, "this isn't a psychiatric hospital. None of the residents—residents, not patients—are here for emotional issues. They're all here because of injury. Accidents, mostly. But everyone here is suffering from permanent brain damage. Our job is to help them adjust to their new reality."

"Okay."

Alonzo leaned back in his chair, folded his hands over his stomach. "Why do you want to work here, son?"

A thousand professional-sounding, bullshit answers rose to my mouth and tangled up.

14

I inhaled slowly and exhaled the truth.

"I want to help."

Alonzo studied me through narrowed eyes, then glanced down at my résumé. "You settled in pretty deep at RRC. Made yourself at home, did you?"

Made myself a home.

"Why not go to college? You want to clean up after sick people for the rest of your life?"

I shrugged.

He pursed his lips. "Don't say much do you?"

"Not much."

"Lucky you, workers standing around yapping is one of my biggest gripes." He extended his hand. "All kidding aside, this letter of rec makes it clear I'd be an idiot not to take you. Jim Whelan, you're hired."

I eased a sigh of relief and shook his hand. "Thank you, sir."

"Only call me *sir* in front of Margery," he said with a wink. "Otherwise just Alonzo. I'm friendly, but I run a tight ship. This place has rules on top of rules to keep the residents safe and comfortable. Breaking them is a one-way ticket out the door. You got that?"

"Yes, sir."

"All right then." Alonzo rose to his feet, and I did the same. "Let's go sign some paperwork, then you be here Monday morning. Seven a.m. sharp. That work for you?"

I nodded. "I lined up a place in Boones Mill. I'll get moved in this weekend."

"Good," Alonzo said. "I'll be needing you to cover breakfast, lunch, exercise, and afternoon recreation. You'll be trained on the duties as you go. We lost two fellas at the same time, so I'm going to need you to think on your feet."

"I'll do my best."

I signed the paperwork then we said our goodbyes.

"Monday, seven a.m.," Alonzo said. "*Sharp.*"

I headed back toward the foyer. Jules had left the front desk, but the room wasn't empty.

A young woman with wavy blond hair stood by the wall, studying the oil painting next to the AC unit. She was shorter than my six feet by a good five inches. Slender. Dressed in shapeless khaki pants, a plain beige shirt, and loafers.

She looked around as my booted steps echoed around the foyer. Large blue eyes in a heart-shaped face watched me approach. A full-lipped smile lit up her delicate features and my goddamn pulse quickened.

"It's beautiful, isn't it?" she asked, nodding her head at the painting. "The way the light falls over the curve of the apple. How it gives the grapes that shine."

I moved to stand beside her. "Looks like fruit to me."

She laughed. "It is fruit. It's the *essence* of the fruit. A gorgeous rendering of something so simple. The light revealing the life within."

"You sound like you know what you're talking about."

"I like to think so. I'm an artist. A painter." Her crystal-blue eyes, fringed with dark lashes, rose to meet mine. "You're the first person I've seen. What's your name?"

"Jim. Jim Whelan."

"Thea Hughes. Pleased to meet you." She took my hand and gave it one strong, hearty pump up and down. "You have kind eyes, Jim Whelan."

You're fucking stunning, Thea Hughes.

She gestured at the painting. "But not a fan?"

I shrugged.

"What's your poison, artistically speaking?"

"Music," I said. "I like… music."

Christ, I sounded like a moron. *Me like music.* But Thea's exquisite face lit up even brighter now.

"Oh hell, I love music." She laughed. "Painting is my jam, but music is *life*. Do you play?"

"I have a guitar…" I said, and the rest died. I wasn't about to tell her I sometimes sang too. Fuck no.

"I love the guitar," Thea said. "What's your fave?"

I rubbed the back of my neck, shrugged. "I don't know. Rock music, mostly. Guns N' Roses. Foo Fighters. Pearl Jam."

Thea cocked her head. "Funny, I don't know those."

"You've never heard of Guns N' Roses?"

She frowned. "I don't know, actually… Should I have?" Then she slugged me in the arm playfully. "Don't music-shame me, James. I'm a techno-and-dance gal. Behold… my sweet, sweet Chicken Neck dance moves."

She thrust her head forward on her neck, over and over, and a laugh burst out of me. I wouldn't have been surprised if a cloud of dust and moths had puffed out too. I envied how easily she inhabited her own skin. No self-consciousness.

She is who she is.

"Jim?"

I blinked.

"You're staring."

How can I not?

"Can't blame you, though," she said and then clapped her hand over her eyes. "Oh my God, that sounded like so egomaniac… ish. Egomaniacal? Is that a word?" She laughed. "I meant that I make a spectacle of myself. Or so my sister is always saying."

"You dance like no one's watching, even when people are watching."

"I hope that's not a subtle jab at my mad dance skills."

"Never," I said. I'd never had a conversation go this easily for me. I talked as easily as she danced. No hesitation.

"What do you paint?" I asked. "Fruit bowls?"

She gave me a sly, playful look. "What do you think I paint?"

I shrugged, jammed my hands in my pockets. "If I had to guess… I'd say big stuff. The Grand Canyon, maybe. I'd guess you use lots of colors, too."

"Big and colorful, eh?" She laced her fingers behind her back. "And what makes you say that?"

"I don't know. Something about you."

That sounded like a bad line, but the truth would have been too much. That in only a handful of minutes in her presence I felt the magnitude of her.

"Well, you have me pegged pretty close," she said. "I mostly paint scenes of Egypt. Pyramids, Cleopatra, the Nile. It's my thing."

I nodded. "Had a feeling."

"Did you?" Our eyes met and her smile turned private. Just for me. "I have a feeling about you too, Jim Whelan."

My heart did a slow roll. "Yeah?"

"Yeah. Outside, you're built like a brick wall with a movie star face and a badass black leather jacket. Inside? Deep as the Grand Canyon." Her eyebrows raised inquisitively. "Am I close?"

I shrugged. "I… I don't know…"

"You shrug a lot too," she said. "Don't do that. Your thoughts aren't inconsequential."

Our eyes met again and the "brick wall" I'd built to keep myself safe felt useless against her. *Inconsequential.* I had to see her again, even if that meant she'd hear the stutter.

I had a feeling Thea Hughes wouldn't care if she did.

"So, are you visiting someone here?" I asked.

Thea's smile froze. "Here?"

"Yeah. I just moved into town and I was—"

"My sister. She's coming here." Her delicate brows furrowed, confusion clouding the crystal blue of her eyes. "And my parents. They'll be here any minute."

"Okay." Inhale. Exhale. "I was wondering if maybe, you'd like to—?"

"How long has it been?" Thea hugged herself and looked around as if seeing her surroundings for the first time. Her breath shortened. "I don't know this place." Her gaze darted to me. "How long has it been?"

"How long…?" I blinked. "I don't know—"

"Who are you?" Thea's eyes were wide now, panic bright in their light blue depths. "How long has it been?"

Did she want the time? I started to check my watch, and then it dawned on me. Like a tidal wave of cold water dousing the tiny, flickering flame between us.

Oh, fuck, you jackass. She's a patient. A resident.

"How long has it been?" Thea shrieked, her voice echoing through the foyer.

"I d-d-don't know…" I stammered to the pounding of my pulse.

She took a step back from me. "They're working on my case," she said. "The doctors. I had an accident. How long has it been?"

I glanced around the empty foyer, looking for help. "I… I d-don't…"

"Miss Hughes, there you are."

I spun to see a small woman with dark hair and eyes in a nurse's pale blue scrubs striding quickly down the hallway. Relief lanced through me. The nurse shot me a curious glance and gently took Thea by the arm.

"Miss Hughes always seems to find her way to the front door."

Thea turned her wide-eyed gaze to the nurse, whose nametag read Rita. "How long has it been?"

"Two years, Miss Hughes," Rita said. "The doctors are working on your case."

"Right," Thea said, taking a deep breath and clutching Rita's arm. "They're going to figure out what's wrong with me."

Rita smiled and nodded her chin at the oil painting. "This picture is lovely, don't you think?"

Thea relaxed and her smile started to return. "Absolutely. Look at the way the light shines over the curve of the apple." She turned to me. "Isn't it beautiful?"

I nodded, staring. "Yeah. Beautiful."

She beamed and offered her hand. "Hi. I'm Thea Hughes."

"Jim Whelan," I murmured. My hand rose on its own and took hers, feeling as if I were having an out-of-body experience.

What the fuck just happened?

Thea gave my hand a strong, one-pump shake. "Nice to meet you, Jim."

Rita cleared her throat. "You must be our new orderly?"

"I start Monday."

"I'm Rita Soto." Her smile was warm. "Welcome to Blue Ridge." She nodded at the empty front desk with a frown. "I see Jules is on another smoke break. Thank you for keeping Miss Hughes company."

"Sure," I said, unable to look at Thea any longer; my eyes ached. "I better go."

"Bye, Jim," Thea called. "See you again sometime?"

I stopped. It was the exact question I'd been ready to ask her.

You got your answer, you big dummy. Doris cackled in my head. *You're going to see her every day.*

Every. Day.

CHAPTER 2

Jim

I spent the weekend in a rented U-Haul, making the three-hour drive between my shitty little apartment in Richmond and the shitty little house I'd rented in Boones Mill. After my successful interview at Blue Ridge, George Hammett—my new landlord—practically threw the keys at me from the cab of his truck, then screeched away before I could change my mind.

He didn't have anything to worry about. I didn't need much. The house was shabby as hell but livable. During two days of unpacking and cleaning, I managed to not think about Thea Hughes for a grand total of eight minutes.

Fuck me. She's a resident.

A resident.

Stupid of me to not see it. I should have paid better attention.

What was her diagnosis?

Maybe something minor.

Maybe she was recovering…

Then Alonzo's words rattled in my head: *Everyone here is suffering from permanent brain damage. Our job is to help them adjust to their new reality.*

Thea Hughes wasn't recovering and wasn't going to get better, and I had to adjust to that reality too. She was a resident of Blue Ridge Sanitarium. I was an orderly charged to take care of her, end of story.

End of *our* story.

I took my attraction to her—an attraction I'd never felt toward any woman—and shelved it away with the speech therapist dream.

Sunday night, I fired up a frozen dinner in my new house's old microwave. After, I set my guitar on my lap and played Guns N' Roses "Sweet Child O' Mine" quietly, so the neighbors wouldn't hear. I sang about eyes like the bluest sky, belonging to a woman who exuded warmth and safety.

She's a resident.

I put the guitar away.

Later, I lay in my bed, listening to the crickets grow loud as summer approached while reading my worn out, dog-eared copy of *Fight Club*. My fingers turned pages I'd read a hundred times, and the dim light made the scars across my knuckles gleam white against my tanned skin. The scars came from countless fights during endless school days. Days when the soundtrack of my life was taunting voices and the rattle of chain-link in the yard where they always cornered me.

I hid my bruised face from Doris as best as I could when I got home, but she always found out.

What happened this time?

N-N-Nothing—

Spit it out, you big dummy!

I did get big. Bigger. Stronger. I lifted weights and started winning every fight. By senior year of high school, no one dared to fuck with me. Including Doris. I moved out of her house the minute I turned eighteen and never looked back.

The scars on my knuckles were badges I'd earned, as was the silence when the taunting stopped. But it lived on in my mind—a poisonous voice of someone who was supposed to watch out for me and tormented me instead.

Watch out for yourself. Keep your head down. Do your job.

Thea Hughes, I thought with a pang in my chest, wasn't going to be anything but part of my job. I could watch out for her too.

I rolled into the Blue Ridge Sanitarium at 6:45 a.m.

"Happy to have you on the team," Jules said, shooting me a wink. "*Very* happy."

"Break room?" I asked.

She rolled her eyes with a sigh. "You're no fun. Back there, second door on the left."

The employee break room consisted of a few lockers, a card table, and men's and women's bathrooms. A white uniform consisting of pants and a button-down, short-sleeve shirt was waiting for me in an open locker, along with my badge and nametag.

Just as I'd buttoned up my shirt, a wiry guy entered the break room. He looked to be about thirty, with a full head of brown hair and friendly dark eyes.

"It's too early for this shit, am I right?" Laughing, he extended his hand. "Joaquin Reyes. You must be the new guy."

"Jim Whelan," I said, shaking his hand.

"Good to meet you, Jim. Alonzo comes on in a few hours. I'm going to show you the basics. The layout of this joint, where shit is stored, all that."

"Sounds good."

Joaquin showed me around, cracking jokes and flirting with the nurses we passed. I braced myself to see Thea Hughes around every corner but saw no sign of her.

While Joaquin sped around the place like he was born there, I made a mental map: resident rooms and nurses' station on the top floor.

Therapy rooms and the medicine room on the second floor.

The break room, supply storage, cafeteria and rec room on the ground floor.

Blue Ridge was much larger than the exterior led me to think. The additions built to accommodate the residents had newer paint and prison-like barriers. Like the fence that surrounded the nurses' station and another blocking off the resident quarters from the downstairs.

"Think of them like child-proof gates," Joaquin said. "Most of the residents can't remember shit, and they'll wander right out the door if we're not careful."

"They have amnesia?" I asked, my thoughts darting directly to Thea.

"Some worse than others," Joaquin said, heading down the stairs. "But Alonzo will tear me a new one if I say any more. He's in charge of training new hires how to talk to the residents so you don't freak them out."

"Yeah, he mentioned that," I said, remembering Thea's panic because I couldn't answer her question, *How long has it been?*

We arrived on the ground floor, where Joaquin unlocked the door to a cleaning supply closet. "Once a month, the director of the place shows up," he said. "And we all gotta be on our best behavior. Then there are the doctors." He rolled out a mop and bucket. "The neuropsychologists come up from Roanoke Memorial to do rounds. Specialists are in and out. Some are decent, but most won't even acknowledge an orderly's presence. When in doubt, just stay out of their way."

I nodded.

Joaquin pressed the mop handle into my hand. "Not a big talker, are you? But you got a phone? If not, we got some old pagers lying around."

"I have a phone."

"We'll get you all the numbers. You gotta keep your phone on you at all times. We're always short-handed. Lots of turnover. Hours can be grueling. Late nights. All-nighters."

"I'm on the day shift."

Joaquin smirked. "Technically. You'll end up working at least three night shifts, rookie. Lunch is forty-five minutes unless you're needed for a resident and, like I said, we're always short-handed. You do get a fifteen-minute break every four hours. You smoke?"

"No."

"We'll see how long that lasts. Orderlies in other facilities don't do janitor work, but that's not the case here. We gotta take on multiple jobs." He pushed the mop and rolling bucket to me. "Mop up the cafeteria, now. Later, you'll work at the rec room and help supervise FAE."

"FAE?"

"Fresh Air Experience. It's a therapeutic way of saying exercise. Residents who are up for it go outside and walk around the grounds. Usually, a nurse is assigned to each resident, but we're short nurses, too. So either the orderlies help out, or it's skipped altogether."

"You mean the residents don't get to go outside?"

"Don't get your panties in a twist. Most days they do. Other days, it's just not in the cards." He peered up at me. "You've probably seen *One Flew Over the Cuckoo's Nest* too many times. This is a good place. Everyone's treated well. The funding's not exactly pouring in, but it's better than a hospital. Or a psych ward. Cool?"

"Cool."

Joaquin narrowed his eyes. "How old are you?"

"Twenty-four."

"Got family near here?"

"No."

He leaned in. "Okay, so listen. This job has a way of latching on. I know I said there's a lot of turnover, and there is. Mostly because decent employees who don't fuck up aren't all that easy to keep. But those that stick, like me and Alonzo, we tend to *stick*. I came here for a summer job. That was eight years ago. Point is, don't get stuck on this mountain."

He slugged my shoulder and left me to mop the cafeteria floor. Breakfast was over and the room was empty. Alone, moving the mop in figure eights over the linoleum, I turned his words over in my head.

Don't get stuck on this mountain.

Getting stuck is what I did best. I'd probably have worked at my last job forever if it hadn't shut down. I didn't want much in the world. Just a place where I could work and be of help to people. And no one to bother me.

Being stuck on that mountain didn't sound bad at all.

While the residents were all at lunch, I cleaned three rooms. Each had its own bathroom and was identically furnished with a bed, closet, small dresser, and a table and chair under a window.

All the doors locked from the outside.

I met Alonzo downstairs in the recreation room that consisted of a nurses' station, a dozen small tables, a TV mounted on one wall, shelves full of games and puzzles, and a storage closet at the rear. Alonzo had a stack of file folders under his arm and greeted me with an approving look.

"Joaquin tells me you catch on quick," he said. "Let's sit."

We took a table in the corner that had a vantage of the entire space. Only one resident was present—the older man with the dented head. He worked slowly and laboriously over a puzzle while his attendant stood at the station, chatting with the duty nurse.

"You need to get to know the residents," Alonzo said. "That there is Richard Webb. Mr. Webb to you and me."

I nodded.

"They each have a nurse assigned to them. Most nurses work more than one resident though, so we step in and help, time to time. But carefully. Be friendly, but don't talk their ear off." His eyebrow raised. "I have a feeling I won't have that problem with you."

The door to the rec room opened. I looked back and recognized the nurse I'd met yesterday, Rita Soto.

Thea Hughes was beside her.

She wore shapeless beige pants, a plain shirt, and loafers, but she was jaw-droppingly beautiful. A stunning work of art wrapped in a paper bag. Her blond hair fell around her shoulders in soft waves, and she regarded the rec room with bright if hesitant eyes.

Rita led Thea to a table and set her up with paper and colored pens. Within moments, Thea was bent over her work, drawing. Like a child making doodles after school.

"That's Miss Hughes," Alonzo said, tapping his pen on the file folders. "Of all our residents, she needs the most care. Which means she's got the most rules."

I tore my gaze from her and forced my voice into a neutral tone. "What's wrong with her?"

"Only one of the worst recorded case of amnesia in medical history."

I stared. "Are you sure?"

Alonzo chuckled. "Am I *sure*? That's one I haven't heard before. But I get it. Miss Hughes is young and beautiful and looks healthy as a horse, but that just ain't the case."

He shuffled through his files until he found hers, opened it, and spoke in a low voice as he read.

"Althea Renée Hughes, age twenty-three. Two years ago, she was in a head-on collision while driving with her parents. Drunk-driver plowed his pickup truck right at 'em. Parents were pronounced dead at the scene. Miss Hughes was Life-Flighted to Richmond General where she spent two weeks in a coma. They treated her for a broken arm, broken clavicle, broken femur, and internal injuries. But it was her head that took the worst of it."

I swallowed. "What happened?"

Alonzo read from her file. "Catastrophic brain injury sustained in a motor vehicle accident with intracranial hemorrhage and increased intracranial pressure resulting in trauma and damage to the hippocampus." He looked up. "In English: her long- and short-term memory are shot to hell. She's got no memory of her life before the accident and no memory of her life now."

"What do you mean? No memory at all?"

"She has semantic memory, which means she remembers factual information such as words, concepts, numbers. She still knows how to wash her face, use a fork, put on her clothes. But she has no episodic memory. No personal experiences, events, or details about people or places. Meaning, she knows what a dog is but can't tell you if she's ever pet one in her life. She remembers the history of Egypt she's studied but can't tell you if she's ever been there herself."

"Okay," I said slowly. "But she knows what's happening to her? She's aware of...?" I gestured to indicate the room.

"Where she is? What happened to her? What she was doing five minutes ago? Nope. She has a few minutes of consciousness and then she has to start over. She resets."

"Resets?"

"Yeah, when her minutes are up, the slate gets wiped clean again, so to speak. We call it her reset."

He's messing with me. How can anyone survive with only a few minutes of memory?

"That's crazy."

"Sounds that way, but it's her truth. You can hear it happen. She says the same thing, asks the same questions, every few minutes. All day long. Day in and day out. Going on two years now."

How long has it been?

That was Thea's reset. I'd heard it yesterday.

"She don't stray from her script much unless she's drawing. Or you get her in a conversation," Alonzo said. "Then she's good for a few minutes more. And just when you think 'Hey, this gal's all right. Why is she here?' *Bam*. Reset."

"What happens?"

"She'll pause and get all blank and confused. Then start her script over again. When she first came to us and a reset hit, she'd throw a fit. Like a little seizure. Now she only has fits when something upsets her. That's why we keep her on a strict routine, and you have to know how to talk to her so you don't set her off."

Too late.

"What does she think is happening when the reset hits?"

"She knows there was an accident. She knows she was hurt and something's going on with her brain and the doctors are working on her case. That's all she needs to know. Her older sister, Delia, is her guardian now. She directs Miss Hughes' care, and she's adamant we don't spill the beans that their parents didn't survive. No need to upset her. Even if she won't remember it a few minutes later."

I frowned, trying to wrap my mind around Thea's condition. "But... if Thea's—"

"Miss Hughes," Alonzo said. "Always Miss Hughes."

"If she's taking a bite of food or in the shower and the reset hits, what does she think is going on?"

"She goes with the flow," Alonzo said. "The brain is a complicated mechanism, but its basic function is survival. The way her docs tell it, Miss Hughes' memory resets, but she continues on calmly because she's in this facility, and the facility doesn't change. Calm is our number one goal. And since you're so chatty all of a sudden, lesson one: you go up to Miss Hughes and what do you say?"

I'm sorry. I'm so fucking sorry this happened to you.

"I'm n-not sure what you mean."

"Most people would say, 'Hello, Thea. How are you, today?'"

"Okay."

"Wrong. Three huge mistakes in that sentence. One: using her first name implies you know her, but she don't know you, so that upsets her. You gotta call all residents by their last names. It's polite and respectful, too."

I nodded.

"Two: never ask how she's doing. She don't know. She has no idea how she should be feeling in the few minutes since she 'came awake' again, so don't ask."

Came awake again. I still couldn't grasp having only a few minutes' worth of consciousness.

"Three," Alonzo said, "never use words like *today* or *this afternoon* or *good evening* or *Merry Christmas*. She don't know one day from the next, one minute from another. No sense of time. When she asks, 'How long has it been?' she means since her accident."

"Two years," I murmured.

"Yep," Alonzo said. "And reassure her that the doctors are working on her case. No more than that. If she talks to you, listen. If you get in trouble, redirect her to whatever she's doing. Like her art. She can hold a conversation for longer than a few minutes if she's occupied. When her attention is pulled—*bam*. Reset. You got all that?"

I nodded, but my expression must've given me away.

Alonzo leaned back in his chair. "Spit it out."

"How can she live like this?"

"Quite happily. Calmly. And it could be worse. A fellow in England's only got forty-five seconds' worth of memory. Miss Hughes can go as long as seven minutes before reset, but that's not usual."

"How does that happen?"

He tapped a finger to his skull behind his ear. "A truck plowing straight into your gray matter will do the trick." He held up his hands at my sharp glance. "I don't mean to sound cold, but that's just what happened. Our job isn't to ponder it or feel sorry for Miss Hughes. We don't waste time talking ourselves into thinking she's fine just because she looks high functioning. She's got permanent brain damage, but she's not suffering. She don't know what she don't know. Our job is to take care of her and keep her calm. Okay?"

A thousand questions crowded in my mouth and I couldn't get out a single one. I recalled our conversation yesterday. The best I'd had in years and then… gone. Erased. And Thea—Miss Hughes—living only a few minutes at a time. For two years now.

Alonzo stared me down. "I know it's hard to take, son, but that's the reality." He tapped the file folder. "Come on. We got twenty-five more residents to talk about."

28

We went back to work, going through case files, but I could hardly concentrate with Thea sitting behind me. The desire to talk to her was like a hunger in my gut. I didn't talk to anyone and now I wanted to sit down across from her and demand to know if she was suffering. Was she happy?

Don't be stupid. It's none of your business. Do your job.

After the case files, Alonzo went out for a smoke. Mr. Webb and his nurse left, so I cleaned up his jigsaw puzzle. My eyes kept stealing glances at Thea.

She smiled as she worked. Maybe Alonzo was right. Maybe Thea's amnesia kept her from the horrifying reality of her situation. She didn't know what she didn't know.

But what if she did?

Thea looked up and gave me a friendly, polite smile. Then her entire face froze. I froze too, watched her *reset*. Her clear blue eyes clouded with confusion and she leaned toward me from her seat.

"How long has it been?"

I glanced around for Rita but the only other person in the rec room was the duty nurse watching a soap opera on a small TV propped on her desk.

I took a step toward her.

"How long—?"

"Two years, M-M-Miss Hughes."

Fuck, there it is.

Thea didn't seem to notice the stutter. She nodded, her hunched shoulders easing back down. "I had an accident," she said. "You're the first person I've seen since I came back."

I took another step toward her. Inhale, exhale. "Came back?"

"I've been away for two years. But I'm back now and the doctors are working on my case." She looked at my nametag. "Jim."

"Jim Whelan," I said.

I have a feeling about you, Jim Whelan.

I silently willed Thea to remember, for recognition to light up her eyes. For her smile to turn familiar and warm as she recalled our conversation yesterday.

She held out her hand. "Nice to meet you, Jim Whelan. I'm Thea Hughes."

CHAPTER 3

Jim

She'd introduced herself to me three times now.

Three of hundreds to come, if not thousands. Her brain was damaged. She's not going to magically remember you.

It was hard to believe her amnesia was so severe, when she sat there looking this vibrant and sharp. I recalled Alonzo's instruction to redirect her after a reset and glanced down at her work. She'd drawn a pyramid. On closer inspection, she'd built one out of words. Strings of words written in ballpoint pen, colored over with Magic Markers.

"That's really good," I said. More than good.

"Thank you," Thea said, frowning at the paper. "It's okay but there's something missing. It feels…"

"Small."

She glanced up at me with a wry twist to her lips. "Are you an art critic, Jim Whelan?"

"N-N-No, I just meant—"

"I'm teasing," she said with a sigh and turned back to her drawing. "It *is* small. I wish I had a canvas as big as a wall. And paint to last me for months."

"That's exactly what I meant," I said, still standing over her awkwardly. "Your talent is bigger than paper and pens. Grand Canyon-big."

I hoped the cue from yesterday would spark her, but Thea blushed and grinned playfully at me. "I take it back. You can critique my art any time you want."

The moment caught and held, and again, I saw the depths of Thea Hughes. Miles instead of minutes.

"Jim?"

"Yeah?"

"You're staring at me."

"Sorry."

"It's okay. I don't mind being stared at by you. You have kind eyes."

Déjà vu to the fucking extreme.

I felt my skin burn hot and *redirected* my own damn self away from her. I craned a little lower to read one of the word chains comprising a slope of her pyramid.

Carried buried bury born torn mourn moan loan alone lone lonely lonely lonely

"What do these mean?" I asked, tapping a finger over the words. "If you don't mind…?"

Thea cocked her head at the words as if they were foreign to her. "I don't know. I wrote them before the accident. Two years ago."

"You drew this two years ago?" I felt I was on shaky ground, testing the limits of her understanding and possibly setting her off.

She nodded. "I must have. But now that I'm back, I can finish it."

"Okay," I said.

Thea's brows furrowed, and she tucked a lock of blond hair behind her ear as if puzzled by her own words. "It sounds strange, doesn't it? I've been away for a long time."

"It's what happened."

Her smile was grateful. "That's a good way to put it. I feel like…"

"Like what?"

"Like there's more to it, but whenever I try to remember more, there's nothing. I don't even remember how I got here, to this table. With you."

I had no words that could help her understand. I hardly understood her situation myself.

"But I know the doctors are working on my case," she said. "I'll let them worry about it. I'm just happy to be back."

"Me too."

Thea's smile grew more brilliant, and she picked up her ballpoint pen again. "Tell me about yourself, Jim. And sit down, for crying out loud. You're hovering."

I glanced around for Alonzo, but he was nowhere in sight. I sat down across from Thea, telling myself I was only doing my job.

"That's better," Thea said, beaming. "What do you do?"

"I'm an orderly."

"Oh, yeah? Where at?"

Alonzo might tear me a new one for talking to Thea mere seconds after telling me not to fuck up and say the wrong thing. The rising anxiety brought out the damn stutter.

"At the B-B-Blue Ridge Sanitarium."

Shit.

Thea glanced sharply at me, then her gaze softened. "Do you have a stutter, Jim?"

No one had asked me in years, I'd kept it hidden so well. Humiliation dug deep claws into me as I inhaled and exhaled. "Sometimes. It shows up when I get n-nervous. Or pissed off."

Her brows rose. "You don't look pissed off. Do I make you nervous?"

Christ, was she flirting with me?

Thea patted my hand. "Don't be nervous. I don't bite… *hard.*"

A flush of heat on my skin where her soft fingers touched me quickly became a jolt that surged through my arm, my spine, down to my groin.

She's a resident, for fuck's sake.

I gently pulled my hand away.

"I heard that line somewhere. A movie, maybe." She cocked her head. "You don't talk much, do you?"

"Not much."

"Because of the stutter?"

I nodded.

"My sister says I never shut up." She laughed and shrugged. "Guilty as charged. I say what I mean because life's too short, right?"

Now she leaned closer to me. The scent of plain, industrial soap wafted from her warm skin.

"I'm just going to come out and say I have a feeling your stutter is not the most interesting thing about you, Jim Whelan."

I stared. No one had said anything like that to me before. This girl was a magnet of push and pull—drawing me in, though I had to keep a professional distance. She was direct as hell but smiled at me as if there was a secret between us that only we knew. She was *here*, but any minute now, she'd be gone.

And this moment, right here, right now, never happened.

I cleared my throat. "I wouldn't call it interesting."

Thea rested her chin on her hand. "Did you have a hard time with it growing up?"

"You could say that."

"I'm sorry. You probably don't want to talk about it. I only brought it up because I don't care."

"Don't care?"

"If you stutter. We all have something, right?"

"Yeah," I said. "We do."

"Don't let it stop you from talking to me. I like talking to you, Jim."

"I like talking to you too, Thea."

Her name came so easy to me. An inhale, and then a soft exhale with my tongue behind my teeth. No effort. No force. No stutter.

The moment grew warm and long, then shattered like glass as the rec room door opened behind me. Thea glanced over my shoulder and her beautiful smile collapsed. Her expression turned blank and her entire body stiffened. The ballpoint fell out of her fingers and rolled toward the end of the table. When it clattered to the floor, Thea snapped out of the rigidity, and a jubilant smile broke over her face.

"Delia!" She jumped up from her chair and ran past me.

I let out the air trapped in my lungs and got to my feet. A woman in a navy suit with dark hair pulled into a severe bun had walked in with Nurse Rita. Thea threw her arms around the woman's neck, nearly knocking her off her feet. Delia's lips pressed together hard. Over Thea's shoulder, the woman's eyes met mine and I quickly busied myself gathering Thea's pen off the floor.

"You're here," Thea said. "I'm so happy to see you. How long has it been? Where are Mom and Dad?"

"It's been two years," Delia said. "Mom and Dad are on their way." Her tone was weary, as if she'd answered these questions a thousand times. She probably had.

"Let's sit," she said, moving her sister back to the table.

I stood frozen, waiting for Thea to see me and remember we'd been having a conversation. She had to remember. No one had amnesia this badly. Alonzo had told me a bunch of bullshit. This was a prank on the rookie. Initiation for all new orderlies.

Thea finally tore her adoring gaze from her sister and looked at me with polite curiosity.

"Hi," she said, her gaze darting to my nametag. "Jim? This is my sister, Delia."

I stared.

Gone. It's all gone.

Just like our conversation in the foyer the other day. Vanished. Like it never happened.

Delia cleared her throat, a hard sound that yanked my attention. "Can I help you, *Jim*?"

"Jim Whelan is our newest orderly," Rita said, moving to stand next to me.

Delia looked me up and down with shrewd, dark eyes. She was the exact opposite of Thea in every way—stiff, cold, and tight-lipped, with a stony dark stare. Though she likely wasn't more than a few years older than me, something had stolen the vitality out of Delia, so she looked like someone who'd aged a decade in two years.

She lost her parents and her sister's in a sanitarium. Give her a break.

I offered my hand. "Hello, Ms. Hughes."

She glanced at my hand as if I'd offered her a dirty diaper.

Thea laughed. "Delia, you're such a crank." She took my outstretched hand and gave it one, hearty pump. "Thea Hughes. So nice to meet you."

That's four.

I let go of her hand but kept staring into her eyes, searching for a sign this was all bullshit. Thea was acting. She wasn't delirious from an injury or wracked with Alzheimer's. I recalled my Grandpa Jack's vacant gaze from his deathbed. How his memories floated in and out, and once they were gone, they were gone. It had been obvious something inside him was broken and falling away. Thea was young and beautiful and perfectly healthy.

Except she wasn't.

"Take a picture, it'll last longer," Thea said, laughing while Delia's cold stare pierced me.

"I'd like to be alone with my sister now," Delia said, pulling out a chair at the table. "I'm sure you have work to do?"

Thea shot me an apologetic smile and wiggled her fingertips at me in a little goodbye.

Rita pulled me away from the sisters. "Don't take it personally. Delia's like that with everyone. And thanks for keeping Miss Hughes occupied. How'd you do?"

"I can't fucking believe it," I murmured.

"I know. It takes some getting used to. It feels like she's faking, right?"

I nodded.

"Her being high functioning almost makes it worse."

"I think she had a small seizure."

"That's to be expected," Rita said. "They're called absence seizures. They don't hurt her."

"Do they happen a lot?"

"Not too many now. It used to be worse. When she first arrived, she was panicked. Seizures every day, all day. Screaming and hysteria, the poor thing."

"S-S-Screaming?"

Rita nodded, not hearing my stutter. "The reset would hit, and she didn't know what was happening. Imagine coming aware in the middle of taking a sip of water or taking a walk outside. Or waking up, not knowing if it's morning or night. But she's been at Blue Ridge two years now, so she's grown used to it."

"So she *does* remember where she is."

"No, honey," she said. "She can't remember anything. Most of what she says is out of habit."

"Does she remember you?"

Rita shook her head. "Nope. She doesn't know my name. Or her doctor's name. She eats in the dining room every day, three times a day but couldn't tell you where it is. She can't make her own way from this room to her bedroom. If you turned her loose outside, God forbid, she'd be lost within minutes. But she knows routine. We've been careful to build a *sameness* into her days, and that's grooved itself into her subconscious. Consistency keeps her calm."

I shook my head slowly. "Unreal."

She put her hand on my arm. "I know it's hard to understand, but the brain is an amazing mechanism with billions of outlets. When they're damaged, the results can be random and fascinating."

I didn't find Thea's situation fascinating.

Fucking horrifying, maybe…

Thea suddenly jumped out of her chair. "Delia!" she cried. She bent over her sister, hugging her tight. "I'm so happy to see you. How long has it been? Where are Mom and Dad?"

"It's been two years," Delia said. "Mom and Dad will be here soon. Tell me about this pyramid."

Rita leaned in. "She's redirecting Miss Hughes to the drawing to keep her from asking about her parents, the poor thing."

"Does she do the same Egypt stuff every day?"

Rita nodded. "Every day."

"What's the deal with the word chains?"

"They're extraordinary, aren't they? The detail. Miss Hughes is a talented artist."

"Do they mean anything?"

"Her neuropsychologist, Dr. Stevens, says they're echoes of her life before her accident. She attended an art college and was considered one of its best and brightest, according to Delia." Rita quirked a funny smile. "However, Miss Hughes sometimes claims that she was an etymologist."

"A what?"

"Someone who studies the origins of words," Rita said. "Dr. Stevens says it's a confabulation. That Miss Hughes made it up. He thinks it's her poor brain trying to create a history for herself because she has none." She glanced at the cubby full of drawings. "Almost time for a clean out."

"You just throw them away?" I asked.

"What else can we do with them?"

I didn't have an answer, except that the art was too good for the trash. Thea was too good for Magic Markers and scratch paper.

Rita studied my expression and put her hand on my arm.

"She'll draw more," the nurse said. "And she'll never know these are gone because she can't remember she did them in the first place."

I nodded vaguely, though I didn't like it. Not one fucking thing.

"I'd better get back to work," Rita said. "You'll get used to Miss Hughes. Just give it time."

Time. I had plenty of that. Years and years. Thea had a few minutes.

It's Miss Hughes to you. Let her go. Do your job.

As I swept the rec room floor, my eyes kept stealing glances at Thea. My stupid heart ached the way it did the day Grandpa Jack died. Grieving for something lost that could never be regained.

This was Thea's loss, not mine.

You sure about that?

I nodded. I hadn't lost Thea. She wasn't mine to lose and she never would be.

CHAPTER 4

Jim

Joaquin was right; Alonzo gave me two night shifts in a row. I met Mary Flint, the duty nurse who worked every night—a middle-aged woman with short dark hair and a pronounced nose. The biggest part of her job was dispensing nightly doses of medications from a locked mini-pharmacy on the second floor. Once the residents were out for the night, Mary didn't have much to do. Every time I passed her station on my rounds, she was dozing.

Fine by me. No small talk.

The first night at Blue Ridge was like the first night in my new house. Getting used to the sounds and the silence. I welcomed the solitude and the guarantee I wouldn't have to interact with anyone. I roamed the halls like a ghost, conscious of my feet on the linoleum and the sound of my breath.

Don't get stuck on the mountain.

Made yourself at home, did you?

I'd bounced around the foster care system my whole life. The concept of home or family didn't have any meaning for me. Grandpa Jack once said, "Make the best out of what you got."

So that's what I did.

After my night shifts, I had a full day off to recover before going back on the day shift. I spent it sleeping and messing around on my guitar. Grandpa Jack had gotten me a second-hand acoustic for my eleventh birthday. Doris wouldn't allow "noise" in the house, so I took it to the yard and plucked out songs I'd heard on the radio. I couldn't read music but turned out I had a good ear.

In my house in Boones Mill, I set it on my lap to try a Mumford and Sons song I'd heard the other day. A couple of lines from "Sweet Child O' Mine" came out instead. I slammed my hand on the strings.

"Fucking stop. Leave her alone."

I read a little, trying to stay awake and get back on a normal schedule. By four in the afternoon, I was stretched out on the little couch in my living room, watching *Die Hard* on a local channel. The movie was interrupted by commercials every three minutes and the swearing was dubbed over.

Bruce Willis, barefoot and bloody, stormed into a room. "Yippie kai yay, mother-flipper."

My eyes drooped. My thoughts broke apart. Sleep dragged me away from the noise of the movie...

The chain-link fence at the rear yard of Webster High School made a distinctive noise when a body was shoved against it. A scraping, metal-against-metal song. Most days I remembered to come around the front of the school, but I was running late today. The gap in the fence was close to the little house I shared with Doris. I squeezed through.

Toby Carmichael was waiting.

He gave me a rough shove and the fence gave a rattling twang as I bounced off it, the hard wire diamonds stabbing my shoulder blades.

"Why don't you go to the special-ed school with all the other losers?" Toby said. "Everyone knows you're r-r-retarded."

The three friends he brought along cheered and laughed, egging him on.

Toby shoved me again. "Say something, Wee-Wee-Whelan."

Don't say anything, *I told myself.* Don't give him ammo.

I was a freshman with a slight, undernourished body. Toby was a husky junior, fed on a steady diet of buffalo wings and bacon

39

cheeseburgers at Mill's Place, where all the kids hung out after school.

All the kids except me.

His shove bounced me against the fence and it sang its song, like a metallic cricket rubbing its legs together. I fucking hated that sound.

"I said, say something."

Toby lunged at me again and I dodged, my hands balled into fists. "F-F-Fuck off."

All four guys stopped, stared, and then erupted into laughter, mimicking me. "Fuh-Fuh-Fuck off."

Toby gripped me by the collar of my second-hand windbreaker jacket. "If I see you looking at Tina Halloran one more time, I'm going to break your stupid fuh-fuh-fucking face."

I struggled to remember who Tina Halloran was. She must've been the pretty girl who smiled at me while I was putting my stuff away in my locker yesterday. A short moment of sun in a perpetually gray sky.

"Hi, Jim," she'd said, wagging the tips of her fingers at me in a little wave.

I'd never talked to her. Of course not. I never spoke, not in class and certainly not in a crowded hallway full of students. Never to pretty girls with friendly smiles. Someone must've put her up to it. Maybe Toby...

"She doesn't want anything to do with a retard like you," he bellowed, bringing me back to the present. "You got me?"

Rage burned hot in me. Rage at the unfairness, the taunting, the goddamn stutter that caused me so much misery. My hands balled into fists and I drove one into Toby's stomach.

He gasped, sucking in air, but didn't let go of my jacket. His eyes widened with murderous anger. "You are so dead."

Hit me, I thought. Fucking hit me. Beat the stutter out of me for good.

Toby's left fist connected with my jaw and pain exploded across my mouth. I staggered back, reeling, and crashed to the ground.

He jabbed his finger at me. "That's your only warning. Next time, I smash your teeth out. Not that you need them."

The guys left with a few more sneering comments. I slowly got to my feet. Rubbing my aching jaw, I gathered my backpack and the notebooks that had fallen out. I spit out a wad of blood and watched it splatter to the ground. I imagined it was my stutter, finally ejected from my mouth, bloody and dead. It was gone now. Gone for good. I inhaled like Mrs.

Marren taught me. Exhale. Inhale, exhale, then let the words fall out…

"M-M-My n-n-n-name's Jim…"

Fuck.

I would have spat a curse, but that would have tripped on the way out too. I hurled my backpack at the chain-link fence and stared at the ground, breathing heavily. Slowly, I dragged dirt over the splotch of blood with my worn-out Chucks. Tried to bury it forever…

I woke up in a dark house with a fading, phantom ache in my jaw.

"Fucking pathetic," I said.

That stutter was buried now, even if only in a shallow grave, and no one had to know how bad it had once been. Those days were gone. Hours upon hours piled up between then and now like bricks. I'd keep piling them up until the memories were only a bad dream and nothing more. I'd wipe them clean away, the way Thea's mind wiped away her every waking moment.

Jesus, stop making everything about her.

I threw on my leather jacket and headed into town, prepared to erase my memory the old-fashioned way—by getting wasted.

In Boones Mill's tiny downtown, I found a bar called Haven. Small, dark, and with a tiny stage, where a guy plucked out a song on his guitar. A flyer on the table said local acts were welcome. A fleeting image of me on the stage with my guitar came and went.

I nearly laughed out loud.

I ordered a beer from the waitress and listened to the guy warble out a country song to a bored audience of ten people. The waitress came back before I was halfway done with the beer.

"Ready for another?"

"Uh, sure."

She leaned a hand on my table and smiled. Pretty. Her dark hair was in a ponytail and a tight black T-shirt strained over the curves of her breasts.

"Haven't seen you here before and I've seen everybody." She cocked a hip. "I'm Laura."

"Jim."

"New in town, Jim?"

I nodded.

"I thought so." Laura's smile turned private as she leaned closer. "Need someone to show you around? I make a pretty good welcome wagon."

What she was offering was clear. No reason I shouldn't take her up on it, except that Boones Mill was a hell of a lot smaller than Richmond. I didn't take women home regularly, but when I did, it was for one and only one night. With minimal verbal interaction.

I don't care if you stutter, Thea whispered in my ear. *I just want you to keep talking to me.*

"No, thanks," I said. "I'm good."

She pouted. "You sure? This town is so small and—"

"I'll take that beer." I raised my bottle.

Embarrassment flitted over her face, which she quickly covered with a scowl. "Sure thing."

She stomped off, and I watched her go, her ass looking perfect in her tight jeans, and inwardly cursed at myself. Small town or not, it was a while since I'd had company.

And what the hell was I doing thinking about Thea Hughes? Her memory was fucked. She wasn't capable of anything, not even friendship.

Her brain is broken. Leave her alone.

But she wouldn't leave *me* alone.

Laura plunked a new beer on my table and walked away. In my pathetic imagination, Thea sat next to me, listening to the music, swaying in her seat.

"Music is life," she said, her hand slipping into mine. Her blue eyes bright with recognition and light.

My life was a set of hours to be endured, not lived. My light low and sputtering. But I could take care of Thea Hughes. That was something I could do.

I left Laura a generous tip and rode back to my house without so much as a mild buzz. I hit the sack early and made sure my alarm was set.

I had a job to do.

In the dining hall the next morning, Thea looked up from her breakfast of eggs and toast, as I helped Mr. Webb take a seat at the table beside her.

"Good morning," she said, squinting at my nametag. "Jim."

"Good morning."

"How long has it been?"

Anna Sutton, the head nurse, joined us and set a cup of orange juice in front of Thea. She was in her fifties, dark hair always tied back neat and tight.

"You can answer," she instructed me, like a grade school teacher.

"Two years," I said. "It's been two years, Miss Hughes."

"Two years," Thea said. "God, that's so long. But I'm back now and the doctors are going to tell me what's wrong with me."

"They will," Anna said with a prim, reassuring smile.

"I'm Thea," she said, offering her hand and introducing herself to me for the fifth time.

Stop counting.

"Nice to meet you," I said, the words sounding so fucking wrong in my ears.

Thea glanced down at her food. "I've never eaten scrambled eggs before. Have I?"

"Yes, Miss Hughes," Anna said. "You love them."

Thea made a face, contemplating the truth of this statement before shrugging. She shot me a grin. "You're hovering, Jim. Come sit and eat scrambled eggs with us."

Anna arched one eyebrow at me, silently conveying that only one right response was correct here.

"I gotta get back to work," I said.

"Bummer," Thea said. "Where do you work?"

I glanced at Anna. She shook her head. The word "here" was forbidden.

"I'm an orderly."

If God were merciful, Thea would wrinkle her nose in distaste or snobbery and I'd be able to stop liking her so damn much. But no, she flashed that smile of hers.

"Groovy. Will I see you again?"

"Y-Yeah. Sure."

Again and for the first time.

Again turned out to be later in the afternoon, in the rec room. She was bent over a drawing, markers spread all over the table and a ballpoint in her hand. No doubt making her word chains. I swept the floor and kept my eyes on my work.

"Damn." Thea shook her pen hard, put it back to the paper, then frowned. She gave it another shake then abruptly froze. Her reset hit. Her hand trembled and she glanced around, confused.

We were short-handed as usual. Only the duty nurse was at the station. I had to do something before her panic took hold. I put down the broom and strode over. I nearly asked if she was all right before catching myself.

"Hi," popped out instead.

"Hi," she said, looking relieved. "How long has it been?"

"Two years, Miss Hughes."

She took a steadying breath and a faltering smile touched her lips. "That's a long time to be away, but the doctors are going to tell me what's wrong with me." Her eyes found my nametag. "Jim? I'm Thea Hughes."

That's six, I thought. *Cut it out.*

"Is your pen out of ink?" I asked, redirecting like Alonzo instructed.

Thea frowned and put her pen to paper. It scratched alongside the pyramid constructed out of words, but nothing came out. "How did you know?"

"I'll get you a new one."

I went to the storage supply closet and unlocked the door. Inside, I yanked the chain and the light bulb came on, illuminating racks of jigsaw puzzles, board games, magazines, and old books. I found reams of paper, boxes of ballpoint pens and Magic Markers. All the art supplies Thea had.

"That's it? Pens and paper?"

I jumped back as a rat scuttled across the closet's rear wall. Crouching on my heels, I found a crack in the drywall, revealing a sliver of daylight. I made a mental note to tell Alonzo about it, then shook a ballpoint pen from a box and hurried back to Thea. She was still trying her empty pen on her paper.

"Here you go," I said.

"Thanks, Jim," she said, taking the new pen. "You're a pal."

Amnesia or not, Thea was inherently friendly and cheerful to everyone she met. Buoyant. I'd bet good money she was effortlessly popular in school. The kind of beautiful, talented girl you wanted to hate but never could.

"Jim?"

"Y-Yes?"

"You're staring." She fluttered her eyelashes at me. "What are you thinking about?"

"You." Something about her directness demanded the truth in return. "I was wondering if you were as good of an artist in high school."

"I was an Egyptologist," she said with a nod at her drawing.

"An Egyptologist?" I said. "Not an etymologist?"

Her face scrunched up. "A what?"

"Oh. N-N-Nothing. Rita said..."

"Who's Rita?"

Shit. Fuck. Redirect.

"You studied Egypt?" I said and gestured at her drawing.

"I think that's what this must be. My old work." Thea's smile widened as she craned back to look up at me. "Sit down, will ya? You're hovering."

Now I'm on her loop.

"I love all things Egyptian," Thea said. "Their history is so rich with the rituals and gods, the monuments and the romance. All good stories have a romance. Love. Without love, what's the point?"

"Not my area of expertise," I said slowly.

"No?" Her grin widened. "Not a romantic? Are you sure? You look like Marc Antony to me. Lots of armor on the outside, but on the inside..." She made a face. "Yikes. There I go again. I have zero filter, if you haven't noticed. My sister is always telling me to tone it down, but I call it like I see it. Life is short, no?"

So short, Thea. Five minutes.

"You don't say much do you, Jim?"

"Not much."

"Am I talking your ear off?"

"No, it's fine."

It's fine. Jesus.

"Jim, Jim, Jim." Thea cocked her head. "Short for James, right? But you look more like a Jimmy to me. Jimmy with the kind eyes. Do you mind if I call you Jimmy?"

Why the hell that simple request sent my heart crashing, I didn't know, but it felt as if she drew us together across years instead of minutes.

Be professional. Tell her to use Jim.

"N-N-No," I said. "I d-don't mind."

Thea leaned over the table, compassion softening her features. "Do you have a stutter, Jimmy?"

I almost told her it only showed up when I was nervous or pissed off. Then she could ask if she made me nervous. She'd give that flirtatious laugh of hers, then tell me she didn't mind that I stuttered, but to not stop talking to her, and that my stutter wasn't the most interesting thing about me...

God, this is fucked up.

It occurred to me that I could change the script. I could tell her anything. I could fuck with her, and in a few minutes, she'd have forgotten all about it.

The notion made my stomach roil.

A cruel person, a bully—a Toby—would fuck with her. He'd laugh at her confusion and fear and justify it for the same reason—she wouldn't remember.

But I'd remember.

Someone needs to watch out for her.

"I stutter only sometimes now," I said. "It was worse when I was a kid."

"Did you get bullied for it?"

"Yeah, I did."

Her lips curled in a scowl. "Fucking bullies," she said. "I'm sorry, Jimmy. All bullies are cowards trying to hide their own weakness by directing attention to someone else." She glanced at me. "That doesn't make what you endured easier, does it?"

"It happened. Nothing can change it now."

"Tough guy, are you? Like Marc Antony. A stoic soldier, but your eyes give you away."

I coughed. Redirect.

"Marc Antony," I said and nodded at her drawing. "Part of your Egyptian studies?"

Thea leaned her cheek on her folded hands like she was warming herself before a fire. "Marc Antony is part of the romance. A love story with Cleopatra. He went to war for her. Died for her. When they told her he was dead, she put her hand in a basket with an asp. Can you imagine? Loving someone so much that the thought of life without them is too unbearable?"

"No," I said. "I can't."

Her gaze dropped to my hand on the table and her fingers reached to trace the scars on my knuckles.

"These tell a story, don't they?" She traced one of the fine lines on my first knuckle. "You put your hand in with the snakes, too."

I nodded slowly, savoring the feel of her warm skin on mine. "So they'd leave me alone."

"And did they?"

"Eventually."

"I'm glad." She put her hand in mine completely, her fingers wrapping around and holding tight. "I'm being too... something. Personal. Delia would throw a fit, but I feel like..."

"Like what, Thea?"

"Like I have to hold on to this moment, you know? Or you... I don't even know you and yet I don't want to stop talking to you." Her hand squeezed mine. "I don't care if you have a stutter, but please keep talking to me, Jimmy. Okay?"

My mouth went dry at the nameless desperation in her eyes.

Jesus, does she know she's trapped? She can't. Impossible...

"I won't," I said. "I'll talk to you every day. I promise."

Thea breathed a small sigh of relief and released my hand. "Thank you, Jimmy. That makes me feel better."

With a final smile—a parting smile, I realized—she took up her pen and then froze.

She's resetting.

Confusion passed over her features. She looked up at me, flinching a little to see a big man in close proximity. I instantly leaned back to give her space.

"How long has it been?" she asked.

"Two years," I said, my voice hardly more than a whisper. "But the doctors are working on your case."

"Yes, they are." She smiled hesitantly and found my nametag. "I'm Thea Hughes."

Seven. Seven times now.

"Jim Whelan," I said.

She offered her hand. Again. I took it robotically, enduring her one-pump shake. Again. Her fingers didn't linger in mine but released immediately, the way you do with a stranger. Again.

"Nice to meet you, Jim Whelan."

Fuck. I can't do this.

I rose to my feet. "I have to get to work."

Her face fell. "Oh. Bummer. Will I see you again?"

I could promise her I would, but she wouldn't remember. There was no promise. I could tell her the sky was falling or my name was Abraham Lincoln and she wouldn't know the damn difference. It'd vanish, like every other word we'd ever spoken to each other. *I* vanished every time her reset hit and was recreated over again in Thea's eyes. I could be whatever I wanted; whomever I wanted. And yet she was the one woman I might've had a chance to be myself with.

The terrible irony of it was like copper in my mouth.

"Sure, Miss Hughes," I said. "I'll see you tomorrow."

CHAPTER 5

Thea
(five minutes earlier)

I open my eyes for the first time.

A beautiful man sits across from me. Strong and built. His hands are large, his knuckles scarred. His biceps and forearms are cut with lean muscle. He's wearing white. A uniform?

At the next table sits an old man with a dent in his head.

Am I in a hospital?

Yes, because there was an accident and now I'm back.

Jesus, how long have I been away?

My heart pounds and blood rushes to my ears. My hand is clutching a pen and my knuckles hurt. It's hard to breathe. There was the accident, and now I'm here in this room. But how long between then and now? How did I get here? How much time have I lost?

"How long has it been?" I ask the beautiful man.

"Two years," he says in a low voice, almost a whisper. "But the doctors are working on your case."

He's right. The doctors are working on my case. That's one of the Things I Know.

My name is Thea Hughes.

There's been an accident.

The doctors are working on my case.

This man knew that, which means he must know me somehow. My hands unclench a little.

"Yes," I say. "They are."

But two years? God, I've been away a long time, but I'm back now. I ease a sigh of relief and the panic ebbs. Still, I can't find… something. Something is lost and I need to find it. If only I knew what it was.

I find the guy's nametag. Jim.

Jim is beautiful. And sexy. His sexiness is like a black leather jacket—it makes any outfit look good on him. He doesn't sprawl in the chair, doesn't man-spread like he owns the furniture or like he's commanding the room to pay attention to him. His posture is quiet, arms crossed on the table, shoulders a little hunched. He doesn't know how sexy he is, which makes him even more delicious. I fight a crazy urge to press my face into the crook of his neck and inhale him. Can't help it. I haven't been touched in forever. No sex. No food. No drink. Nothing.

Instead, I offer my hand. Delia is always yapping at me to be polite. And not that I mind touching this guy. "I'm Thea Hughes."

He sounds almost disappointed as he answers, "Jim Whelan."

Even his name is sexy. Masculine. Solid. But a softness lurks in him, making him more like a Jimmy than a Jim. I'm about to say so when a sudden, pained look crosses his handsome features and he rises to his feet.

"I have to get to work."

Disappointment bites me deep. I don't like being alone. A silence loiters on the outskirts of Jim and me—tight and airless—and it's so scary.

"Oh. Bummer," I say casually, hiding my desperation. "Will I see you again?"

Please say yes, Jimmy Whelan.

He hesitates, his dark eyes gazing intently into mine. I don't know what he's looking for, but whatever it is, I want him to find it.

"Sure, Miss Hughes," he says. "I'll see you tomorrow."

Then the beautiful, handsome man in a white uniform gets up and walks away.

A FIVE-MINUTE LIFE

I miss him already. I wish he'd come back. He has such kind eyes. Built like a brick wall with a sturdy jaw shaded with stubble, yet he's not intimidating to me. He's a good man. I want to keep talking to him.

He seemed reluctant to leave.

Maybe he's lonely.

Maybe I'll go find him and ask if he wants to hang out. Nothing serious. We just met, for crying out loud. But seeing him again feels like something that would be good for me.

I start to rise out of my chair when my eye catches a drawing on the table in front of me. It's an Egyptian landscape—a tall pyramid casting a long shadow under a blazing sun.

Did I draw this? Of course. Obviously, it's here in front of me, along with pens and colored markers. I must've started it before the accident. I should finish it. It's been two years. I'll finish it now. I uncap a Magic Marker, wishing I had canvas and paint. Maybe Delia will bring some for me when she comes. Or Mom and Dad.

I miss them. I try to remember their faces, to recall one moment of our lives before the accident.

I can't. When I look, I see emptiness. Like a vast desert of space with no walls but no air moving either. Fear starts to dig into my stomach, and I reach for the markers. Something I can hold in my hand. I add color to the sky. When it's done, I pick up the ballpoint. Tiny words loop out from under my pen and fill the shadow beneath the pyramid.

Strong stone moan groan lone alone lonely lowly low slow such scratch scar scar scar

It doesn't make sense. Words and words and words, saying nothing.

A person who studies words is an etymologist.

How is this a Thing I Know? Did I study words in college? Did I go to college? I try to remember. Something. Anything.

Silence in my mind.

Emptiness.

I'm lost…

My heart pounds and blood rushes to my ears. I read the words beneath the pyramid again.

Strong stone moan groan lone alone lonely

Jimmy is lonely. The words are about Jimmy.

Who is Jimmy?

Dark hair and eyes. Kind eyes. And a uniform. Was it white…?

Was what white?

I don't know. I can't see anymore. I can't remember…

I open my eyes for the first time.

There's an old man with a dented head at the next table.

Am I in a hospital?

Yes, because there was an accident and now I'm back.

Jesus, how long have I been away?

My heart pounds and blood rushes to my ears. My hand is clutching a pen and my knuckles hurt. It's hard to breathe. There was the accident, and now I'm here in this room. But how long between then and now? How did I get here? How much time have I lost?

A petite woman in a blue uniform is hurrying to me. A nurse. Her nametag says Rita.

"How long has it been?" I ask.

"Two years, Miss Hughes," Rita says. "The doctors are working on your case."

She's right. The doctors are working on my case. That's one of the Things I Know.

My name is Thea Hughes.

There's been an accident.

The doctors are working on my case.

This nurse knew that, which means she must know me somehow. My hands unclench a little.

Still, I can't find… something. It's lost and I need to find it. If only I knew what it was.

"This is a beautiful pyramid," Rita says, tapping the paper on the table in front of me. It's a picture of an Egyptian desert under a blazing sun, a pyramid casting a long, dark shadow.

I smile. "Thank you. I must've done it before the accident."

Rita has a sweet smile and I feel safe with her. There's a terror lurking in being alone. I think I've been alone for a long time.

I wish I had a canvas and paint. Maybe Delia will bring me some when she comes. Or Mom and Dad. I miss them. I try to remember their faces, to recall one moment of our lives before the accident.

I can't. When I look, I see emptiness. Like a vast desert of space with no walls but no air moving either. Fear starts to dig into my stomach. I'm holding a pen. It's solid and real in my hand and the panic ebbs. I put it to the paper and tiny words loop out and fill the shadow beneath the pyramid.

Was what white wrote rote rip trip snip snap map mapped trapped trapped trapped

It doesn't make sense.

Rita touches my arm. "This is coming along beautifully."

I smile back with relief. I need her words. I'm starving for them. For touch. Sound. Conversation. It's so quiet in here.

"Thanks," I say. "Have you worked here long?"

I feel like I should know the answer to that question. I feel like I should know Rita but I don't.

"A few years," Rita says. "Would you like something to drink?"

God, yes. I haven't had anything to drink in years. "A lemonade would be perfect," I say.

Is it? I know what lemonade is but I can't remember how it tastes. Or how I got here.

Rita smiles. "I'll be right back." She taps the corner of my drawing. "Can't wait to see what you add next. You're very talented, Miss Hughes."

"Thank you."

Rita gets up and I go back to drawing. I add some color to the words within the pyramid's shadow. Magic Markers aren't really my preferred medium, but Delia's always telling me not to be so picky. I can't help it if I prefer paint to pens. Painting is like breathing. Egypt is life.

A person who studies Egypt is an Egyptologist.

How is this a Thing I Know? Did I study Egypt in college? Did I go to college? I try to remember. Something. Anything.

Silence in my mind.

Emptiness.

I'm lost...

My heart pounds and blood rushes to my ears. It's suffocating, this quiet. Vast but constricting. A little box with no walls.

I read the words within the pyramid. *Trapped.*

Trapped where?

I don't know. I don't know where I am anymore. I can't remember.

I open my eyes for the first time…

CHAPTER 6

Jim

My mornings blurred into a routine of sameness. My own endless loop. The alarm went off at six; I made coffee and showered while it was brewing. Poured a cup and took it back to the bathroom. Wiped steam off the mirror to trim my thin beard. The guy in the mirror looked tough. Muscles built up from long hours in the garage lifting weights. Hard eyes. Mouth a grim line that rarely opened to speak.

Tough guy, eh? You're a coward. Doris sneered. *She compared you to Marc Antony? What a crock.*

"She's none of my business," I said.

The guy in the mirror mouthed along, but I'd been keeping a mental clock in the back of my mind all morning. Making coffee: five minutes. Drinking a cup: five minutes. Showering: five minutes. Shaving: five minutes.

A progression throughout the morning while Thea was trapped in minutes of consciousness at a time. A fucking nightmare. Not mine but terrifying anyway.

I had to believe Thea wasn't aware of her prison. I'd seen a desperation in her eyes, but I wasn't qualified to say what it meant. She looked happy enough with her pens and paper, working on her endless word chains, sometimes with a faint smile on her face.

Who was I to say she was suffering?

No one, Doris supplied helpfully. *You're no one.*

My shift at Blue Ridge began with a frantic text from Alonzo, ordering me to Mr. Perello's room on the third floor. Perello was an Army vet who served in Afghanistan. A roadside explosion sent an iron rod through his eye socket. He was a friendly guy until his traumatic brain injury triggered bouts of angry hysteria.

"You don't know where I've been!" he cried, fighting the combined efforts of Joaquin and Alonzo to restrain him while the duty nurse prepared a sedative. "You don't know what I've seen!"

His flailing arm caught Alonzo across the face. Alonzo staggered back, and I quickly stepped in. Quickly and carefully—the man was Army tough, and the rage gave him added strength. It took everything I had to hold him against the wall so he wouldn't hurt himself or anyone else.

"You don't know!" Mr. Perello seethed, his face inches from mine. A black eye patch over his left eye. "You fucking assholes think you got it all figured out. But you don't know *shit.*"

"Now, Mr. P," Joaquin said. "Calm down—"

"Don't fucking tell me to calm down. I'll teach you to show some respect. You don't know what I know."

"You're right," I said. "We don't know."

Spittle hit my jaw as his head whipped toward me. "Shut your mouth," he cried. "Don't fucking patronize me."

"I never would, sir," I said.

"I've seen shit."

"Yes, you have," I said. "We can't even imagine what you saw."

"I earned some respect, goddammit," Mr. P said, the fight draining out of him. "I *earned* it over there in that goddamn desert that you'll never have to see."

"You did. And we're grateful for it."

Mr. Perello stopped struggling and the duty nurse swooped in with the syringe.

"There you go, Mr. P," Joaquin said, easing the man on his bed. "You're going to take a nap now and feel much better when you wake up."

Mr. Perello went limp and we let him go.

"You okay, boss?" Joaquin asked.

"I'm okay." Alonzo wiped a trickle of blood from his lip. "Getting too old for this."

Joaquin slapped my shoulder as we exited the room. "Well, holy shit, rookie. I was beginning to think you didn't talk at all, but you knew just what to say to Mr. P."

I shrugged. "I told him the truth."

Alonzo nodded. "Indeed. You did good, Jim. Real good."

"Thanks."

I coasted on that *real good* the rest of the day, Joaquin's shoulder slap boosting me along. Fate kept Thea out of my sight and work kept her easily out of my thoughts. My job felt solid in my hands.

Late in the afternoon, I took the mop and bucket into the rec room, just as Thea left with Rita. She had a small smile on her face.

Because she's happy enough. Keep doing your job. Just like you did with Mr. Perello.

I hummed a little "Sweet Child O' Mine" as I moved to clean up Thea's table. Rita had left Thea's markers and a few sheets of paper behind. I gathered them and the markers to take to her shelf.

I stopped in mid-stride.

I'd seen Thea's drawings before, but I hadn't really *looked*. I was looking now.

The word chain I'd asked Rita about had been one of hundreds. Thousands. This drawing of a pyramid under an Egyptian sun was crawling with them. Tiny, precise penmanship as small as typeset. Every detail of the drawing crafted from words, with the marker colors over them.

Are they all made out of word chains? Impossible.

I grabbed the stack of drawings on Thea's shelf. The first showed another pyramid in the Egyptian desert. So did the one beneath that. And the one beneath that. The entire stack was drawings of ancient Egypt, some with Cleopatra wearing her blue and gold-striped headdress and gold bracelets circling her upper arms. Some showed Marc Antony at the head of a fleet of warships, his sword held high and glinting in the sun.

Every single image was crafted out of words. Chains of words. Pointillism paintings made of letters instead of dots.

Tomb loom soon moon moan groan grown sown lone lost lost lost

I turned one page at an angle to read the tiny script that created a black cat basking in the sun.

Cat sat sang sting wing wasp was wasn't mustn't must trust lust last gasp gone gone gone

Shadows cast across the desert sand were a sea of words in black ink and shaded over in gray. One line jumped out at me.

Dark mark lark line sign sing screen scream scream scream

"Holy shit."

These weren't just word chains. These were strings of pain. And at the end of every one, the theme. The period at the end of Thea's sentence. A repetition, like the echo of a voice calling out from somewhere deep and dark.

Lost. Gone. Scream.

My hands were shaking now. There were weeks of drawings, and I shuffled through them, picking out more word chains at random, my breath coming short. One that terrified me more than any other. A short coil of words that made up a little shadow under Cleopatra's throne.

Love live life knife near tear seer fear wear where? here here here

"Here," I whispered. "She's here."

I wasn't stupid enough to believe her doctors hadn't seen these drawings, but why the fuck hadn't they done anything about them? Didn't this mean Thea was conscious of her situation?

It's all right here. She knows what's happening to her.

The thought sank like a stone in my heart.

"Jesus Christ." Inhale. Exhale. I gripped the edge of the chair as twilight fell outside the windows. "She knows. She fucking knows."

This was more than regurgitation. Had to be. Thea was there, trapped in her own mind, and had been *for years.*

Nurse Rita entered the rec room, this time with Nancy Willis clinging heavily to her arm—another resident who was suffering from permanent dizziness due to an injury sustained twenty years ago. Rita set the old woman down in a chair and brought her a set of dominoes.

"I'll be right back, Ms. Willis," Rita said, reading my expression. "Jim? You're pale as a ghost."

58

I started to show Rita the drawings but stopped. She'd seen them. She'd been working here for years too. Anger burned in my veins which meant the stutter was lurking.

"N-Nothing. I'm fine."

She frowned but Ms. Willis dropped a domino on the ground and called for help to retrieve it. Rita left me to assist her so I could get to work. I was supposed to take out the trash. Do my job. Throw out all of Thea's drawings.

Her cries for help.

I dumped Thea's drawings into a trash bag but didn't tie the bag. I lifted it from the can and gathered the ends in my fist to take outside to the dumpster.

What are you doing?

I had a vague idea I'd take the drawings and… what? Mail them to Thea's doctor? Mail them to another doctor? A better doctor who would actually do something about the fact she was fucking trapped in five minutes at a time?

Outside, the air was thick and sticky; the summer sun brilliant in a clear blue sky. At the dumpster at the side of the building, I reached into the bag and grabbed three or four of Thea's drawings, rolled them into a tube and stuffed it into my back pocket, then tied the bag and tossed it into the dumpster.

"Whatcha got there, Jim?"

Shit…

The dumpster lid slammed down, nearly smashing my fingers. I turned my back to it, my heart pounding as Alonzo approached.

"N-N-Nothing," I said.

"Mighty hot out for chattering teeth." He cocked his head. "Nervous? Show me this 'nothing.'"

Now you'll lose your job, you big dummy.

I inhaled, exhaled, and handed over the rolled-up drawings.

Alonzo unrolled the papers and tucked a cigarette in his mouth. "You an art fan?"

"No, sir," I said.

"You mind telling me why you're saving Miss Hughes' drawings from the trash?"

I straightened, crossed my arms. If he was going to fire me, may as well tell the truth. "Didn't seem right to throw them away."

He nodded and rolled the papers up again. "Come sit."

My arms dropped, and I followed him to a bench that faced the Blue Ridge's west wing. Crickets chirped and flitted in the tall grass as Alonzo lit his smoke.

"The word chains, right?"

I nodded. Alonzo started to speak when movement above caught our eyes. Thea appeared in the window of her room. She didn't look down but put her hand on the glass and stared out over the forest, to the mountains in the distance.

"You can't be looking at her like that," Alonzo said.

I flinched and tore my gaze from Thea. "I'm not—"

"And you can't be taking nothing from the sanitarium. If Delia Hughes knew you did this, she'd have your ass, no questions asked."

"They feel important," I said in a low voice. "Those word chains—"

"They aren't your business, son. We been over this. She isn't like you or me. She looks pretty. Healthy. She smiles a lot. But she's brain damaged. *Brain damaged*."

I shuddered. "I know."

"Do you?" Alonzo cocked his head. "You're reading into her scribbles like they're a secret code. You look at her like there's *hope*."

"Hope…?"

"Hope she's going to get better."

"Don't we all want that for these patients?"

Alonzo narrowed his eyes. "We do, but I told you, they're not going to get better. Miss Hughes isn't going to get better. Not today or tomorrow. Not ten years from now. The doctors have been all over her case. They've seen these." He waved the drawings. "And there's nothing they can do."

I shifted on the bench, the weight of his words like a prison sentence being handed down to Thea. Twenty-three years old, with no other health issues. She could easily live to be… seventy? Eighty? Sixty more years in this place? Sixty years of drawings, introductions, and *How long has it been?* All the while, somehow knowing she was trapped with no way to get out.

I couldn't fucking imagine it.

"There's nothing they can do?" I asked. "Nothing at all?"

"Althea Hughes has one of the worse documented case of amnesia in medical history," Alonzo said. "If there were something to be done, her doctors would do it."

I sank back against the bench. "She's trapped."

Alonzo studied me a moment more then ground out his cigarette and picked up the butt. "Watch yourself, son."

My head whipped up to meet his gaze. "I would n-n-never—"

"Never take her personal property home with you?"

He's right. I sound like a fucking stalker.

"I get feelings about people," Alonzo said. "Been good at reading them. I suspect you're a good man, but this is your warning. Watch yourself and watch your hope. Watch that you don't want Miss Hughes to get better just for her sake but for yours too."

He handed me the drawings.

"I take it you know where to put these?"

I nodded.

"Good. See you in there."

He walked away and when he was gone, I let the drawings uncurl in my loose grip.

Leave this to her doctors.

They were neurosurgeons and psychologists with years of training and education. I was an orderly with a high school diploma.

I stood up and headed back toward the dumpster. I shot a last glance up at the window, but Thea wasn't there anymore.

She's not there anymore.

Feeling more and more like a stalker infringing on patient privacy, I hoisted the heavy dumpster lid with one hand. It felt almost obscene to put artwork of this caliber in the garbage, but I should've left them alone in the first place. It was wrong to take them. Unprofessional. I was lucky Alonzo hadn't fired me.

I reaffirmed my vow not to get involved in Thea Hughes' care any more than an orderly should. It was none of my business.

I stuffed the pages in, and the heavy lid slammed down, pinning a drawing so that its corner stuck out against the rusted green metal. A word chain jumped out at me, like a goddamn five-alarm siren.

Bye lie cry try fly sly sigh high hail hell help help help

CHAPTER 7

Jim

I was in the employee break room, taking my fifteen minutes off when Rita burst in.

"Oh Jim, thank God, you're here."

"What's up?"

"I have to attend to Ms. Perkins right now and Nurse Eric is out sick today. Would you mind taking Miss Hughes out for her FAE?"

I hesitated. Over the last few days, I'd been good at avoiding Thea. Doing my job. Keeping my head down. I didn't talk to her in the rec room, and I sure as shit wasn't going to think about her word chains. I had to believe Alonzo when he said the doctors knew what they were doing or else I'd lose my mind.

"I'm sorry, I know you're on break," Rita said. "I wouldn't ask but there's no one else—"

"N-No, it's fine," I said. "I can take her."

So much for keeping my head down.

"Thanks a ton. She's in the cafeteria finishing a snack." She tapped the doorjamb. "If you could hurry before she wanders to the front door again…?"

I headed to the dining room. In the hallway outside, I spied a doctor I hadn't seen before conferring with a few other specialists from Roanoke. Mid-thirties, sleek black hair, intelligence sharp in her eyes.

"Hey, Joaquin," I asked as he passed. "Who's that?"

"Dr. Christina Chen," he said. "New arrival from Australia. Word is, she's interested in Miss Hughes."

"Interested? What's that mean?"

Joaquin shrugged. "Have you seen Dr. Stevens around at all? Me neither," he said before I could answer. "*Interested* is better than nothing."

I nodded. For days, I'd been telling Thea the doctors were working on her case. Maybe this meant it was finally true.

In the dining room, Thea sat at a table, an empty plate and a half glass of lemonade in front of her. She wore the usual drab clothes they put her in but beautiful in the summer light streaming in from the tall windows.

Her nervous glance told me a reset had just hit. I hurried toward her.

"How long has it been?" she demanded before I was halfway across the room.

"Two years, Miss Hughes."

She nodded and eased a sigh, her eyes going to my nametag. "Thanks… Jim. I had an accident. The doctors are trying to figure out what's wrong with me." She stuck out her hand. "I'm Thea."

I'd forced myself to stop counting her introductions and endured her vigorous handshake for what felt like the millionth time.

"Would you like to go for a walk?"

Thea's luminous face broke out into a smile that made my chest ache. "I would love to. Are you my escort?"

I nodded.

She raised an eyebrow. "Well?"

"Oh, right…"

I offered her my arm and laughing, she took it. I led her to the back door that opened on the fenced grounds.

"It's such a beautiful day," Thea said, turning her face to the sun.

The heat wrapped around us in a thick blanket of humidity. Insects buzzed. The lush, green grasses threatened to overtake the stone path through the grounds. The high fencing was just visible on our right, with the thick forest on its other side. I wondered if Thea saw only the trees and plants and not the fence that kept her in.

"You're awful quiet, Jim," she said. "Not a big talker?"

"Not much."

"I'm the opposite. My sister says I never shut up." Thea peered up at me. "Jim is short for James, yes? You don't look like a James. Or a Jim, even. Jimmy, I think. You have kind eyes. Do you mind if I call you Jimmy?"

"I don't mind," I said, my heart aching and glad at the same time. The same every time.

"Something bothering you, Jimmy?" Thea gave my arm a squeeze. "Contrary to what Delia thinks, I'm a good listener too."

"N-Nothing's bothering me," I said.

Nothing was what I could do about Thea's predicament. I suddenly regretted this walk.

Thea cocked her head. "Okay, but I'm all ears if you change your mind. Especially now. It's so quiet out here."

Twice she'd brought up the quiet. I wondered if the silence of her mind—empty of memory—bothered her more than the quiet of the grounds on this humid afternoon.

Of course, it bothers her. Because she knows. Her word chains are proof.

That line of thinking wasn't going to get me anywhere. There was nothing I could do to change the future, but I could do something for her at the moment. For the five minutes she had.

"Do you like music?" I said.

Thea's face lit up. "*Like* it? Music is life. I'd kill for some tunes right now."

I reached for my phone to play something for her and realized I'd left it in my locker.

Shit. So much for that plan.

"What about you, Jimmy?" Thea asked. "What do you listen to?"

"Old school rock and metal, mostly," I said.

"Right on. Dance and techno are my jam. Do you play an instrument too?"

"Not really."

She gave my arm a nudge. "Not really usually means yes, but you don't want anyone to know."

What difference does it make if you tell her? In about three minutes, she won't remember anyway.

"I play guitar," I said. "And I sing a little." The words flew out before I could catch them back.

Thea stopped walking and stood in front of me on the path. "You sing?"

"A little," I said. Fuck.

"You sing and you play rock music on the guitar. Good grief, Jimmy. You have to know how hot that is, right?"

I coughed. "N-N-No…"

She cocked her head, her expression softening. "Am I making you nervous?"

Inhale. Exhale. Hell, I told her before.

"I have a stutter. It was worse when I was younger. A teacher told me singing can help."

Thea nodded, then her smile returned. "I'd love to hear you sing."

I stared. I hadn't sung in front of anyone. Ever.

"No one's around for miles," she said. "And it's so quiet. Please? Just a little sample?"

"I don't have my guitar."

"A cappella works for me," she said.

My stomach tightened and my palms got sweaty. "I don't think so."

"Are you sure? Because—"

"*I'm sure.*"

Thea flinched and looked away. I cursed myself, aware of the sheer volume of trust Thea had to place in everyone around her—whether she knew it or not. Except for Delia, everyone in Thea's life was a stranger.

"Sorry," I said. "Didn't m-m-mean to bite your head off."

"No, it's my bad. Delia's always telling me I'm pushy as hell. Guess she's right." She slugged my arm half-heartedly. "You're off the hook. I just feel like…"

"Like what?"

"Like it's so quiet, you know? Not just out here." She gestured at the grounds. "But all the time. Always. I know that doesn't make sense. Not even to me…"

Just fucking sing for her. Make her happy. Her reset is coming. She won't remember.

The ache in my chest tightened like a hand squeezing. I dreaded singing out loud, but I dreaded the reset more. How it would tear down everything we built. Another introduction. Another request to call me Jimmy. But in these few minutes, she'd have what she wanted. A change from her endless cycles of sameness.

It wasn't about me anyway. If she really was aware of her situation, deep down, the very fucking least I could do for her was anything she wanted.

"Okay," I said. "I'll sing."

"Really?" Thea's face lit up. "Score. I am so ready."

"Let's walk. I can't do it with you staring at me."

We began to walk. Years of taunting and bullying nearly changed my mind, but before I could think about it for another second, I began to sing "Sweet Child O' Mine," low and rough. A slowed-down a cappella rendering of the rock song as we walked the silent grounds.

I sang of a woman's blue eyes that thought of rain, her smile, and the beauty of her face that could make me cry if I stared too long. I lost myself in the words, inhibitions falling away with every syllable because I was singing to Thea. I was singing *about* Thea and it was the easiest thing in the world…

"Are you *kidding* me?" Her hand clutched my arm, cutting me off.

Shit. Here it is. The reset.

But gazing up at me, those crystal blue eyes were only full of wonder, awe and—God help me—want.

"You're so good." She yanked up the sleeve of her ugly beige shirt. "It's a million degrees out but I have goose bumps. Look."

Her pale, perfect skin was raised in gooseflesh.

"You have a beautiful voice," she said, her tone lower now. "Rough and deep and… sexy."

I swallowed. Jesus, I wanted to kiss her. Her cheeks were dusted pink, and the sun glinted on her hair. I wanted to bury my hand in it, haul her to me and kiss her. Feel her smile against mine and taste the sweetness of her mouth.

"And you play guitar too?"

"Y-Y-Yes."

She gave herself a little shake and her eyes filled with the desperation I'd seen the other day. "God, if only..."

"If only?"

"I don't know," she said. "I feel so comfortable with you. It doesn't make sense. We don't know each other. You're the first person I've seen since I came back."

"Thea..."

"Whatever happens, Jimmy, please don't stop singing to me. Okay?"

I swallowed hard. "What do you think is going to happen?"

It wasn't an Alonzo-approved question, but I had to ask. I had to know if she knew.

"I might go away again," she said, her voice strangely hollow. She glanced around the silent grounds under a blanket of thick, heavy air. Her hand in mine. "I don't want to go away again."

I gripped her fingers hard. "I don't want you to either."

Now her eyes filled with tears and she moved closer to me. "Jimmy," she began, but the rest of the sentence was lost forever. Time was up. Our five minutes was over.

I watched myself disappear in her eyes, then reappear as she glanced around.

"Who...?" She pulled her hand out of mine and took a step back, brows furrowed.

Remember me, Thea. Please.

Her gaze dropped to my nametag. "Jim?"

I nodded, my breath held tight.

"How long has it been?"

I exhaled all my stupid, baseless hope.

"Two years, Miss Hughes," I said.

Two years and five minutes.

CHAPTER 8

Jim

Alonzo was in the rec room when I brought Thea in for her drawing time. As I collected pens and paper, I felt his gaze at my back.

"Thank you, Jim," Thea said with a bright smile. "You're a pal."

"Yup."

A pal. Not Marc Antony. Not the guy who sang to her and gave her the chills. I was no one again.

Walking toward the door, I felt ill.

"You look like you just came back from a date that crashed and burned," Alonzo said.

"Rita needed help," I said, crossing my arms. "So I helped."

My boss narrowed his eyes. "Uh-huh. I hired a new guy. Starts in a week. That'll *help* too."

I nodded.

"You remember what I said about Miss Hughes?"

Every muscle in my body tensed, my stomach tightened. "I remember."

"See that you do, son," he said, pushing off the wall. "Because she never will."

A FIVE-MINUTE LIFE

That night, I picked up my guitar and sang "Sweet Child O' Mine." The lyrics came out fluidly, without hesitation or self-consciousness. The music drowned my life's customary soundtrack—the rattle of a chain-link fence, the taunts of bullies and Doris's poisonous commentary.

I'd sung to Thea Hughes. Out loud. Because she liked my voice. It made the hairs stand up on her arms. She thought it was sexy.

It turned her on.

I buried that thought deep. Thea wasn't capable of consent and it'd been wrong to fantasize about kissing her. But I could take care of her. Protect her from the deafening silence of her mind. Maybe do what Mrs. Marren had told me years ago.

Find your voice, Jim. Don't let it fade away because the words don't come easy. Or because you're afraid of looking weak. You're not weak. Not so long as you do what's right for yourself.

What was right for me was doing right by Thea Hughes.

I put my guitar away and read some of *Fight Club.* A story about a guy who created another version of himself. A stronger, better self who didn't give two fucks what anyone thought of him. Who had no failings. No stutter.

I read until my eyes drooped, then slept.

I dreamed I had two selves, like the narrator in *Fight Club,* and I met up with the two selves of Thea Hughes. The four of us stood before the oil painting in the foyer of the Blue Ridge Sanitarium: the stuttering orderly and the resident with unalterable brain damage. The orderly did his job and gently assisted the resident back into the dim confines of the sanitarium.

But the beautiful artist took the stutter-less version of me by the hand and led him out into the bright light of day.

That morning, before shift, I sat around the employee table with Rita, Joaquin, and the head nurse, Anna Sutton. Over snacks and sodas, they shot the shit about the Netflix shows they'd seen lately, while I struggled for a way to bring up Thea without sounding like an obsessed psycho.

"What's our budget for rec rooms activities?" I said at the first lull.

All heads turned toward me. "Why do you ask?" Anna said.

"Mr. Webb does the same jigsaw puzzle, day in and day out," I said. "And Thea Hughes needs better supplies. A canvas. Real paint and brushes. I was wondering what the budget is for getting some new stuff in here."

Anna gave me a dry look. "Mr. Webb does the same jigsaw puzzle every day because it's part of his therapy. When he's ready for a new puzzle, he will begin a new puzzle."

Fuck. Stepped in that one.

"As for budget," she continued, "we have none. Blue Ridge Sanitarium is a rarity. Not many memory care facilities deal solely with brain injury. The money goes toward staying open. Paying salaries."

"Why would Miss Hughes need a bigger canvas anyway?" Joaquin asked. "She can't remember that she's only had paper. She doesn't know one way or the other."

Inhale. Exhale. "What if she does?"

Joaquin laughed and kicked his feet up on the table. "Please welcome our new neuropsychologist, Dr. James Whelan."

Under the table, my fists clenched.

Sure, tell them about the word chains. Doris sneered. *I'm sure they'll come as a huge shock to everyone who's been working with Thea for* years.

"The *actual* neuropsychologist has been all over this case a hundred times," Anna said. "And in any case, Miss Hughes is regurgitating what her brain picked up. That's all."

"Isn't that memory?" I asked.

"No, Jim," Anna said slowly, as if I were a child. "It's a groove of routine. She cannot bring anything to mind, therefore she has no awareness of her quality of life, so long as we keep her calm."

Rita put her hand on my arm. "Is that what you're worried about? That Miss Hughes is suffering?"

"How could she not be?"

"Because she can't remember," Anna said, shooting Rita a hard look. "Without conscious awareness of her situation, how can there be suffering?"

It sounded plausible, but the itch in the back of my mind wouldn't leave me alone.

"Why is she so accepting of her situation—wherever she is and whoever she's with—when a reset hits?" I asked.

"Didn't Alonzo give you the rundown?" Joaquin asked.

I crossed my arms. "I want to hear it again."

"Miss Hughes didn't accept *anything* after her accident," Anna said. "It took months before she stopped becoming hysterical with every reset. She's calm now because underneath the bells and whistles, the brain's most basic function is survival." Lips pursed, she stood up, checking her small gold watch. "Time to clock in. Are we satisfied, Dr. Whelan?"

I shrugged. *Not fucking remotely.*

Joaquin clapped his hand on my shoulder. "If there was something more to do for Miss Hughes, one of them smart neuro-psychs would have put it together by now."

"Are they still looking?" I asked. "What about that new doctor? Christina Chen?"

He shrugged. "I don't get involved in resident care and neither should you. If Delia Hughes finds out you're messing around with her sister, she'll have you canned."

Because Thea should have paint instead of goddamn Magic Markers? Or some music? A better quality of life?

After the others left, I turned to Rita. "Why would it bother Delia to know we give a shit about her sister?"

"Delia has her reasons," she said gently. "She's protective. Afraid of upsetting her, afraid of any publicity. And she's also watching the money."

"What money?"

"Their parents had a life insurance policy that left them a million dollars each. Blue Ridge's funding isn't consistent. Some years, we have cutbacks. *Most* years. Delia wants to save every penny if Thea needs care somewhere else. She's cautious."

She's got a million bucks in the bank and won't buy her sister some fucking paint?

"It doesn't make any sense."

Rita checked her own watch and stood to go. "It's sweet you want to make things better for Miss Hughes," she said. "But if you bought her a canvas and paint, she'd forget all about it the second they were out of sight."

But she'd have it in the moment. Doesn't that count?

"Rita."

She stopped at the door and looked back at me.

"I think she knows," I said.

"I don't know, honey, but she isn't hurting."

"But—"

"It's like Anna said. If she has no conscious awareness about her situation, she isn't suffering."

"What if the awareness is deeper than consciousness?"

"There is no awareness without consciousness." She smiled gently. "That's why they call it *un*conscious."

I rubbed my hands over my face. "What about music? Thea loves dance and techno.

"She listens to a classical station sometimes. Delia's orders. She'd read Mozart stimulated the brain."

I stared. "That's it? That's Thea's entertainment?"

"Well, no. She has a TV. Her favorite show was *The Office*. She watches that, though I don't know that she can keep up with the plot. Like being here, it's just routine." She smiled gently at me. "And when I shut off the radio or TV, she doesn't remember they were ever on."

Her expression was full of pity as she left. Joaquin had looked amused. Anna wanted me to mind my own business and stop trying to diagnose a complex neurological situation I had no training or education for. They'd all given up on Thea.

Rita popped her head back into the room. "Before I forget, Jim, can you take Miss Hughes for her walk today at one o'clock? I know it's your break time but—"

"Yeah, I can do it," I said.

Because I wasn't going to give up on her.

CHAPTER 9

Jim

The day dragged until one o'clock. I grabbed my phone and a set of earbuds from my locker and shoved them in my pocket. I approached Thea at her table in the dining room, a half-finished plate of cheese, crackers, and sliced green apples in front of her. I let her see me first.

"How long has it been?" she asked.

"Two years."

She nodded. "I just came back. You're the first person I've seen." She looked at my nametag. "Hi, Jim. I'm Thea."

"Would you like to go for a walk and get some fresh air?" I asked.

Her smile was painfully stunning. "I'd love to."

We stepped out the back door and into the stifling heat of the summer day. Instead of wilting in the humidity, Thea came alive. Despite her bland clothing, she was vibrant and beautiful. I suspected that Thea Hughes, pre-accident, wouldn't have been caught dead in khaki pants and loafers.

"It's so nice out, Jim," she said. "Is Jim short for James?"

"You can call me Jimmy," I said because I was sick of our usual script.

She nudged my arm with a laugh. "I was about to ask, mind-reader. You are a Jimmy. You have kind eyes."

At least that line I could listen to a hundred more times.

"It's so quiet," Thea said.

I gripped the phone and cords in my pocket, wondering if introducing music was a good idea. What if it set her off? But Thea's five-minute world was always quiet, and I was tired of second-guessing myself. So fucking tired of not *doing* something.

"I was thinking the same thing," I said slowly. "Do you like music?"

Music is life.

"Do I? Music is *life*. What's your fave?"

I wasn't going to let her turn the conversation on me. "This and that," I said. "What do *you* like?"

"I'm a dance and techno gal." She frowned. "But funny… I can't think of anyone I listen to."

"Hold on," I said, pulling out my phone and earbuds. I quickly scrolled iTunes for popular dance songs. "Bad Romance" by Lady Gaga popped up first.

"Try this." I gave her the earbuds and hit play, bracing myself.

Instantly, Thea's face broke into pure joy and she began to bob her head, eyes closed, listening to her favorite music for maybe the first time in two years. "Oh my God, this is *amazing*," she cried. "Here. Share."

She took one bud out and gave it to me. We stood in the heat of the afternoon, face-to-face. She was lost in the music and I was lost in her. I'd never seen anything so beautiful in my life. She swayed like a willow tree, slender and delicate, while I was the oak rooted in front of her. Between her and the world, protecting her as best as I could.

The song ended and Thea took out her earbud. "*I want your love… Love, love, love…*"

I stared. *That's the song, you idiot. Not her.*

Thea laughed and gave me a playful shove. "I love it, but I can tell it's sooo not you. You are not a dance house, club kid kind of guy, am I right?"

"Not really."

She tapped her fingers on the muscles of my forearm. "I can't picture you on the dance floor. You'd be the bouncer at a club, making sure everyone behaved themselves. A Marc Antony. Have you heard of Marc

Antony?"

"Sounds familiar."

"Marc Antony was a general who fought with Julius Caesar during the civil war. After Caesar died, Antony was put in charge of Egypt, where Cleopatra was queen. They had an affair that nearly started another war. He was Cleopatra's love. Strong. Noble. A soldier, but he fought only because he had to." She raised her eyes to mine. "You look like you'd fight, but only if you had to."

"Only if I had to."

I'd fight for you.

Our eyes held another moment, then Thea drew a deep breath. "Oh my God, Jimmy," she said, her arms out wide. "I feel so *awake.*"

"Yeah?"

"Like I just drank six Red Bulls or something." Her smile turned warm and flirty, and she tapped my phone. "You got one more song in there for me?"

"I have hundreds."

She raised her crystal blue eyes to mine and for one precious moment, something deep in her connected to something deep in me so hard and fast that my chest constricted, trying to hold on to the air that had been punched out. Thea's eyes widened and so did her smile. The radiance inside her burst through the cracks of her broken mind and I saw her. This girl whom, if we had longer than five minutes, I'd make mine.

But no sooner did I get a sweet taste of *mine* when the familiar confusion rolled through Thea's gaze. She was resetting. *I* was resetting, going from protector to threat. From friend to stranger. From Jimmy to…

No one, Doris finished. *You're no one.*

My hands itched to grab Thea and hold on, so I didn't vanish.

She took a step back. "Who…?"

"Jimmy," I said. "My name's Jimmy."

We did that scene three times that afternoon. Three times, I waited for the curtain of her mind to close and open again and we started over. Actors in a movie, reading a script, but the cameras and crew were hidden from sight. The same words, take after take.

Every time, the confusion swept across her eyes, wiping everything away. Erasing our five minutes. Erasing who and what we were to each other.

Nothing. We can't be anything to each other because she has nothing to give. No way to give it.

Eventually, we made our way back inside, each still with an earbud in our ear, listening to a dance song together. We sat at Thea's table, still tethered, a techno beat thrumming in our ears.

"You like this one?" I asked. "BOOM" by X Ambassadors.

Thea nodded to the beat. "I love it."

She loves it. She's happy. Delia can shove it up her—

"What is going on here?"

I flinched, and the earbud fell out of my ear. Delia Hughes stood by the table, her hard stare going between me and her sister.

"Delia!" Thea shot to her feet, then immediately froze, gripped by an absence seizure. I watched her to make sure she was okay until it released her, then turned to her sister.

"Hello, Ms. Hughes."

Delia started to speak, and I was pretty sure it wasn't to tell me what a great job I was doing. But Thea came around the table and threw her arms around her neck.

"You're here. How long has it been? Where are Mom and Dad?"

Delia's voice was a stone. "Two years, and they're on their way."

"I'm so glad you came." Thea hugged Delia again, then stopped short when she saw me. A shy, soft smile came over her features. "Oh. Hi."

"Hi."

"I'm Thea Hughes." She stuck out her hand, and I shook it, drowning in déjà vu.

"Jim Whelan."

"So nice to meet you. This is my sister, Delia." Thea laughed at her sister's sour look. "Oh my God, Deel, you're such a crank."

"You're an orderly, yes?" Delia asked me. "Where is Nurse Soto?"

"We're shorthanded today," I said.

Delia pursed her lips. "I see. Well, I'm here now. You may go."

I glanced at Thea who rolled her eyes and mouthed *I'm sorry* at me.

An hour later, I was pushing a mop down the hall outside the rec room and saw Rita, Alonzo, and Delia in a huddle. They looked up as I approached and Delia turned to me, arms crossed.

"We can ask him, himself. What were you doing with my sister?"

Shit. I'm going to lose my job. Thea will be alone in the silence.

"N-N-Nothing," I said. "Just listening to music."

"Is that in your job description?"

"N-N-No."

"Are you nervous? Guilty? What's wrong with you?"

Rita interjected. "Jim's been taking Miss Hughes for her daily exercise on days when I—"

"When you can't because you're short-staffed," Delia finished. "I don't pay to have Thea cared for by an orderly."

"Jim is a fine employee," Alonzo said. "One of our best."

Delia sniffed, shouldered her purse and leveled her gaze at me. "Stay away from my sister unless you want to find another job. I can't imagine your stutter would make that easy."

Rita's eyes widened and Alonzo cast his gaze to the ground. Silence fell as Delia's short-heeled footsteps clopped down the hallway and vanished.

"I'm sorry, Jim," Rita said. "She's upset because she's protective of Thea. I'll talk to her."

"Don't," Alonzo said. "We should just do what she wants."

"I've got three other residents to deal with since Nurse Fay quit," Rita said. "Unless Jim takes her, Miss Hughes misses her FAE. I'll explain it to Delia. She may be a grouch, but ultimately she only wants what's best for her sister."

Alonzo frowned. "I suppose," he said. "But Jim shouldn't take Miss Hughes for FAE until you get the okay from Delia. The last thing we need is for her to get Dr. Poole involved."

Dr. Poole was Blue Ridge's director of operations whose favorite pastime was firing personnel to save money.

Rita patted my arm. "Sorry for the... unpleasantness, Jim. What Delia said—"

"It is what it is," I said, my blood burning.

Alonzo was about to say something when Joaquin appeared at the end of the hallway.

"Hey, boss, got a second?"

"Coming." He gave me a curious glance, then walked away.

Congratulations. Doris cackled. *Now they all know you have a stutter and Delia is probably going to get your ass fired.*

She was right. If I wasn't careful, if I didn't leave Thea's case to the professionals, I'd have to start over somewhere else.

And never see Thea again.

That afternoon, as I cleaned up the empty rec room, I found a new drawing on Thea's shelf. I glanced at the door before picking up the paper. Marc Antony stood at the prow of a warship, clad in silver armor under a burning sun of orange and red. His sword in the air, his expression stoic and calm. Every detail crafted out of word chains.

She's not just good. She's a genius.

As I read the word chains making up a side of one ship, my heart stopped.

Rue true blue bluest sky eye my smile rile rain pain pain pain

"Holy shit," I whispered.

The lyrics to "Sweet Child O' Mine." Distilled down to their essence. The way the song would sound in Thea's looping mind.

I gave the page a quarter turn, following the words up the ship's mast.

Wish kiss kind eyes my mist mystical miracle lyrical lyrically utterly utter mutter stutter strum sting sing sing sing

Slowly, calmly, I folded the drawing and stuffed it in my back pocket. This one was mine.

Thea was down in the dark, but I was down there with her.

CHAPTER 10

Jim

"Jim, this is Brett Dodson," Alonzo said. "Our newest hire."

"Good to meet you," Brett said, giving my hand a shake. He was stocky with dark hair and icy blue eyes that went over my shoulder, straight to Thea.

"I have to attend to some matters upstairs," Alonzo said. "Jim, can you show Brett around? I haven't had a chance to go over the resident files with him, so no interaction yet. Capisce?"

"Sure," I said.

I took Brett around, finishing at the rec room. I pointed out the residents' shelves, the game storage, and the supply closet.

"You got a hole in the wall," Brett said, nodding at the crack in the closet's sheetrock.

"Alonzo knows," I said. "He's called someone to fix it."

Brett's face was narrow and angular, with a small curl to his lips. "He's kind of obsessed with this place, yeah?"

"He has high standards," I said.

I wondered how Brett would stack up. He seemed friendly enough, I thought, following him back into the main room. As usual, Mr. Webb was at his table, working his puzzle.

"His head looks like the fender on my last car," Brett muttered under his breath.

"That's Mr. Webb," I said pointedly. "He works that puzzle every day. It's okay to box it up after he leaves, even if he's not done. He'll start it over tomorrow."

Brett stared until Mr. Webb looked up, scowling.

"Hey, Mr. Webb. How ya doing?"

Mr. Webb narrowed his eyes and went back to his puzzle. Brett's gaze turned to Thea.

"What's her story?"

I stood straighter. "That's Thea Hughes. Her case is severe. Alonzo will explain it to you."

"She looks all right to me," Brett said. He grinned and elbowed me. "You sure she's a patient?"

"A r-r-resident," I said, trying to gauge this guy, my hackles up. But he shrugged and smiled.

"Right." Brett laughed. "Gotta use the terminology."

I nodded. "Come on. I'll show you the dining room."

"You like working here?" Brett asked along the way.

"Sure."

"Kind of weird, isn't it? All these people with fucked-up brains. Like that dude with the dent in his head?" He whistled between his teeth. "That's fucking wild."

I stiffened. "It's what happened."

"Alonzo was telling me there's a guy here who'd had a metal rod go straight through his eye and he *lived*. Perello-somebody."

"Mr. Perello," I said. "He's a veteran."

Brett laughed. "*Mister*. Right." He rummaged in his pants pocket. "You smoke?"

"No."

"Suit yourself."

Brett sauntered toward Jules at the front desk. He spoke to her a moment and her laugh echoed down the hallway as they went out to smoke.

I found Alonzo in the break room, stacking case files.

"You done for the day?" he asked.

I nodded. "You went over those with the new guy?"

"Not all of them. We'll finish the rest tomorrow." He cocked his head. "So? What do you make of him?"

"I don't know," I said. "You're the one who can read people."

"Yep, and I can read a schedule too. We're shorthanded. I don't need to tell you—you been working fifteen-hour shifts for three straight weeks. We got no applications in a month and we need the help. We'll keep an eye on Dodson and give him the night shift, if need be."

He got up to go and paused at the door.

"Rita says Delia will allow you to take Miss Hughes for her FAE every day."

I kept my expression neutral. "Great."

"That means giving up your fifteen."

"It's fine."

"Great. Fine. Mm-hmm," Alonzo said. He started for the door again, then turned back. "I *can* read people, Jim. And you're barking up the wrong damn tree." He shook his head. "Hell, son. You're in the wrong damn forest."

"I want to get Thea some better art supplies," I told Rita that afternoon in the rec room. "A canvas and some paint."

Rita bit her lip. "It's so sweet of you, Jim, but we talked about this. No budget."

"I'll pay for it myself."

"Slow down, honey. Delia Hughes will flip her lid if a male staff member starts buying things for Thea. You could lose your job. I could lose *my* job."

"Over better art supplies? Thea's too good for pens and paper."

"I know," Rita said. "And Delia knows it too, but she has all kinds of rules. She worries that painting will upset Thea. And she's afraid of the publicity if Thea creates a masterpiece. Which she will."

"Why would that be a bad thing?"

"The world's worst recorded case of amnesia is a prodigal musician. He's been featured in documentaries, books, and medical shows. The second-worst case is Thea Hughes, a genius artist." Rita shook her head. "Delia's already had to fight off the press. She wants none of the attention. She thinks it would be too much for her sister."

"But that kind of attention might get her case in front of doctors, right? Better doctors who might be able to do something for her."

"Her case has been written up in medical journals," Rita said. "It's not a secret."

"Are her word chains in the journals too?"

Rita sighed. "I don't know. Look, as long as the doctors tell Delia that Thea is happy as she is…" She shrugged. "That's all Delia wants to hear. That her sister's okay. Not upsetting Thea takes precedence over everything else."

"That's fucked."

Rita put her hands on her hips. "I beg your pardon?"

"I said it's fucked, Rita. Why would Thea get upset if she had no awareness of her situation? And if she *is* aware, shouldn't we do everything we can to improve her quality of life?"

The nurse's mouth fell open. "I don't believe I've ever heard you speak so many words in a row."

I crossed my arms. Shrugged like it was nothing, because nothing had ever been important enough.

"I understand your concern, but Thea has no awareness of what upsets her because she has no memory. Her upsets aren't conscious, they're instinctual. Mindless. You didn't see her in the beginning, Jim. Episodes of hysterical screaming. I had to sedate her more times than I want to remember."

She glanced at Thea, who was bent over her drawings.

"So long as Dr. Stevens tells Delia her sister is fine as she is, Delia wants to stay the course. So, we stay the course."

I nodded even though the scenario felt ridiculous. I knew Blue Ridge was short-staffed and under-funded, but it seemed a no-brainer to give Thea paint or music or anything she enjoyed before the accident. Why her sister kept such a chokehold on her treatment made no damn sense.

"You have a little bit of a crush on her?" Rita asked, jerking me from my thoughts. "I understand. She's beautiful but—"

"*N-N-No*," I said. "Nothing like that. I just want her to have a life. A happy one."

"She does seem happy. Happier than I've seen her in months."

"Doesn't that mean something?"

She gave me a sly smile. "I think it means she likes you. But let the doctors worry about her, okay? They know what they're doing."

I didn't argue, but it seemed what the doctors were doing was a whole lot of nothing.

Rita took Thea back upstairs. I cleaned up the pens and paper, and another of Thea's word chains jumped out at me like a striking snake.

Wish miss kiss kill will fill fall fail faint paint wait wait wait

"Jesus."

Stay the course. For how long? Another two years? How long did Thea have to wait to at least be allowed to do what she loved?

Fuck that. After work, I'd ride directly to the nearest art supply store.

Then hang a left at the unemployment office once Delia finds out. Doris sneered. *And then how will you take care of your broken-down girl? Who will protect her then?*

I had no reply, other than it was the right thing to do.

I found a small arts and crafts store in Boones Mill and bought a canvas, brushes, and a set of acrylic paints. They weren't cheap but living like a miser for six years meant I had money to spare. It felt good to spend it on something that mattered.

The following morning, I went to work with the supplies tucked under my arm.

"Whatcha got there, honeypie?" Jules asked as I strode past the front desk.

"Nothing."

"Hey, when are we going to go out after work? I'm ready when you are."

I ignored her. After weeks of working at Blue Ridge, Jules rubbed me the wrong way. Nothing terrible I could put my finger on, just an itch I couldn't scratch.

I put the new supplies on a high shelf in the rec room closet. The hours dragged until one o'clock when it was time for Thea's FAE. I endured our usual script until finally, we were alone in the brilliant sun. Her hand nestled in the crook of my elbow and her face turned up to the light, a dream-like smile on her face. She looked so peaceful. What if Delia was right that painting was too much for Thea? What if it triggered something deep in her sleeping memory?

Through the doubt, Thea's own words spoke up: *I'd kill for a canvas, as big as a wall.*

"Thea," I said.

She grinned. "Jimmy."

"Would you like to start a new painting?"

"Would I?" Her hand on my arm tightened. "I'd love to. I love to paint the pyramids. Ancient Egypt. You need a canvas as big as a wall to do Egypt justice. Have I told you I was an Egyptologist?"

Fifty-four times. Then I made myself stop counting.

"No. Tell me."

Her smile widened. "I love everything about ancient Egypt. Especially the pyramids. The idea that Egyptians would take the time and manpower to create gigantic monuments to the dead is just amazing to me. That's all a pyramid is. A place where a dead king or queen is given all they need for the afterlife. It's packed with supplies and the things they loved. All down there in the dark..."

Thea's expression darkened too, her brows furrowed, as if she were close to touching something she couldn't quite grasp.

Redirect.

"I know where there might be a canvas and paint," I said.

The shadows fled from her eyes. "No shit?"

"No shit."

"Where? Can you show me now?"

"Sure," I said. "Let's go."

Her happiness invaded my cold brick wall. I knew by the time we reached the rec room and I got the supplies set up, her reset would hit. But she was happy *now*, at this moment, and I'd made it happen.

I fucking did something...

I guided her to her table. "Be right back."

I hurried to the supply closet and grabbed the paints, brushes, and tucked the canvas under my arm. If Delia wanted to fight me on this, I'd stand up for the both of us. Because painting wouldn't upset Thea. It would help set her free, at least for a little while.

A man's booming laugh filled the rec room. I dropped the canvas and strode out to see Brett Dodson sitting across from Thea, his back to me. Thea's face was closed down, her shoulders hunched up, her hand holding tightly to her pen.

"How long has it been?" she asked.

"Twenty-four billion light years," Brett said. "Give or take five minutes."

Thea's eyes widened and her chest hitched. "What do you mean?"

I strode over, anger running hot in my veins. "It's been two years, M-M-Miss Hughes," I said quickly. "T-T-Two years and the doctors are working on your case."

Thea's gaze darted between the two strange men in her space.

I wheeled on Brett and hissed, "What are you d-d-doing?"

"I had to see it with my own eyes. Dude, it's nuts. Check this out." He turned to Thea and pointed at his nametag and said slowly, as if she were dumb, "I'm Brett."

"Hi," she said, not offering her hand. "I'm Thea Hughes."

"Brett *Favre*," he said. "Ever heard of me? I used to play for the Packers. Two Super Bowl titles. I'm retired now—"

I grabbed his arm and yanked him out of the chair. "Wh-What the f-f-fuck?"

"What?" Brett laughed as he staggered back. "What's your deal man? She's not gonna remember. They told me all about her… what's it called? Her reset. I thought it was a joke—"

I gave him another rough shove. "She's not a j-j-joke. And you can't talk to her like that."

I wasn't much taller or bigger than him, but I put on the suit of armor that made the bullies leave me alone in high school. Standing tall, feet planted, still as stone. I was ready for a fight, but Brett's expression instantly turned remorseful.

"Shit, hey, I'm sorry, man. I didn't realize it was such a big deal."

My fists unclenched and I studied his face, looking for sincerity or bullshit. "It's a big deal that you don't f-f-fuck with her."

"I'm sorry, really," he said, and then jerked his chin over my shoulder. "Damn, I think she's in trouble."

I looked back. Thea sat ramrod straight, the absence seizure clamping her like a vise. Frozen except for her hands that twitched on the table, the pen clattering.

Inhale. Exhale. I wheeled back around to Brett and concentrated every ounce of mental will I had to enunciate the words, "Get the fuck away from her."

"Woah, be cool, man. Honest mistake." He held up his hands and walked backward toward the door. "Won't happen again."

I had no clue if I could believe him or not. I wasn't good at "reading people." I stared him down until he was out of the rec room, then hurried to kneel beside Thea.

"Hey," I said gently.

She looked at me fearfully, her breath coming in short gasps. "How long has it been?" she whispered.

"Two years," I said. "The doctors are working on your case. They're going to figure it out."

And if they're not, I'm going to make them.

She nodded and sucked in a few deep breaths. "I've been away. But I'm back now."

"I'm glad you came back," I said.

A slow smile broke over her face, like a sunrise. "You're the first person I've seen." She offered her hand, her voice strengthening. "I'm Thea Hughes."

"Hi, Thea. I'm Jimmy."

Her friendly expression was back. "Jimmy," she said. "That name fits you. You have kind eyes."

I smiled. "So I've been told."

I found Alonzo outside on a bench, smoking a cigarette.

He held up his hands. "I know, I know. I heard everything. Brett apologized. He couldn't believe Miss Hughes' situation and took it too far. It won't happen again."

"You're not going to f-f-fire him?"

Alonzo's eyes widened slightly, and humiliation crawled over my skin like red ants, making my face burn. The goddamn stutter stealing away any authority or clout I might have had.

"I thought Delia was just being rude the other day," Alonzo said, his voice softer than I'd ever heard it. "You could have told me."

I stiffened. "I don't tell anyone. Why would I?"

Alonzo watched me almost sadly a moment, then waved a hand. "Never mind. Brett's on notice. Any more antics and he's out of here." He gave me a dark look. "I heard you got pretty rough with him."

My chin lifted. "Thea had a seizure."

"Christ." Alonzo blew smoke out. "Look, I'm getting old and I'm tired. We need Dodson. I'll put him on the night shift for a few weeks where he can't talk to anyone, how's that?"

I crossed my arms.

Alonzo sat up and jabbed the two fingers holding the cigarette in my direction. "Don't give me that look, Whelan. I'm this close to putting you on the night shift too, you got me? Brett was out of line but so were you. You can't be getting in pissing matches over Miss Hughes. It's unprofessional, for starters. Moreover, *she's not yours.*"

My shoulders tensed. "I know she isn't."

"Do you? I hear you want to buy art supplies for her."

"They're bought."

"Lord above, did Delia approve that?"

I said nothing.

"That would be no." Alonzo sighed. "I knew it. You're falling for the poor girl."

My arms dropped to my sides. "I'm not f-falling for her. She can't—"

"That's right. She can't *nothing.*" He chucked his smoke down and ground it under his boot.

"She can paint," I said. "She's an artist. She should be painting."

I braced myself for Alonzo to blow up at me, but he sank back on the bench. "I know. It's a shame, watching her make do with pen and paper, day after day."

"So? Tomorrow?"

"Tomorrow at rec time, give it a shot. But if Miss Hughes shows any kind of upset at all, that's it." He made a slashing motion with his hand. "No more paint."

"Got it."

"We'll see. You recall Delia nearly had you canned last week. Or you got amnesia too?"

"I remember."

"She doesn't like strange men taking an interest in her sister. You can see why, can't you?"

Inhale. Exhale. "I would never hurt Thea in any way. I swear it."

It came out perfectly. No stutter.

Alonzo eyed me a good, hard minute. Then, with a small groan, he bent and picked up the butt of his smoke off the ground with two fingers. "All right, Jim. I'll have your back on this," he said. "Don't make me regret it."

The gravel crunched under his feet as he walked away, leaving his words hanging in the sticky air.

You're falling for that poor girl.

I was. I'd quit my job before I hurt her, but it didn't stop my stupid heart from wanting an impossible life. I was a dying man in Thea's Egyptian desert, and she was a mirage. An oasis that didn't exist.

And I had to stop turning my empty soul in her direction.

CHAPTER 11

Jim

After the previous day's attempt to let Thea paint had been ruined by Brett, I decided to make up for it. I went back to the art store and purchased an easel, a smock, and one of those paint trays with a hole for the thumb. I'd found a tarp in one of the supply closets and set it underneath the easel in the rec room to protect the old linoleum. I had a feeling that Thea, when she painted, didn't hold back.

Job done, I shot a glance at Alonzo who stood at the nurse's station. It wasn't Delia's day to visit, but he was there to run interference, just in case. The trust he'd placed in me felt impossibly good. If this went south, it wouldn't just hurt Thea but ruin that too.

Alonzo glanced down the hall and then back to me. "Here she comes."

Rita brought Thea in, and I joined them at the door.

"Hi, Miss Hughes."

Thea glanced at my nametag. "Hi... Jim?"

"It's Jimmy," I said. "I have something for you."

Her smile widened. "Oh yeah? Is it my birthday?"

I stared and my brain went into a tailspin.

Was it? Did she think it was? Did she know one way or the other?

"Oh my God, calm down, Jimmy. I'm teasing." Thea laughed, but the smile fell off her face as she caught sight of my setup. She walked slowly toward the mini art studio. "Is this... for me?"

"Y-Yeah," I said. "Do you like it?"

"Like it?"

Thea whirled on me and threw her arms around my neck. For a split second, time stood still, and I had this girl in my arms. I had her warm embrace wrapped around me after years of going without. She let go quickly, leaving me reeling, and went to the easel, where she traced her fingers down the edge of the canvas.

"Holy shit, Jimmy, this is amazing. I haven't painted in... how long has it been?"

"Two years, Miss Hughes," I said, stuffing my hands in my pockets. "You're long overdue."

She gave me another beautiful smile. "Thank you. I think so too."

As she set up her paints, I shot a glance over my shoulder. Rita beamed and mimed clapping her hands. Alonzo nodded at me with quiet approval. Like the proud parents I never had.

Fuck, don't get stupid now.

I concentrated on Thea, making sure she was okay and not overwhelmed. Just the opposite, Thea smeared paint on her palette in blotches of color and got to work. No word chains. Not even a pyramid. At least not that I could tell.

For twenty minutes, with Rita and Alonzo at my side, Thea painted. Bright blue swaths across the top of the canvas, dark gray along the bottom with tall, rectangular columns rising from the gray into the blue. Outlines only, so far. Hints of what was to come. Whatever Thea was doing, it was too big for one session.

"Obelisks?" Rita murmured. "Is this Egyptian?"

"Don't know," I said.

Rita and Alonzo drifted away from the corner to work with other residents in the rec room. I busied myself straightening up but did a half-assed job, always keeping an eye out for any signs of distress in Thea. None. She was consumed. I doubted she'd have heard a window shattering.

And no reset. Holy shit...

"Rita." I waved her over. "When was her last reset?"

"Before she came down."

"That was what, twenty minutes ago? She'd have had three or four by now, right? But she…"

"Painted right through them."

We shared triumphant glances. Thea painted for another thirty minutes straight and then Rita checked her watch.

"I hate to stop her, but I have to take her back," Rita said. She stepped forward and touched Thea on the arm. "Miss Hughes?"

Thea froze and blinked. "How long has it been?"

"Two years," Rita said. "The doctors are working on your case."

Thea looked at the palette and brush in her hand, the smock over her drab clothes and back at the unfinished painting.

"I did this," she said. It wasn't a question.

"You did," Rita said. "It's beautiful and you can work on it again after a rest."

Thea beamed and her body relaxed. No seizure.

I slumped back against a wall as relief coursed through my veins. Happiness so potent it felt illegal.

It worked.

"Awesome." Thea set down her paints, removed the smock. "Not too shabby, right? I mean, it's a start. Not done yet, obviously. Not at all. But I can come back and finish?"

"Of course," Rita said. "Are you hungry? Would you like a snack?"

She thought for a second. "Starving."

Rita shot me a smile as she led Thea out of the room. In a few minutes, everything she's accomplished would be wiped clean.

But she can come back tomorrow. Or have an easel in her room. She doesn't have to stop…

"Okay, cool your jets," Alonzo said, chuckling. "I know where your thinking's going, but let's take it one step at a time."

"She looked pretty happy, right?"

"She looked *a lot* happy." He crossed his arms, not quite meeting my eye. "You know I run around this joint trying to keep it from falling apart. Because that's important."

I nodded.

"But that's not all that's important." He patted me on the shoulder, meeting my eyes. "You did good, Jim."

The father-son feeling came over me again, and I crossed my own arms over my chest, not sure if I wanted to keep it out or hold it in. "Thanks."

Alonzo coughed and looked away. "Speaking of falling apart, I called a guy to fix the hole in the supply closet ages ago. Better go see what's keeping him."

He hurried out of the rec room and I turned to Thea's painting. Tall, rough, rectangular cuboids reaching into a sky of blue. I didn't know what it meant, but there were no word chains, no cries for help, and that made the unfinished painting a masterpiece to me.

Seven a.m. the next morning, and the heat was already intensifying. I entered the cool confines of the sanitarium to see Brett Dodson leaning over the front desk, laughing with Jules.

"How's the night shift treating you?" she was asking.

"Boring as hell," Brett said. "I'm scheduled for three weeks. Alonzo's a dick."

I let the front door slam shut.

They both turned. Brett's face broke out into a grin as if he hadn't a care in the world.

"Hey, Jim. How's it going?"

"Good morning, Jim," Jules said. "Whatsa matter? Cat got your tongue?"

Brett coughed a laugh into his hand.

Fear, anger, and humiliation all tied up in a knot in my stomach, just like they had every day of my life when I was a kid. But I didn't get this far from the high school bully bullshit just to have it start up all over again here.

"Cat got your tongue?" I said, dragging my glare between Brett to Jules. "That's the best you got? You didn't even stutter the *t*."

"Hey," Brett said. "It's cool, man. I was just telling her what happened yesterday." He turned to Jules. "Don't make fun."

Jules stared at him and burst out laughing.

He's full of shit. They both are.

Inhale. Exhale.

"Enjoy your three weeks of night shifts," I told him as I went past.

Brett smiled lazily. "Oh, I'm sure I'll find a way to keep them interesting."

Thea stood in her corner, humming to herself. My earbuds in her ears, my phone in her pocket. Her hips swayed side to side as she painted.

"I've never seen her so happy," Rita said. "These last few days, it's like a light turned on. And it doesn't shut off, even with the resets. It's like…"

"She knows," I said.

Rita's eyes filled with tears. "God, maybe she does. When I think about all the times I've been busy and overworked… Delia said she loved *The Office,* so I plunked Thea down in front of the TV, for hours on end, when she could have been doing this…"

"She's happy now," I said. "That's what counts."

"Yes, I think so. Thanks to you." She shook her head. "God, look at that painting."

The rough obelisks were now the towering skyscrapers of New York City, with the Empire State Building front and center. A forced perspective, as if the viewer were looking down at Manhattan from a high angle, making the building facades sprout from the grid of streets like a bouquet. Yellow cabs and cars, like children's toys, dotted the boulevards. Puffy clusters of green made up Central Park. The sky was clear blue, with a blazing sun glinting off the metal skyscrapers in perfect bolts of silver and copper.

It's a masterpiece, just like Delia predicted.

"What the hell is going on?"

Rita and I turned. As if my thoughts conjured her up, Delia Hughes marched across the rec room in her navy suit, staring at her sister, who was still lost in her work and the music. For a moment, Delia's dark, hard eyes softened. I could almost see her remembering Thea before the accident. Maybe painting just like this at home with their parents alive and well.

"She always wanted to go to New York," Delia murmured softly. Sadly.

Then her entire expression turned stony, and she whirled on Rita and me. "Whose idea was this? Not Dr. Stevens, I presume."

I opened my mouth to speak but Rita cut in.

"Mine," she said. "I felt two years was adequate time to acclimate Thea to Blue Ridge, and it's time she resumed the activities she enjoyed before the accident."

Alonzo came rushing into the rec room, then stopped when he saw Delia. He smoothed the front of his white uniform down and joined us. "Ms. Hughes," he said slowly.

"Why was I not consulted about this?" Delia flapped her hand in Thea's direction.

"It's non-medical care," Alonzo said. "We are authorized to—"

"And if she had a seizure? Those are medical in nature, are they not?"

"Yes, but—"

"But you feel it's perfectly acceptable to send my sister into a medical seizure with your non-medical care and then what? Did you think further than that?"

"She hasn't had a seizure, Ms. Hughes," Rita said. "Not in days."

"Not *yet*."

"She loves it. She's vibrant in a way I haven't seen before."

"And painting a masterpiece, no less," Delia said. "I told you, I don't want a media circus over Thea. I don't want the entire world watching a beautiful young girl exhibit her brain damage as if she's some kind of sideshow."

"We can ensure that no word gets out about her painting," Rita said. "It's part of the HIPAA policy. Anyone here who shares her work outside of this facility can face termination or even a lawsuit. I'll ensure the staff understands that implicitly."

Delia held Rita's gaze for a minute, thinking. Then she whirled on me. "And you. Do you understand implicitly?"

I nodded, meeting her gaze. "I do."

"What do you have to do with this?"

"Jim works with Thea every day," Rita said carefully. "We are all involved in her care. Allowing Thea to paint makes her extremely happy."

"She can't be happy," Delia said. "She can't *remember* happy."

"Delia," Rita said in a gentle voice. "Look at her."

Delia's eyes softened as she took in her sister. "Well," she said, after a minute. "We'll see. I'd like Dr. Stevens to be made aware of this. And it looks like I'll be driving over for the next few days to keep an eye on Thea. If she has even the slightest of tremors…"

"Delia," Thea called, taking the earbuds from her ears. No sooner were they free when she froze, an absence seizure shook her. Her first in days. I glared at Delia's back as she joined her sister.

The only thing that sends Thea into a seizure is you.

"You didn't have to cover for me," I said to Rita.

"I think I did," Rita said. "Delia doesn't want male attention on her sister. And anyway, I support this." She motioned at Thea, who was now animatedly discussing her painting. "I wasn't kidding. In all the years I've worked with Thea, I've never seen her so happy."

I took that victory—and my broom—and got back to work. I swept the hallways and the foyer, happy that Jules was off on another smoke break. I made my way to the dining room, where I found Delia Hughes sitting alone at a table near the window, a cup of coffee in front of her. Her gaze on the surrounding forest outside the sanitarium.

She heard my footsteps and turned. "I know you're behind getting my sister the paints," she said. "I see how you look at her."

There was no sense in backing away or running like a coward. I crossed the room and sat at a nearby table, setting the broom over my knees.

"It was my idea," I said. "Rita covered for me because I know what it looks like."

"Do you?"

"I just want Thea to be happy. That's it. Nothing else."

"I told you, she can't remember happy."

"Maybe she can."

Delia whipped her head to me. "You are not a doctor."

"No," I said, my jaw stiffening. "But I've seen her word chains."

"Dr. Stevens says they're nothing to be concerned about."

"But—"

"Let me be more clear," Delia said. "He says there's nothing they can *do* about them. Do you understand the distinction?"

She glared, challenging. The orderly's guess against the neurosurgeon's professional diagnosis. I tried something else.

"Why do you come here twice a week? An hour and a half from Richmond, each direction. Why?"

Delia scoffed. "Because she's my sister."

"You could live on the moon for all she'd remember, right?"

"She needs me. When I visit, she gets…"

"Happy?"

"Upset, Mr. Whelan." Her voice was bitter. "She has a seizure every time. She's so *happy* to see me, her brain short circuits."

The grief of losing her entire family was written in every hard line of Delia's face.

"I know everyone thinks I'm too harsh with her care," she said into my silence, almost to herself. "Too *disciplined.* Thea was always the fun one. Constantly making dumb jokes, even at the most serious times. She could make everyone smile just by walking into a room. I walked into a room and nobody noticed. She laughed too loudly and cried easily. When our cat was run over by a car, Thea cried enough for the both of us, so I didn't."

She straightened and smoothed her skirt. "But that's okay. Someone had to take care of things. Someone had to be responsible. Someone had to make funeral arrangements for our parents. Someone had to find a place that would take care of Thea. One that wasn't an ocean away or wouldn't drain the money within a year. Someone had to do those things, right?"

I nodded.

"And so I'm the bad guy because I don't want Thea to paint. Because I'm afraid it will bring on seizures. Because *I* bring on seizures. I hurt her…" She swallowed. "I hurt her with my mere presence."

"I don't think that's true," I said.

"No? I'm the only person she remembers by name. I'm the only link from her past she's been able to hold on to. Me and her art." Delia sniffed and dabbed the corner of her eye with a napkin. "I'm afraid if she paints, it will hurt more than it helps. I'm afraid one day she'll have a seizure—a final seizure—and then she'll be gone too."

Now I felt like shit for not trying to see her point of view. "I'm sorry,

I—"

"Sorry you acted without thinking? Or that you were thinking with another part of your anatomy?"

"Never," I said in a low voice. "I would never."

"And I have no choice but to believe you," Delia said, setting down her napkin. "I have to go."

She shouldered her purse and began to rise.

Speak now or forever hold your peace.

"Ms. Hughes, I think Thea has seizures when she sees you because she remembers her life with you."

"No," Delia said. "She can't."

"I think she does," I said as gently as possible. "In her own way."

Delia stared, frozen, and her hard eyes began to shine. "I… I don't want her to suffer. I can't imagine she suffers. If I thought that…" She straightened. "Her neuropsychologist should know whatever you think you know. He makes her treatment plan. He says keeping her calm is right for her."

"What about doing things that give her a chance?"

"A chance at what?"

"At life."

"What life?" Delia cried. "She has no life, but she's alive. And she's all I have left." She sneered now. "What do you know about it? You're an orderly. Go mop a floor and leave my sister alone."

She stormed out, heels clopping, leaving me with a broom in my hand and an empty dining room to clean up.

CHAPTER 12

Jim

The bar was nearly empty that night. The stage dark but for a cone of light shining down on a guy in jeans and a plaid shirt, an acoustic guitar on his lap. Thankfully, the overly welcoming waitress I met when I first came here wasn't working. Unbothered, I nursed a beer and listened to the guy make his way through covers of modern songs. The listless crowd eked out a clap or two at the end of each tune.

But at least he's up there.

I had no aspirations to be a singer. I wanted to help kids who stuttered not to have the shitty childhood I had. Eventually, I'd have to put myself out in the world. Onstage, not in the audience.

I'd put myself out there for Thea. Taking a stand for something and then defending it out loud felt good. Watching Thea light up as she painted a masterpiece was worth everyone at Blue Ridge hearing my stutter. The desire to make her better was growing stronger than the pain and humiliation I might face because of it.

And that's how it might be if you go back to school and get a speech therapy license to help those kids.

"Thanks, you've been a great crowd," the guy said. "I'm going to close with a favorite called 'I Will Follow You into the Dark.'"

I drained my beer and pushed my chair back to go when the song's lyrics grabbed my attention. A man telling his love he'd follow her into the dark, but it was nothing to be sad about. They'd go together, hand in hand.

I went home and pulled up "I Will Follow You into the Dark" by Death Cab for Cutie on my phone. It was a simple song—but powerful. I set it on repeat and sat with my guitar, listening for the chord changes. I had to put it in a lower octave for my vocal range, but in an hour, I had mastered it.

For Thea.

Lately, everything in my life was for her. To try to help her as much as she was helping me.

Her happiness, in however small of increments it might come, was all that mattered.

And then it all fell apart.

The next day, Rita caught up with me as I was taking resident bedding to the laundry room. "Something's going on with Thea," she said. "She's hardly said a word, and she didn't touch her breakfast."

The words sunk into the pit of my stomach like a heavy stone. "Maybe she didn't sleep well?"

"She does look tired." She forced a smile. "Maybe that's it. I'm sure she'll perk up once she gets to rec time. Her painting looks just about finished. You'll take her on her FAE today?"

"Of course," I said.

The hours crawled until one o'clock and I practically ran to the dining room. Thea sat alone at a table, a plate of untouched food in front of her. Her head was bowed, her wavy blond hair spilling down to curtain her face.

"Miss Hughes?" I said gently.

She raised her head and that unease in my stomach tightened like a vise. Her sky-blue eyes were red-rimmed and glassy, ringed with shadows. She glanced at my nametag.

"Jim," she said dully. "How long has it been?"

"Two years," I said. "The doctors are working on your case. Would you like to go outside? Get some fresh air?"

"Sure," she said. "Sounds good."

I offered her my arm, and she stared at it for a moment, then slowly put her hand on my skin, hesitantly, as if I would burn her. Her hand found the crook of my elbow, as usual, and she got to her feet.

Maybe Delia was right that painting stirred up too many memories that hung just out of Thea's reach. Outside, the heat was stifling, and Thea turned her face to the sun as she always did. I wanted to ask if she was okay, but Alonzo had warned against those types of questions. She had no way of knowing.

I took a chance.

"How are you today, M-Miss Hughes?"

"You can call me Thea," she said. "And I'm... I don't know. Tired. I've been away awhile and just got back. You're the first person I've seen." She raised her glance to study me. "You have kind eyes, Jim."

"You can call me Jimmy. If you want."

"Jimmy. Okay."

We walked a few more steps in the quiet afternoon, where only the buzzing of insects and our feet on the gravel were the only sounds.

"It's so quiet here," Thea said. "Talk to me, Jimmy. Tell me about yourself."

"Not much to tell," I said. "I work here."

Shit. There was no "here" for Thea. Only now.

"Here," she said and glanced around at the green grounds and forest on the other side of the fence. "It's pretty here."

"Yeah, it is."

"Tell me more. Keep talking to me. Please."

"I play guitar. And sing a little."

I waited for her to break out of her sadness to demand I sing. Or listen to music. Instead, she nodded absently.

"What else?"

"I like helping people."

Though I might be terrible at it.

Her smile was a dimmer, sadder version of her usual beautiful smile.

"I can see that about you," she said. "That's why you're *Jim* on the nametag but *Jimmy with the kind eyes* in real life. Very kind for such a strong, intimidating man." Her hand on my arm tightened its grip. "Like Marc Antony. A soldier who doesn't want to fight but will if he has to."

She turned to me suddenly, fear swimming in the blue depths of her eyes.

"You'd fight for me, wouldn't you, Jimmy?" she asked. "Like Marc Antony?"

"Yeah." I swallowed. "Yeah, Thea. I would."

She nodded but didn't look reassured. Only confused, as if she were trying to work out a problem by talking it out.

"Antony fought for Cleopatra," she said, as we started walking again. "He fought so bravely for her. But their enemies were liars. Cowards. They told Antony that Cleopatra had died, and so he stabbed himself with his own sword. And when she heard that, she became weak with grief. Undone. Funny how that works. The stronger the love, the more helpless the person feels in the wake of its loss."

Like one of her word chains, Thea's pain rose to the surface through a murky swamp of amnesia. I listened, struggling to understand.

"Antony was dead," she said. "Cleopatra was alone. So she put her hand in the snake's basket to end the pain. The alone-ness. It's not the same as loneliness. Alone-ness is an abyss. It's being alone even when you're surrounded by people. It's vast and empty and silent."

My mind was blank. At a loss for a way to help her. Her next words chilled me to the bone.

"Cleopatra thought she'd be alone forever. Death was the better choice." She looked up at me. "Maybe she's right. Anything is better than alone."

Jesus.

Thea knew what was happening to her and no one could help. She was alone in her prison. Painting had somehow deepened the understanding of it in a way I couldn't have anticipated. I wasn't a doctor. Doctors swore an oath to do no harm.

I'd harmed Thea badly.

I tried one last time. "Would you like some music?"

Because music is life. Remember?

She shook her head. "I want to go inside."

"Sure," I said, my stomach twisting tighter. "Whatever you want."

I led Thea inside to the rec room, where Delia was already waiting. Keeping her promise to come every day to monitor her sister. She watched me with a dagger-glare. Her moment of weakness in front of me the other day was hard and clear in her eyes.

"Delia!"

Thea's voice was frayed at the ends and then cut off with a strangled sound as she suffered an absence seizure. When the seizure released her, Thea ran to her sister and held her tight.

"How long has it been? Where are Mom and Dad?"

My heart fucking broke at the pain in her voice.

"Two years," Delia said. "They'll be here soon."

Thea didn't let go of her but clung to her, face buried in her shoulder. Rita hurried over, her hands twisting, her face a mask of worry.

"What's going on?" Delia demanded over Thea's shoulder. "Why is she like this?"

"We don't know, Ms. Hughes," Rita said, glancing at me.

Delia said a few words to Thea then gently extracted herself. She sat her sister down at the table and pulled us aside.

"She can't know what happened to our parents," she hissed at me. "You didn't tell her, did you? Is that why she's so upset?"

"I didn't tell her," I said.

"Someone said something. Something's happened. If I find out it was you—"

"I swear, I haven't told her."

She lifted her chin. "This is the second time in two days I'm discussing my sister with an orderly," she said. "You are to leave her alone, do you hear me? This is your last warning."

With a final, parting glare, she went and sat beside Thea, her arm around her, murmuring comfort in her ear.

I pulled Rita aside.

"It's because of the painting. I never should've bought the canvas."

"I don't know," Rita said, biting her lip. "She's been so happy. I think you were helping."

"Maybe I wasn't," I said. "Maybe I made her worse. I should stay away. No more walks."

Rita shook her head, her eyes on Thea. "I don't know, Jim. I just don't know."

I didn't sleep for shit that night, and as much as I needed to see her, the following day I didn't give Thea her FAE. I waited with my guts twisting in knots until it was rec time.

Thea stood in front of her painting in the corner, studying what she had created over the last few days. New York City under a brilliant summer sky.

A masterpiece.

"How is she?" I asked Rita.

"Not good," she said. "Worse, I think. She's not herself. But she's with her painting now. Maybe it will help."

For long minutes, Thea didn't move, and I wondered if she felt the painting was finished. Then she reached for the tube of black paint and squeezed a huge dollop onto the palms of her hands. With a small cry, she slapped the canvas and dragged her hands across it.

"*No!*" The word erupted out of Rita.

Oh fuck...

We watched in horror as Thea smeared black paint across her beautiful cityscape. Once. Twice. Black swathes across the perfection of her Empire State Building and the pure blue sky.

Rita and I broke from our shock at the same time and rushed forward. Rita took the paint out of Thea's hands, while I gently guided her a step back from the ruined canvas.

"Miss Hughes," Rita said. "It's okay. Oh, honey, it's okay."

You done fucked up now, you big dummy.

Thea was crying, her breath coming in silent, choked gasps. She stared in horror at her hands covered in black paint. Before we could stop her, she raised them to her face and dragged her palms down her cheeks.

"Jesus, honey, no," Rita cried. She looked over at me fearfully, confused.

I could only shake my head, slack-jawed and my heart thumping in my ears.

I did this. I did this to her.

We took hold of her arms and started her away from the canvas. A voice rang out from the rec room door.

"My God…"

Delia was there with Alonzo, staring in horror. Alonzo's dusky skin was paler than I'd ever seen it.

"Delia," Thea cried. She went rigid in my hands as an absence seizure made her stiffen and tremble.

"What in the hell is happening?" Delia said, rushing forward. Her blazing gaze swept over Rita and me. "What is happening to my sister?"

"Delia," Thea said, before we could speak. Her voice was a watery croak. "You're here. How long has it been? Where are Mom and Dad?"

"Jesus," Delia breathed, then hurried to add, "Two years. They'll be here soon."

Thea slipped out of my grip and collapsed in Delia's arms, sobbing, black paint smearing Delia's hair and the shoulder of her suit jacket.

Delia held her sister tight, stroking her blond hair. Her glare was both murderous and terrified.

"I told you," she said, her voice shaking with tears and anger. "I told you painting would be bad for her. But did you listen? No, not to me. Not to her doctor."

Rita shook her head, tears in her own eyes. "I don't understand. She was so happy."

"Help me get her cleaned up," Delia snapped. She kept an arm around Thea as they walked to the door, Rita following. Delia stopped and stared at Alonzo and me.

"I think it's time we had a meeting with Dr. Poole and Dr. Stevens."

"Yes, ma'am," Alonzo said to the ground.

Pain wracked my chest as if I were having a seizure too. "Alonzo—"

He held up a hand. "Don't." His brown eyes were heavy as he looked to the ruined canvas in the corner. "Best go clean that up."

I put the canvas away. Cleaned up the paint splatters. Stored the brushes in the supply closet. The next day, Thea was back at the table, markers and a sheet of paper in front of her.

I went to get a broom, to do the job I should've been doing all along, instead of interfering where I had no business.

I swept the rec room, working around Mr. Webb doing his jigsaw puzzle and Ms. Willis playing dominoes with her nurse. Mr. Perello spoke about the war to his attendant. All the while, I stole glances at Thea, hoping to see her with a pen in her hand and that smile on her lips.

But she sat with her hands folded in her lap, staring at nothing.

Rita met my gaze and shook her head, saddened and helpless too.

I hurried in my tasks to avoid Delia, but she showed up early and strode directly to me.

"Why are you in here?"

"Just cleaning up," I said. "I haven't spoken to her, Ms. Hughes. I promise."

"I would goddamn well hope not. You need to leave. Now. I don't want you anywhere near my sister. In fact, the next time I see you will be at the meeting I've arranged with Drs. Poole and Stevens."

I nodded. I hurt Thea and would probably lose my job over it. A small price to pay.

"Delia," Thea called weakly from her table behind us. No energy. Hardly a smile. "You're here. How long has it been?"

Before Delia could reply, the skin-shivering sound of a rattle filled the rec room. My stomach clenched and my palms went sweaty at the sight of a snake, striated silver with dark gray diamonds, gliding out of the supply closet and across the rec room floor, silent but for its tail.

For a split second, everyone stared, no one moved. Time stopped.

"*You gotta watch for pit vipers, Jim,*" Grandpa Jack said from the recesses of my memory—a fishing trip to Lake Murray. "*'Round here, the Massasauga rattler is the deadliest. Black and silver beauties, they are, but bad news.*"

Bad news.

Someone screamed, and time lurched forward. Residents scrambled out of their chairs and backed away. Delia stumbled in her hurry to reach Thea and fell against the table.

And Thea...

My stomach recoiled in horror as Thea calmly watched the snake make its way toward her. With perfect calm, she kneeled on the floor. Her expression blank but almost peaceful. Serene. Resigned. She held out her hand.

The snake's tongue was a flicking black fork in a mouth that opened to hiss and show its elongated fangs, less than a foot from Thea's fingers.

I gripped the broom in both hands like a baseball bat, and in three longs strides, I was there. Thea snatched her hand back as I brought the broom handle down on the snake's head. It made a sickening *splat* as it connected. Blood and brain matter spurted across the linoleum in a halo beneath its crushed head, but its body still writhed.

Again and again, I brought the broom down, hating the destruction of the animal, hating what Thea had been doing more.

The Massasauga was dead, and I stood, panting, adrenaline coursing through me instead of blood. Rita and the other residents stared. Delia crouched beside her sister, staring up at me with a mixture of fear and shock.

Thea trembled in her arms, locked in a seizure.

CHAPTER 13

Jim

"Well, Rita?" Delia demanded as the nurse came down the hallway toward the rec room.

"I gave her a mild sedative," Rita said. "She's calm and resting."

Delia sniffed, checked her watch and continued her pacing.

Now Anna Sutton, the head nurse, joined the gathering. It was her only day off, but when Rita couldn't get Dr. Poole to answer his phone, she begged Anna to come in. She smoothed her skirt and blouse, clearly wishing she were in her uniform.

"Where is Dr. Poole?" Delia asked, arms crossed tight and fingers gripping the sleeves of her blazer. "Or Dr. Stevens? I told you, I want a meeting with both, Monday morning."

"Dr. Stevens is at a conference in Miami until tomorrow," Anna said. "Dr. Poole is unavailable. But we'll arrange—"

"Unreachable, you mean," Delia said. "Disgraceful."

"Rita, I want a nurse stationed in Miss Hughes' room for the next twenty-four hours," Anna said. "Alonzo, what's the situation in the rec room?"

"Joaquin's cleaning up. All other residents are safe."

The rec room door opened, and Joaquin came out with the mop bucket and a plastic bag, heavy with the bloody coils of the dead snake. I'd offered to do the cleaning, but Delia didn't want me out of her sight.

"All good, boss," he said. He gave me a sympathetic glance and rolled the mop bucket down the hall.

"How on earth did a snake make its way into our walls in the first place, Mr. Waters?" Anna asked.

"A hole in the exterior wall that should have been fixed days ago," Alonzo said. "I take full responsibility."

I whipped my head toward him. Alonzo had called maintenance a dozen times to fix the hole in the supply closet, and no one showed up. I opened my mouth, but he shot me a hard look and shook his head.

"I see," Anna said.

"Do you see?" Delia snapped. "A deadly rattlesnake got into this facility and my sister—under your care—tried to kill herself with it."

I flinched at the words.

Like Cleopatra. She put her hand in the snake's basket because she's so fucking alone…

"Given the eyewitness reports," Anna said slowly, "I'm not sure that's an accurate assessment of what Miss Hughes was doing."

"No, she's just an animal lover," Delia said, her voice dripping with sarcasm. "She was merely trying to pet a deadly snake. And you forget—I was an eyewitness too. I saw what she did."

"Ms. Hughes—"

"Thea was doing just fine until he showed up." She jerked her chin in my direction.

"Jim saved her life," Rita said quietly.

"*Jim* put her life in jeopardy in the first place," Delia snapped. "Thea was perfectly happy drawing her drawings. But he took it upon himself to alter her treatment plan, without her *unavailable* doctor's consent or consultation, and this is the result."

She was right, but something still itched the back of my thoughts. Thea had been happy for days before, creating her masterpiece. It'd only been recently that she'd spiraled down.

Still trying to play doctor? Doris sneered. *You big dummy.*

Anna folded her hands in front of her. "Ms. Hughes, I can assure you—"

108

"You can assure me of nothing," Delia said. "Dr. Stevens has vanished. Unqualified staff members are deciding what's best for Thea. And there was a poisonous snake inside the recreation room."

She fixed us each with a cold stare, then gave an irritated sigh and checked her watch again.

"I have to go. I actually have a life of my own that needs attention. I'll be back on Monday for a meeting with Dr. Poole and Dr. Stevens." She gave Anna a hard look. "Make it happen. Meanwhile, I don't want this man"—she jabbed her finger at me—"anywhere near my sister. I want him gone. Now."

"Ms. Hughes," Anna said. "We do not have all the facts. Dr. Stevens needs to hear the entire story and examine Thea himself before we begin arbitrarily releasing staff members."

Delia's eyes flared. "Arbitrarily?"

"However, given the severity of the situation and the fact Mr. Whelan and Nurse Soto both acted without authority or permission…" She gave first me, then Rita a hard look. "I feel a three-day suspension for Mr. Whelan is appropriate. Unfortunately, I simply can't afford to have Nurse Soto absent."

"Of course not," Delia said. "This place is barely functioning as it is." She shouldered her purse. "I'll be back on Monday for that conference. If either of the doctors fail to show up, I will remove my sister—and her money—and find another facility that cares about its patients."

When she was gone, Anna turned her hard look on all three of us. "There is a temporary fix to the outer wall, Mr. Waters?"

Alonzo nodded. "Yes, ma'am."

"And Miss Hughes is stable?"

"She is," Rita said.

"We'll keep her on twenty-four hour watch," Anna said. "If there's no improvement in her condition tomorrow morning, we'll extend it to forty-eight. Hopefully, no further measures will need to be taken."

She turned to me. "Your three-day suspension begins now, Mr. Whelan. Be ready to attend the meeting with the director and Dr. Stevens on Monday. I suspect they'll want to hear from you."

I nodded. In the past, the idea of talking in front of people would have made my blood run cold. Now my thoughts were for Thea. She'd been so happy painting and then it all went to shit.

"Jim?" Alonzo said, weighing my name heavily with disappointment.

"I'm going," I said.

On the way to the break room to change out of my uniform, Rita caught up with me.

"I'm sorry, Jim," she said. "This isn't right."

"You're working tomorrow?"

"Yes. They can't spare a single nurse or else I'd be going home, too."

"Will you text me that she's okay? Please?"

"Of course."

I walked out of Blue Ridge feeling like I was betraying Thea. Breaking a promise. I was supposed to fight for her, but what could I do? If I refused to leave, they'd think I was a psycho and have me arrested.

You didn't protect her. Doris sneered. *You fucked her up more. Go home, you big dummy, and leave your broken-down girl to the professionals.*

That was likely the truth—I'd hurt her when I was trying to help, but the gnawing in my stomach grew stronger and stronger the further my motorcycle took me away from Blue Ridge.

At home, I sat on my couch in the falling dark, wracking my brain for what went wrong. Thea had been so happy, dancing to her music, and her painting was perfect until...

Black streaks across the blue of the sky. Black against the perfection of the Empire State Building. Black mourning bands. Something lost. Something ruined.

I pulled my guitar on my lap and sang Pearl Jam's "Black."

All the pictures, washed in black...

I sang and played, not caring if the neighbors heard. My hands hit the strings harder, slapping instead of strumming. My voice raised until the lyrics vibrated my bones.

Turned my world to black...

The last notes faded. Something turned Thea's world to black, and I was going to get kicked out of Blue Ridge before I could find out what. I put the guitar away, disgusted and helpless, and fell into a fitful sleep.

Around nine the next morning, when I knew Thea would have eaten breakfast, I texted Rita: **How is she?**

The answer came a few minutes later: **Was just about to text you. Better. She ate something today, seems a little more like herself.**

Relief and pain gripped me as I typed, **Glad she's okay.**

Because I'm not there. It's better for her. This is better.

So far so good, Rita texted. **I'll keep you posted.**

The hours crawled. The day was hot and sticky and quiet. My phone chimed with another text from Rita around two o'clock. Thea's rec time.

She's drawing again. Word chains. Egypt. Darker stuff than her usual, but Anna's taking her off watch.

I stared at the words. Good. Thea was better. It was all that mattered.

Thanks, Rita. I guess it was painting that triggered her after all.

The reply came quick. **IDK. She was happy painting. And happy taking her FAE with you. But maybe the painting was it.**

Point taken. I fucked up because I was just an orderly. Not a damn doctor. Stupid of me to try.

I heated a frozen dinner in the microwave, hardly tasting it. The night grew blacker. The silence outside deeper. Like Thea's silence, I imagined. Deep and dark and endless.

Around ten, I thought about going to sleep, but something kept scratching at the inside of my consciousness. I grabbed my phone and scrolled through Rita's texts.

She's drawing again. Word chains. Egypt. Darker stuff than her usual...

Darker than usual. What did that mean?

It means she's still recovering from the snake incident.

But the answer wouldn't stick. The itch dug in deeper, with claws.

I typed a text to Rita, **Send me a photo of Thea's drawing?**

A pause. The rolling dots of a response came then, **I'm in the parking lot.**

Please. I need to see it.

Another pause, and then, **Hold on.**

My chest was tight as I waited. Finally, a photo appeared on my phone. A desert bathed in shadow. Clouds darkening the sky. A pyramid casting a long slant of darkness. And in the center, a coiled snake made of words. If Thea was talking through her word chains, then this was her story.

Asp rasp gasp last late hate help hell fell flesh flush force flow know no no no

That collection of words made my throat go dry. Help. Hell. No.

I went back to the word chain. Round and round the coil. I had to hold the phone still and tilt my head, reading upside down and sideways.

Touch much crush creak weak wake why cry stop stop stop

My heart began to pound so loud that blood thrashed in my ears.

Cleopatra was alone, Thea had said. *She put her hand in the snake's basket to end the pain.*

"What pain, Thea?" I whispered.

I put the phone down on the table and walked around the image, as the chain kept coiling tighter and tighter. The words lashed out at me, piercing my heart.

Hand man pan pant grip grope groan lone alone alone alone

"No," I whispered, the blood draining from my face. "Holy fuck, *no.*"

I hit Call on my phone. It rang once and Rita picked up.

"Jim, I'm going home," she said. "Enough. It was the painting. You... *we* shouldn't have messed with it. And I shouldn't be sending you photos—"

"You said she was better this m-m-morning," I said, cursing my goddamn stutter. Inhale. Exhale. "But last night, she was watched, right? A n-n-nurse was in her room?"

He's been going in her room.

"Yes, but—"

"That's why she was better," I said, rage and horror flushing through me, washing out my stutter, flooding every particle of my being. "Because *he* couldn't get to her. But the nights before that..."

"What are you talking about?"

Brett Dodson's lazy smile rose up in my mind, along with his promise that he'd find a way to keep his night shifts interesting.

Fuck, what's he been doing to her?

Words flashed before my eyes.

Flesh. Force. Grope. Stop.

Three times, she's screamed *stop* on the page. And *no.* She screamed *no.*

I was holding the phone so tightly; it was in danger of being crushed.

112

I squeezed my eyes shut against the constriction in my chest.

"He couldn't get to her, Rita. But tonight he can."

"Who?" Rita asked. "No one can get into resident rooms. They're locked. Only the duty nurse has the key."

"Mary Flint?" I shouted. "She sleeps all night. He took the key. He's been going in her room."

"Who?"

"Brett Dodson," I said. "He works the n-n-night shift…"

I couldn't get another word out. God, I was so fucking stupid. He all but *told* me his plan, and I hadn't heard. But Thea told me… Told all of us.

Inhale. Exhale. "Go back," I told Rita. "Please, go back to her room."

"Jim, I'm tired. I've been working six fifteen-hour shifts in a row. My husband hasn't seen me—"

"Brett Dodson is why she's been melting down," I said, fighting for calm. "Please, Rita. It's him. He's the reason she did it. He's why Thea…"

Put her hand in the asp's basket. Because she thought she was alone. My enemy made sure she was alone.

"The resident rooms are locked," Rita was saying. Her voice sounded different now. Cooler. Calmer. The way she spoke to residents who were irrational and upset. "I'm going home now."

"Rita."

"No one can get into resident rooms," she said again, louder. "It's not possible. Mary Flint is a friend of mine. I have to go."

"Rita, wait—"

"I'm hanging up, Jim."

The click in my ear was soft but might as well have been a door slamming.

Alonzo. I had to call him and tell him…

Tell him what? That I had a completely unfounded accusation against Brett? One that conveniently took the blame off me? I already looked like a pathetic loser with a crush on a brain-damaged girl, one step away from obsessed.

But fuck, what did it matter what they thought of me? I knew I was right. Every time I thought about Brett, the surety was like a bucket of ice water dumped on my head. Over and over again. Putting his hands on Thea. Doing things to her...

I called Alonzo but got his voicemail.

"Alonzo, this is Jim. Where are you? Pull Brett from the night shift. Tell him to go home. Order him to go home." I yanked on my boots. "He's hurting Thea. Call me back."

I threw on my jacket, grabbed my keys and helmet and headed out. The moon was a huge silver orb in a black sky. I rode my bike to the sanitarium and pulled up to the guard booth. Ted Johnson was on night shift. He raised his brow when I lifted my visor.

"Word is you're on a three-day suspension, Whelan."

"Yep," I said. "But I left my cell phone in the break room. Let me just run in and grab it? Five minutes."

Ted frowned. "All right. But Hank Morris is on patrol tonight. I'm going to radio him if you're not out in five."

Good, I thought. Hank was a former college linebacker. If my suspicion was correct, I might need him to keep me from killing Brett.

"Thanks, Ted."

I rode up the hill, then shut off the engine before I got to the parking lot to keep it quiet. I speed-walked the bike to the front door, leaned it against the wall and went in. George Baker was at the front desk. Unlike Jules, he actually did his job.

"Forgot my cell," I said. "Ted said I could get it."

Slowly George reached for his desk phone. "We'll see." He pushed a button. Sweat dripped down my back as precious seconds slipped away. Was Brett already in Thea's room? I closed my eyes against the thought and when I opened them again, George was off the phone and waving me in.

"Five minutes."

"Yep."

I walked casually past George, and once out of his sight and hearing, I took the stairs two at a time, racing up the two flights to the residents' quarters. I forced myself to slow down and get my breathing quiet. I prayed I'd catch Brett as he was unlocking the door to Thea's room. Prayed I'd get there before he did anything to her.

Most of all, I prayed I was wrong about everything. I wanted nothing more than to see Brett shooting the shit with Mary or playing solitaire at a table in the corner. I'd gladly lose my job or be thrown in jail if it meant I was wrong.

I wasn't wrong.

Mary Flint was fast asleep behind her fence at the nurse's station; door was ajar. The key to room 314 was missing from its hook.

Now I didn't care about silence. Blood burned through my veins as I pounded down the quiet hall to Thea.

CHAPTER 14

Thea

The bed dips behind me, making the mattress creak. In a half sleep, I become aware of someone lying next to me. A body curled into mine, a broad chest to my back. Stubble on the back of my neck.

It's a man.

His panting breath—sour with cigarette smoke—wafts over my cheek. My arm is pulled back and his hand grips mine. Behind me and between us, my fingers are curled around something both warm and hard.

The man holds me there. His fingers guide my hand. Warm skin slides over the hardness. Up and down. Over and over. He groans and my heart crashes in my chest.

I open my eyes for the first time.

It's dim. A shaft of moonlight falls over the bed.

I crane my head to look behind me. Beady eyes in a pale face that is silvery in the moonlight. Black hair. The man is silver and black.

My heart pounds and blood rushes to my ears. It's hard to breathe. There was the accident, and now I'm in this room. With this man. Touching him. He's making me touch him.

This isn't right.

How did I get here? How much time have I lost?

"Wh-Who are you? How long has it been?"

"Goddamn, you're a broken record," he says, laughing. "You don't remember, but this is our thing. We had to skip last night, so now I need it more."

I struggle to pull my hand away but he's crushing my fingers. Squeezing harder. Up and down.

"No," I say. "Stop."

I pull away but I'm under the covers and he's on top. Pinning me. I can't move but for my hands. I reach over my shoulder and slap him. The sting flares over my palm. The man grunts, and with his free hand, he grabs my hair and yanks my head back. Terror slithers over my skin with the pain.

"You don't do that again."

"You're hurting me," I gasp.

"Shh," he whispers over my ear. His grip on my hair softens. He strokes it as his other hand makes me stroke him. "Don't fight me. You're my girl, remember? You want this."

"No," I whisper. "This isn't right…"

"You promised. The other night. The hand stuff has been fun, but you promised more tonight."

I shake my head. Hot tears are gathering in my eyes. "I don't… I don't know you."

"Sure you do. I told you. I'm your boyfriend. Brett. You had an accident, but you're back. And now we're going to do all the things boyfriends and girlfriends do."

I squeeze my eyes shut and curl into myself. I search my memory for Brett but find nothing but emptiness. He moves to sit up and makes me sit up beside him. He's stroking himself now, jutting out from white uniform pants.

I'm alone. The man is here with me but I'm so alone.

He chuckles at my expression. "You don't like this? Don't worry. In a few minutes, you won't remember anyway." His hand slinks back into my hair, to pull my head down. "And you promised—"

The door slams open so hard, it rebounds off the wall. The mirror over the dresser falls and shatters. A scream erupts out of me as a man in black leather and heavy boots crosses the room in two long strides. The shadows and light dance over his handsome face that's twisted in rage.

Brett jumps to his feet. "Jesus Christ—"

The man grips Brett by the collar of his shirt with both hands, swings him—like a shot-putter—and sends him crashing into the dresser. Wood splinters and shatters. He's not jutting now but flaccid and trying to climb to his feet.

"M-M-Motherfucker," the man in black cries.

Brett holds his hands in front of him. "Jim, wait..."

Jim doesn't wait. He grabs Brett around the shoulders and drives him out into the hallway. I hear another crash and then a smack of fist against flesh. I crawl farther on the bed, curl up against the wall. I pull my knees to my chest and hug my legs as there is shouting and an alarm sounds.

"What did you d-d-do to her?" I hear Jim shout. "Tell me!"

"Nothing! Jesus, I didn't fuck her, and it's not like she'd remember anyw—"

The voice cuts off with another smack of Jim's fist.

The alarm goes silent. I hear a woman crying.

"I'm sorry," she says tearfully. "I had no idea. I must've dozed off."

I hear a buzz of static, followed by another man. "Hey, it's Hank. We got a situation. I got him contained but call 911."

More people talking in low voices and then the man in black—Jim—comes back into the room. His silhouette fills the doorway, hands still clenched into fists. Gradually they loosen and his breath slows.

"Are y-y-you okay?" he asks softly. His tone is low and gravelly around the stutter.

I nod, yes. Then shake my head, no. God, the silence in my mind is so vast and deep. Like a desert. I don't know if I'm okay. I don't know if I should be afraid of Jim.

He saved you.

He saved me but I don't know him. Maybe he's just as bad. Maybe he wants a turn.

But somewhere, beneath thought, I know that isn't true.

I don't want him to leave.

Sobs pour out of me, and I bury my face against my knees.

"Thea…" Jim's voice sounds like it's breaking.

He knows my name.

He knows me.

I peek up through strands of hair and blurry tears. Jim's taken a step closer but no more.

I hold my shaking arms out to him. I don't know why. I need him. I need someone so I don't feel this alone. Jim sits on the bed. Gathers me to him. I climb into his arms. He smells clean. Warm. Hard and soft. Hard leather and a soft shirt. Hard muscles of his chest under my cheek and his soft hand that strokes my hair, and it's so easy to feel the difference between him and Brett; his every intention is in his touch. This man would never hurt me.

Jim holds me tight as I tremble in his arms. And then he begins to sing. His low and gravelly voice rumbles beautifully under my ear. I feel safe enough to slip my hand into one of his. Big. Strong. Scarred along the knuckles. Red and swollen now. Because he fought for me. Saved me.

Other figures fill the doorway, other people talking, but Jim keeps singing to me. The silence in my mind is defeated by his voice. My eyes close. I'm so tired. It's safe to sleep now because Jim is coming with me.

He'll follow me into the dark.

CHAPTER 15

Jim

Thea's sobs quieted. The rise and fall of her chest against mine became deep and even, and at last, she slept. Gently—reluctantly—I laid her down on her pillow and covered her with her thin blanket, then slid to sit on the floor, my back against the bedframe. I couldn't hold her anymore, but no way in hell was I leaving her room.

The staff saw what had happened. They all watched as I held Thea and sang to her. They knew I wasn't going anywhere without a fight and there'd already been enough violence for one night.

They let me be and guided the residents back to bed. I sat with my knees drawn up, arms resting on them. Hands dangling but ready to fight again. As the sanitarium went quiet, sleep toyed with me, coming and going. Then a hand on my arm gently shook me awake.

It was Sunday morning. The watery light of dawn filtered in from the window.

"Jim?"

I jerked my head up and winced at the crick in my neck. Rita crouched next to me, her expression a myriad of gratitude and regret. Another nurse stood by the door, a syringe pack and a blue plastic box in her hand.

"Jim, you can go," Rita whispered, blinking against the tears in her eyes. "The police are still here, waiting for a statement. Sarah and I need to sedate Thea now."

"What for?" I said, my voice a croak.

"We have to know what happened. Brett said he never…"

I shut my eyes, shook my head. "Don't."

"We need to examine her," Rita said softly. "Thea can't tell us if he's lying or not. Not with words."

My glance went to the plastic box in the other nurse's hands. A rape kit. My stomach churned and bile rose to my throat.

Inhale. Exhale.

I hauled myself off the floor and glanced around Thea's room for the first time. A twin-sized bed, a small desk with pens and paper. A ruined dresser, its wooden shelves cracked and splintered. My shoulders ached at the sight, remembering how I'd ripped Brett off of Thea in a black haze of rage.

Aside from the wrecked dresser, the room was the same as most other resident's quarters but for the papers taped all over the walls. Reminders and notes.

Bathroom is here.

This is the closet.

Two years living at Blue Ridge, and Thea still didn't know her own room.

I gave her a final glance. She slept peacefully, but they'd stick a needle in her to send her down deeper so that she wouldn't wake up to an examination she needed.

She can't consent to that either.

"Thank you for taking care of her," Rita said. "You were right. I'm so sorry. I wish I'd listened."

"I wish I hadn't been right."

I forced myself to leave Thea and stepped into the hallway. Alonzo and Anna were conferring in low voices. They stopped when they saw me.

"My damn phone was off," Alonzo said. "I didn't get your message until late. Too late."

"Too late is right," Anna said. "Get your résumés ready, my dears.

When Delia Hughes hears about this…"

"Where's Brett?" I spat the name through gritted teeth.

"Jail," Alonzo said. "He was in her room, his privates hanging in the wind. Even without your statement, it was obvious what was happening."

"Come on, Jim," Anna said. "The police are waiting downstairs."

In the foyer, two uniformed officers were interviewing Jules at the front desk.

"He made a lot of crude jokes," she said. "But he was so fun. And nice. I never…"

"Crude jokes in general," an officer asked. "Or jokes with specific innuendo toward residents?"

"Both. He made a lot of jokes…" Jules swallowed and tried again. "I never thought it was real. I never did."

My hands balled into fists. He joked about Thea. About touching her…

"Jim Whelan?" one of the officers said. "We need a statement."

I told them everything I'd seen and heard before I'd bashed the door in. Which wasn't much. The only reason I'd heard anything at all was because I'd been momentarily petrified with rage at the sight of that bastard's dick in his hand and Thea's teary, fearful expression.

"He said she wouldn't r-r-remember anyway," I said. The rage returned on a red haze, awakening the stutter, but the cops didn't notice.

Rita came down with the results of the examination. "Negative," she said, and my eyes fell shut in relief. "Seems Brett was telling the truth about the nature of his assaults. Good news, if you can call it that."

Anna nodded, her lips pursed. "I'm glad, but the damage is done."

As the police conferred with Rita and Anna, Alonzo pulled me aside.

"The damage *is* done," he said. "Not just to Miss Hughes but to us too. It's going to be bad at that meeting tomorrow. But no less than what we deserve, I reckon. And by 'we,' I mean myself. Not you. You did right, Jim. Since the beginning, you been doing right by that girl."

"So have you," I said. "You've been doing right by all of them, with no help from the director. They have to see that."

Alonzo put his hand on my arm. "Go home, Jim. Get some sleep and I'll see you tomorrow."

I walked out the front door to my Harley. I'd already been dreading the meeting with Delia, the doctor, and the director. But now, with that bastard assaulting Thea... When I walked out of Blue Ridge tomorrow, it might be for the last time. Delia Hughes might have the entire sanitarium shut down. Good people would be out of jobs.

And Thea would remain trapped in her five-minute prison for the rest of her life.

CHAPTER 16

Jim

Monday morning, I showered and put on my only dress shirt, jeans, and my leather jacket. I rode to Blue Ridge with my guts in a knot.

The parking lot was fuller than usual, with a few sedans and one medical van with Roanoke Memorial emblazoned on the side. Inside, the normally hushed sanitarium echoed with footsteps and voices.

I found Alonzo, Joaquin, and Anna in the hallway outside the rec room huddled up and talking in low voices.

"What's going on?" I asked.

"The new doctor is in there with Delia and Thea," Alonzo said, inclining his head at the rec room door. "They've been in a serious pow-wow with board members and other doctors for an hour."

I frowned. "Is the meeting with Poole and Stevens still on?"

"Poole and Stevens are no longer affiliated with Blue Ridge," Anna said. She tilted her chin. "Neither is Mary Flint."

"Dude, it's nuts," Joaquin said. "Delia Hughes blew a gasket—"

"As well she should," Alonzo said.

"—and heads rolled."

"Somehow, none were ours," Anna said dryly.

"Okay," I said slowly. "Delia isn't taking Thea out of Blue Ridge?"

"Don't think so," Alonzo said. "The new doctor—Christina Chen? She's in charge now and somehow, she's convinced Delia to stay. Said she's going to be more involved in Miss Hughes' care." He nodded at the rec room again. "Starting now."

"And that's it? Delia was satisfied with that?"

"Strangely enough." Alonzo scratched his chin. "Something's going on with her. I can't put my finger on it…"

"Agreed," Anna said. "She seemed almost eager not to have to pull Thea out of Blue Ridge. As if she were grasping at any reason to stay."

"Snakes and all," Joaquin said.

Alonzo gave him a dirty look.

"I meant Brett too," Joaquin said, holding up his hands.

"Miss Hughes was grossly abused while under our care," Alonzo said. "Delia Hughes would be well within her rights to sue us into oblivion. The fact we're still here is a blessing."

"It's a miracle," Anna said. "As much as I loathe what happened to Thea, it was the wake-up call the board needed to fix so much of what was broken."

"We're not out of the woods yet," Alonzo said. "Delia's got us by the balls." He clapped me on the shoulder. "Needless to say, your suspension is over."

Joaquin chucked my other arm. "You did good for Miss Hughes, man."

"Indeed," Anna Sutton said. She patted my hand. "Thank you, Jim."

I looked around at them—Anna and Alonzo like proud parents and Joaquin the brother I never had. A family. My family.

Dream on, you big dummy. Doris scoffed. *They just feel sorry for you.*

But her words didn't stick this time. No one lost their jobs and Thea was still here with a new doctor. I went to the break room and changed into my uniform, feeling lighter than I had in days. A new era was beginning. I just wished Thea hadn't had to suffer to make it happen.

I pushed the mop bucket out into the hallway and began the stretch of the linoleum that led to the front foyer.

Maybe Thea will start a new painting. Maybe this Dr. Chen will have some ideas about her word chains. Maybe I could help—

"You," a familiar voice said behind me.

"Ms. Hughes," I said, turning.

"I suppose I should thank you for coming to Thea's rescue the other night," Delia said.

"Just doing my job," I said warily.

"And you did it well. Got to her right at the nick of time, didn't you?"

I cocked my head. "Sorry?"

"You busted through the door like a superhero. Perfectly timed to catch that man in the act."

"Not perfectly," I said, feeling the stutter right there, rising with the anger at her insinuations. "I was t-two nights too late."

Delia tilted her chin. "And holding my sister? Singing to her? Is that in your job description as well?"

I gripped the handle of the mop. "She was upset. Music helps her calm down."

She pursed her lips, watching me. "I'm torn, Mr. Whelan," she said. "I'm grateful to you, and I don't trust you. You're not—"

"Yeah, I know," I said, cutting her off. "I'm not a doctor. I'm just an orderly."

"You are. Thea is so defenseless, I've always mistrusted male staff around her. Turns out I was right to be wary."

Tears shone in her eyes but she blinked them away.

"Dr. Chen assures me Thea is in safe hands now. A new director will be appointed, more funds allotted for hiring staff and Dr. Chen herself is committed to Thea's case. The only thing that would reassure me more, is if the man who seems so taken with my sister no longer worked here."

The words to defend myself rose to my lips but I bit them back. They'd come out stuttering and weak anyway, making my poor excuses sound desperate. Or obsessive. I knew what my fierce protection of Thea looked like to everyone else: a male orderly paying too much attention to a beautiful, vulnerable patient. Stopping Brett only compounded Delia's worry. In her eyes, I was just another man who had access to Thea. Another predator who could put his hands on her when no one was looking because who would suspect me now?

"One of the stipulations of my keeping Thea at Blue Ridge," Delia continued, "is that under no circumstances are you, or any other male staff, to have direct contact with my sister. If what you say is true—you're just doing your job—this shouldn't be a problem for you."

I tilted my chin up. "Not a problem."

"Good. Because if I hear that you so much as looked her way, I'll call in another demand." She gave me a humorless smile. "You'd be amazed at how amenable a facility can be to client's wishes when it's within that client's ability to sue said facility into the ground."

She started past me, then stopped. For a second, her dark eyes softened beneath the hard mask of her face.

"I am grateful you stopped that man. I know it sounds like I'm not—"

"I don't need your gratitude, Ms. Hughes."

She stiffened. "I disagree. My *gratitude* is the only reason you still have a job, Mr. Whelan."

I didn't take Thea on her FAE that day, and I never would again. I had to be content the new doctor was interested in Thea's case. Still, the idea of working under the same roof with Thea every day and not talking to her was a kind of torture.

Jesus, I really am a creepy stalker.

Maybe it would be better if Delia had me fired after all.

I should do what she wants and quit. Start over somewhere else. Keep my head down. Do my job.

Rita and Alonzo fumed about Delia's edict in the dining room after lunch.

"That's some bullshit," Alonzo said. "I can talk to her."

"Have you met Delia Hughes?" I asked with a wry smile. "Forget it. My job's hanging as it is."

"But after how you saved Thea?" Rita said, shaking her head in disbelief. "When I think of Brett in her room…" She shivered.

"Delia's protective," I said. "Can't blame her for that."

She and Alonzo exchanged glances, and I felt the pity roll off of them in waves.

"No big deal," I said shortly. "There are plenty of residents who need help. You can assign me to one of them."

Alonzo watched me through narrowed eyes. "Mr. Perello," he said after a long moment. "He needs someone with him for his daily smoke."

"Great," I said. "I'll do it."

Alonzo went back to work, and Rita reached her hand across the table and gave mine a squeeze. "I'm sorry, Jim. I wish things were different with Thea. For her sake, but for yours too."

"For m-m-my sake?"

Her smile tilted toward pitying. "You seem so taken with her. And in her own way, she cares about you."

I stared, my skin heating.

The stuttering orderly and the broken-down girl. I could practically see Doris shake her head. *What a pitiful pair you make.*

Now my skin burned with humiliation and I pulled my hand away. "I gotta get back to work."

I rose from the chair and headed out without looking back. I cleaned up a few resident rooms and took Mr. Perello for a walk outside. He sat on a bench and savored his one cigarette.

"This is a life, isn't it?" he asked, watching the smoke curl up and hang thickly in the humid, summer air. "Not *the* life. *A* life. I guess that counts for something."

A life.

That's what I had before Thea. It wasn't much, but at least there hadn't been so much damn confusion. Or this ache in my chest that didn't quit. A longing. Strange emotions I'd never experienced before, like bright swaths of color over a drab gray sky. They swept through me when I thought of Thea. I remembered the softness of her hair and how good it felt to hold her, even if it was to keep her from falling apart.

It wasn't right to feel like this. It wasn't right to feel anything for a girl who had no control over who was in her life. Who couldn't make a single informed decision. Who smiled her brilliant smile at those around her because what choice did she have but to trust us?

I wanted to be a choice she made, not a stranger she was forced to contend with. And it wasn't fair to put that pressure on her, even if she never knew it. *I* knew it, and it wasn't right.

I needed to quit.

After I walked Mr. Perello back to his room, I headed for the break room, hoping to catch Alonzo. I'd hand in my resignation. It'd be hard on the staff to fill my hours until they found a replacement, but they'd manage. Especially with a new director and increased funds. Blue Ridge would survive without me. Like Thea after a reset hit, they'd never know I was gone.

Pity party, you big dummy?

I shrugged Doris off. No pity. Just facts.

But Alonzo wasn't around, and I figured I should finish the full day's work. I went to the rec room to clean up.

I stopped short to see Dr. Chen at the shelf along one wall. Even from the door, I knew she was looking at Thea's drawings. Dr. Chen held the paper and turned it slowly, reading the word chains.

The broom handle banged against the door as I entered the room and Dr. Chen looked up.

"Hello," she said. She couldn't be more than thirty-five, with a sharp intelligence in her eyes and a kind smile. "Don't think we've met. I'm Dr. Christina Chen."

"Jim Whelan," I said. "I can come back."

"You're the one who stopped the orderly from assaulting Miss Hughes," Dr. Chen said. "We're all so grateful to you. Truly." The doctor looked back at Thea's drawings. "Have you seen these? Quite extraordinary."

"Yeah, I have," I said, glancing behind me, expecting Delia Hughes to materialize in a cloud of green smoke. "Thea uses them to communicate. I think they're her memory."

"Do you?" Her tone was inviting, not derogatory. "How so?"

I crossed over to her. Hell, if I were going to quit anyway, I had nothing to lose. I pulled out the folded drawing I kept in my back pocket. "You see this one?" I pointed to the word chain:

Rue true blue bluest sky eye my smile rile rain pain pain pain

"Those are song lyrics," I said. "'Sweet Child O' Mine.' I played it for her when I took her for a walk, and she drew this the next day."

Dr. Chen's eyes widened. "Has this happened more than once?"

I found and showed her more examples, along with the drawing that clued me in to Brett's assaults.

Dr. Chen nodded. "I see."

Hope took flight in my heart. "D-D-Do you?"

She nodded. "Dr. Stevens' notes regard the word chains as Thea's brain exercising itself the only way it knows how. But perhaps that's because he had no context for them."

My heart skipped a beat. "Do they m-m-mean anything to you?" I asked, my jaw stiffening at that damn stutter.

She cocked her head. "You have a slight disfluency, Jim?" Before I could answer, she said, "I only bring it up so that we can acknowledge it, and you don't have to feel self-conscious." Her focus went back to the word chains. "I heard about Thea's painting. She ruined it as a result of the abuse happening to her at night?"

"Yes," I said. "Exactly. She r-r-remembers."

Dr. Chen studied the drawing a final time. "We'll see. Some tests need to be run, of course."

"You can help her?"

The doctor gathered the drawings into a stack and tucked them under her arm. "Before coming here, I completed a fellowship with Dr. Bernard Milton, one of the premiere neuropsychologists in Australia. He's doing amazing, groundbreaking things to restore memory loss in special candidates, using stem cells and nanotechnology."

I listened, rapt. As if this woman were unspooling the secrets of the universe.

"When my fellowship ended, I knew at once where I wanted to devote my attention—to Thea Hughes. I had no idea what I would find in her, but my professional curiosity demanded I work with one of the world's worst cases of amnesia." She gave me a wry grin. "Maybe my ego had a little to do with it, too."

My throat was dry. "And?"

"Her file reads as if she were a typical traumatic brain injury patient with no hope of recovery. But between seeing her in person and this conversation right now, Mr. Whelan, I'm quite dumbstruck at how Thea's case and Dr. Milton's recent work might intersect."

I stared. "Is Thea a candidate for whatever he's working on?"

Dr. Chen smiled. "We'll see. Can we speak again? I find those who work with patients on a daily basis often know more than their physicians."

"I'm not sure I'm going to be working here much longer."

"That's a shame. Well, if you change your mind, I'll be here." She held up the drawings. "I'm going to be here quite a lot."

CHAPTER 17

Jim

For the next few weeks, Dr. Christina Chen kept every one of her promises to Delia. She spent hours with Thea, observing her, asking careful questions and taking notes. Pages and pages of notes.

Not that I witnessed it myself. I kept my own promises, staying away from Thea, and Rita kept me updated.

"I think Dr. Chen has a plan," she said. "I think she might be able to do something for Thea."

I sank into the chair in the break room. "That's good."

"Good?" Rita laughed. "Dr. Chen knows you knew Thea needed more than Magic Markers and scratch paper. You should—"

"I'm leaving," I said.

Rita stared. "What do you mean?"

"I'm going to put my two weeks in with Alonzo. I should have done it two weeks *ago,* but..."

But I wanted to make sure Thea was going to be okay first.

"Nope," Rita said. "I won't let you."

"It's okay. It's better this way."

"For who? Delia? But not Thea." She leaned toward me. "She's doing well, painting again, but she's not like she was. She's not as happy as she was when you were taking her for walks and—"

"She's not as happy because she's still recovering from Brett," I said. "It's not me."

Rita crossed her arms and flumped back against her chair. "You were right about what made Thea happy, Jim, except you forgot to include yourself in that equation."

"It's better—"

"Stop saying that," she cried. "It's not better for you and Thea."

"There is no 'me and Thea,'" I said, my skin burning. "F-F-Forget it." I got to my feet and went to the door.

"Jim," Rita said, her soft tone stopping me. "You're a good man. That you're willing to leave her only proves it. But what about you?"

"What about me?"

"You put Thea's happiness in all our faces. You made it important."

"Because it is."

"And yours? What about your happiness?"

I don't know what that is.

"I gotta get back to work."

I found Alonzo on a bench outside, having his smoke break. He held up his hand before I could speak. "I know. Rita got to me first. Why?"

I shrugged. "It's just time."

"Is it about Miss Hughes?"

"Maybe I just don't want to work here anymore."

He narrowed his eyes. "So this is two weeks' notice?"

I nodded.

Alonzo took a long pull off his smoke. "Okay. Can't stop you. Can't say that I'm glad though."

"It is what it is," I said.

He snorted. "If there was ever a more empty phrase in the English language—"

"Hey, boss." Joaquin rounded the corner. "Dr. Chen wants a meeting."

"All righty." He hauled himself off the bench with a groan. "This should be interesting."

"She wants you there too, Jim," Joaquin said.

My head whipped up. "Me?"

Alonzo chuckled. "You ain't done with us yet."

In the conference room, Dr. Chen sat riffling through a stack of notes and open leather-bound files in front of her, conferring quietly with a young, female intern.

Anna and Rita sat together, talking in low voices. They both stopped and beamed when Alonzo and I came in.

Delia Hughes did not beam. "What is he doing here?" she demanded.

Dr. Chen muttered something to the intern who nodded and left the room, then she folded her hands on her papers and smiled warmly.

"Mr. Waters, Mr. Whelan. Happy you could join us." She turned to Delia. "I wanted everyone who's been involved in Thea's care present for what I have to say." She glanced at me. "All things considered, I feel it's only right."

Delia didn't argue but watched as I took a seat beside Rita, who was vibrating with excitement that jumped to me like an electric current.

"I'll get right to it," Dr. Chen said. "Dr. Stevens' standing diagnosis of Thea states she's unable to lay down new memories, and any memories of her life before the car accident have been washed away. The word chain phenomena in her artwork is, in his words, nothing more than her brain utilizing whatever limited means it had to express itself. I believe he's wrong."

"Wrong," Delia said. "In what way, exactly?"

"Given my observations and the information provided me by the staff here, I feel there is a correlation between Thea's artwork and what she experiences in her short window of consciousness." Her smile widened. "I am prepared to change her diagnosis."

"To what?" Delia asked, while in my chest, my heart began to thud, as if counting off the seconds until Dr. Chen said something that was going to change Thea's life forever.

"Brain damage can result in the patient losing their long-term memory or losing the ability to create new memory. Or, as in Thea's case, both. But current, new developments are revealing that there are rare instances in which a patient is able to retain and make memories, but the mechanism to *recall* them is what's damaged. I believe that this is true for Thea."

"You mean… she *hasn't* lost her memory?" Delia asked.

Dr. Chen smiled. "Rather, she's misplaced it. We're going to help her get it back."

Holy shit, I thought. *Hold on, Thea. They're coming. They're coming to get you out.*

Dr. Chen's next words confirmed it.

"Therefore, I believe she would be an ideal candidate for the procedure Dr. Bernard Milton is performing at the Sydney Medical Foundation."

"What kind of procedure?" Delia said.

"Dr. Milton has developed a treatment involving stem cell surgery combined with a powerful binding agent that allows patients with this specific memory loss to repair the mechanism for recall so that memories—new and old—can be accessed."

As the words hovered in the air, Rita reached under the table to give my hand a squeeze.

"Dr. Milton has already begun a trial of patients," Dr. Chen continued. "They're a few weeks ahead of us but their results, so far, have been encouraging. Though the risks are not inconsequential."

"What risks?" I asked, drawing everyone's eye.

"Are we talking *open* brain surgery?" Delia asked, giving me a sharp look to remind me Thea was her concern, not mine.

Dr. Chen shook her head. "The surgery is a minimally invasive endoscopic, endonasal procedure, which also involves stem cell extraction from the pelvic bone and cerebrospinal fluid…" She waved her hands. "We are getting ahead of ourselves. There are preliminary tests that need to be done to ensure Thea is a proper candidate. Dr. Milton will want to fly in to perform them and the procedure himself. With your consent," she said to Delia.

A quiet descended over the room.

"You're saying this procedure might restore Thea's memory," Delia said slowly.

"It's a possibility, yes."

"All of her memories? From her life before the accident?"

"Correct."

Delia's glance flickered to each of us, watching her. Waiting. Holding our breath.

"And if it works…"

"If it works, Ms. Hughes," Dr. Chen said, "this treatment will bring Thea back to life."

CHAPTER 18

Jim

"I'd like to be alone with Dr. Chen," Delia said. "I have questions."

"Of course," Anna said.

"Thank you, Jim," Dr. Chen said as we headed out. "Your information was particularly helpful."

I nodded, feeling Delia's eyes on me.

In the break room, Rita gave me a hug, her eyes shining. "You did this. Everything good that's going to happen for Thea is because of you."

I slipped out of Rita's embrace. "That's not true."

"It is true, and you need to own it," she said.

"All right, I agree it's very exciting news," Anna said, "but we still have work to do."

The importance of Dr. Chen's words sank in. I tried to imagine how Thea would be, out of her prison. Talking to her for longer than a few minutes. Her calling me Jimmy with the kind eyes. Her remembering me...

Not gonna happen, you big dummy. Doris chuckled. *Delia will see to that.*

Alonzo clapped me on the back. "Still putting in your notice?"

"I don't know…"

He stared. "How do you not know?"

Because nothing good lasts. I have to be able to walk away. It's how I've survived.

"If you're worried about Delia, forget her," he said. "If this miracle works on Thea, she'll have something she hasn't had in two years. Free will. Let *her* decide what she wants."

"Alonzo—"

"You think you're so replaceable?" he demanded with sudden fury. "You think I can pick up the phone and just find someone else? You think it's gonna be easy for me not having you around?"

To my shock his eyes were shining.

"Forget it," he said, shaking his head and heading out the door. "Do what you have to do. What do I care?"

Over the next few days, the sanitarium was crawling with doctors. Dr. Bernard Milton and his team from Sydney flew in and began running tests on Thea. It only took two days to come to their conclusion.

"They're going to do it," Rita cried. "Dr. Milton said she's the perfect candidate and Delia's given consent. Can you believe it? I'm so excited for her."

"Me too."

And scared shitless.

I'd looked up Dr. Milton's procedure. He'd performed it on a test group of patients in Australia a few weeks ago. I didn't understand all the technical jargon, but I grasped the surgery involved drawing bone marrow from Thea's hip bone. The stem cells would then be processed in a lab and married with neurons drawn from her spinal fluid. A procedure called neuroendoscopy would implant the cells into the damaged areas of her hippocampus via her nasal passage. After, she would take an oral medication—a sort of bonding agent—that acted as a bridge between neurons to facilitate the memory recall.

The potential complications from surgery were aneurism, blood clots, and infection. The medication—which she'd have to take for the rest of her life—had its own risks, including elevated blood pressure and stroke.

But if that's what it took to break her out of her prison, then there was no choice, in my mind.

The day came when Thea was transported from Blue Ridge down to Roanoke Memorial. Delia and Rita went with her, gently guiding Thea toward the medical van, talking soothingly to her along the way.

"When she comes back," Alonzo said, standing next to me at the front door, "she'll really be back."

I nodded, watching her disappear into the van. His hand landed on my shoulder.

"She'll be okay," he said. "She's survived the worst thing already. She's a tough girl."

I nodded again. Thea was tough. Stronger than anyone I knew to endure her amnesia for years without going crazy. Still, I felt like I was holding my breath as the days creaked by, one by one.

At night, I sat on my couch in my empty house and played "I Will Follow You into The Dark" and prayed that they'd bring Thea out of the dark for good.

Thea came back on what was technically my last day at Blue Ridge, although Alonzo refused to acknowledge it. Joaquin needed me to cover his midday/evening shift, so I rolled into the sanitarium around noon. The parking lot was fuller than usual, and the medical van was parked out front.

In the break room, I began to change into my uniform, fumbling over the buttons, my heart pounding.

She's here. She's right here.

Footsteps pounded down the hall and the door burst open.

"You're here," Rita cried, breathless. She grabbed my hand. "Come with me to the rec room. Now."

"I can't," I said, my throat dry.

"You have to," she said, her smile bursting over her face. "I insist. You have to see this."

"But Delia—"

"Delia can suck it. Come on."

I followed her upstairs to the rec room. It was full of doctors and staff, clustered in a loose circle. In the center was Thea. She wore pajama pants and a matching shirt. Barefoot, her hair tousled as if she'd just woken up. Her face was free of makeup and her luminous blue eyes looked as if they held all the happiness in the world.

She's so fucking beautiful...

Alonzo stood off to the side, watching with a joyful smile on his face. Delia kept close to her sister, her expression wary, not daring to let herself be happy yet.

Anna led Thea around, introducing her to the people who had been taking care of her for two years.

"And this is Nurse Sarah," Anna said. "You remember her?"

"I do," Thea said. "Hi, Sarah." The doctors all bent their heads to take notes as Thea threw her arms around the nurse's neck. "I'm so happy to meet you. Again and for the first time." She laughed, a ripple of pure joy that filled the rec room. "I remember all of this. All of you. It's like a dream slowly coming back."

My goddamn eyes stung, and I bowed my head, jaw clenched. The last time I'd cried was at Grandpa Jack's funeral and I hadn't done it since. But the tears that tried to get me now were different. Good. So good they scared me.

But I didn't cry. I never cried. Thea was okay. She was there and she was okay. Free. I didn't need anything more.

I can walk out of here with my head up.

I turned to go.

"I think that's everyone," Anna said. "Dr. Milton, would you like to—"

"Guns N' Roses," Thea said suddenly as if the name had been on the tip of her tongue and she'd just found it.

I froze.

"Sweet Child O' Mine," Thea said. "Oh my God, I remember."

I turned around. Thea was walking between all the people, wending her way toward me. Her eyes wide and taking me in, a shy smile on her lips.

"And... Lady Gaga. One of my faves."

My heart stopped then jolted again, double-time. Delia was scowling, but now Thea was singing softly, "I want your love. Love love love…"

She was all there. Standing right in front of me.

I waited for our usual script—one that we'd played out a hundred times.

How long has it been?

The doctors are working on my case.

Can I call you Jimmy? You have kind eyes…

"Hi," Thea said.

I swallowed hard. "Hi."

She cocked her head. Her gaze roamed my face, my eyes, my mouth, studying me. "You're Jimmy. Right?"

I wasn't wearing a nametag. Rita had pulled me out of the break room before I could put it on.

"Yeah." My voice was gruff. "That's me."

Thea's smile broke free, like a goddamn sun after a decade of gray clouds and rain. She stuck out her hand and said, "It's nice to officially meet you, Jimmy."

I had no words. None I could trust. I took her hand, soft and warm in mine, and she gave it her signature, one-pump shake.

"Wow, this is crazy," she said with a laugh, glowing with happiness. "Crazy and good and just…"

"A miracle," I breathed.

"Yeah. Exactly." She moved closer to me, as if we were alone instead of in a room full of people. "And I was right."

"About wh-what?"

"About you."

Her smile was brilliant, shy, and bold all at once. She still hadn't let go of my hand. "You aren't just a dream at all."

PART II

CHAPTER 19

Thea

I open my eyes for the first time…

A hospital room, gauzy white in my blurred vision. Doctors surrounded me. One, a pretty young woman named Dr. Chen, told me I'd had surgery to restore my memory. I nodded that I understood, but I didn't. Not truly. My memory had been lost? They said I had only a few minutes of consciousness, but that made no sense. I was always there. Awake and asleep. What they called my amnesia to me felt like an endless dream in a tiny, airless box. The surgery pulled me out, woke me up. I could breathe again. Think again.

I'm alive…

Joy suffused me like adrenaline.

Another doctor, this one with an Australian accent, asked me questions:

Did I remember my name? Date of birth?

Yes and yes.

Did I remember the car accident?

No.

I remembered the four of us—me, Delia, Mom and Dad—in the foyer, taking a photo on my phone. For Delia's... graduation. Yes. She was wearing a cap and gown.

That memory was one bookend. The other was the hospital, and in between, empty books with their pages slowly filling back up with words. The pages were being filled in, lines at a time, cued by words or scents or the snippet of a song. One familiar face blowing open a whole new avenue of memories.

Delia stayed by my side for the two days I was in the hospital. My sister looked like she'd aged more than the two years I'd been gone. Every time she hugged me tight, she stared at me as if I were an alien life form. Everyone stared at me—specialists, nurses—while I stared at this life that was so much brighter and richer than I'd remembered.

"When are Mom and Dad coming?" I asked.

"Soon," Delia said. "Get some rest."

I was so tired from the surgery. I wanted to sleep, but I was scared if I closed my eyes, it would all disappear.

I don't want to sleep ever again. I want to live.

But I slept and woke, and all that had come back was still there.

I was still here.

When I was well enough, I was taken back to Blue Ridge Sanitarium, which, apparently, had been my home for the last two years. Everything about the old building was strange and familiar at the same time. The sights and smells. The wood and the dust. The disinfectant and the potpourri. I moved through a perpetual fog of déjà vu.

"I know this place," I said in the foyer, standing in front of a still-life painting of fruit in a bowl. "I know this picture, too."

It's beautiful, isn't it? The way the light falls over the curve of the apple...

The words were my own. I'd been talking to someone in front of this picture. A man. Tall. Dark hair. Dark jacket. I could almost see him... A mirage in my vast desert of nothingness.

They took me upstairs to the rec room and there he was.

He stood near the door. In white, not black, but he was there, looking as if he were about to leave. I recognized the angle of his jaw and the softness of his eyes. Another flood gate of memories opened up. Sun-drenched afternoons. Music. This man sang to me. He played my favorite dance songs on his phone for me. He saved me when—

I brushed that dark memory aside. I'd deal with it later. The same way I'd deal with whatever Delia wasn't telling me about our parents. Later.

As I crossed the room, more came back to me—sun and music and... paint. Yes. He brought me paint. A canvas. He brought me back to life...

And now I stood in front of him, my heart pounding like a drum.

Holy crap, he was gorgeous. Beautiful brown eyes. Stubble along his square chin. Muscle and strength and gentleness too.

"Hi," I said. This guy made me shy, and I had never been shy in my life.

I watched his Adam's apple bob as he swallowed hard and said, "Hi."

That's Jim. The name bubbled up from the recesses of my mind.

I saw it carved in black letters on white plastic. A nametag. But he wasn't wearing a nametag and I hadn't needed it anyway. I remembered his name on my own. Just as I remembered it wasn't Jim, but...

"You're Jimmy. Right?"

"Yeah. That's me."

That's him. My Jimmy.

I nearly laughed at the silly thought. He wasn't mine, but I was bursting with happiness that he was here. I stuck out my hand.

"It's nice to officially meet you, Jimmy," I said, his impending touch making me shy again.

His large, strong hand with scars across the knuckles engulfed mine. I gave it a shake but didn't let go.

"Wow, this is crazy," I said. My cheeks hurt from smiling. "Crazy and good and just..."

"A miracle," he said.

God, the way he was looking at me. I searched my memory for some moment with Jimmy that was more than talk and music. There had to be, given how insanely attracted I was to him already. I found only echoes of conversations about Marc Antony and Cleopatra. And Jimmy protecting me from the sick asshole who'd made me touch him. Jimmy hauling him off of me, making him go away. Jimmy holding me and singing, promising that he'd follow me into the dark.

"Yeah. Exactly." I moved closer to him, my hand still in his. "And I was right."

"About wh-what?"

"About you," I said. "You aren't just a dream at all."

He was taller than me by a good six inches. His head inclined slightly as if he was going to kiss me. Which was nuts. I just met him, for crying out loud.

Only I didn't. We met a long time ago. We met over and over again. This time, instead of slipping away to wherever the amnesia took me, I was staying right here. If Jimmy wanted to kiss me in front of all these people, that was fine with me because I wanted to kiss him too. Badly. It would be a bow on the momentous gift of waking up, so to speak, because my God, this man was sexy in both the most obvious *and* understated of ways.

"Thea," Delia said from behind me, jerking me from my thoughts. Her tone like a cold shower. "It's time you rested. Say goodbye to Mr. Whelan."

"Why?" I said.

Before she could answer, an older man with a grandfatherly face spoke up.

"Because your sister is right," he said. "You should rest. You can talk with Jim again later. Tomorrow, maybe. Or the next day. Or the day after that."

Something passed between the two men. An inside joke, maybe, because Jim looked like he was biting back a smile. I stared at the older man, my brain working as if I were on *Jeopardy!* and the seconds were counting down until the buzzer.

"Alonzo," I blurted. "You're Alonzo."

He tipped an imaginary cap to me. "Indeed, my dear. And may I say it's so very good to have you back, Miss Hughes."

"Thank you," I said. My gaze returned to Jimmy like a tractor beam. "I'm glad to be back."

"Come, Thea," Delia said stiffly. "The doctors have more questions."

Nurse Rita stood beside me. "Let's take you to your room."

I loved Rita so much—thousands of memories of her taking care of me with kindness and patience clogged my brain, as each day was almost identical to the next.

Until Jimmy came. Bringing music and singing, paints and canvas.

Delia took my arm and physically pried me away from him. I gave him a parting smile I hoped wasn't too desperate and let my sister and

Rita drag me away.

Dr. Chen and Dr. Milton followed us up to the third floor of the sanitarium. We passed a dining room on the way to the elevators, and the scent of fried chicken wafted out.

"I'm super hungry," I said. "I haven't eaten anything in two years."

"Of course you have," Delia said. "Don't exaggerate."

"Wait, please explain, Thea," Dr. Chen said. "What do you mean by that?"

"I mean that I know that I ate, but I can't remember eating. Does that make sense?"

She and Dr. Milton exchanged glances.

"Is that bad?"

"Not at all," Dr. Milton said. He had a silver beard and a full head of hair the same color. He reminded me of Jeff Bridges but with Hugh Jackman's accent. "Do you find you can describe many of your memories this way?"

"I can clearly remember things from before the accident. With details. But my time here…" I gave my head a shake. "The details are fuzzy. Maybe they're not all back yet?"

Like Mom and Dad. They're not back yet, either.

A soul-deep fear dug itself into my heart, and suddenly I lost my appetite.

"I want to lie down," I said.

Rita led me to a door with 314 on it. I noticed the lock was on the outside of the knob. Inside, the room was spare and drab. No color. No art on the walls or decor of any kind, unless you counted all the papers taped everywhere.

This is the closet said one taped to what was obviously a closet.

"Was I not only an amnesiac but a moron too?" I teased.

Rita laughed. "We figured better safe than sorry."

Inside, the clothes were nearly all white and beige. Nothing with a pattern or color.

"Who was in charge of my clothes? Let me guess." I shot my sister a look.

Delia lifted her chin, wearing her stiff, stubborn, I'm-always-right expression, which meant she was the guilty party. "I've been managing your money on things you need. Flashy clothes aren't on the list."

"Obviously," I said, wandering the tiny room. Examining the little reminders on every wall.

This is the bathroom, on the bathroom door.

Smell your breath, said the one taped to the bathroom mirror. *If it's not minty, brush your teeth. If it is, you already brushed.*

"Unreal," I said, and then I realized I *was* tired. My lower back ached from the bone marrow extraction they'd said I had, and sensory overload made my eyes want to close. I climbed into the twin bed, propped up on the pillows. "Why is this room so godawfully boring? I didn't stop loving art. Or Egypt. Or color. What gives?"

Delia started to speak up, but Dr. Chen intervened.

"Until the advent of Dr. Milton's research, you were misdiagnosed," she said. "Stevens believed you were completely unable to lay down new memory. That your few minutes of consciousness were all you had."

"So it didn't matter what I wore or what my room looked like? I wouldn't remember it anyway?"

"Essentially, yes."

Delia looked guilty again. "I felt the less stimulation, the better. To keep you calm."

"I guess I understand. I can hardly explain what it was like for me. I was here, but I couldn't grasp anything. Like trying to climb out of a box and constantly sliding back down. No thoughts. None that I could hold on to, anyway."

I looked to Delia, sitting on the edge of my bed.

"But I know things," I said. "I know things from these two years since the accident that I can't actually remember knowing. I wanted to paint. Constantly. I was starving for it. I can't *remember* feeling that, but I felt it." Tears started to sting my eyes. "And music. And color. I wanted those things."

"You had seizures, Thea," Delia said. "Do you remember those?"

I met her gaze. "I remember wanting to be with you, every minute. Seeing you made me so happy but somehow, I knew you'd vanish. And it scared me. Terrified me. I know that without remembering it."

I swallowed hard; the tears threatening to overwhelm me now.

"I remember asking you when Mom and Dad were coming," I said, my chest hitching, my hands clutching the sheet. "But they never came. Not in two years. I don't remember how I know that, but I know that.

Tell me now, Delia. Tell me the truth. Where are Mom and Dad?"

From my other side, Rita suddenly took my hand, tears in her own eyes.

"No," I said, looking between her and Delia, shaking my head. "No, please…"

"The accident was bad," Delia said, her voice hardly more than a whisper. "It's a miracle you survived."

"But Mom? She didn't make it?" I had to stop to breathe, the sobs wanting to erupt as the horrible truth bloomed in me like an icy black hole sucking the light and warmth out of the room. "And Daddy? He… He's gone? They're both *gone*?"

Delia's eyes filled and spilled over as she nodded.

"Oh my God," I whispered, tears streaming. I let go of Rita and held my arms to my sister. "Oh my God, Delia…"

Wordlessly, Delia moved to sit beside me, and I clutched her to me, sharp angles and all, and we cried. Her body shook soundlessly while the sobs tore out of me. Mom and Dad were gone, and now the memories were all I had.

Delia brushed the hair from my wet cheeks. "Get some sleep now." She sniffed and turned to the doctors who were watching in solemn silence. "No more questions today."

"Of course," Dr. Chen said. The team filed out, Rita last.

"I'll be right outside the door if you need anything."

"Thanks, Rita," I said, my voice a croak. "Deel," I said, the tears starting again. "For two years, you didn't tell me."

"How could I? What would it do to you, to tell you over and over—?"

I was shaking my head. "I meant, for two years, you dealt with them being gone alone. And me. I was gone too."

Delia straightened, dabbed her eyes with a Kleenex from her purse, shifting back into her business mode. "I did what I had to do. And I wasn't…"

"What?"

She patted my hand. "Sleep now. We'll talk more later."

"We have lots to talk about now, don't we?"

Her smile was stiff as she left, quietly closing the door behind her. Memories of my parents—thousands of them—swarmed up at once, bursting through as if making up for being barricaded for so long.

I curled into a ball on my side, like a burnt leaf, and cried until my stomach ached. I wished Delia hadn't left. Maybe I could call Rita in. I didn't want to be alone. So fucking exhausted by it. I wanted to be touched. Human contact. Someone to hold on to so that I didn't slide back into oblivion.

I want Jimmy.

My lungs sucked in a huge breath. Just thinking of him brought relief. With tears drying on my cheeks, my sobs hiccupping, and grief a heavy stone in my heart, I slept because Jimmy was there. I listened to his voice. I felt his arms around me.

He was all there, in my memory.

CHAPTER 20

Jim

When I walked into the break room at seven the next morning, Alonzo and Rita were there, wearing identical, bemused smiles.

"Shut up," I said, turning to hide my own smile in my locker.

Alonzo chuckled. "Glad to see you've come to your senses."

"I'm only here because…"

"It made Thea so happy?" Rita finished. "Good enough answer for me."

"She wasn't happy long," Alonzo said.

I turned around. "What do you mean?"

"Delia told her about their parents."

"Shit."

"Poor thing." Rita checked her watch. "I want to be there when she wakes up." She started out the door then stopped. "Jim, would you take her on her FAE today?"

I frowned, even as my stupid heart leaped at the idea. "She's back on a regular sanitarium schedule?"

"For now," Rita said. "Dr. Chen wants to integrate her back into life slowly."

"Delia's not going to allow me anywhere near her."

Rita gave an arched smile. "It's not up to Delia anymore now, is it? I'll ask Thea what she wants." Her eyebrow waggled. "And if she says she wants you...?"

Jesus, Rita.

"Yeah, okay," I said, my skin heating. "I can take her. But only if you square it with Delia too."

"Right," Alonzo said, chuckling. "Jim didn't rescind his bullshit resignation just so Delia Hughes could fire his ass. Am I right or am I right?"

I glared at him, but he only laughed harder. "You can't blame me for giving you a hard time," he said, standing up. "I'm too relieved you're still here."

I kept my expression blank, so he couldn't see how deeply his words sank. Thea wasn't the only reason I was staying at Blue Ridge, though the way she looked at me yesterday... Christ, I nearly kissed her. Because she looked as if she were waiting for me to. *Wanting* me to.

I shut the locker door.

I stayed because I wanted a conversation with her that lasted longer than five minutes. And I stayed because if I left, I'd lose Alonzo and Rita and Joaquin too. Too many hits I couldn't take.

This is bad, I thought, heading to the dining room to help Mr. Webb with breakfast. *I need to be able to walk away at any time. Keep my head down. Do my job...*

But somewhere over the last few weeks, keeping my head down and doing my job was no longer enough.

Around one o'clock, Rita grabbed me in the hallway outside the dining room. "Thea's ready for her walk. She asked for you specifically."

I swallowed my heart that was apparently trying to climb out of my chest. "She did?"

Rita nodded. "Like I said, she has free will now. Delia threw a fit, but she had to go back to Richmond at least until tomorrow afternoon." She inclined her head toward the dining room. "Thea's in there, finishing lunch. Heads-up, she's having a rough day."

That's all I needed to hear. I went inside. Thea sat a table by herself, in beige pants and a plain white T-shirt. Remnants of lunch in front of her. Her eyes were puffy and red, but a smile found its way to her lips when I approached.

"Hi," she said, her voice raw from crying. "How long has it been?"

I froze, and the blood drained from my face.

Oh fuck. Oh no.

Thea laughed tiredly. "Oh my God, Jimmy, I'm kidding. I'm sorry. I didn't mean to..." She folded her arms on the table and hid her face in them. "Bad joke. I'm so sorry." She peeked up. "Do you forgive me?"

"No," I deadpanned, before relief burst out of me on a laugh, and I slumped into the chair opposite her. "It's not funny. Why am I laughing?"

"Because I make jokes at the worst times. Now you're going to discover all my worst qualities. Lucky you." She smiled wanly, and then the dark cloud of her grief thickened the air between us.

"I'm sorry about your parents," I said quietly.

Her eyes filled with tears. "I am too. Didn't stop me from wolfing down a huge lunch."

"You probably needed it."

"Coming back from the dead is hungry work." Her eyes spilled over and she covered her face with her hands. "See? I keep making dumb jokes."

"You deal how you deal," I said. "It's a lot to take."

"How do you deal? Do you have a dark sense of humor?"

"Me? No, I have no sense of humor whatsoever."

She laughed a little. "Oh good. I get to discover your worst qualities, too."

I kept my expression blank as my heart filled with possibilities. Thea was free and she wanted to get to know me. We had longer than five minutes. We had time to explore who we were...

Together?

Doris sneered. *Aren't we full of ourselves today?*

Thea pushed her tray away with a little shove. "I need some air."

I got to my feet and offered my arm.

"Thank you, Jimmy."

We left the dining room and stepped outside into the humid air. She turned her face up to the bright sun the same way she had on every other walk we'd taken. Because she'd always been herself. Even then.

"Everything is so real," she said. "Like I've had blurry vision and now I can see." She inhaled deeply. "We've done this walk a few times, haven't we?"

"Yeah, we have."

"Were we friends?" she asked. "I think so. You're the only one who treated me like I was still here."

"Because you were."

Her small hand tightened on my arm and she buried her face in my shoulder for a second, a little nuzzle.

We came to a bench and sat next to each other. Insects buzzed in the tall grasses and the wisps of clouds streaked the perfect blue sky. I could see the delicate curve of her neck, disappearing down into the collar of her shirt. It was perfect, too.

"How did you know that I was there?" she asked. "Even the doctors thought I was a lost cause."

I shrugged.

"Don't shrug," she said. "Your thoughts aren't inconsequential." She clapped a hand over her mouth. "I said that before, didn't I? Wow, déjà vu on steroids."

"You said it to me the first time we met," I said. "We were in the foyer, looking at a painting of a bunch of fruit."

"*A bunch of fruit*," Thea said with a laugh. "I remember. Was that when you knew I was still here?"

"Lots of things added up. You were like a bright light in a dark room," I said slowly. "It didn't seem possible you were only as deep as a few minutes. Then I saw your word chains and I knew I was right."

"My dad used to say I could light up any room." Her eyes filled with tears. "Did you know they were gone?"

"Yes."

"But you didn't tell me. No one told me. And I kept asking and asking…"

"We were ordered n-n-not to."

Shit.

She frowned, studying me. "Are you cold?"

"I have a stutter. It comes out when I'm stressed. Or pissed off."

Recognition lit up the sky blue of her eyes. "That's right. I remember."

I stiffened. The Thea of Five Minutes didn't mind the stutter. But the Thea of Real Life…?

You don't know her at all, Doris said. *Introduce her to your worst quality...*

"Are you stressed now?" Thea asked.

"A little. Thinking about everything you're trying to process. Paranoid I'll say the wrong thing. Or that I won't be able to say anything that's worth hearing."

Thea pondered this, then nodded. "Holy crap, I'm tired." She threaded her arm into mine and rested her head on my shoulder. "Anyway, big deal, you have a stutter. I have brain damage."

"Show off."

She slid her cheek along my sleeve to peer up at me. "You're just jealous. My pity parties are way more epic than yours."

"Oh yeah?" I asked. "Mine has a DJ that plays nothing but 'Everybody Hurts' on repeat."

"Mine has brownies," she said, "...with nuts in them."

I chuckled. "You win."

"I don't care if you have a stutter, just don't go ever go quiet on me, Jimmy."

"I'll try not to, Miss Hughes."

Thea bolted up, eyes wide. "Oh my God, James—what's your middle name?"

"Michael."

"Oh my God, James Michael Whelan, call me Thea or I'll kill you."

I laughed. "It's against the rules."

Thea settled back against my shoulder. "Fuck the rules."

I grinned over her head. *And fuck you too, Doris.* I gave my ex-foster mother the mental middle finger. *She's exactly who I knew she'd be.*

"You can call me Thea because I know you," Thea said. "We know each other. We're friends, remember?"

"I remember."

She was right. We knew each other. She knew me better than anyone, because she knew how to let me be myself. She didn't have to fear me going silent; I had a voice with her. Humor. The stutter was an afterthought.

We sat for a few long minutes, and then Thea's slender body began to shake with sobs.

"It comes in waves," she said. "Dr. Chen said to just let it flow when it does. Otherwise, it gets scarier and scarier to face all at once."

It was against the rules, but I put my arm around her and held her tight to my chest. She burrowed into me. Fit perfectly against me. Her tears dampened my shirt.

"I'm sorry," she said. "I'm a mess."

"Don't be sorry," I said. "I never liked this uniform anyway."

She laughed around a sob. "You've held me like this before too. When I was scared and crying that night. You were the one who stopped him."

"Do you want to talk about it?"

"No," she said, hunching tighter. "I can't deal with him right now. But this feels good. You're a good hugger, Jimmy."

"I try."

She took a deep, steadying inhale. "What about you? I can't remember that we ever talked much about you on our walks."

"Not for lack of trying. You ask a lot of questions."

Her laugh was a little stronger this time, but she stayed curled against me.

"For real," she said. "What about you? Do you have family near here?"

"No."

"Where are they?"

"Don't know."

"How do you not know?"

I shrugged. "I never knew them. I've been a foster kid forever. My mother gave me up. The state told me she was a teenager and she told them my name. That's all I know."

"Then you were adopted?"

"No. Just bounced around between foster families."

Thea sat up and brushed a lock of hair out of her eyes. Even splotchy red from crying, she was beautiful.

"For eighteen years?"

I nodded. "None of the families stuck. Some were bad. Real bad. The last especially."

"And then...?"

"I aged out," I said. "The stutter made finding work hard, but I got a job as an orderly in Richmond. Then that place shut down, and I got the job here."

And then I met you, Thea Hughes.

Thea frowned, pondering all of this, then settled back against me. "So... where do you live?"

"I rent a place in Boones Mill. It's about fifteen minutes from here."

"Alone? Or do you have a roommate?" I felt her stiffen as if bracing herself. "Or... a girlfriend?"

"No girlfriend. I live alone."

Thea melted against me. I held her tighter.

"Do you have a dog?" she asked. "A goldfish?"

"No pets allowed."

She craned her neck up to look at me, her lips inches from mine. "But Jimmy...?"

I shifted under her questioning gaze. "I know it doesn't sound like much, but I don't need much, either."

Thea frowned. "What about love?"

I frowned back. "What about it?"

"There had to have been *someone.* When you were a little boy...?"

"Grandpa Jack. My last foster mother's dad. He was good to me. He died but... we had some good times."

Thea stared, and I realized the entirety of my life's story had taken minutes to tell.

Five minutes. I've been living a five-minute life.

"I don't need pity, Thea," I said, turning away from her incredulous look. "It is what it is."

Her hand touched my fingers, her soft skin warm in the warmer air, and then slid into mine—palm to palm—and our fingers laced together. Thea settled back against my chest, curving into me again because she belonged there and we both knew it.

"I don't feel sorry for you, Jimmy," she said. "I feel sorry for all the people who had a chance to really know you but didn't. They blew it. They fucked up. I'm proud of myself that I'm not like them."

I stared over her head. No one had ever said anything like that to me. Her words sank some place deep in me that rarely saw the light of day.

Her dad was right. She can light up even the darkest of rooms.

CHAPTER 21

Thea

I opened my eyes and waited for the first grief of the day to whack me. It came but was somewhat gentler than yesterday. I felt okay. No new revelations awaited me, at least. I had to keep going, carry on, and officially start my new life as a real person.

This room, though...

So drab and boring. The morning light's gold brilliance only highlighted how craptastically plain this joint was. I sat up and pushed the covers off, yawned, and stretched.

Rita knocked and came in with my morning dose of Hazarin and a glass of water. The doctors said if I didn't take this pill every single day I'd sink back into oblivion.

"Here you are," she said. On her palm was a horse pill, half black, half gray.

"Looks like poison," I said. "Hazarin. Like hazard. Keep out. But hey, if it keeps me here, they can call it Shitterall, for all I care."

Rita laughed and I popped the pill in my mouth, washed it down with the water.

"I'll be back in a bit to take you to breakfast."

"I'm sure I can find my way down."

She smiled. "Probably. But let's take it slow, okay?"

"Thanks, Rita."

I used the bathroom, washed my hands, and stared at the note taped to the mirror.

Hairbrush is in the first drawer.

I tore it down, and the mirror was clear, showing my entire reflection. A twenty-three-year-old woman with tousled blond hair and blue eyes puffy from crying. I searched my face for signs of the two years I'd lost. Grief for my parents was making it difficult to tell. I bent and splashed cold water on my face.

When I came up, my T-shirt had dropped a little to reveal a scar, low on my neck. I stripped out of the shirt and inspected myself. The scar ran horizontally the entire length of my right collarbone. Another scar ran down the outside of my right forearm. White seams, half an inch thick, with hash marks from stitches.

"Jesus."

Now that I could see those scars, another, thinner one at my hairline jumped out at me. Another small hook over my left eyebrow.

I stripped out of my pajamas completely and stood naked in front of the mirror. My breasts looked the same—B cups with small nipples— but I'd gained a few pounds in the hips and stomach. A six-inch scar ran along the right side of my abdomen.

I kept going down, rediscovering my own body.

There was no sign of Dr. Milton's procedure—they'd gone in through my nose, *gag*—but for a bandage, small and square-shaped on the back of my left hip bone where they'd done a bone marrow extraction. I had another old scar running from hip to knee, on the outside of my right thigh.

"God."

They'd told me in the hospital I'd broken bones and had internal injuries from the car accident, but I couldn't remember any of that pain or the recovery. The one benefit of the amnesia.

My vanity took a hit, staring at my scarred body, but I squashed it. Mom and Dad hadn't survived at all. I'd wear these scars proudly as a tribute to them. Daily reminders that I had to live this life that had been spared in the accident that took two amazing people out of this world and into the next.

I wiped my eyes and went naked through my little room, tearing down the dozens of notes, schedules, and reminders taped all over to give me some sense of orientation when Rita wasn't around, I guessed.

TV is here.

The TV, a small flat screen, lived behind cabinet doors. I'd spent hours and hours watching *The Office*—a show I obsessively binged even before the accident. No doubt I had every line of every episode memorized. But as much as I adored that show, the thought of other people living their lives while I sat in this room watching a screen made me itchy.

I've lost so much time.

I tore the note off the TV cabinet, wadded it up with the others, and chucked them in the trash, then opened the closet to get dressed.

"Jeeeee-sus," I said under my breath. "Fifty Shades of Beige."

I picked out the least "mom-jeans" pair I could find and a white T-shirt with horizontal pinstripes of maroon every two inches, in the dresser. It was the most interesting garment I currently owned.

"Honestly, Delia. Would a print have killed me?"

I brushed my hair in the bathroom mirror, then searched for signs of makeup. Perfume. Jewelry. Anything remotely girly.

Nada.

A knock on my door and Rita peeked her head in. "Miss Hughes? You decent?"

"Not you too, Rita," I said, sitting gingerly on the bed. "You're as bad as Jimmy. Call me Thea."

"The doctors are here. And your sister texted that she's on her way."

"Speaking of texts," I said. "Do I still have a phone? Though they've probably made, like, a zillion new models since I've been gone."

"It's locked away in a safe in the back office with your wallet and other personal items," Rita said. "I can check for you after breakfast."

"Thank you, Rita. For everything."

"My pleasure, Miss Hughes. Thea." She leaned over and gave my hand a squeeze. "I'm so happy for you. And if it's not too much for me to say, I think your mom and dad are happy for you too."

Tears stung my eyes. "I think so too."

Dr. Chen and Dr. Milton, along with their mini-army of interns, crowded into my room for the morning grilling. They took my blood pressure, checked my breathing and asked a bunch of questions about what I could and couldn't remember.

"Memories from before the accident feel normal," I said. "Everything after is still kind of hazy. Dreamlike."

"In what way?" Dr. Milton asked. The interns' pens readied.

The itchy feeling came back. I suddenly wanted to run a marathon or paint a hundred paintings. I could breathe again. I was getting my true self back.

And my true self decided the doctors all looked far too serious.

I squinted my eyes. "I'm seeing something. A vision…"

Chen and Milton exchanged glances. The interns scribbled furiously. "A vision?"

"Yes, it's… It's coming…"

"What's coming?"

"Winter." I rolled my eyes up in my head, showing the whites. "Winter is coming…"

Rita snorted laughter which made me laugh and break character. The doctors stared at me and the young interns looked around, in need of guidance.

"Get it?" I said. "Bran Stark? You guys don't watch *Game of Thrones*? Sorry, I couldn't help myself." Then my eyes widened as I realized I'd missed two years of the show. "Oh my God, do *not* spoiler me or I'll go *Arya* Stark on y'all."

Dr. Milton chuckled while Dr. Chen rolled her eyes with a bemused smile.

"If we could please get back to our questions?" she said.

"Sure. Sorry. Go ahead. I'll behave."

They asked questions, and I answered honestly and without fucking with them, though it was tempting.

When they finished their interrogation, Dr. Milton and Dr. Chen conferred for a moment.

"What's the verdict?" I asked.

"So far, everything you're experiencing is consistent with what the Sydney team is reporting with their first group of patients," Dr. Milton said. "In fact, you're doing so well, I feel confident I can leave you in Dr. Chen's capable hands."

"You're leaving her?" Delia was at the door, staring daggers at Dr. Milton. "She's only been out of the hospital three days."

"Ah, Ms. Hughes," Dr. Milton said, shooting me a wink. "We weren't expecting you until this afternoon."

Delia stood beside me. "When you would've been long gone, sneaking out without talking to me?"

"I had every intention of discussing Thea's case with you," he said patiently. "I'm not leaving like a thief in the night. Perhaps in the next few days, if she continues to do so well. We're pleased with her progress."

"Hear that, Deel?" I said. "I'm doing great, so chill the hell out."

"How about some breakfast?" Rita said.

"Go. Enjoy," Dr. Chen said. "We'll check back with you after lunch."

Delia, Rita, and I headed down to the dining room. Margery, behind the counter, gave me a tray of oatmeal, toast, fruit, and orange juice.

"Coffee too, please," I said.

Margery glanced at Rita who glanced at Delia.

"You're kidding," I said to my sister. "You didn't let me have coffee? And I thought the wardrobe was the torture."

"It's not good for you," Delia said. "Juice is better."

"To be fair," Rita said, "we didn't want the caffeine to interfere with your sleep patterns."

"Decaf doesn't exist in this part of Virginia?" I said with a laugh. I stopped. "Wait. We *are* still in Virginia, right?"

Delia rolled her eyes. "Always, with the dumb jokes."

"Damn skippy," I said, turning to Margery. "Coffee, please. A big one."

"You got it, sweetheart."

She passed me a steaming mug and I took a sip.

"God, even no cream or sugar and it's heaven. But I'm going to need cream and sugar, please, Marge. And lots of it."

We took our trays to a table near the window. Other residents were having their breakfast with the aid of their assistants.

I put cinnamon on my oatmeal and took a bite. Warm and sweet and perfect.

"I haven't had oatmeal in two years," I said, taking another heaping spoonful.

"Don't be silly, of course, you have," Delia said, forking a piece of strawberry from her fruit bowl. "Nearly every morning."

"But I couldn't remember eating it or what it tasted like." My eyes widened, and I glanced back to the counter. "Do they have bacon? Oh my God, I must have bacon."

"Not on Wednesdays," Rita said.

"So let's go out. What are the good breakfast places around here?"

Delia and Rita exchanged looks.

"It's a little soon, don't you think?" Delia said. "You had surgery less than a week ago."

I glanced a table over, at Mr. Webb and his dented head. Then at Ms. Willis who had a hard time holding her utensils. She looked up and gave me a faltering smile. I smiled back though I suddenly felt like crying.

Delia's cell phone rang in her purse and she rose to answer it.

"How are we doing?" Rita asked. She glanced at my tray. "Not hungry all of a sudden?"

"I feel all over the place," I said. "I want to head for the front door and keep running. That's the grief, partly. Like I could escape it if I just went somewhere else."

Rita nodded, listening intently.

"But also, and this is going to sound horrible…" I lowered my voice. "I'm better."

Rita glanced around just as Ms. Willis dropped her spoon for the fifth time.

"Not better like superior," I said quickly. "Literally *better*. I'm not sick. I don't belong here anymore."

"I understand, hon, but it's only been a few days. Dr. Milton's procedure is brand new. Not just for you but the entire medical community. The long-term results aren't yet known."

"All the more reason for me to get the hell out of here."

"And do what? Where would you like to go?"

"New York City."

"That's a little too much to ask for right now. We need to keep you close. In the event of complications."

I pursed my lips and buried my disappointment. Rita was a sweet woman and a friend, but she was a medical professional, first.

"Can I at least go shopping for some new clothes?" I indicated the drab outfit. "I mean… Loafers? Really?"

"You can't leave the premises, honey."

"Why not? I want to go shopping. Not leave the country. I've lost two years. I don't want to waste one more second."

She bit her lip, thinking. "Maybe I can get Dr. Chen to allow a short trip if I go with you."

"A short trip, where?" Delia asked, resuming her seat.

"To the mall," I said. "Any mall. This wardrobe, Deel?"

"I told you, I've been managing our money. High fashion wasn't a top priority."

"Clearly," I said with a laugh and an eye-roll.

"It's too soon," Delia said.

"I think Dr. Chen will sign off if I go with her," Rita said.

"Today?" I said.

"We'll see," Rita said, rising. "I'll go check with her and get your belongings from the safe too."

"Thanks, Rita. You're the best." I felt Delia's eyes on me. "What?"

"If she says yes, we're not blowing a ton of money on clothes."

"Your idea of a ton of money is vastly different from mine," I said. "Speaking of, how are you affording this place? Insurance? Or has healthcare had a miraculous turnaround in the last two years and everyone's finally learned we need to take care of each other?"

My sister sipped her tea. "Mom and Dad had an insurance policy, making us the beneficiaries."

"Oh." I sat back in my chair. "How much?"

"I'd rather not say."

"You have to say. They were my parents too."

"I don't want you to get the idea that you don't need to be careful with money anymore."

I crossed my arms. "I wasn't irresponsible before the accident. I was going to college. Saving up for New York. I'm not a completely lost cause."

"One million dollars," she said as if I'd pried the words out of her mouth.

My jaw dropped. "A million? Between the two of us?"

"Each."

"Holy shit." I sat back in my chair. "That's a lot of shoes."

"I had no idea how much care you would need," Delia said, "long-term or otherwise so I've been careful. Stretching it out to make it last as long as possible. Insurance only goes so far."

"Here we go," Rita said, returning. She laid my wallet on the table in front of me, then hesitated. "I have your cell phone too. But…"

"But what?"

"I need to prepare you. It's damaged from the accident." She handed me the phone and a cord. "You can charge it at that outlet on the wall to see if it still works."

The face of the phone was cracked, and dried blood was smeared across the home button. I couldn't remember the accident, yet I held it in my hand, like a clairvoyant, holding an object and gleaning the truth from it.

With shaking hands, I plugged the phone in. We waited in silence for it to come back to life.

"It's back," I said as the screen came on. "Cracked and bloodied, but it's still here."

Like me.

Memories turned on in my mind with the phone. Texts with my friends, silly apps, and my music. God, my music was there. And photos.

I dipped my napkin in my water glass and gently wiped the blood away, then hit the photo icon. The last photo my phone took came up. Mom and Dad, Delia in her cap and gown, and me in a pink dress with paint splatters across the front. Tears blurred my vision.

"Look, Deel. It's us. All of us." I turned the phone's cracked face to my sister. "Your graduation," I said. "We were so… ourselves that day. I was aggravating you. Mom and Dad were so proud. And you were rushing us out the door so we wouldn't be late."

Delia looked away, blinking hard. "I should've been in that car."

I dropped the phone in my lap. "No. No, don't think that. Ever."

She didn't meet my eye, and I reached over and touched her hand.

"Hey. I know it's been hard for you, dealing with everything alone. But I'm only awake because you took care of me. And if there's one thing me waking up has taught me, is to be grateful for everything. Every minute. I'm so grateful for you, Delia."

She nodded reluctantly. "Okay, Thea. Thank you."

I tapped my chin. "It was Richard… No, Roger. Roger Nye. He's the reason you weren't in that car. If he were here, I'd give him a huge hug. Where is he now? What's he been doing? What have *you* been doing? God, I don't even know. I've been so wrapped up in—"

"You've been wrapped up in getting better," Delia said. "And that's exactly what you should be doing. Not running out the door the first chance you get."

Delia hadn't run away, though she could have at any time. She could've left thinking I'd have forgotten all about her, but she stayed.

I reached over and hugged her. "I love you."

"Love you too," she said and extracted herself from me. Back in Business Mode. "Well. I guess it wouldn't hurt to go shopping."

Dr. Chen gave me the okay to go to the Westfield Mall at Roanoke, provided Rita was there and we took the medical van with the driver on standby. The staff had already made a medic-alert bracelet for me and Rita clasped it to my wrist as we left Blue Ridge.

"*Wearer of this bracelet may appear disoriented or confused,*" I read off the silver band. "*If found, please call 911.* If found? Like I'm a lost puppy?"

"It's a smart precaution," Delia said.

I didn't argue. *Precaution* was Delia's middle name, and the doctors had to protect me in the event their medication failed. But the bracelet felt heavy and pessimistic. The medication wasn't going to fail. And if it did, all the more reason to get out in the world and not sit around a sanitarium waiting for the ax to fall.

At the outdoor mall in Roanoke, I found some better clothes at H&M—colorful peasant blouses, cut-off jean shorts, off-the-shoulder shirts. Delia insisted on finding sales and paying with a special card that accessed my life insurance bank account.

I started to tell her I could pay myself. At the time of the accident, I had over three thousand dollars in savings.

But is it still there?

I planned to wear my new clothes out of the store. In the fitting room, I ditched the khakis forever and changed into cut-off shorts and a green tank top with embroidered yellow daisies on the front. I slipped my wallet into a new, colorful Boho-style stitched bag, wondering if the cards still worked. If my driver's license was expired. Can I drive again? Be independent again?

Suddenly I was desperate to know my money was there. Not the million from the insurance policy—that was too much and felt more like Delia's. The three thousand dollars was *mine*.

"I want to hit American Eagle and Urban Outfitters next," I said. "But first I need a Wetzel's pretzel like nobody's business."

Rita fanned herself with her hand. "And a lemonade."

We took our food to an outside table under a large yellow umbrella, and I spied an ATM near the bathrooms down a corridor.

"I gotta pee," I said, grabbing my bag. "B-R-B."

"Someone should go with you," Delia said.

"Nah," I said casually and popped a pretzel bite in my mouth. Salt and breaded goodness made me close my eyes in ecstasy. "Lord, Wetzel's knows their shit." I patted Delia on the top of her head. "I'll be back in five or you can send the SWAT."

Without waiting for her permission, I hurried toward the bathrooms. Instead of going inside, I went to the ATM just around the corner and jammed my bank card in. For a half a second, I panicked when it asked for my PIN and then it came to me.

"Keep doing your thing, Hazarin," I muttered, then let out a little cry of joy. My card worked and my bank balance showed more than I thought. Nearly four thousand dollars.

Plenty.

I don't know what I had "plenty" of money for, only that hell would ice over before Delia gave me access to the money our parents left me. At least not yet. And I couldn't wait for that day to come.

I couldn't wait one more day for anything.

I slipped my card in my wallet, the wallet in my bag, and headed back to Rita and Delia.

"Ready?" I asked. "Time to shop."

We went into Urban Outfitters where I tried on a low-cut sundress in white with little laces at the bodice.

"Pretty sexy," Delia said. "Where do you plan on wearing that?"

"I don't know. Maybe a date."

"With whom? You don't know anyone."

Jimmy Whelan popped immediately into my thoughts, making my skin shiver pleasantly. "Yes, I do," I said, almost to myself.

Rita's face turned pink as she riffled through a rack of denim jackets. Delia's eyes widened.

"Who?" she asked. "God, don't tell me you mean that orderly?"

"*That orderly?*" I said. "Elitist, much? Yes, I mean Jimmy. We're friends but… who knows what could happen? And who cares about his job? He could be a janitor at a nudie club for all I care."

"Jesus, Thea."

"It wouldn't change who he is."

"And who is he to you?"

I shrugged, swaying the dress's skirt side to side in the mirror. "I don't know. A friend, for sure. My best friend, all things considered." The girl in the mirror smiled and her cheeks turned pink. "Maybe more."

"More?" Delia stared. "How can he be more? You don't know him."

"That's not true," I said. "I didn't meet him for the first time the other day. He's been taking care of me for weeks."

"How do you know?"

"I remember, Deel. I remember *him*."

She sniffed and perused a rack of blouses, but I'd been turning thoughts and feelings about Jimmy around and around and needed to let them out. To hear how they sounded outside of my own head and heart.

"There's something about Jimmy that I really connect with. He's the only one who understood I was still in there. No judgment," I added for Rita's sake. "I just… I don't know, I feel comfortable with him. Like I've known him forever. Not gonna lie, it doesn't hurt that he's drop-dead gorgeous."

Rita coughed, and a pleasant, zingy panic shot through me. I whirled on her.

"Oh my God, you cannot go reporting to Jimmy anything that is spoken here," I said, laughing. "Girl code, Rita. *Girl code.*"

"I am sworn to secrecy," she said, laughing.

"What do you have against him, anyway?" I asked my sister. "He saved me. In case you've decided to forget, he's the one who stopped that man…" I gave myself a shake as gooseflesh broke out over my skin, this time cold and unwanted.

Rita put her hand on my arm. "Are you ready to talk about that night?"

"Nope," I said, shaking my head. "Not going to let that asshole ruin my day." I heaved a sigh. "As I was saying, Jimmy's a good man. One of the best."

Delia snorted. "I don't trust him. I don't trust any man who would take so much interest in a girl who had no way of speaking for herself or making decisions."

"I remember him, Deel," I said again. "I had a way of speaking for myself, through my drawings, and he saw it." I gave her a pointed look. "And now I can actually speak for myself and make decisions. You're going to have to get used to that."

My sister looked ready to argue when her phone rang again. She put it to her ear and turned away from us. "Hi," she said, her voice soft. Over her shoulder, she caught us watching her and made a face, then walked to the other end of the store.

"What do you think, Rita?" I asked, twirling in the mirror. "Am I crazy to feel anything about Jimmy? Not that I do. I mean… I don't know how I feel. Not exactly. Except that when I look at myself in this dress, there's a part of me that wants to buy it and wear it for him. Be pretty for him. And another part that wants to put it on just so he can tear it off me."

Holy shit, where did that come from?

Rita's eyes met mine in the mirror, identical expressions of shock on our faces. My skin flushed red against the white dress.

"I said that out loud, didn't I?"

"Yes, you did."

"Girl code, Rita. *Girl. Code.* But you know what? I'm not even embarrassed."

Turned on? Yes. Embarrassed? Not so much.

"I'm alive. I'm here. And I want to live. That means everything, you know? All the experiences I've missed out on." I lowered my voice confidentially. "I'm talking about sex, here, Rita."

"Yeah, I got that."

"A girl has *needs.*"

Rita glanced over her shoulder for Delia. Seeing the coast was clear, she leaned over my shoulder, our faces close in the mirror.

"Between you and me, I think Jim would lose his mind to see you in this dress."

"And that's your professional opinion. So it's extra legit."

"Extra legit," she said. She gave me a squeeze. "Come on. Let's buy this dress."

I bought the dress.

After, I bought a few little things to liven up my wardrobe—sandals, sunglasses, perfume, and a little peridot gem on a delicate gold chain from a jewelry store.

"For Mom and Dad," I told Delia. "Their birthstone."

"They were born in the same month?" Rita asked.

I nodded. "Same day, actually. August twentieth."

"They were born on the same day and died on the same day," Delia said.

"There's a poetry in that, don't you think?" I asked, my throat thick. "They were meant to be together, from the very start."

Delia said nothing but bought a little necklace for me without complaint.

After, we hit a Michael's craft store and Delia spent a good wad of cash on three large canvases. Also, without argument. She felt guilty, but I wanted to tell her not to be. The past was done, and the future wasn't created yet. All we had is now.

And I was going to live in it.

Just not in the Blue Ridge Sanitarium.

But the thought of not seeing Jimmy every day hurt my heart more than I expected.

He went into my world in order to bring me out. Maybe it's time for me to return the favor.

CHAPTER 22

Jim

I was outside with Mr. Perello when Thea came back from a shopping excursion with Rita and Delia, looking as if she'd been on a beach vacation. I nearly dropped the lighter as I went to light Mr. P's smoke.

Gone were the bulky khaki pants and shapeless tops. Thea wore sandals, shorts that revealed approximately eighty-two miles of gorgeous legs, a tank top that clung to her curves, and sunglasses. She popped bubblegum while she hauled shopping bags over her shoulders. Her blond hair was a tousled mess that I wanted to sink my fingers in to.

She caught sight of me, lowered her sunglasses with one finger, and wiggled her pinky at me in hello.

"Well?" Mr. Perello said from the bench. "You just going to stare at her like a dope? Say hi back."

But by the time I got my shit together, Thea was stepping through Blue Ridge's front door. Delia gave me a hard look before she disappeared inside.

"That's a grade-A stink-eye right there," Mr. Perello supplied helpfully.

"Tell me about it."

Inside, I made my rounds, and then it was rec time. I found Thea sitting with Rita and Delia, surrounded by her doctors, just about to start a post-excursion barrage of questions.

"How do you feel?" Dr. Chen asked. "Was it difficult to process being in a crowded place like a mall?"

"You mean after being cooped up here for so long?" Thea replied. "No, it was easy but…"

She found me in the corner and smiled as if we hadn't just seen each other minutes ago; better than a million compliments. Then her smile turned sly, and she winked at me.

"But what?" Dr. Milton prompted.

"But… I don't know. I feel like…" She shook her head, confusion filling her gaze.

A few days ago, I'd panic but now I immediately knew what she was up to. I put my palm on the top of the broom and settled in to watch the performance.

"I… I'm… my…" She worked her jaw as if it had suddenly become stiff.

There she goes…

"My… may…" She glanced around in a panic. *"Mais, qu'est-ce qui m'arrive?"[1]*

Dr. Milton gave a start. "Beg your pardon?"

I stifled a laugh in my shoulder as Thea's eyes widened and her hands flew to her throat.

"Je ne peux pas m'arrêter de parler français!"[2]

Dr. Milton stared at Thea, his jaw opening and closing. Dr. Chen, however, crossed her arms and mutely shook her head at an intern to stop taking notes.

"C'est normal?" Thea begged of Dr. Milton. *"Qu'est ce qui cloche chez moi?"*

"There is nothing wrong with you," Dr. Chen answered, a bemused smirk on her face. "Nice try. Four years of French, here. *Et vous?*"

"Six," Thea said with a giggle.

"What…?" Delia stared in alarm, then slumped in her seat.

---

[1] What is happening to me?
[2] I can't stop speaking French!

"Honestly, Thea, there *is* something wrong with you. Very wrong."

Thea burst out laughing. "Couldn't help myself. I finally found a good use for it."

Dr. Milton chuckled. "Quite a prankster."

"It gets old, trust me," Delia said.

"If we could get back to our evaluation?" Dr. Chen said.

Thea shot me another smile and a sheepish shrug. I held up both hands, giving a ten-out-of-ten score, then the doctors closed in around her.

Rita meandered over to me, her hands behind her back and a shit-eating grin on her face.

"What?"

"Can't say," she said. "Girl code. I *can't say* that Thea talked about you at the mall."

"She did?"

"And at the risk of sounding like we're back in junior high, I also can't say the words drop, dead, and gorgeous were thrown around quite liberally."

I inhaled the possibilities, then sighed them out. "Chapter three of the employee handbook, Rita. You know nothing can happen."

Between Thea and me. Us. Whatever that might be.

"I do," she said. "But if Thea continues to do well, she won't be a resident much longer."

"Really? It's only been a few days."

"I know and the doctors—not to mention Delia—are going to want to keep her for observation."

"Is it dangerous for Thea to leave Blue Ridge?" I asked.

"For longer than a trip to the mall?"

I nodded.

"In my professional opinion? Not necessarily. If she had someone with her at all times, at least at first. And I'd prefer she have a roommate, once she gets her own place, just to be safe." She raised her eyebrows. "Any volunteers?"

"I'm being serious."

"So am I," she said. "Why are you asking?"

"I don't think she's going to be happy here for long."

"Neither do I. She's strong-willed. I don't think any of us can talk her out of wanting her life back. But it's too soon. Dr. Chen says so and she's the final authority, not me."

"But there's no real danger?" I asked. "Medically speaking?"

"Honey, there's danger in getting in a car to head to the corner store," Rita said. "Thea knows that better than anyone. But Delia has power of attorney over her. It was set up when Thea was incapacitated." She looked over to where Thea was answering the doctors' questions. "Does she look incapacitated to you?"

She looks fucking perfect.

"Exactly," Rita said, reading my expression.

"So Delia has to call off her power of attorney, right?"

"I doubt it. Ms. Hughes has been in control of every aspect of Thea's life for the past two years." She gave me a sympathetic glance. "She's not going to give it up without a fight."

Later, when I figured the doctors had cleared out, I went back to the rec room. Thea stood in front of a blank canvas, a tray of paints beside her. She turned and gave me another of her so-happy-to-see-you smiles. It sent a warm feeling through my chest and heated my blood too. Being near her was becoming something more than good. Or casual.

I still wanted long conversations with Thea, only instead of having those talks while out on the grounds or in the rec room, my imagination conjured her in my bed, with her hair splayed over my pillow. The morning light revealed the marks we'd put on each other's body the night before. Her lips were swollen from my kisses, and my shoulder blades stung where she'd raked her nails. We'd talk and kiss until kissing wasn't enough. Then I'd take her hard and she'd come undone beneath me. We'd eat and talk and kiss some more, then do it all over again. Because we had all the time in the world...

Because she's no longer incapacitated. She can make her own choices. I could be a choice she makes.

I pushed the longing away and the heated thoughts that went with it. Nothing could happen, at least while she was still a resident and I was an orderly.

"New stuff?" I asked with a nod at the canvas.

"Yeah," she said. "But I'm not feeling it right now."

"Painter's block?"

Thea laughed. "Exactly. Before the accident, I couldn't go three days without painting. I've only done one here. One in two years. It'd be zero if not for you."

"They didn't know."

"What did I draw?" She thought for a second. "Egyptian scenes. One after the other."

"You made a lot of word chains. It's how you communicated."

"That was all I had. Words instead of sentences or paragraphs. No chapters in the Book of Thea."

She stared at the blank canvas and a shiver came over her. She hugged herself, her eyes shining.

"Are you okay?"

"I ruined the last painting I made… Because of *him*. He was making me do things. I couldn't remember but I knew. I know that doesn't make sense…"

"It does," I said. "I get it."

"You did," she said, looking at me. "You knew what I was trying to say when I slashed my New York painting with black. I ruined it because he was ruining me."

Her voice broke on the last words, and without thinking, I put my arms around her. She clung to me a moment, before pushing herself away and wiping her eyes.

"No more crying," she said. "I don't want to be inside anymore. I don't want to be *here*, anymore. Inside these walls."

"Come on," I said. "Let's go for a walk."

"On the grounds? With the fences hidden just out of sight? Sure, why not?"

But she went and once outside in the fresh air and sunshine, she heaved a sigh.

"I'm sorry I snapped at you, Jimmy. I'm stir crazy. I feel like I could run a marathon, but they still got me on a hamster wheel."

"It's early yet," I said. "Give them time. They need to make sure you're okay."

"I know. I'm not ungrateful, just ready to move on." She peered up

174

at me. "What about you? Did you ever want to do something besides work at a sanitarium?"

I started to shrug but told her the truth instead. "I wanted to be a speech therapist for kids."

She stopped walking, her lips parted in surprise. "That's brilliant. Why not do that?"

"College means more talking. It was hard enough to finish high school."

Her brows furrowed. "Wait, I remember now. You were bullied." Her expression hardened. "I hate that. I hate they did that to you. But you can't give up on your dreams, Jimmy. I know that sounds super after-school-special, but it's true."

"A stutterer helping stuttering kids?"

"A stutter makes you perfect for the job. Those kids need to see someone who's just like them. Someone who had it tough too but made it through."

We came to the bench we'd sat on the other day. The one that faced the north facade of Blue Ridge and the surrounding forest beyond.

"You don't know how amazing you are, Jimmy, because no one's told you." I stiffened, but she put her hand on my arm. "It's not pity, okay? Just the facts. You've helped me more than anyone. I don't just mean with the painting and the music. I mean... that night."

She faced forward. Her voice was shaky, but she didn't crumble.

"Earlier today, Rita asked me if I wanted to talk about him and I said no. But I guess today's the day, after all."

"I'm here," I said.

She inhaled and let out a ragged breath.

"I know I talked a lot about Antony and Cleopatra. Constantly. I even told people I was an Egyptologist of all things. But of course, I wasn't. I love Egypt and its history and the pyramids. Painting them was my forte before the accident. But after, I needed a story. I think it was the only way I knew to keep from going crazy. To borrow Cleopatra's history since I had none."

"It makes perfect sense."

She nodded and smiled gratefully. "When Brett started coming at night, he told me there was no one I could call for help. Just him and me."

"He lied," I said in a low voice full of grit for not realizing what he'd been doing sooner. "He lied to make you feel helpless."

"Yes," she whispered. "So I borrowed Cleopatra's story. Marc Antony was dead, and she was so alone. She put her hand in the snake's basket. And so did I. But I wasn't alone, was I?"

I shook my head. "No, Thea."

"I wasn't trying to kill myself," she continued. "I know it probably seemed like it. I only did it because that's what Cleopatra did, and she was me. Her story was mine, so I told it the only way I knew how."

She squinted up at me.

"You were there. You snatched my hand out of the basket. Because you heard me telling the story when no one else did." Her voice quavered but didn't break. "And you stopped Brett. Not just stopped him; you made him a human bowling ball and sent him crashing into my dresser."

"He deserved it," I said. "I'd do it again."

"What was the song you sang to me after?"

"'I Will Follow You into the Dark.'"

She leaned her head on my shoulder. "Will you sing it for me?"

"Now?"

"There is never a better time."

"I guess not."

I cleared my throat and sang to Thea as the afternoon fell toward twilight and the sky deepened to purple and orange. This wasn't in the job description. It wasn't in *my* description to feel whatever I was feeling for Thea. She was too good. It felt too good to be with her.

Nothing good lasts…

I finished the song.

"You're a beautiful singer, Jimmy." She sniffed and sat up. "Jimmy with the kind eyes. That's how I remembered you. Right here." She put her hand between her breasts, over her heart.

I nodded, staring at her mouth. Ready to kiss her. Fucking dying to kiss her. To fill my hands with her face and her hair. To delve into her mouth and taste the sweetness of her.

But her eyes were still shining with tears over what Brett had done. I had to take care of her. That was my job.

"We should g-g-go inside," I said.

"Jimmy…" But then she nodded. "Okay. I guess we should."

I led her back inside the sanitarium, but as the door shut behind us, I felt like I was betraying us both.

CHAPTER 23

Thea

One week later, Dr. Milton flew back to Sydney.

"If he can leave, why can't I?" I asked Dr. Chen during one of my morning checkups.

Delia sat on the edge of the bed, scrolling on her phone. Even this early in the morning, she was here, hovering over me.

She heaved a sigh. "Here we go again."

I made a face at her while Dr. Chen listened to my heart.

"It's still too soon to know the long-term effects of the medication," she said, looping the stethoscope around her neck. "We need you in a controlled setting for your safety. Not to mention, you're only the eleventh candidate in the history of medical science to undergo this procedure. It's far too early to send you off into the world without precautions."

"I'm fine. I feel great. I remember more and more every day. I want to leave Blue Ridge, rent my own place, get a job. And if there are side-effects to the medication, I don't want to sit around in here waiting for them."

I shot her my brightest, most charming smile. The one that used to make Dad melt but never worked on Mom.

"Let me go and we'll jump off any bridges when we get to them."

"I'm afraid I can't condone that at this time," she said and made a note in her chart.

Dr. C's a mom.

"This isn't a prison," I said stiffly. "I'm not an inmate. I'm a patient. I should be able to leave whenever I want."

"I have power of attorney," Delia said and exchanged glances with Dr. Chen. "And so long as the doctors think you're safer here, then that's what I want too."

"That made sense when I was incapacitated. But I'm not anymore. You can't keep me here against my will."

"Don't be so dramatic." Delia crossed her arms. "We have to wait and see—"

"God, Deel. If the medication stops working, it's all the more reason for me to get out now. I need to live. I'm not sick. I'm me. I'm right here."

"Is this about the orderly? Is he putting ideas in your head?"

I threw up my hands. "You know what? I'm actually capable of having my own ideas. And dreams. I want to take a trip. To New York."

"That's hundreds of miles away."

"Do they not have hospitals in New York?" I tapped a finger to my chin. "I can't remember…"

Delia rolled her eyes.

"Oh, come on," I said, trying to lighten them up with a laugh. "It's not like I'd be stranded in a desert if something went wrong."

Delia gave Dr. Chen a pleading look. "Can you reason with her?"

Dr. Chen shifted, looked uncomfortable. "The bottom line, Thea, is that it's far too early to gauge any long-term side-effects. I'd prefer to keep you under observation."

"Fine," I spit the word. "But how long?"

"A month, minimum. Maybe two."

A month? Holy fuckballs, no way.

"I did two years," I said, biting out each word, so they wouldn't put me on watch. "I guess a few more weeks won't matter."

But it did matter. Those years were a long, endless reel of sameness. Wake up, eat, watch *The Office,* take a walk, draw pyramids, scream for help, eat, go to sleep, wash, rinse, repeat. In five-minute increments. Until Jimmy heard my cries and added music and color to my monotone, monochrome existence.

Now I had a real life in all its beautiful, painful, amazing glory, and they wanted to keep me in prison. Seconds ticked away. I could practically count them with the beat of my heart.

Dr. Chen finished her exam and Delia stood up.

"I need to run an errand in Roanoke. I'll be back later." She gave me a stiff hug. "Be good."

"No promises."

I sat in the quiet of my room. It wasn't as vast and empty as the horrible silence of the amnesia, but it wasn't living.

I took my cracked cell phone out of the top drawer of the new dresser they'd given me—taking a peak under a stack of new, lacy underwear that my wallet was still there—and scrolled through iTunes. I put on "Tidal Wave" by a new band who'd come up in the last two years while I dressed in a pair of those new lacy panties, jean shorts, and a pink T-shirt.

I took my phone with me as I headed downstairs. It was technically breakfast time but screw my routine. I needed to paint.

The rec room was deserted, only the empty canvas waiting for me. I squeezed paint dollops onto my palette and reached for a brush. No, a brush wasn't going to be loud enough.

I put the canvas on the tarp on the floor, and using my hands, scooped a handful of purple acrylic paint. I let a stream of drops fall, like tears, then kneeled and swept my hand over the canvas.

For the next twenty minutes, I attacked the canvas with different colors, using drips, or swipes, or handprints. Letting the paint speak for me. A Jackson Pollock-like mess of pure emotion. I cranked my music up higher, let the paint flow as it would, an extension of me.

Purple that wept for my parents.

A snake of black that might suffocate me back into amnesia.

Yellow for the hope that it wouldn't ever again.

And swirls of paint, a riot of color for all that I felt inside me. For Delia and Rita. And for Jimmy. For freedom on the other side of these walls and a life I might have with him if we were brave enough to explore all that lay between us.

A FIVE-MINUTE LIFE

He is so much more than he knows.

I sat back on my heels, paint smearing my clothes and my palms covered in yellow. I wiped a sweaty lock of hair off my forehead with the back of my hand and studied what I'd done.

It was a pretty, messy, chaotic painting, reflecting all that was inside me... and going nowhere.

I should have painted another pyramid.

A tomb.

CHAPTER 24

Jim

My shift started with a spill of maple syrup in the dining room. Minor catastrophes continued through lunch and I was kept busy for hours. My thoughts were on Thea every other minute.

"She's in the rec room," Rita said as she rushed by me in the hallway, as if reading my mind. "Can you check on her?"

Thank you, Rita.

"Sure."

In the rec room, Thea crouched over a canvas, drizzling yellow paint on it with her hands. She worked feverishly, as if someone were timing her. It was a beautiful mess of big bold splashes of color, spilling over the sides of the canvas and onto the floor.

Her gaze flicked to me as I approached, then back to the paint. Sweat glistened on her chest and made her little necklace with the pale green stone stick to her skin.

"No more painter's block," she said.

"I can see that."

"This is what I feel, Jimmy," she said, swiping her hands, covered with yellow paint, across the top. "And this little canvas is the sanitarium. It can't contain me."

She gave her painting a final swipe, then rose to her feet. We stood, side by side, over it.

"Have you ever been to New York City?" she asked.

"No."

"Me neither. I always wanted to, ever since I was a kid. I want to see the lights of Times Square. I want to go to the top of the Empire State Building and see how the world looks from up there. I want to walk in Central Park and eat a hot dog from a street vendor. I want all that and I don't want to wait."

"Thea..."

She turned to face me. "I wanted this before the accident. That's always been my vision of life. But I was put on pause for two years and the vision kept growing. Outgrowing me. The life I'd had while I was away has been building up, and I'm going to burst if I don't live it."

"I want it for you, too."

"You do?"

"But I think you should wait a little longer and see—"

"Is that what you're doing?" she asked softly. "Waiting to go back to school to be a speech therapist? Until when? Do you know what happens while you wait? Nothing. And then next thing you know, years have gone by. I can't do nothing anymore. I can't."

I lifted my chin. "What are you saying?"

"I'm not going to stay here. I'll walk out the front door and hitchhike to New York if I have to."

I thought of her, young and beautiful, walking along the road in her short-shorts with her thumb out for any asshole to pick up. A Brett-type who seemed friendly as hell on the surface, but underneath...

"What's that look for?" she asked, the backs of her hands on her hips.

"I don't like the thought of you hitchhiking."

"Is that so?"

"Yeah, it is."

"And what will you do about it? Tell my sister?"

"Maybe."

Her eyes narrowed. "Liar."

We stared each other down, emotions broiling in both of us. Her cheeks were flushed, and my hands itched to grab her and kiss that brassy mouth of hers. Both of us daring the other to say what was behind our heated words.

I care about you.

Prove it.

I blinked first. "Fine," I said. "I wouldn't tell her. But I don't want you to get hurt."

Thea's arms dropped and her voice softened.

"And I don't want to waste away in a box. Blue Ridge is bigger than the little prison I was trapped in for two years, but it's still a prison." She stepped closer to me. "An invisible clock is hanging over my head and the minutes keep ticking away. I lost two years. Now every second I'm not out there, doing what makes me happy, is just more time lost."

She moved closer. I could feel the warmth of her skin and the scent of her perfume—something flowery and light—mixed with the harsher scent of acrylic yellow paint all over her hands.

"I want to live, Jimmy. Don't you?"

"I don't know what that means," I said, my own autopilot existence feeling like a prison too; one I'd made for myself.

"Really live," Thea said. "Not just exist."

I nodded.

"You should have it, Jimmy." She tilted her head up. "Go out in the world and…" Her hand came up between us, on my chest, over my heart. "…take what you want."

Her breath caught as my arm slipped around her waist, pressing her to me. *Taking* her to me. My head bent down to hers, drawn by an invisible force I couldn't stop. The tiniest smile tugged at her lips until they parted, ready for my kiss. My eyes drank in every detail of her exquisite face, while my other hand slid into her hair that was softer than it'd been in my fevered imaginings. I made a fist, pulling gently, eliciting a little gasp from her. Her lips parted wider, inviting me in.

I never wanted anything in my life like I wanted Thea…

"Yes, Jimmy," she whispered.

Take what I want…

Inhale. Like a diver ready to submerge into her depths. Exhale.

Our lips touched.

"What the hell is going on?"

184

The air shattered at the intrusion. Our bodies jerked apart, my heart thumping.

"Jesus, Delia," Thea said breathlessly. "None of your business, is what's going on." Her eyes were still locked on mine. "Jimmy, don't," she said, when I started to pull away.

But I let her go, my hands instantly feeling empty and cold without her skin and hair and vibrant life pulsing beneath them.

Not here, I wanted to tell her. *I don't want this here.*

"It's n-n-not... professional," I managed.

"For once I agree with him," Delia said, glaring at me. "He could lose his job for inappropriately touching a resident."

Thea clenched her jaw. "Delia, I love you, but you're crossing the line. Every line. I can't even look at you right now." She turned to me, almost pleading, her voice a whisper. "Don't give up on me, Jimmy. Please."

She ran out of the room, and Delia and I were left alone. She slowly turned to face me, her expression stony.

"My sister is impulsive and emotional after being woken a few days ago from what was essentially a two-year coma," she said, speaking slowly, her voice low and hard. "If you think she knows what she wants under these circumstances, then by all means, put your hands on her again."

"Ms. Hughes..."

"This was your first and last warning," she said. "Emphasis on *last*."

She strode out, leaving me alone with Thea's painting. Not word chains but another kind of cry for help.

I finished my shift and left the sanitarium that night without changing or talking to anyone and rode my motorcycle at unsafe speeds down the winding road from Blue Ridge. I leaned into the turns, feeling the thrill of the danger coursing through me. Trying to recreate the potent feeling of Thea in my arms, her gorgeous face turned up, waiting and ready—wanting—me to kiss her.

At home, in my small, dark house, I went to the bathroom to splash cold water on my face. Then stared at the dripping reflection in the mirror.

I was still wearing my uniform—plain white shirt and pants. But now the white was slashed with yellow along the right side of my waist, where Thea touched me. And in the middle of my chest—Thea's handprint in stark yellow, small and delicate, fingers splayed like a star over my heart.

CHAPTER 25

Thea

"Dr. Chen said a month, minimum. Maybe two," I said when Rita came to bring me my morning dose of Hazarin.

"The procedure is so new, they're scared if they declare victory and something happens, they'll lose face," she said. "Or worse, funding. The patients in Sydney are in lockdown too."

"It's not right," I said. "Giving us the awareness of our freedom and then keeping it from us."

"I don't like it either."

"Then help me bust out of this joint, Rita."

A short silence descended. She knew what I meant. *Give me the Hazarin.*

"You know I can't do that," she said.

"I know," I sighed. "I don't want you to lose your job." I took the one pill she'd brought with her from the locked medicine room and downed it with water.

"Try to make the best of it," she said. "In a few weeks, you'll be free to go."

"And if the medicine stops working before then? What will I have to show for it?"

"I wish I knew how to answer that," she said.

She left and I stared at the ceiling. The walls. The tiny window. Suddenly it was hard to breathe. I needed to be outside, even if that outside had fences too.

It was early yet; a little after seven. The heat and humidity hadn't yet taken hold. Morning light slanted silvery and gold over the grass. I walked the circumference of the grounds along the fence and came to the side that fronted the parking lot. The rev of a motorcycle's engine sounded, and I watched a man ride up.

He wore jeans, a black leather jacket, and boots. He maneuvered the bike with a casual sexiness that glued my eyes to him. I knew who it was even before he took off his helmet.

"A motorcycle, Jimmy?" I murmured. Heat flushed through me when he removed his helmet and ran his fingers through his dark hair. "Not fair. Not fair at all."

He plays guitar, sings like Eddie Vedder, and rides a motorcycle. A girl's ovaries can only handle so much.

"Hey," I called from my side of the fence, stopping him in his tracks on his way to the front of Blue Ridge. "What is that? A Harley?"

"It is," he said, striding over. "How'd you know?"

"Lucky guess." I watched him approach the chain-link fence.

"You're up early," he said. "Feeling better?"

"I feel great. Stir-crazy but great. And I've never seen you out of uniform in real life. You look so different. I'd never have known…"

That you were all this, Jimmy.

"I guess that's the point of the uniform," he said. "Keeps the focus on the work."

I nodded. "Delia put me in a uniform too. All those boring clothes. This is the real me." I coughed, suddenly shy again, the way only Jimmy could make me.

I expected his eyes to rake me up and down—I wanted them to. The desire to feel desirable to him came over me again like it had in the mall. To be pretty for him. But his dark brown eyes never left my face. They held mine with an intensity that stole my breath.

"I like the real you, Thea," he said. "I always have. Doesn't matter what you're wearing."

My fingers on the chain-link squeezed as another flush of heat swept through me.

"You keep saying things like that, Jimmy and I'll..." I sighed. "Nothing, actually. I can't do anything from behind this fence. Quite the metaphor."

I gave the fence a shake. It rattled, and Jimmy flinched from the sound.

"Oh, I'm sorry—"

"It's n-n-nothing," he said. "Bad memories. I got thrown against a lot of chain-link fences in high school. The sound of it stuck with me, I guess."

"Then I hate this fence even more," I said, wanting to touch him softly. To soothe away the hard memories. "I hate that I'm on this side and you're on that side. You're free and I'm trapped in here. I'm awake and alive and in the exact same place I've been for two years."

"I know," he said.

"Well?"

He glanced around. "Watch out," he said, then tossed his motorcycle helmet over to my side. It landed a few feet from me. Jimmy scaled the eight-foot fence, kicked his boots on the top, then dropped easily down on my side. I could smell his cologne and the leather of his jacket

"Better?" he asked.

"Not really. I'd rather you'd have lowered a rope made out of sheets tied together and hauled me out on *that* side. Neither of us belongs here."

He squinted, his gaze taking in the grounds and the sunlight spilling over the grass.

"I'm late for work." He rubbed the back of his neck. "You want to go for a walk later?"

I cocked my head. "Is that the Blue Ridge Sanitarium version of a date?"

Unfazed, he shook his head. "Dating isn't allowed."

"Do you always play by the rules?"

His mouth was grim. "When your safety is on the line? Yeah, I do."

"What does my safety have to do with you and me on a date?" I gave him a flirty smile. "Are you dangerous?"

I already knew the answer to that. To anyone who would hurt me, Jimmy was dangerous. But not to me. Never to me.

"They want to keep an eye on you a little longer."

My smile collapsed. "And I should be reasonable and just go along with it, but I feel like I'm squandering this gift I've been given every second I'm in here."

"I know, but it was hard for us too," he said. "Hard for Delia, I mean. Seeing you trapped in that five-minute loop. The absence seizures."

"But everything's different now. I'm here. I'm awake."

He looked about to say something, then changed his mind.

"She got to you, didn't she?" I asked. "What did she say?"

"She told me I shouldn't take advantage of you. And she's right. It's not professional. It's…"

"Wrong? Because I'm a mental patient who can't make decisions for herself? And let me guess, she threatened to have you fired."

He nodded.

The fight started to ebb out of me. "Honestly, part of me wants you to get fired. So you'll go back to school and follow your dreams. You're not trapped here, Jimmy. You can leave at any time."

He shook his head. "Someone has to watch out for you."

Another flush of warmth surged through me. "I don't need protection anymore."

"I know," he said. "But for so long it's what I've been d-d-doing…" He broke off, carved his hand through his hair and took a step away from me. "Goddamn, this f-f-fucking stutter…"

I pulled him back to me. "You only stutter when something is important to you."

Jimmy nodded, his brown eyes darkening. "You're important to me."

He stepped closer and I felt the pull between us, inevitable and potent. My body trembled now, wanting his touch so badly. I'd been so cavalier about being held by him a few days ago, but things between us felt deeper. More. Touching him now would be different.

It would be everything…

"You've been important to me for a long time," I said. "I've always felt close to you, Jimmy. No… *connected*. Do you feel it too?"

"Yeah, I do." His hand came up and his thumb brushed my chin and then slid along my cheek. "I shouldn't be doing this."

"I want you to. So badly." My eyes fell shut at the sensation and I pressed my cheek into his hand. "In my Cleopatra story, you were my

Antony."

"God, Thea." His voice hoarse with need and raw emotion.

I opened my eyes and he was right there, breathing my breath as I inhaled his. I could feel his body along every part of mine, a vibration running along the length of me. My cheek where he touched me, down my neck, down to the tips of my breasts that ached and hardened. My hand came up to hold his wrist, and I tilted my chin up to him.

"My Antony..."

His lips brushed mine. The lightest touch, yet the sensation drew a moan from me and an electric current wrapped around my heart. It pulsed as his kiss came again. He captured my upper lip briefly, then the lower, sucking lightly. Exploring.

I clung to him, hardly able to keep my feet, as his hand slipped into my hair, angling my head. My lips parted, ready for him. He made a sound deep in his chest, and his mouth took mine completely, pushing in—the sweetest invasion—and I opened to take it all.

Another moan rose in me at the first taste of his tongue sweeping along mine, and I sank against him. His kiss gave me every part of him—the lust and raw need wrapped around a core of reverence. He kissed me completely, as if his every intention was pouring into my mouth. To take care of me. To cherish me.

To fuck me...

"Oh my God," I whispered. The thought made me dizzy.

Every electrified particle in my being knew Jimmy's kiss was a preview of what he would give me in his bed. I'd surrender to my warrior while he worshipped me as his queen. Reverence and need in perfect, equal amounts. I'd come screaming his name.

The thought set my blood on fire. I found my feet, wrapped my arms around his neck, my fingers sinking into his hair, pulling. He dropped one hand to my waist, pressing me to him. Heat flushed my core, aching with want. Lust. Happiness. The intensity of him made my heart pound, overwhelmed by this much need in a man pressed against me, his every muscle and bone and sinew tensed with it.

Now Jim's other hand came up to hold my face. He turned my head to the other side, and a fresh rush of heat surged through me as he gave me more of his kiss. He gave and gave, while his mouth greedily delved into mine and took what it wanted. A gentle sucking that accompanied every sweep of his tongue, every nip of his teeth.

We kissed and kissed, our hands roaming, the urgency growing desperate. My entire world became the scent of Jim Whelan's skin, his cologne, the leather of his jacket. I fell against the fence, taking him with me. It rattled, and he broke his mouth from mine, blinking for a moment like a man coming out of a dream.

That sound... Bad memories...

I held his face in my hands, his breath coming hard and warm over my wet lips.

"Stay with me," I whispered. "Right here. Make a new memory..."

Our mouths crashed together again, our tongues tangling, teeth biting. He gripped the chain link above my head, so he could press into me harder. My legs spread to fit him closer to me, angling my hips to feel the denim of his jeans rub the denim of my shorts. His mouth descended to my chin, my neck, down to my collarbone, to the scar there. He kissed it reverently, then ran his tongue over it.

"Jesus, Jimmy." I breathed.

My fingers sunk into his hair, as he kept going. Open-mouthed kisses, the brush of his stubble, the flick of his tongue, all sending shivers over my skin and spreading like wildfire over every inch of me.

My eyes fluttered open. Then they flared wide.

Jules was leaning against the corner of the sanitarium. Arms crossed, watching us over the cigarette in her hand.

Oh shit.

Jimmy felt me stiffen and pulled away. He looked to where I stared; breathing hard. We reluctantly stepped away from each other as Jules tucked her smoke into the corner of her mouth and gave a slow clap.

God, how long has she been there?

"Very nice, Miss Hughes," Jules said. "Making your way through the orderlies?"

"What? No..."

Jules chucked her smoke on the ground and twisted the heel of her boot on it. "Sure looks like it to me." She gave us both a disgusted glance as she strode for the side door. "Watch yourself, Jim. She'll cry rape and you'll end up in jail too."

Her words slapped my face and Jimmy tensed up beside me. I could feel the anger radiating off of him.

"Where did that come from?" I asked after the door had closed behind her.

"She and Brett were friends," he said.

"I can see that now," I said, shivering despite the morning warmth. "She seems like the kind of person who'd send love letters to a serial killer."

Jimmy's hard expression didn't soften as our gazes locked, everything we'd done hanging between us.

"Are you okay?" he asked.

"Yeah. Kind of shocking to hear but just words." I glanced up at him. "Wait. Do you mean us?"

He nodded.

"I regret nothing." He didn't return my teasing smile. "You do?"

"I'm late for my shift," he said and added, "My last shift."

"No, I won't let them fire you."

"I shouldn't have kissed you here."

He trudged to the side door and I gave the road out of Blue Ridge a last, longing look and then followed. I could scale the fence too, but how far could I go without the Hazarin? How many miles to New York would I make before I began to slip back into oblivion?

And would Jimmy follow me? Or try to stop me?

Inside, I gripped his arm, my fingers digging into the leather. "What happens now?" I asked. "Are you giving up on me?"

He moved in, stood as close to me as he could without touching me. "Never, Thea. N-N-Never. I swear it."

"Jim?" Alonzo stood at the end of the hallway, his expression grim and hard but his tone heavy with regret. "Can I see you a minute?"

Jimmy's final parting glance was full of such longing, my heart nearly broke. He walked away from me, down the hall, and around the corner.

It felt like goodbye.

Because it was.

Later, in the rec room, I stood over a fresh canvas but didn't touch the paint. Rita came in, her face pitying and I knew the answer before I asked, "Where's Jimmy?"

How long has it been? Where are Mom and Dad? Where's Jimmy?

The script had been rewritten, but the details were the same—me, stuck here, waiting for other people to tell me how my life was going to be.

Rita started to answer but Anna, walking in with Alonzo behind her, beat her to it.

"Jim has been let go," Anna said.

My heart felt as if it had been stabbed, even if I knew it was coming. "Jules tattled on us?"

Alonzo bowed his head as if in mourning. "It is against the facility's regulations for an employee to have inappropriate relations with a resident. Jim knew that and he left without incident."

He sailed away and left me. Left me without a fight.

I glared at them all. "And what if the relations were completely consensual?"

"That's not possible," Anna said. "Not while you're here, Miss Hughes."

"You all were so happy to see me wake up," I said. "I don't know why you bothered."

Rita looked pained. "Please, Thea. Try to understand—"

"My sister is behind this, isn't she?"

"No," Anna said. "This is policy."

I lifted my head, unwilling to let them see me broken or beaten. "I'm sure Delia will come today to check on me," I said stiffly. "I'll be in my room."

I went upstairs and lay on my bed, sucking deep breaths. Jimmy's kiss lingered all over my lips, my skin, and my heart. And now they expected me to live another few weeks in the sanitarium without him.

Delia came to my door an hour later. I threw it open on the third knock.

"You have no right to do this," I told Delia.

"I suspected you'd throw a tantrum."

"A what...?" I clenched my teeth to bite back a scream.

"I warned him," she said. "And he still couldn't keep his hands off you."

"You don't get to say whose hands I want on me."

"Neither do you." Her expression was smug. "It's against sanitarium policy."

"Fuck the policy and fuck you, Delia!"

She stared as if I'd slapped her.

"You can't dictate my life," I said. "You want him fired because he kissed me? I wanted it, Delia. I want *him*. I want to live. Goddamn, do I need to write it down? More word chains? More paintings? I'm standing right in front of you and telling you what I want, and you can't hear me."

"Are you done?" Delia asked.

I blinked. "Am I... *done*? No. I'm not done. I haven't even started yet. I'm leaving." I went to my dresser, yanked out the entire drawer, and upturned it on the bed.

"You can't leave," Delia said.

"Watch me."

I went to the closet, grabbed my new clothes off the hangers and dumped them too.

"Miss Hughes," Rita said, appearing at the door, breathlessly. "Is everything all right?"

I whirled on her, hand outstretched and fingers trembling. "Give me the Hazarin, Rita."

"She can't do that," Delia said. "Rita, can you leave us, please?"

Rita hesitated.

"Don't go," I said, my voice cracking. "Please..."

"Nurse Soto," Delia snapped.

"I'll be right out here," Rita said to me, her eyes pleading. She stepped outside and closed the door.

"I hate you," I seethed at my sister.

"You are going to listen to reason," Delia said, her eyes blazing. "For the first time in your life."

"No," I said. "I'm not listening to you. I'm going to write a letter to a judge to rescind your power of attorney. I looked it up. I can—"

"I'll fight it," Delia said calmly. "So long as the doctors say—"

"Why?" I demanded incredulously. "What is going on with you? And why do you hate Jim? Why is the idea of me being with him so hard to take? Or me being awake at all?"

"It's not—"

"You act like you wish I hadn't had this procedure."

"That's not true—"

"Then why can't you let me go?"

"Because I was going to leave and now I can't."

I froze. "What?"

The words fell from her mouth like stones. "I was going to leave you and marry Roger Nye. We were going to move to Vancouver. He got a job offer there a few weeks ago. We're supposed to move in a month. But then the procedure came up and…"

I stared until she tore her gaze away.

"I'm a terrible, selfish person," she said. "I know that. But I needed my life back. Then Brett Dodson was caught in your room, and I felt so guilty for even thinking you'd be okay here alone."

I sank down on my bed beside the overturned drawer.

"Not only couldn't I leave," Delia said, "but I had to be here even more. I had to try to put everything back the way it was before you were assaulted. I nearly lost my job." Her voice wavered. "I nearly lost Roger. And then Dr. Chen swooped in with her miracle procedure and the life I tried to scrape together blew up again. For the first time in two years, I didn't know what was going to happen next. The script was torn up. Again, I tried to put things back where they were and keep you safe. I want that more than anything. More than my own happiness, I want you to be safe."

A silence fell as I absorbed her words. "You're going to *marry* Roger?" I asked finally. "You're in love with him?"

She nodded. "Since junior high. Or… since forever, I guess."

"You never told us."

"I would have, eventually. I don't like anyone in my business. You, Mom, and Dad were all so… emotional. They'd make a big deal about it. You'd make fun of me."

"No, never—"

"Yes, Thea. You would."

"I'd tease you, but ultimately I'd be happy for you. I *am* happy for you."

"Despite knowing I was going to leave you?"

I swallowed. "That hurts. That hurts a lot, but I can't blame you."

"I thought you'd never know the difference," Delia said. "All those absence seizures you had whenever you saw me? They'd stop. It would be better. You would be better. But it turns out you would've known I was gone, wouldn't you? Deep down."

I nodded. "You should still leave. You've been chained to me for two years. Maybe it's time you went with Roger and built a life."

"No, I can't."

"You can. I promise it'll be okay."

"You don't understand—"

"I do, and I—"

"They *died,* Althea," Delia cried. "The last time I left with Roger, our family was destroyed. Mom and Dad died. And now you want to run away and... What if something happens to you? I can't do it again."

I shook my head, my voice wavering. "You can't live like this, Deel. You can't make all of your decisions based on fear. You have to let go of it. Let me go. You don't *have* to do anything anymore."

She looked away, wiped her nose. "Someone has to."

I saw her so clearly now. How she was forced to handle everything in the wake of the accident. How her fist clenched tight in a semblance of control.

"There's no such thing," I said.

She raised her head, confusion in her shining eyes.

"Control," I said. "It doesn't exist. You can try to control your life. You can try to get your family to your graduation early and a truck can still come smashing through it, shattering it to pieces. But you can't live in the fearful moments just before the truck hits. I know what it's like to live in those few minutes and it's not living, Deel."

Her eyes widened until I could see the whites. Her pulse pounded in a vein on her neck.

"I see," she said, her tone chilled and low while her body trembled with raw emotion I'd never seen in her before. "So it's my fault you got in the car when you did."

I gaped. "What?"

"It's my fault. I was pushing you out the door to my graduation."

"No."

"I skipped out to be with Roger."

"I'm not saying that. Delia—"

"I left you to get smashed by that truck."

"I wasn't saying that at all. Jesus, listen to me—"

"It's true," Delia said, biting the words out. "All of it. And I'm not going through it again. I refuse."

She rose to her feet, shouldered her purse with hard, jerking movements.

"You never take anything seriously. Not even your own life. I may not be able to control what happens to you out there, but in here there are doctors and nurses and safety. You can stay put a few more months. It won't kill you."

I shook my head. "No."

She went to the door. I rushed to it and shut it when she tried to open it.

"Let me go," I cried. "Please, Delia. If something's going to happen, it will. But let me be happy until then. Don't let all of my memories be of this little box of a room."

My sister jerked the door open, her gaze never leaving mine, her composure—her control—returned.

"It's for your own good."

Then she was gone, shutting the door tight behind her.

CHAPTER 26

Thea

I backed away from the door and sat on the bed, all that I didn't know about my sister crashing over me like a wave.

I don't know her at all. I never did.

I curled up on the bed as the sobs came. I cried for all I lost. For all I never had. My sister, Jimmy, Mom, and Dad. The alone-ness of the amnesia loomed, closing in on me.

A soft knock came at the door. "Thea?" Rita called.

I didn't answer. She could come in whenever she wanted. The door locked from the outside.

The door opened. "Oh, honey."

She sat beside me and I curled toward her, needing the human connection. I wrapped my arms around her knees and cried as she stroked my hair.

"She's like the witch in a fairy tale," I said between sobs.

"She's trying to protect you."

"I want to fight her in court, but she said she'd fight back. It could take months."

Rita sighed and I peered up at her. Conflicted thoughts played behind my nurse's eyes. A tiny flicker of hope sparked in me. Rita was my last chance. My only chance.

I sat up and wiped my eyes.

"Every morning," I said, "the doctors come in here and they ask me their questions. They want to know what the amnesia was like and I never could explain it properly. An airless box. A vast desert that was infinitely huge and yet claustrophobic. None of that is accurate."

"What is it then?" she asked softly.

"It's like death, Rita," I said. "Because what are we if we aren't our memories? Who are we without them? *Where* are we in this life? They anchor us to all the who, what, and where. Without memory, we might as well be dead. Inside the amnesia, I'm not physically dead but I'm stuck in between both worlds. Like a ghost. And now that I'm here, my sister wants to cram me back in that purgatory."

"Is Blue Ridge so bad? We want to take care of you—"

"It's my pyramid. A tomb stocked with all the things I need for the next life I can't get to." I sat up and took her hands. "Help me, Rita. Talk to Delia. Or Dr. Chen. Make them see. Time is ticking away. I can't explain it. Maybe because my consciousness is determined by a chemical reaction in a pill. It's all I have, and sometimes it feels like the thinnest thread. Help me live before it snaps."

Rita looked away. "Dr. Milton reports that the patients who have undergone the procedure ahead of you are doing well. There's no reason to think the medication will fail, but if it does…"

"If it does and I'm still here, then I came back for nothing," I said.

She pressed her lips together. My hope guttered out.

I let go of her hands and curled away from her. I stifled my cries but what difference did it make? I could scream from the rooftops, in my paintings, in word chains, and they wouldn't hear me.

They can hear me. They just won't listen.

A hand shook me awake as dawn's light filtered through the window.

"Get up," Rita said. "Get dressed, quick. I'll help you pack."

I sat up, blinking. "What…?"

"Hurry," she said, grabbing the backpack I'd bought on our mall excursion. "Shit, I'm going to be *so* fired for this."

I watched, slack-jawed, as Rita pulled the Hazarin pill bottle from her front pocket.

"I was tired," she said. "Had a bad night. Instead of bringing you one dose, I grabbed the entire bottle without thinking and you swiped it. Okay? That's our story. It might not be enough to save my job, but it's worth a shot."

Hope flared like an inferno, but I tamped it down. "No, Rita. I don't want you to get fired."

"I don't either," she said with a rueful laugh. "But I have a lifetime to remember the choices I made. And you only have right now."

I flew off the bed and hugged her tight. "Oh my God. Are you sure?"

"I didn't sleep at all last night, thinking of what you said. That part of my alibi is true."

She gave me a motherly pat on the cheek, though she wasn't quite old enough to be my mother.

She's the sister I never had.

The thought felt ugly and unfair. Delia was doing her best. It's all anyone could do.

Rita pressed the bottle in my hand. "It's got thirty pills after you take today's dose. One month and then you have to come back. I don't know what will happen when you do…"

"I don't either, but right now, I don't care."

I swallowed that morning's pill dry and stuffed the bottle at the bottom of my backpack. While Rita dug through my clothes for the essentials, I got dressed and hit the bathroom, grabbing toiletries and makeup, plus the birth control pills they had me take to keep track of my periods because I hadn't been able to do it myself.

Jimmy flitted into my thoughts at what else the pills meant, but I pushed him out.

"Take my number," Rita said. "Let me know how you are. Do you want Jim's?"

"I don't know. Not yet. I need to get out of here first and then sort out how I feel about him."

Rita nodded. "You're going to New York?"

"Hell, yes. There's a Greyhound bus ticket out there somewhere with my name on it."

She quirked a funny smile, but it vanished quickly. "Ready? Okay. Shit. Here we go."

"We?"

"We have to get past Jules at the front desk and then I'm going to smuggle you out in my car. Tell the outpost security I need to run home for my phone or something."

"No way," I said. "That, plus the missing meds? You'll be busted for sure."

"How do *you* plan to get past them?"

"I'll figure it out," I said. I gave her a peck on the cheek and a hug. "Love you. I can't thank you enough."

Rita hugged me tight. "Be careful. Please. If you start to feel fuzzy or disoriented in any way, you call me. Or get to an ER. Promise?"

"Promise."

We crept down the silent hallway together, every creak of the floorboards like a siren. We stopped in the stairwell on the first floor.

"Jules will go on her first smoke break any minute now," Rita whispered. "She usually goes out the side door that leads to the parking lot."

I made a face. "I'm well aware."

"That means you'll have to walk out the front door."

That's exactly how I should leave here. Waltzing right out the front door.

I huffed a breath. "Okay, here goes."

Rita gave me a final squeeze. "Good luck."

Her footsteps faded away up the stairwell, then I was on my own.

I watched through the little window in the door between the hall and foyer, ready to dive into the broom closet if someone came along. Thankfully, Jules slipped out for a smoke break after only a few minutes. I waited twenty seconds then crossed the foyer, passing the pretty oil painting—*a bunch of fruit.* I opened the door on the brand-new Virginia morning.

Holy shit, I did it.

I kept to the side of the road that led down to the security checkpoint, glancing over my shoulder now and then to make sure Jules was still around the corner and out of sight and not ready to jump out and yell

"Gotcha!" for the second time.

The road curved and the checkpoint outpost came into view; I ducked behind a tree.

Now what?

The security wasn't too tight—except for me, the residents were there voluntarily. But unlike the parking lot, the fence here in the forest had barbed wire coils along the top. It became a solid brick wall on either side of the road at the checkpoint. Red and white striped boom barriers kept traffic from coming or going unless raised by the security guard. The forest was cleared for a good ten yards on either side of the road, and more fencing buffered it all the way down the hill. Even if I managed to sneak past the guard, I'd be a sitting duck.

I gnawed my lip, half-wishing I had taken Rita up on her smuggling plan. Waltzing out the front door was the easy part.

A plan of my own popped into my head then: keep waltzing. Hide in plain sight.

Not a great one, I admitted, but the only one I had. I popped a piece of bubblegum into my mouth, put on my sunglasses and crouched low. My heart pounded in my chest and I prayed the guard was tired this morning. Dozing. Maybe reading a paper.

Moving as fast as I could while crouched over, I dashed toward the outpost and flattened myself against its left side. I squeezed my eyes shut, waiting to hear the door open and the guy bust out to grab me.

Nothing. Only the tinny sound of a small TV. *The View.*

That show is still on? I thought those gals would've killed each other by now.

Breath held, I scooted along the edge of the checkpoint and peered over the window. The guard had his back to me, feet kicked up on the desk, absorbed in the show.

Let's do this.

I ducked under the boom barrier, crept along the brick wall, then simply turned around and walked right back up to the outpost. Casual as fuck, as if I'd been strolling up the road this entire time.

Toward a sanitarium. At seven in the morning. As one does.

The guard did a double-take to see me, his eyes widening, and his feet dropped to the ground.

"Hi," I said, snapping my gum.

"How did…?" The guard looked all around, over his shoulder and then back to me. "Can I help you, miss?"

"Maybe," I said with a flirty smile. I folded my arms on the window, pushing my breasts up.

Hell, it worked for Erin Brockovich.

"I think I'm lost," I said. "I'm in town for the Celebrity Rabies Fun Run Race for the Cure? They said it was supposed to start around here."

I held my breath. If this guy was a super-fan of *The Office* I was toast, but it was all my brain could come up with on the fly.

The guard squinted. "The *what*?"

"Haven't heard of it? Bummer. Wi-Fi up here is shitty. My GPS must've sent me the wrong way."

His eyes narrowed suspiciously. "It's a long wrong way up this hill."

Slow down. Be cool. Act natural.

"You're telling me." I smiled bigger, leaned closer. "What is this place, anyway?"

"Blue Ridge Sanitarium," he said. "Brain injury cases."

I widened my eyes and lowered my sunglasses to show him I had nothing to hide. "No shit?"

He nodded, and his glance went longingly back to his TV. Immune to my charms. And, apparently, my boobs.

"No shit," he muttered. "Hope you find your fun run."

"Me too." I blew a bubble and let it pop. "Have a good one."

I patted the window frame in parting, turned, and sauntered down the winding road as fast as I could without looking like I was trying to hurry. When the curve took me out of sight of the outpost, I ran like hell. Any second, the security guard was going to wonder who in their right mind did a fun run for rabies.

Michael Scott, that's who…

A relieved laugh burst out of me and morphed into a gasp as I rounded the last bend in the road and came to where the sanitarium drive met the main road. I stopped short, staring.

Jimmy leaned against the driver's side door of an old green pickup truck, mind-blowingly handsome in his leather jacket, jeans, and boots. His hair was slick with a morning shower. He nervously checked his phone then glanced around. His arms fell slack when he saw me.

"What are you doing here?" I asked.

He pushed off the door. "I heard you needed a ride to New York."

I stared, happiness exploding across my heart. "I thought you left me."

"And I told you I'd never give up on you."

Tears threatened, and I crossed my arms, refusing to turn into a complete puddle at his feet.

"How did you know I'd be making my escape this morning?"

"Rita texted me her plan last night. She didn't tell you?"

"She failed to mention it." My cheeks warmed. "I guess she wanted it to be a surprise."

He smiled one of his rare smiles. "I hope it was a good one."

"The best." I tore my gaze from him and looked at the pickup truck behind him. "Where's your motorcycle?"

"I traded it. I didn't like the idea of driving from here to Manhattan with you on the back. If you had a seizure—"

"I'm not having seizures, Jimmy," I said.

He shrugged. "I'm not taking any chances. Besides, if you were behind me the entire time, I wouldn't be able to…"

"To what?" I asked, moving closer. "See me?"

"Talk to you."

His words sank into my heart, better than any compliment. The *ultimate* compliment from Jim Whelan.

"God, this is *so* much better than my Greyhound bus plan," I said. "But I can't ask you to—"

"You don't need to ask. I'm here."

My eyes stung at his quiet humility. I didn't know how to thank him for everything he'd done for me. I knew I'd burst into tears if I even tried. I glanced around, blinking hard, struggling to find something to say.

"You sold your motorcycle for me?"

"Yesterday."

"Right after you were fired?"

He nodded.

"You lost your job because of me, so you traded your beloved motorcycle for this truck?"

The truck was old with a dented fender and scratches in the paint, which meant Jim took a loss on his bike, probably in order to sell it fast.

"I was fired because I broke the rules," he said. "But yes to everything else."

I threw my arms around him. He held me close, my feet dangling off the ground, and my body reacted instantly. Every part of me wanted every part of him.

He's it. He's what I want. In every way.

"Thank you," I whispered against his neck, which was wet with my tears. "I should say it a hundred times..."

"Don't," he said into my hair. "You don't have to."

I slid down the length of his body until my feet touched the ground but left my hands around his neck. I brought one to his cheek, my thumb brushing the corner of his mouth.

"Jimmy..."

He stiffened in my arms.

"What's wrong?" I sniffed a laugh. "You don't want to kiss me anymore? Granted, I'm a little snotty right now, but that's your fault."

"I... That's not what this trip is about. You don't owe me anything."

"*Owe* you? I—"

"Hold up."

His glance darted over my head, eyes widening at the road leading up to Blue Ridge. As I turned to where he was looking, I heard the slow crunch of tires on gravel.

I looked at Jimmy. "Oh shit."

He stared back. "Oh shit is right." He yanked the passenger door open for me. "Get in. Get down."

I crouched on the floor of the cab as he raced to the other side of the truck and jumped in. A pleasant panic bloomed in my gut, like the feeling you get right before a roller coaster drops. My stomach sent flutters up to my heart, adding to the adrenaline rush that was already coursing through my veins.

Jim scooted down below window-level and we listened, our breaths held, as the security car slowly rolled past. When it grew fainter, he ventured a peek and then I watched him follow the vehicle down the road.

"Gone," he said. "I don't think they know you've escaped yet, or we'd be screwed." He laughed at me, curled on the floor of the cab. "You ready?"

206

I gave him a thumbs-up. "Born ready."

I buckled myself into the passenger seat while Jim stripped out of his jacket and tossed it in the small space behind our seats, then fired the ignition. He filled the truck with the scent of denim and his clean, unfussy cologne. I leaned back in my seat and just drank him in.

Jimmy's large hands gripped the wheel as he drove. His forearms were perfection, and my fingers itched to run them along the striations of his muscles under that tanned skin. My eyes blazed a path up to his bicep that strained the short sleeve of his black T-shirt. Up, up, to the corded muscles of his neck, to his strong jaw brushed with stubble.

He's like a shot of booze, or a drug that feels too good to be legal.

I welcomed the lust. The slow roll of want shuddering through my entire body made me feel alive. I hadn't felt it in years and never this powerful. Never.

Jimmy drove with confident precision, taking me wherever I wanted to go. He'd given me so much and never asked for a thing in return, and there was no place on earth I'd rather be than with him.

PART III

CHAPTER 27

Thea

"It's a seven-hour drive," Jimmy said. "I figure if we push straight through, only stopping for lunch and gas, we'll get you there fast. Sound good?"

"Sounds perfect."

The adrenaline rush from nearly getting caught faded, leaving me a pleasant buzz of happiness. Blue Ridge couldn't stop me, but they could make things difficult if they got the police involved. But I was out in the world. The green of Virginia in summer outside our rolled-down windows and the wind played in my hair.

"Music?" Jimmy asked.

"You read my mind."

He picked up his phone from the dash and handed it to me. "The truck's too old for Bluetooth, but if you put the volume on high…"

"On it."

I scanned through his music.

"You sure have a lot of dance and techno here for a rock n' roll guy."

"I loaded it up before your procedure," he said. "For our walks, or while you were painting."

"Damn, Jimmy. For a guy who doesn't talk much, you always say the perfect thing."

He kept his eyes on the road, but the corner of his mouth turned up in a half-smile.

I found "We Are Young" by Fun., featuring Janelle Monáe. I hit play.

"I love this. Janelle is my girl-crush," I said after a few moments. "But it's not techno."

"I know but I heard it and thought you'd like it."

"You were right."

I cranked up the volume when the chorus hit. It filled the cab like an anthem of everything I felt in that moment. I was alive, I was free, and I was with the man I wanted to be with more than anyone in the world.

For the next few hours, Jimmy and I listened to music and talked. About his Grandpa Jack, because it was the only bright spot in his childhood. About my parents, and Jimmy held my hand while I cried for them. As we crossed into Maryland and I peppered him with questions about pop culture in the past two years.

"Which movie won Best Picture last year?" I asked. "Something with Steve Carell, I hope."

"Who?"

"You're kidding, right? The brilliant actor who played Michael Scott? The World's Best Boss. From *The Office*? The World's Best TV Show?"

He shrugged. "Couldn't say. I don't watch much TV."

"Everyone needs *The Office* in their life," I said. "Who won the Super Bowl?"

"This year? The Patriots."

"Last year?"

"The Patriots."

"Should've guessed," I said with a laugh. "Who is the president?"

"You wouldn't believe me if I told you."

My phone rang. "This can only be one person…" I fished it out of my bag. "Yep." I hit answer. "Greetings, sister."

"Thea, where are you?" Delia crowed in my ear.

"Honestly, Deel, it's none of your damn business. Not anymore."

"You shouldn't be alone. It's not safe. If something happens—"

"I'm not alone," I said. I glanced at Jimmy. He nodded. "I'm with He Who Shall Not Be Named."

"Of course," Delia said, her tone bitter with sarcasm. "The orderly. Who else? For God's sake, Thea…"

I covered my phone with my hand. "Delia says hi."

"I'll bet."

"You are toying with your life," Delia snapped in my ear. "And for what? That man? Did he put you up to this? Of course, he did. He's been trying to get into your pants for months."

"He's a perfect gentleman, though I'm going to try my hardest to cure him of that."

Jimmy coughed, and his ears reddened.

"Althea Renée Hughes…"

"No, Delia," I said. "You don't get to talk to me like that. If you're not careful, I'll end this call and you'll never hear from me again."

"Until you need more Hazarin," Delia said. "Did Rita Soto give it to you?"

"I stole it from her. She's got nothing to do with this."

"Don't insult my intelligence."

"Leave her alone. She's a good person."

"You need to come back, Thea. You have—"

"Brain damage? I'm not sick, Delia. I'm finally well, and I'm done wasting time."

A short silence and I could practically hear her desperate attempt to hold on to control.

"I'll have him arrested."

I barked a harsh laugh. "For what?"

"Kidnapping a brain injury patient—"

"You try to have him arrested and we're done forever. I swear it." Frustrated tears stung my eyes. "Don't do this, Deel. Mom and Dad would *hate* this."

"They would," she said, her own voice cracking. "They'd hate how you're risking your life for a man—"

"I'm hanging up now."

"And going where?" she said quickly. "To New York City? For how long?"

"I don't know yet. A week, maybe more. And when I come back, it won't be to Blue Ridge. I'm going to get my own place. Go back to art school."

"So you'll come back to Richmond?"

My gaze slid to Jimmy. Who lived in Boones Mill.

"I don't know all the details, yet," I said. "I'm going with the flow. But whenever I come back, I'm going straight to a judge and rescinding your goddamn power of attorney."

"That's not important. You're—"

"It is to me. I want my life back. And I'm taking it."

"Thea…"

"Go marry Roger," I said. "Be happy, Deel."

"Wait—"

I hung up and dropped the phone in my bag. I wiped my eyes. "It's amazing how you can feel anger and frustration and love for the same person, all at the same time. That's how family works, I guess."

"I wouldn't know," Jimmy said with a grim smile. "Keep checking in with her."

"She threatened to have you arrested."

"She's worried about you." He raised a brow. "She's angry and frustrated and loves you, all at the same time."

I shook my head, marveling. "You're amazing, James Whelan. Maybe the last of the truly good men."

His phone in my lap rang with Delia's number.

"She's persistent, I'll give her that," I said, offering him the phone. "You want?"

"She got my number from Alonzo, probably. And yeah, I'll talk to her." He hit a button and put it to his ear. "Ms. Hughes."

He's so polite and chivalrous. I wonder if his grandpa Jack taught him how to treat women.

Jim got an earful from my sister for a good minute, watching the road as he listened.

"It's not up to me, Ms. Hughes," he said, finally. "It's up to Thea."

"Amen," I muttered.

"We won't," Jimmy said into the phone. "I promise."

He listened for another ten seconds then pulled the phone away. "I think she hung up on me."

"Typical. What did you promise her?"

"That we wouldn't vanish."

"Fine, but I'm not going to tell her where we're staying in New York. Let her try to find us. What else did she say?"

"Various threats about what she'd do to me if anything happened to you. Death. Dismemberment. Castration."

"She watches *Game of Thrones* too."

We shared a smile, but the unease of Delia's threats settled into my gut like carsickness, until he indicated a sign for a roadside diner a few miles outside of Baltimore. Then I was ravenous for a burger and fries and a chocolate milkshake.

"This good?"

"Works for me."

Jimmy took the exit and parked the truck in the diner lot. He started to get out, but I stopped him with a hand on his arm. "Delia can't really have you arrested, can she?"

"Don't know. Maybe if you were incapacitated?"

"And I'm not. I can speak for myself if she tries something. But I don't want to get you in trouble. You already lost your job for me."

"I'll be fine."

"Why risk it?"

Is it because you're as crazy about me as I am about you?

Jimmy shrugged slightly, glanced down at my fingers on his skin. "You wanted this. You deserve it. I wanted to make it happen."

I lowered my gaze, traced a scar on his knuckle with my fingertip. "What else do you want, Jimmy?"

His dark eyes met mine and he swallowed hard. I felt the need in him under my hand. I saw it burning in his eyes. I heard it in the words he'd just swallowed down, and my heart pounded, waiting.

"I want to eat," he said finally. "I'm starved."

He pulled from my touch and climbed out of the truck.

"Ouch," I said to the empty cab.

Maybe I was all wrong about Jimmy. Maybe he didn't feel for me what I felt for him. Maybe he truly only wanted to do this for me, like some kind of field trip.

After he kissed me the way he did? I thought, going back to that beautiful morning. *Impossible.*

But I was suddenly too afraid to push it. Like waiting for biopsy results—maybe just better to live in blissful ignorance. Except it wasn't blissful. It was torture.

I'll just have do things the old-fashioned way and seduce him.

Jimmy came around and opened my door, sending a waft of summer humidity to wrap around me. I lifted my hair off my shoulders as we headed to the restaurant, feeling Jimmy's gaze sweep the curve of my neck and my breasts.

"See something you like?" I teased.

He looked away and held open the door to the diner for me. The hostess at the front greeted us.

"Two? Right this way."

She seated us at a wide table that made me feel like Jimmy and I were separated by a mile of sticky Formica.

"Cozy," I said, as we slid into our seats on opposite sides.

A tired-looking waitress came by. "Drinks?"

"Chocolate milkshake, please," I said. "Extra cherries."

She turned to Jimmy. "For you, sugar?"

"A Coke."

I opened the menu. "God, I want one of everything," I said. "It's been forever since I've eaten a burger and fries. I mean, I know that's not true, but I feel like my entire life is a menu and I'm starving. For food, music, art, for experiences, for sex…"

Jimmy shifted in his chair and toyed madly with his fork.

"Can't help it," I said. "I've missed so much."

The waitress returned with his soda and my shake. I took a long, deep pull from the straw and moaned as cold chocolate deliciousness poured into my mouth.

"Oh my God, brain freeze," I said with a laugh. "But *so* worth it."

I plucked a cherry and sucked the whipped cream off before biting it from the stem. Across the table, Jimmy stared, eyes dark under furrowed brows, fists clenched on the table.

"What?" I said.

"N-Nothing."

I leaned over the table. "Your kind eyes don't look so kind right now. You look as if you have some thoughts about what else I might be able to do with my tongue."

Jimmy shifted in his seat. "You're not making it difficult."

"Is that a bad thing?"

"No, but—"

"But what?"

When he didn't answer, I tossed my cherry stem on the table and sat back with a frustrated sigh.

"No bullshit, James. What's going on? Why haven't you tried to kiss me when we were practically sucking each other's faces off in the parking lot yesterday morning." I leaned forward again. "Even if the answer breaks my heart, I'd rather live with that pain than none at all. So I'm going to ask. Do you care for me, Jimmy?"

"Yeah, I do," he said, meeting my gaze. "But I shouldn't have kissed you."

"So you mentioned," I said with a wince. "Why?"

"I have to be careful."

"Because you don't trust me to know what I want?"

"Something like that."

My eyes flared open. "And here I thought you weren't like them. You were the only one—"

"Thea," he said, his voice harder than I'd heard him take with me. I fell silent.

"I knew you before the procedure for longer than I have after," he said. "For all those weeks, we talked and listened to music and every conversation we built was torn down again by the amnesia. Over and over again. A part of me is scared shitless you'll suddenly..."

"Go away again?"

He nodded. "I never want to cross a line with you. Which is why I shouldn't have kissed you at Blue Ridge. I should've waited until we were outside of those gates."

"We are now," I said, my hand wanting to slide across the table and take his. "We're here now. Together."

"But we're not here for me," he said. "We're here for you. I don't want you to think I'm trying to get something out of you."

"I don't think that," I said. "But we *are* here for you. You're a good man. You deserve some happiness too. Don't you?"

He shrugged, lifting the weight of his loveless life on his strong shoulders. No self-pity, just a heartbreaking gesture of resignation.

The waitress arrived, her arms laden with burgers and two baskets of fries.

"Here we are." She set them down. "Anything else?"

"We're fine, thanks," I said. I ignored the heavenly scent of greasy food curling under my nose and kept looking at Jimmy, who stared back. I'd never seen him so hard and intimidating. A stone wall built up year by year, to protect a child who had nothing and no one.

"You want to know if I think I *deserve* happiness?" he said to my expectant gaze. "No, I don't. Life doesn't work that way. The world doesn't owe me anything, and I stopped asking a long time ago. End of story."

A short silence fell. Neither of us spoke or moved to touch our food.

"I think that's exactly how life works," I said gently, conscious I was talking to a man for whom life had provided only the barest of essentials. "I think everyone deserves happiness. It's out there, waiting to come to us, but we have to be open to receiving it. We have to *know* we deserve it, in order to give it a chance."

"Simple as that?"

"Yeah," I said. "It's that simple and yet, sometimes that hard to do."

He jerked his chin at my food. "Eat," he said, a faint smile on his lips. "It'll get cold."

My appetite was gone. It was more important to make him see I knew what I wanted. To shout that I trusted him with every fiber of my being, and he could trust me. But James Whelan took nothing for himself, even when he deserved everything. Quite possibly, the idea of being loved was so foreign to him, he wouldn't know it if it slapped him in the face.

Or if it were sitting right across from him.

We ate in silence, the air between us tight with possibilities. A humming live wire connected us. Its tension strained tighter and tighter, waiting for something to break it.

I watched Jimmy take a bite of his burger. A dollop of mustard stuck to the corner of his mouth.

Without hesitation, I crawled up onto the table, clattered over silverware, and nearly knocked over a water glass. Jimmy stared, his eyes wide to see me on my hands and knees on the tabletop, my face inches from his. His shock mellowed into want, a heat emanating from his skin.

216

A FIVE-MINUTE LIFE

"You have some mustard on your face," I whispered. "Let me."

I bent my head toward his and licked his lips in a long, slow swipe. My mouth lingered on his, wanting his kiss so badly. Hungrier for it than any food.

"Got it." I climbed backward into my seat, vaguely mindful of other patrons watching and whispering. I sipped my cold shake, casual as hell on the outside while inwardly, I was on fire for him.

I'm yours, Jimmy, I thought. *Come and get me.*

CHAPTER 28

Jim

Thea on all fours, her necklace swinging between us and her breasts pushing out of her bra from under her shirt. Her tongue on my mouth.

This is going to get me arrested. I'm going to take her right here in the restaurant.

She climbed back into her seat, and I took a long pull of the cold soda when I really needed an icy shower to cool my blood.

It seemed so easy; to have her. To be with her. But having something this perfect and good didn't happen to me. Like being dirt-poor for years and suddenly having a bucket of gold dumped in my lap. I didn't know what to do with it all.

You're going to fuck it up, is what you're going to do, Doris offered.

I paid the bill while Thea used the restroom. I came out into the sticky heat to find she'd slipped past me and was now leaning against the truck.

"Only a few hours left to go," I said. "Should be in Manhattan at dusk."

"And then what?" she said. "I wish you would tell me what you're thinking. After you kissed me yesterday morning, I thought…" She shook her head. "Never mind."

She pushed herself off the driver's door and walked around to her side.

I climbed in on my side and started the truck. I said nothing but let Thea be upset with me. Getting her to New York City was the priority. Everything else could wait.

Thea put her music back on, humming along or singing while I drove us across Pennsylvania. She napped for the last few hours and woke as the sun was sinking in a cloudy gray sky. We hit the Lincoln Tunnel and went north for ten blocks, to Midtown Manhattan in crawling traffic.

Thea craned out the windows, taking in the sights, her smile stunning in its happiness.

"Oh my God, there it is," she said, jostling my arm and pointing. "The Empire State Building."

"You want to go there now?"

"No, I'm going to save that for last." She grinned. "It's getting dark. I want to see Times Square."

Of course, she does. All that light and color.

I found a parking spot a few blocks away. The air felt heavy with rain—a summer storm looming. We walked with the crowds of tourists in humidity that felt different from the green heat of the South. New York smelled like heated metal and concrete. Hot dogs and falafel. Garbage and perfume. Thea inhaled it with the same exhilaration she had on our walks on the Blue Ridge grounds.

We stood at the corner of Broadway and Seventh Avenue and I understood Thea's need to be here. New York teemed with life in a way I'd never experienced. People strode past, arguing, laughing, talking into their phones in different languages. Hawking wares, swearing, or meandering like tourists, taking photos of the glowing billboards surrounding us on all sides.

For a small-town kid like me, it was a lot to take, but Thea stood in the center of that bustling sidewalk, her eyes drinking it all in, the color and light playing over her face. Her smile was radiant, and I wished Delia could see how happy her sister was at this moment.

Thea glanced up at me, her smile never wavering, only softening. "Isn't it amazing?"

I nodded. She turned her gaze back to the lights, but I just watched her; drank *her* in because she was all the light and color I could ever want.

She must've felt my eyes on her; she turned to me again, delicate brows furrowed.

"What is it?" she asked. "Tell me everything. Even if it's hard."

"Nothing good lasts," I said. "That's been a truth of my life. Being with you? Here? It's too fucking good."

"*Nothing* ever lasts, good or bad," she said, her eyes alit with a thousand different colors. "That's why we have to live as much as we can, as hard as we can, every moment."

Every fucking moment.

My arms slipped around her waist and I pulled her close. Her hands slid up my chest and clasped behind my neck.

"Are you going to kiss me now?" she asked. "Please say yes. I'm saying yes, Jimmy."

Because I'm a choice she's making.

I bent my head to her until our lips brushed and then I kissed her. No fences or rules or hesitation. I kissed her with my entire heart that had been so fucking vacant until Thea.

Her mouth opened for me with a little sigh, almost like relief. I drank it down and when she moaned softly; I took that too. Inhaled it. Sucking gently because the need to have this piece of happiness was all-consuming. I'd been starving for it my entire life.

The first raindrops began to fall, lightly at first, then harder.

"Oh shit," Thea said with a breathless laugh.

Lightning crashed, and the sky tore open. The downpour scattered the tourists and sent them running for store awnings while the native New Yorkers calmly opened umbrellas or pulled up hoods on jackets, unfazed.

I ducked into my jacket and shielded Thea with it as we made a mad dash back to the truck. We were drenched by the time we climbed in, Thea's shirt clinging to her every curve.

"We've only been in New York for a few minutes, and I already love it," she said, her eyes luminous in the dimness. "It doesn't give a shit that we were trying to have a moment."

"Not remotely," I said. "Where to?"

"A close hotel," Thea said, leaning to kiss my ear. "As close as humanly possible."

I drove the truck to the closest hotel, the Hilton Times Square, grateful my jeans and the dark concealed how badly I wanted her.

Thea bit her lip as we pulled into the valet. "The parking is as much as the room."

"I have it covered," I said. "Let's do the first night here. We'll figure the rest out later."

She grinned. "No script?"

"None."

We climbed out of the truck, her with her backpack and me with the small duffel I'd packed after I'd received Rita's text. Thea's eyes widened as she watched me pull my guitar case from behind the front seat too.

"Are you trying to kill me, Jimmy?"

I shrugged, feeling self-conscious. "I don't know. You keep asking me to sing. I felt like the odds were good you'd ask me again on this trip."

"A billion to one, for." She grinned. "But I have money too," she added as I tipped the guy at the valet. "You're not paying for everything. I'll get the room."

I didn't like the idea of Thea spending a dime on me, but this was her trip and part of it was paying her own way after years of dependence on everyone else.

"Do you have something high up with a view?" Thea asked the desk clerk.

"We're pretty booked…" He tapped his keyboard. "A-ha. You're in luck. I have a standard room on the thirty-third, two queens, non-smoking."

"Queen-sized," she said, heaving a dramatic sigh. "I suppose we can make do."

He smirked. "Do your best."

Key cards in hand, we rode the elevator up to the thirty-third floor. The air seemed to thin out as we rose higher and higher, anticipation rising with it. I glanced down at Thea beside me. She looked up, rainwater dripping from her hair, glistening along her skin. Without a word, she stood on tiptoe and planted a kiss on my mouth. Soft lips and the smallest touch of her tongue before pulling away.

Goddamn, if nothing else happens, tonight is already perfect.

The lamps in our room were off, the drapes drawn. The lights of New York City were the only illumination. The grid lay spread below us or rose high in towering pillars. Obelisks of light.

"It's so perfect," Thea murmured, echoing my thoughts. She dumped her bag on the bed and moved to stand at the window.

I set my guitar against the wall and my duffel on the other bed, claiming it as mine if that's what she wanted. For so long, even sitting across from her felt like an invasion of her privacy because she had no way to know if she wanted it. No memory to ask or answer.

Now she can tell me what she wants.

I joined her at the window, and we watched as lightning cracked across the dark night.

"I talk a good game," she said. "But I'm suddenly really nervous. My heart is racing."

She took my hand and laid it on the warm skin her tank top didn't cover. Her pulse thudded under my palm.

"We do what you want to do, Thea." I brushed a stray lock of damp hair from her cheek. "Whatever you want or nothing at all."

"I don't want to do nothing," she said. "Not ever again. But…" She broke off with a small laugh, looking away.

Inhale. Exhale. "Is this your f-first time?"

"No." She ran her fingers over my jacket, her gaze following, until she raised her eyes to mine. "But right now, standing here with you, I can't remember anyone else."

She moved into the circle of my arms, pressing against me. Every molecule in my body wanted to grab and take but I held her gently. Loosely.

She tilted her head up to mine. "Just kiss me, Jimmy, and let's see what happens."

No script. The entire night waiting for us to make of it what we wanted.

I bent and kissed her softly, tasted her lips that parted for me at once, despite the nervousness I felt trembling through her body like an electric current. I deepened the connection, my tongue venturing into hers and she moaned. God, Thea's moans were like matches tossed on a smoldering fire.

She kissed me back, her tongue sliding against mine, exploring, while her hands slipped into my hair, then to either side of my face, holding me like I was something valuable.

We kissed with growing urgency. When thunder boomed, neither of us flinched. Thea pushed my jacket off my shoulders, her hands roaming as our mouths devoured and plundered, biting and clashing, with our breaths rasping between little sounds of want neither of us could control.

"I'm not nervous anymore," she breathed. "Because I remember all of you. Us. Everything you ever said or sung to me, Jimmy. Not in my broken mind but here." She laid her hand over her heart. "I kept you here. Even when my memory wouldn't let me tell you."

"You told me," I said, my own breath coming hard. "I heard you."

"You fought for me," she said.

I kissed her again and lifted her up. She wrapped her legs around my waist, never breaking our kiss as I took her to the bed. I laid her down, and she shoved her backpack to the floor, then reached for me as I sank down on top of her. Her body beneath me, straining for me, was driving me out of my mind. I'd never wanted a woman like this in my life. I'd never *had* a woman like Thea, one I wanted and who wanted me just as I was.

Her hands slid down the sides of my body to my waist. She pulled me against her, lifting her hips to mine, and I ground down on her while I kissed her, sucking gently, eliciting more of those soft little moans that made me crazy.

She tore her mouth from mine, gasping. "Jesus, how do you do that?"

"Do what?" I asked, kissing her neck, her throat, and the delicate skin beneath her ear.

"Kiss me so it feels like I'm falling into you."

I didn't answer but kissed her like that again and again, until our hands craved skin. I sat up and kneeled on the bed, to reach behind and pull my shirt over my head by the collar. Thea's eyes widened at the sight of me. Unabashed, she slipped out of her tank, then reached behind her to unclasp her bra.

I'm a dead man...

Her skin was luminous in the dim light. The green gem on its gold chain glinted between her breasts that were fucking perfection. I bent and kissed her there.

"You're so fucking beautiful," I murmured against the beat of her heart. I closed my eyes and inhaled the scent of her, savoring this moment. Her arms cradled my head, fingers sinking into my hair.

She gently raised my face to hers, eyes and fingers trailing over my lips and nose and eyebrows. The moment held and then we kissed, a last, gentle touch. Then Thea got up on her knees and pressed her body against mine. Skin to skin, her breasts against my chest. My hands slid down the silken skin of her back to the waistband of her jean shorts, then around to undo the buttons. Her fingers tore at the zipper on my jeans, our eyes meeting between frantic, biting kisses.

I kicked out of my pants as she stripped out of her shorts. Clad only in lacy pink underwear, she leaned back, propped on one hand while her other trailed down between her legs. My erection grew painful as her fingers made circles over her panties. In answer, my hand went down the front of my boxer briefs, and I stroked myself while her fingers rubbed and dampened the silk of her underwear.

Holy fucking shit…

"Oh God, Jimmy," she said, watching me, her breath coming short. "No man's ever made me feel like this. Made me want this so bad."

"Good," I said.

I withdrew my hand and hauled her onto my lap so she straddled me, her dampness tight on my erection; her silk against the cotton. I kissed her raw and deep.

She whimpered into my mouth and rolled her hips against mine. I gripped her with both hands to grind her harder while my mouth found one of her nipples. I sucked and bit as she rode me. Her head fell back, fingernails scraping the back of my neck as I moved her on my lap, tortured by the clothing still left between us, and savoring what was to come when I tore it away.

"No more, I can't…" she cried. "Jimmy, please. Now…"

I took her nipple mercilessly one last time, before laying her roughly down on the bed. I tugged off her panties and stared a moment at the sight of her, naked and perfect and mine. Then I stripped out of my underwear and Thea let out another of those little moans.

"God, you're going to ruin me for anyone else."

I kneeled above her. "You've already ruined me."

She ringed her hands around my neck and pulled me down. I lay

224

over her, straining to be inside her but holding back by a damn thread.

"I'll go slow," I said, bracing my arms on either side of her face. "Whatever you want. Tell me and I'll do it."

Her body beneath mine softened everywhere at those words, melting against me, her legs opening to take me, and I settled between them. Every molecule in my body screamed to feel the wet heat that was between her legs and sink myself deep into it.

"I want you inside me," she whispered against my lips. "Right now."

"Wait, I need a condom," I gasped.

Thea shook her head. "I'm on the pill and I want to feel everything."

She tilted her hips up, offering. My need to have her roared in my ears so I couldn't hear my own thoughts. She reached between us; her brazen eyes holding mine as she rubbed the tip of my cock against her soft wetness.

"Thea..." I gritted out. "Jesus..."

"I want you to feel everything," she said and then moved her fingers to spread herself for me. "I want you so bad..."

It took every ounce of self-control I possessed to slide slowly into her instead of thrusting hard and deep. Her tightness gripped me like a fist, wet and hot and slick. My eyes fell shut, and a moan rose out of me when she lifted her hips to take more, her hands at the small of my back, clinging to me as I sank inside her.

"Oh God," she breathed, her voice in whispery tatters. "God, yes. Just like that. Ah, *God*..."

She bit her lip, her eyes squeezed shut as I entered her completely, hip to hip, her body taking all of me.

I searched her face and she nodded quickly.

"Yes. So good, Jimmy. Please, more... More..."

I rolled my hips, pulling back and thrusting in, building a slow rhythm. She responded to every movement with the same vigor she treated everything else in life. She gave me all of herself and I took more and more, greedy for every moan, every soft sigh of ecstasy.

I pistoned my hips harder and faster and our kisses turned sloppy, a desperate mashing of mouths and clacking teeth. Her legs came up to wrap around my waist as I reached between us and under her, my fingers splayed on her ass, spreading her wide, trying to drive in deeper.

Her nails raking my back. "Oh God... I'm going to..."

"Come," I grunted, my face buried in her neck. "Come for me, Thea."

Our bodies crashed over and over, flesh slapping flesh, until Thea tensed, back slightly arched, as if offering herself to me completely. I took her, hard and deep and relentless, her cries filling the hotel room, then tapered to whimpering moans.

"Now you," she managed between ragged breaths. Her knees fell open and her hands pulled me to her mouth for a kiss. "Fuck me, Jimmy. However you want. Come inside me. I'm yours. No one else's. Ever again…"

The release that had been building in me rose into a crescendo. I let go instead of holding back, thrusting hard and spilling deep inside her. Wave after wave of it, rolling through me and into her until I was utterly spent.

I collapsed on top of her and she wrapped me in her embrace. I closed my eyes, floating in a perfect delirium of sweat-slicked skin and hard breaths and pounding hearts.

"I was right," she said, catching her breath. "You ruined me in the best way. And you've ruined this trip. I'm not going to be able to get out of bed for a week."

"That works for me," I said, starting to move off of her.

"Don't go," she whispered. "Stay right here forever."

She was teasing, and yet she meant it. Her eyes held mine intently and her face was so beautiful in the city lights; her happiness full in every curve and line. Right there in my hands.

Too good…

"I'm too heavy." I kissed her softly and pulled out of her, my body missing hers instantly. My thoughts already whispering there was no such thing as forever.

Shut up. Let me have this.

We lay entangled in one another as the rain smattered the windows. My head in the crook of her neck and her fingers toying lazily in my hair. My entire view the soft hills and valleys of her body.

Tiny tentacles of fear wormed into me as sleep came on.

It's too good. Nothing good lasts.

"Thea," I murmured.

"Hm?" Her fingers in my hair grew still as sleep came for her too.

Nothing lasts at all…

A FIVE-MINUTE LIFE

I closed my eyes. "Nothing."

CHAPTER 29

Jim

I dreamed her…

My body weighed a thousand pounds. Heavy and sated. Thea was wrapped around me, still, the ghosts of my past whispered this was all a lie.

She raised her head, her hair tousled and smiled sleepily.

"Hi," she said.

"Hi."

She propped herself on an elbow and made circles on my bicep with her fingertip. "So last night was… um… pretty mind-blowing. Wasn't it?" She plucked at the sheet now. "It's been a while for me."

"Fucking mind-blowing," I said, brushing a lock of hair out of her eyes.

"I'm a mess," she said. "Hungover from you."

"You know what they say about curing a hangover."

"Hair of the dog that bit you?"

I nodded and leaned in to nuzzle her neck, then lightly bit the skin above her collarbone.

"Mm," Thea sighed. "I see what you did there."

She writhed as I worked over her neck and jaw, one hand cupping her breast and running my thumb in circles over the nipple.

"And just like that, I'm wet for you," she whispered.

I hauled her on top of me and watched her ride me as morning light streamed in from the windows. When she came, I flipped her onto her back and took her hard—as hard as she wanted and as hard as I needed—to prove this was my life.

Nearly an hour later, we collapsed in another tangle of arms and legs, her head pillowed on my chest.

"Jesus, you're a beast," Thea said. "No, a warrior. My warrior."

I kissed her, slow and deep, running my tongue over her swollen lips.

"No, no, no, I will not succumb to your manly seductions again," she said, hauling herself from the bed. "Today is our first full day. We have so much New York-ing to do. You care if I shower first?"

"Help yourself."

She bent to smack a wet kiss on my lips and headed to the bathroom.

I lay back on the bed and watched the light grow stronger outside. The storm had passed in the night. A new day. Mine and hers.

Don't let all that old shit from the past fuck it up.

Thea's phone rang from inside her backpack.

Delia.

Not my business.

Thea's phone went silent and my phone rang ten seconds later.

"Ah, hell."

I went to the window and dug it out of my jacket pocket.

"Ms. Hughes."

"Why isn't she answering her phone? What's happening?"

I glanced down at my nakedness and smothered a laugh. "She's in the shower," I said, climbing back into bed and pulling a sheet over me.

"You're sleeping with her."

I wouldn't call it sleeping.

"It's none of your business, Ms. Hughes. Thea is fine."

"Fine," Delia said. "Because you would know."

"I knew how she was in the amnesia better than you ever did," I snapped, then rubbed my eyes. "Sorry. I didn't mean that."

Delia sniffed. "She has to take the Hazarin at seven. Every morning."

I glanced at the clock. 7:09 a.m. "I'll make sure."

A pause.

"I should have you arrested."

"For what? Taking an adult woman exactly where she wants to go? She wants to be here. With me."

"And where is here?"

At a hotel in New York City. Maybe you could try calling around to each one until you find us.

My bitterness didn't hold. Delia was scared for her sister.

"I'll tell her to call you," I said.

"James?"

"Yeah?"

"She's the only family I have left."

I gritted my teeth. Delia didn't give a shit that Thea meant everything to me too. I wondered how many snakes I'd have to kill to prove it.

"I won't let anything happen to her," I said. The water shut off in the bathroom. "I'm going. Goodbye, Ms. Hughes."

I hung up and put my phone on mute. A few minutes later, Thea emerged from the bathroom, wrapped in a towel, her hair falling around her shoulders in damp waves.

"Your sister called you," I said. "And then she called me."

"Did you tell her I was in the shower, rinsing off bodily fluids and sweat from our fourteen-hour sex-a-thon?"

"Didn't mention that."

"She's a smart gal. I'm sure she'll put six and nine together. Get it?" She waggled her brows.

"Yeah, I got it—"

"Six and nine. *Sixty-nine.*"

I rolled my eyes with a laugh. "She said you need to take the Hazarin at seven every morning."

"On it."

Thea tucked the towel tighter around her body and dug the pill bottle out of her backpack. "I'm going to splurge on an eight-dollar water from the mini-fridge."

I watched her swallow the capsule that kept her tethered to the present. Infinitesimal molecules forming a bridge between the damage done in the accident and the repairs from the surgery. A bridge she crossed every millisecond to stay on this side of consciousness.

I wondered if the bridge were rickety and frail, doomed to fall apart piece by piece. Or if it were iron and steel, engineered to last for decades.

I sat up and swung my legs over the side of the bed. "No side-effects?" I asked, then wished I hadn't. It felt like kicking the foundations of that bridge to see if they'd hold.

"Not a one," Thea said. She started to put the pill bottle back in her backpack.

"You should put that in the hotel safe," I said. "In case your backpack gets lost or someone swipes it."

"Good thinking." She kneeled and created a code for the safe and stowed the medicine. "The code, should you need it, is nine-nine-eight-six."

"Because?"

"Because Michael Scott worked at Dunder Mifflin for..." She inhaled and sang slightly off-key to the main tune from *Rent*. "*9,986,000 minutes. That's like watching Die Hard eighty thousand times.*"

She laughed and took another swig of water, completely unaware of what she was doing to me, minute by minute.

I've never loved anything as much as Thea loves that TV show. Until I came to Blue Ridge.

"You should call Delia back," I said.

"Later."

"She's worried about you."

Thea slowly bent and captured my lower lip between her teeth, sucking gently before letting go. "Later."

"I thought we had New York-ing to do."

She cocked her head and lifted the edge of the towel. Offering.

I tore it off her. "Later, it is."

Thea called Delia while I showered. I changed into the other pair of jeans I'd brought and was pulling a fresh white T-shirt over my head when Thea rolled her eyes and ended the call.

"She wanted to know which hotel we're staying in. As if. I should have taken a photo of us in bed together just to piss her off."

"Keep checking in with her. Let her know you're okay. It's all she wants."

Thea gave me a dry look. "She wants your head on a platter, James," she said. "As if I have zero ability to think for myself."

She tossed the phone into her backpack with a disgusted snort, then hopped to her feet, her blue eyes alit from within. She wore her jean shorts and a maroon tank top with a drawing of a turtle on the front in white. She'd tied her hair up into a high ponytail that showed off the curve of her neck and small ears pierced with tiny silver hoops.

"First on my list," she said. "The Met."

"The Mets?" I asked, hiding my smile while pulling on a boot. "You want to watch baseball?"

"You're so cute. The Metropolitan Museum of Art. I checked on my phone while you were in the shower, and they have a ton of amazing exhibitions right now. One is a collection of paintings by the classic Dutch masters, and the Drawing and Prints Department is showing a bunch of stuff from my boy, Leo DaVinci. Not to mention they have one of the largest collections of Egyptian antiquities eh-vah."

"Sounds good."

"You sure? You won't be totally bored? I remember you said art wasn't your thing."

"But it's your thing," I said. "This is your trip."

"It's *our* trip. I only have a few must-sees on my list. Anything else you want to do is gravy."

"I'm good with whatever, Thea."

She pursed her lips at me. "Okay, well, I was thinking we should probably check out of here. The Met is up in Central Park. I found this cute hotel nearby that looks perfect, and the parking isn't going to wipe us out. Check-in at the new place isn't until four. I figure we can get out of here, drive up to the park, and grab some breakfast before the museum. Sound good?"

"Great."

We checked out and drove a slow crawl from the Times Square area, up the West Side of Manhattan, parked the truck at a public garage, then walked to a café for breakfast. Thea chatted animatedly the entire time, telling me about her life before the accident.

232

"I was a year away from graduating from the VCU School of Art in Richmond," she said over eggs, bacon, and coffee. "I was hoping I was good enough for a scholarship for the Academy of Art here for my grad studies. Then a truck smashed my parents' car and smashed all my plans too." Her eyes filled with tears. "But so what? I'd never paint again if it brought them back."

I reached across the small table and held her hand as she sniffed and dabbed her eyes with a napkin. "But I'm going to start over again. Go back to school. I think that's what they'd want me to do."

"I'm sure they do."

"What about you? Have you thought at all about going back to school for speech therapy?"

I shrugged. "Not much."

"If it's something you really want to do, you should do it. I think you'd be amazing at it."

She dropped the subject, but I turned it around and around in my head. Being with Thea was a doorway to a real life opening and possibilities pouring through. A future vision unfurled in my mind: Thea in a studio painting, a ring glinting on her left hand, and me sitting with a little boy who couldn't talk, and I was telling him things were going to be okay. Because they'd turned out okay for me. More than okay.

You're going to tell him he can have everything he's ever wanted? Doris sneered. *Bullshit and lies. Life doesn't work that way and you know it.*

I tried to ignore the insidious thoughts, but they were ingrained in me. Part of the fiber of my being, woven by years of abuse and neglect in a fucked-up system.

I looked at Thea across from me, radiant and beautiful and full of love. Love was a stranger. Fear had been my constant companion.

Take care of her. Give her this trip. That's your job. Your only job.

"Are you okay?" she asked. "You look sad."

"I'm good," I said.

The waiter came by and dropped the check.

Thea made a grab for it, but I was faster. "I got it."

"Jimmy—"

"I *got* it, Thea." I forced a smile to soften the harsh tone. "Come on. Let's get you to that museum."

CHAPTER 30

Thea

Jimmy and I walked through Central Park, from the Upper West side to the Upper East Side, under a brilliant sun and thick humidity. The city still smelled of the rain that came through last night, but the sky was a perfect blue, empty of clouds

"It's beautiful," I said as we strolled along a path. "I love this piece of the green in the midst of all the concrete and steel."

Jimmy made a sound in his chest but said nothing else. He'd snapped at me pretty hard over the check in the restaurant, and now a hard glint was in his dark eyes, a thousand unspoken thoughts lurking behind them.

All morning, I talked about myself and my past. Telling him was remembering and remembering felt like a gift I got to open every second.

But maybe Jim wanted—or needed—to talk about his own childhood. I could hardly fathom eighteen years in the foster care system with no good memories to show for it.

Remembering might not be such a gift for him.

Still, Mom and Dad always said talking about the bad stuff was a way of taking away some of its power.

"Hey," I said, slipping my hand into his and giving it a squeeze.

"You okay?"

"Sure." He squeezed back. "Tired, maybe." He gave me a knowing look. "Not much sleep last night."

"Spoiler alert: you're not going to get much sleep tonight either."

He let out a laugh that softened the hard edges of his features.

He's okay. We're okay and we're in New York. Not everything is everything.

As we strolled the museum galleries, my art school education came back to me, along with my love of painting. We stood in front of Vermeer's *Young Woman with a Water Pitcher,* and I stared in awe at its beauty.

"It's the sunlight," I said. "See how he floods the room with it? How it glints on the pitcher and the glass in the window. All that blue and gold…" I shook my head, drinking it in. "It's such a simple moment, it becomes almost spiritual. Something divine about that young woman, in her home, opening a window to let the morning in."

I filled my eyes with the painting until I felt Jimmy's on me, a strange, nostalgic expression on his face.

"What is it?" I asked.

"I was remembering our first conversation," he said. "Standing in front of the painting at Blue Ridge. You described how the light touched the fruit."

"I remember."

"Even then?"

He nodded. "But it didn't last. That perfect moment."

"Not then," I said. "But I'm here now."

His eyes took me in the way I'd gazed at the Vermeer, the strange nostalgia returning. He nodded and moved on to the next painting.

We continued through the museum and to the Egyptian galleries I'd been so excited to see. But once there, I wasn't as moved as I'd been by the Vermeer.

"I love the artifacts," I said as we passed a bright blue hippo in its glass case. "I love the history and rituals. That's all still there but…"

"But what?" Jimmy asked.

I put my hand to the glass display that held a fragmented stone sculpture of a king's face, nothing left of his eyes or head.

"I don't know," I murmured. "It feels different. Like that part of me that was obsessed with Egypt is gone now."

I couldn't describe it any further until we headed to the Sackler wing and stood in front of the Temple of Dendur that had been moved from Egypt, brick by brick, across the Atlantic and reassembled here.

I expected my breath to be stolen away at the sight of the temple and the two huge statues that sat guard over it. But I shivered and rubbed my arms.

"A tomb."

Jimmy glanced down at me.

"It's not," I said. "That's a sanctuary, not a tomb, but the amnesia… That's what it felt like. A tomb, and Blue Ridge was the pyramid in which all things I needed for life were stored. But it wasn't life. This is life, and I don't need the pyramid anymore. I'm free."

We stood side by side in front of the monument. I inhaled through my nose and let it out.

"Okay," I said, slipping my hand into Jimmy's. "I'm ready to go."

We headed to the Leonardo Da Vinci exhibit and stayed until we'd seen as much as I felt Jimmy could take before he grew bored—and we headed back into the brilliant sunshine, and the space between us didn't seem so far anymore.

"Item number two on my list," I said. "Have a picnic in Central Park, then walk across the Bow Bridge. I'm starved."

"How about a hot dog?" Jimmy asked with a nod at a vendor on the street a little way from the museum.

"I am in desperate need of a hot dog." I gasped, and I gripped Jimmy's arm, staring at him with wide eyes. "That's what she said."

He smirked. "Let me guess. *The Office*?"

"I've been waiting *two years* to say that," I said. "My life is complete."

He rolled his eyes. "Come on, woman. Let's go get you a hot dog."

We bought two hot dogs, two lemonades and two little bags of chips, and took them to a bench shaded by a huge oak tree to eat.

After we ate, Jimmy balled up his napkin. "I think I need seconds."

"I'm on the job," I said, jumping to my feet.

"No, I got it."

"Not this time." I kissed his cheek. "B-R-B."

I came back with another hot dog for him, extra mustard and relish, like his first.

"Shit, I forgot napkins."

"Thea, wait. I'll go."

"Nope. You're eating."

I went back to the vendor, practically skipping with happiness and returned with a pile of napkins.

"Here you go," I said, plopping back down on the bench beside him. I took a swig of my lemonade. "God, today could not be more perfect."

Jim hadn't touched his second hot dog. I gave him a quizzical look and he turned his gaze away, to the park in front of us.

"What's next?" he asked. "Bow Bridge?"

I nodded. "It's one of the most photographed landmarks in New York. So beautiful and romantic." I nudged his arm. "And if you're totally done with paintings and pretty bridges, tonight we can go to… I don't know. WrestleMania or something."

He didn't smile but got up and gave his uneaten food to a homeless man sitting on a nearby bench.

"He needed it more," he said, answering my look.

"Okay."

It was a sweet gesture, but that heaviness was in his eyes again.

We walked to Bow Bridge, the graceful arch spanning The Lake and crossed its length along with a dozen other tourists.

"We don't have one photo of us together," I said, fishing my phone out of my backpack. "It'll be the first on this phone since the accident. I think that's fitting. My old life right alongside the new with nothing in between."

We moved close together, and I held the phone up, turned the cracked screen around to capture us, the green waters of The Lake, and New York City rising behind the treetops beyond that.

"Say cheese doodles," I said, my throat threatening to close on me. Hearing the tears in my voice. Jimmy turned to me just as I snapped the pic.

I opened it back up and we leaned in to examine it.

"Not very cheery. I'm obviously about to cry and you're looking at me." I shook my head, swallowed. "You're looking at me with so much…"

The words fell apart. Jimmy pulled me to him.

"I never used to cry this much," I said against his chest. "Or maybe I did. But not for so many intense emotions. Horrible grief and pure happiness, both."

We stood for a few minutes on the bridge, our arms wrapped around each other. Jimmy still didn't say a word.

I sniffed and glanced at our photo one more time.

"I've taken better. Although the tears in my eyes make them really blue."

"You're blue and gold, like that painting," Jimmy said. "Nothing's more beautiful than the way the sunlight touches you."

Before I could answer, he pulled me back to him and kissed me hard. Fiercely. Almost possessively. My eyes fluttered open to see his eyes shut tight, his brows furrowed as if kissing me caused him pain.

"Damn, Jimmy," I searched his face as I caught my breath back. "What is going on with you today?"

"Nothing."

"That kiss was *not* nothing."

"Let's get to the hotel and I'll kiss you like that again."

"You're trying to change the subject with promises of sex. It's not going to work."

He cocked his head.

"Okay, it's working a little." I slipped back into his arms. "Are you sure you're okay?"

"I'm fine, Thea," he said in nearly the same tone he'd told me he'd pay for breakfast. "Let's go."

His mood swings between brooding and grouchy, to romantic and considerate were driving me crazy, but I decided to bite my tongue until we were alone in our room.

"The ArtHouse," Jimmy said, reading the marquee. "Of course."

"It's kind of my theme," I said with a grin.

The room was cozy and clean and had a partial view of the park.

And a king-sized bed.

"Oh my God, we are going to have so much sex on this bed," I said, kicking off my sandals and jumping up and down on the king-sized mattress. "Come here, Jimmy."

I suddenly needed to hold him, he seemed so far away. He moved to where I stood on the mattress and wordlessly slid his arms around my waist. He kissed my middle, breathing hotly through the thin cotton of my shirt. I wrapped my arms around his head, holding him close, raking my fingers through his hair.

"You're a good man. I want to be a good woman for you."

"You are," he said gruffly.

I shook my head. "I'm going to take care of you," I said, trailing my hands over his shoulders and down his chest. "You've taken care of me for months, and now it's my turn."

He stiffened in my arms.

"What is it?" I asked. "And don't say nothing."

"I don't know," he said. "I'm not used to being taken care of."

"I got that," I said softly. "I saw your face when I brought you a bunch of napkins. Just napkins…"

He started to answer when his eyes widened. "Holy shit, your medication," he said. "Did you remember to get it from the safe at the other hotel?"

I froze and turned my face into a perfect mask of *oh shit*. My eyes widened and my lips parted.

"Fuck." His face went white, and he tore his hand through his hair. "We have to go back. N-N-Now…"

"Jimmy, wait," I said, reaching for his sleeve. "I'm kidding. I have it. I grabbed it after I found our new hotel. You were probably in the shower. It's in my backpack."

He stared at me for a solid ten seconds then tore his hand from mine. "The fuck, Thea?"

"What…? I-I'm sorry," I said, my heart pounding as liquid guilt surged through my veins, sludgy and thick. "I'm so sorry, Jimmy. It was a joke. I—"

"A b-b-bad fucking joke." I could see the frustration ratchet up with the return of his stutter. He hadn't stuttered once since we arrived in New York.

I jumped off the bed. "I'm sorry. I didn't think—"

"You didn't think I'd be scared shitless for you? Or you d-d-didn't think at all?"

"The second one," I said in a small voice. "It's what I do. When things get heavy, my instinct is to go for the joke. To lighten the mood. I'm so sorry."

He stared at me again, his brows drawn tight, then he turned away, hands on his hips. "It's fine. I'm just… tired."

"It's not fine and you don't have to be tired to be mad," I said, slipping into his arms. "You should be mad at me if I do stupid shit. We'll still be okay. And I promise to think before I do any more stupid shit. And then *not* do it."

He nodded stiffly and pulled away. "It's early yet," he said. "Let's go out to… wherever you want to go next."

"Wait, Jimmy. We should talk."

"About what? I freaked out, and you apologized. Nothing to talk about."

"You've been off and on, all day," I said. "Sometimes right here with me, and sometimes a million miles away. Or even angry with me."

"I'm not."

"Since breakfast, when I talked about my life before the accident. I was thinking, maybe you wanted to talk about yours too. Maybe you need to—"

"I don't."

"Jimmy…"

"There's nothing to talk about. It's done."

"Yes, but—"

"Why is it important, Thea? Just drop it."

I stared. "Why is it important? Because you are. You're important to me." He started to turn, but I grabbed his arm. "No. We're going to talk about this."

"About what? My fucked-up childhood?"

"Yes," I cried. "Or whatever it is that's making you so upset right now."

"You want to hear about it, Thea? Why? What fucking difference will it make?"

"I don't know," I said. "But it will. Because I care about you."

He flinched as if the words whipped him. "You want to know what it was like? Fine. Let's talk about it. Let's talk about how one foster mother came home from her job every day and locked me in a closet until dinner so she wouldn't have to deal with me. Or about the racist asshole who saw me hanging out with a black friend after school when I was in third grade. He chained me to a fence in the backyard in the dead of winter and said he'd leave me there for a week if he saw me with that friend again. Or how about Doris, the foster mother I was with the longest? She insulted me day in, day out until I thought my n-n-name was Fucking Moron, or Big Dummy. She made sure I knew every fucking day of my life that I was n-n-nothing and no one."

His skin reddened, his face a mask of rage and humiliation.

"And this f-f-fucking stutter," he seethed. "Are you listening to it, Thea? Is this the shit you want t-t-to hear?"

"Yes," I said, tears streaming down my cheeks and my voice quavering. "Yes, I want to hear it."

"It's fucking pathetic."

"It's not. It's what happened to you and it *matters*."

"Yeah, it happened, Thea," he said, breathing heavily, in and out. "You wanted to know what it was like? That's what it was like. That's what I *know*. That's life."

"So is this," I whispered. "You and me. Right here. Now."

He stared at me and my heart broke for him, ached for him. Yet it filled with a fierce pride that he had endured all that he had and didn't let it turn him rotten. He was still a good man.

The best kind. He deserves everything.

I moved in. My hands holding his face, my forehead pressed to his. His eyes fell shut.

"I'm going to fuck it up," he said hoarsely. "Or your meds are going to fail."

"Neither of those things is going to happen," I said. "Or they both might. Or maybe *I'll* fuck us up with one too many bad jokes. But we can't live waiting around for that."

He pulled back enough to hold me with his hands and his gaze. "I've never had anything as good as this."

"Neither have I," I said. "I've never felt this way about anyone. Ever." I kissed him once. Twice. "I'm scared too. But let me…"

Love you.

"… take care of you."

I kissed his lips. Each corner of his mouth.

"Please, let me. Let me be there for you the same way you've been there for me. You brought me back to life."

"God, Thea." He kissed me between words. "You're doing the same."

His hands came up, one in my hair, the other at the small of my back. Pressing me to him. I felt the need in him ignite under mine that roamed his back, his neck, his hair.

"We'll take care of each other." My head fell back as his mouth moved over my neck. "No matter what happens."

His arms around my waist tightened. I took his strong, chiseled jaw in my hands and kissed him slow and deep, giving him everything. Sealing a promise to him.

He made a sound, deep in his chest, and then his kiss turned hard and biting. I whimpered into at the flush of heat that surged through me. Again and again, he took my mouth with his magnetic, sucking pull that made me dizzy and delirious. He stripped me out of my shirt. I tugged his over his head.

"Shower," I murmured as his hands roamed me. "I want you in the shower. Like the rain of our first night…"

We moved to the bathroom, stripping each other of clothes as we went. I turned on the water, and we stood under the stream, skin to skin, wrapped tightly in each other. I felt his cock between my legs, huge and hard, but I forced myself to slip out of his embrace.

"I'm going to take care of you," I said. "Right now."

I moved behind Jimmy, ran soap over his broad back. He tolerated it for a minute, then turned, reached for me again. I gave him one brazen kiss—all tongue and teeth—while my hands indulged in the planes of his chest, the ridges of his abdomen, moving downward.

"Thea…"

I dropped to my knees and took him in my mouth while I stroked the immense, hard length of him.

He groaned. "Ah, fuck…"

The water fell over us, warm and clean. I tasted every inch of his cock with my tongue, then took him deep. His hand smacked the tile above me, bracing himself, and the sound spurred me on. I wanted his release for myself. Greedy for every sound, every low moan. He found my hair, his fingers tangling.

"Harder," I managed.

His hand tightened in my hair, pulling, holding me there.

Yes, oh God, that.

Jimmy tensed and then spilled his release into my mouth. I drank it down, sucking and stroking to take every last bit of it, because it was mine.

"Jesus, Thea."

Jimmy's head dropped, the water streaming across his face to rain over me. It ran in rivulets over the cut planes of his body, the muscles of his arms and shoulders. Sheer masculine perfection. His eyes opened and found mine. My heart thudded at the pure, raw want in his expression.

"Come here." Still breathing hard, he pulled me to my feet. The intensity in his eyes sent shivers dancing over my skin, despite the heat of the water. "My turn."

His words dropped between us, deliciously menacing in the promise of what he was going to do to me. Desire coalesced in a heavy ache deep inside me.

"Oh God..."

He captured my mouth in a searing kiss, while his hand slipped down between us, between my legs. He rubbed circles over my flesh, and then he slipped two fingers inside me.

I trembled, arching my hips into his touch.

"Yes..." I clung to him, my arm wrapped around his neck. "God, yes... Please..."

He pressed me to the wall, pinning me with his body, his mouth, and his fingers that took me to the edge before he pulled back.

I let loose a little mindless cry at the loss. It echoed in the bathroom and morphed into a gasp as Jimmy went to his knees and put his tongue on me. He kissed me with that same sucking pull and I came almost instantly—the ferocious ecstasy tearing through me. I scrabbled to hold on to him, my nails digging, starbursts firing behind my closed lids.

Jimmy rose and held my jaw in one hand. He took a kiss from me, sucking it from my lips with wanton greed. His other snaked out and shut off the water. Without a word, he lifted me out of the bathroom and laid me down on the bed. He stood over me like a warrior, ready to conquer.

And then he did.

He slid into me with one hard thrust. I stretched my arms over my head and arched my back as he braced his weight on one forearm and hooked my leg over the crook of the other, taking me hard and deep.

I gave myself up to him completely—my body and my heart naked and his for the taking.

CHAPTER 31

Jim

Thea nestled into me and nuzzled my neck. "Morning. May I take your order?"

"Surprise me," I murmured sleepily.

She kissed below my ear, my jaw, my lips, then disentangled herself from my arms. I yawned and watched through half-closed lids as she padded naked to the bathroom. After these last three days, I had her morning routine memorized by sight and sound. She'd use the bathroom, brush her teeth, take the Hazarin. Then she got dressed, grabbed her bag and slipped out the door, blowing me a kiss on the way.

I rubbed my eyes and settled in to wait. I was getting better about letting her do things for me, like buying me coffee in the morning or picking up the—very—occasional tab at dinner. Lancing the wound of my childhood and letting her see the venomous details had loosened the grasp of a lifelong fear.

But I'd never fall asleep while she was out there alone.

Fifteen minutes later, Thea returned with two cups of coffee and two sausage-and-egg sandwiches from the shop across the street. She sat cross-legged on the bed beside me while we ate.

Thea sighed happily between bites. "I love this city. We could go to a different restaurant for breakfast, lunch, and dinner every day for years and never eat at the same place twice."

"What's the plan for today?"

Thea's phone rang. Right on schedule.

"Hold that thought." She wiped her hands on a napkin and answered her phone. "Hi, Delia." She climbed off the bed and went to the window to talk to her sister. Their relationship hadn't improved during our time in New York, but Thea never let a day go by without telling her sister she was okay. In return, Delia stopped threatening to have me arrested.

A fair trade.

"I will," Thea said at the window. "We're having an amazing time. The time of my life… Okay… *Okay.* Bye. *Bye, Delia.*" She came back and dumped her phone on the bed beside me. "I wish she'd just marry Roger and leave us alone."

Thea's eyes betrayed the hard words. I knew she hated the estrangement, but Delia couldn't be trusted. She still hadn't rescinded power of attorney.

Thea blinked away her sadness and smiled brightly at me. "Where were we?"

"Today's plan," I said through the last bite of my sandwich. "Empire State Building?"

"Not yet," Thea said. "That's last. I figure I have enough cash for a few more days. And don't tell me you got it. You have rent to pay and no job."

"I have savings."

"We can't drain them down. I don't want to make anything harder for you."

I reached and pulled her on top of me. "You're making it hard for me."

She settled against my groin, grinding on my growing erection. "I see what you did there."

I kissed her, tasting the salt of her breakfast and the sweetness of coffee that was more cream and sugar than anything else. The kiss deepened, and all thoughts of food were forgotten for the next hour. I could've happily remained in the hotel for the rest of the day, losing myself in sleep-sex-talk intervals, but Thea had more New York-ing to do.

"I'd like to wander through Greenwich Village," she said. "No plan. No agenda."

"No oysters," I put in and laughed at Thea's sour expression.

Two days ago, we went to Grand Central Station, where Thea insisted on splurging at the Oyster Bar because it was a very "New York thing to do." When the plate of raw oysters arrived, her eyes widened at the gelatinous goop and her nose wrinkled at the smell. But Thea being Thea, she clinked an oyster shell against mine in a toast and tossed it back. She immediately looked like a beautiful woman who'd knocked back the worst thing she'd ever eaten and was trying desperately to pretend it wasn't so bad.

I can't remember laughing so hard in my life. I chuckled again now, thinking about it.

"You're still laughing at me?" She held up her pinched thumb and forefinger. "I was this close to barfing."

"Is barfing in the Oyster Bar a very New York thing to do?"

She gave my bicep a playful punch. "Shut up. *Anyway,* I'd like to walk around Greenwich, have a late lunch, maybe do some shopping, and then have a cocktail at a jazz lounge or something. Sound good?"

She always asked me that. *Sound good?* And I always pretended to think about it for a half a second, before saying, "Sure."

As if I'd deny her anything.

We showered, dressed, and headed out into another sticky, sun-drenched day. Thea wore shorts and a white tank top with flowers embroidered along the top.

"You're beautiful," I told her on the elevator ride down.

She leaned into me, kissed my neck. "You always say *you're beautiful,* instead of *you look beautiful.*"

I shrugged. "Both true."

"Yes, but one is a sweet compliment about how I might look at the moment, and the other feels like you're describing who I am." She sighed and rested her cheek on my shoulder. "You're very eloquent. Has anyone ever told you that?"

I smirked. "What do you think?"

"I think everyone who missed that about you can suck it."

"It's not like I gave them many opportunities. I didn't say much. But

I had this one teacher, Mrs. Marren. She was nice to me. Said I was smarter than anyone thought, including myself. She's the one who told me to sing to help the stutter."

"I love her already." Thea glanced up at me. "Speaking of singing…"

"Ah, shit."

"How have I completely forgotten you brought your guitar?"

"Because I keep it stowed in the hotel closet?"

She grabbed my arm as the elevator door opened on the lobby. "Promise you'll sing for me? And play? At least once?"

"What do I get out of it?"

Thea tapped her chin, pretending to think. "Sex. *All* the sex."

"I'll sing for you. No sex required." I kissed her softly. "But since you're offering…"

"Oh hell, let's be real," she said, looping her arm with mine as we crossed the lobby. "If you play guitar and sing for me, Jimmy, I'll be naked before the second verse."

We took the subway to Christopher Street and proceeded to walk approximately every square inch of Greenwich Village. Thea dragged me up and down the streets, pausing to admire window displays or pop in every other shop. She took us over to Bedford Street to see the apartment building they used for the exteriors of *Friends.*

"Second best show on TV after *The Office,*" she declared and had us take a selfie while she sang a terrible song about a smelly cat.

We had lunch at a noodle restaurant on Sixth Avenue, then headed back over to Christopher Street for soft-serve at The Big Gay Ice Cream shop on the corner.

The entire time, Thea's happiness wrapped around me like a summer heat—not thick or humid but the kind of heat that thawed a decades-long winter. I wasn't the only one basking in Thea's radiance. Anyone who came in contact with her—waiters, passersby, street vendors—they were in love after one smile, joke or hug.

It's so damn easy.

In the Big Gay Ice Cream Shop, Thea spent half an hour listening to the cashier—Jonathan—vent about his on-again, off-again boyfriend as if Thea were a lifelong friend and not literally someone who walked in off the street. When we left the shop, Thea had the guy's number in her phone and was surreptitiously wiping her eyes.

"Since the accident, all my old friends in Richmond have moved on," she said. "Or maybe Delia cut them out of my life. Other than Rita, I haven't had a friend until you." She gave my arm a squeeze. "But you're my boyfriend now, so that's not the same. Everyone needs that BFF to talk boys with." She waved at Jonathan through the window and blew him a kiss.

He waved vigorously and mouthed *Call me.*

"Boyfriend, huh?" I said, trying for casual when my stupid heart grabbed at the word and held on for dear life.

"Oh shit. Is it too soon? I just thought…"

"Whatever you thought, I'm thinking it too," I said. I pulled her close to me and kissed her, tasting cool vanilla sweetness on her tongue.

"You always say the best things," Thea said.

"I want to get a good report when you call Jonathan."

She laughed and pounced on me, wrapping her arms around my neck. "You're doing all right so far, Jimmy Whelan." She slid down until her feet touched and then her eyes widened at something over my shoulder. "That bookstore is too cute. Let's look."

She took my hand and dragged me down Bleeker to a small shop with carts of books spilling out the front door. We went inside and Thea picked up an old paperback, opened it, and put it to her nose to inhale deeply. "No better smell than an old book."

"Did you read before the accident?" I asked.

"Romance novels, mostly."

I frowned. "I didn't see you with any books at Blue Ridge."

Thea lifted a shoulder. "They probably thought it wouldn't take if I was only 'there' for five minutes at a time."

But did they try?

"I also really dig books *about* books," she said. "My all-time favorite is *Shadow of the Wind* by Carlos Ruiz Zafon. Ever hear of it?"

I shook my head, scanning the Zs on the fiction shelves.

"It's romance, magic, and tragedy set around an old Barcelona bookstore in nineteen forty-five." She toyed with the little green gem on her necklace, her gaze turning distant. "My mom introduced me to Zafon," she said. "He was her favorite too."

My fingers found *Shadow of the Wind* and handed it to her. "I think this is yours."

Thea smiled gratefully and took it. She blinked hard at the cover. "Reading it again will be like coming home. What about you? Do you like to read? If you say yes, I'll have to marry you right now."

"Yeah, I read," I said slowly.

"You do?"

"Yep. Guess you'll have to marry me right now."

Thea hugged her book to her chest, a blush in her cheeks "Guess we should find City Hall."

"Guess we should."

The moment caught and held. Thea looked away first, uncharacteristically shy as she perused the shelves. "What's your fave?"

"Chuck Palahniuk. *Fight Club.*"

"Saw the movie." She wrinkled her nose. "Too violent for me."

"Yeah, it is. But I read the book a hundred times over the years. The idea of creating a better, stronger version of yourself that doesn't put up with any shit appealed to me, I guess."

Thea moved around a table of bargain books. "And now?"

I shrugged. "I don't know. Like your love for all things Egyptian, *Fight Club* doesn't feel like it fits me anymore."

"You don't need a better, stronger version of yourself." Thea pecked my cheek. "You never did."

"What are we going to do next?" Thea asked after we left the bookstore, a new copy of *Shadow of the Wind* for her and *Catch-22* for me in her backpack, and her arm tucked into mine.

"Up to you," I said. "It'll be dark soon. You hungry?"

"No, I mean when this trip is over," she said. "What's next, Jimmy?"

"We go back to Virginia, I guess."

"And then? I'm not going back to Blue Ridge. No chance."

"Neither am I," I said. "Because I was fired."

She didn't smile. "You need a job. I need a job. We both need to go back to school. I mean, if you feel up for it."

"Maybe," I said. "Your art school was in Richmond?"

She nodded. "But even if I went back. I don't know where I'd live."

Inhale. Exhale. "Maybe we could both move to Richmond."

Thea stopped walking. "We?"

It's too much. You're asking too much of her. Of life. No one gets everything they ever wanted...

I pushed the old fear down and kept talking.

"Maybe we get a place together in Richmond," I said. "I'll get a job and you can go back to school. And then, down the road, when we're settled... I can look into programs for speech therapy."

Thea pounced, wrapping me in a choke-hold that softened as she slipped down into my arms. I held her while the pedestrians parted around us like a river around a stone.

"It sounds so perfect," she said against my chest. "This is a dream and I'm going to wake up in that little box again—"

"Jesus, don't say that."

She huffed a steadying breath. "No, you're right. I love your plan."

"Yeah?"

"I do," she said.

We kissed to seal the pact, but it wasn't enough. A feeling I didn't have a word for made my chest expand. I couldn't describe it except that when I looked in Thea's eyes, or held her, or kissed her, or listened to her talk, it grew bigger. Sunk in deeper. Embedded itself into the marrow of my bones, and yet I was fucking petrified it would crumble and vanish.

We passed by a tattoo shop and Thea slowed to peer in the window. "I always wanted a tattoo but as an art student, I had too many design options floating in my head. Want to check it out?"

"Sure."

We went inside the dark, cool confines of the small shop. Art on every wall and R-rated music blasting from the sound system. A guy bent over a woman facedown on his table, inking a design on her calf. Another guy stepped out from the back—thin with tattoos over every inch of skin visible but for his face. The butterfly on the side of his shaved head looked newly inked—darker than the other tattoos.

"Can I help you?" he asked in an almost gentle voice. His eyes were quiet and calm in the middle of the noise and color in his skin.

"I think we're just looking." Thea glanced up at me. "Or... are we?"

"Get one if you want one." I looked to the guy. "She likes to pretend I can stop her from doing anything."

"Ha ha." Thea elbowed me. "I think I do want something. To commemorate this trip to New York."

"Cool," the tattooist asked. "You want to look at some books? Get some ideas?"

"Absolutely," Thea said and offered her hand. "I'm Thea."

"Nicholas."

"Nice to meet you, Nicholas." They shook hands and Thea opened a book of flash tattoos on the counter in front of her. "How about you, Jimmy? We could get matching tattoos." She laughed. "We could get each other's names, thereby guaranteeing we'll be broken up by the end of the week."

"Sure," I said.

"Yeah right," Thea murmured above the flash book.

"Let's do it."

Her head whipped up. "Are you serious?"

"I don't recommend getting each other's names," Nicholas put in, in his quiet voice.

"Not names but definitely something for this week."

"Something that's us," Thea said. She turned to Nicholas. "Any suggestions?"

"For a couple?" Nicholas crossed his lean, tatted arms. "Anchor and compass. Lock and key. His and her crowns."

"You sound like you've done those a hundred times," Thea said.

He smiled. "You could say that."

"Give us a moment, please." She took me to the corner of the waiting area. "What do you think?"

Her eyes were impossibly blue and so full of light, she was nearly blinding. What did I think?

I think we promised to take care of each other.

I think we agreed to move in together.

I think we jokingly-but-not-really talked about getting married.

I thought about our plan to move to Richmond together and the foreign, still-nameless feeling surged in my heart. I wanted that feeling to be permanent, like ink in the skin.

"A lot has happened in a few days," I said. "And I don't mean sightseeing or oysters."

She nodded, suddenly shy again. "I think so too. A lot has happened... between us."

"Yeah, it has," I said. "This week feels like a promise we're making to each other. For the future. That's what I want to commemorate."

She nodded and kissed me softly. "I do too."

We took turns sitting with Nicholas. In his unique, cursive handwriting, Nicholas inked my promise to Thea down the side of her right forearm, above the seam of her scar, *Keep me safe.*

Then down my forearm, Nicholas inked Thea's promise: *Keep me wild.*

We held our arms together for Nicholas to take photos with Thea's phone. "Delia's going to shit her pants," Thea said. "I can't wait."

Nicholas covered the tattoos in plastic and gave us care instructions. After we paid, Thea gave him a hug.

"I hope you don't mind," she said, "but I can't help it. A hundred tattoo shops in New York but we came to you."

"I don't mind," Nicholas said. "Usually I cringe when couples come in for something matching. But you two..." He shrugged, smiling. "I'm not worried."

We continued down the street, wordlessly, hand in hand, Thea's promise to me buzzing on my skin. In front of a small bistro, a waitress was on her knees at a chalkboard, erasing it with frustrated swipes. She sat back on her heels and put the back of her hand to her mouth.

"Hey, you okay?" Thea asked, gently.

"Oh, sorry. I'm fine," she said. "No, actually, I'm not fine. This is my first day on the job and my boss wants me to make the specials board and I have, like, the *worst* handwriting ever. I'm going to get fired, because if I can't even do this...?"

Thea took the written menu from the sidewalk. "This is what needs to be on here?"

"Yeah, but it needs to be 'pretty' and 'eye-catching' and I can barely make it legible."

"I can help," Thea said. "We're on vacation here and I haven't painted or drawn something in days. I'm about ready to burst."

The waitress sniffed and looked up at me, then back to Thea. "No, you're on vacation. You don't need to waste your time on this. I'll... figure it out."

"We have time." Thea looked up at me. "Don't we, Jimmy?"

"You're asking me?" I said with a laugh. "Do your thing, baby."

Thea cocked a brow but her cheeks went pink. "Baby, eh?" She leaned into the waitress. "We're having a big week," she said in confidential tones. Then she clapped her hands together. "Okay, gimme that chalk, and I'll whip something up for you."

The waitress—her name was Paula—and I watched as Thea used the colored chalks to write up the restaurant specials in that same precise handwriting she'd used to make her word chains. She framed it with pink and blue flowers bursting from the corners and green vines that curled and trailed down the sides.

"Holy shit, that's beautiful," Paula said. "You've even added shading. And depth. With *chalk*. Amazing. But... hell, they're going to want me to do this every week."

"Tell them it was a one-time deal. But you can erase the specials as they change and leave the flowers."

"Thank you," Paula said, hugging her. "Thank you so much. You saved my ass."

"Thank *you*," she said to Paula. "That should hold me for the rest of the trip."

Thea wiped her chalky hands on her shorts, promptly covering them in pink and green, and we continued down the street.

After a minute, Thea glanced up at me. "Baby?"

"If you don't like it, I won't use it," I said. "It just slipped out."

"I like it," Thea said. "I went warm all over when you said it. It makes me feel taken care of. Like I'm still myself, but I'm yours too."

"You are yourself," I said, pulling her to me. "You are always one hundred percent yourself. I could see it from the moment I met you in front of that painting. It's what I..." I stopped, that nameless feeling starting to become not-so-nameless. "It's what attracted me to you most."

"You and your perfect words." Thea sighed.

Her eyes fell shut as she leaned in to kiss me, soft and sweet, then reached for her backpack.

"What are you doing?"

"I'm calling Jonathan."

"Reporting back already?" I asked and slung my arm around her neck as we kept walking. "How'd I do?"

Thea grinned. "A-plus, baby."

CHAPTER 32

Jim

We found a little dive bar near the tattoo shop and took a small booth in the back. Loud rock music filled the small, dark space, blaring from speakers tucked in the corners.

"I just sent Delia the pic Nicholas took of our ink," Thea said. "I'm trying not to be in-your-face about it, but she's always hated tattoos."

"Too late now," I said, trying not to be smug myself. I nodded toward the bar. "Drink?"

"White Russian, please," Thea said with a grin. "It's been a while."

I went to the bar, ordered the cocktail for Thea and a beer for myself. When I returned, Thea had her phone pressed to her ear, a finger plugging her other, and a look on her face I didn't like.

Damn you, Delia, I thought, sliding back into the booth. *Leave her alone. Let her be happy.*

"What?" Thea shouted. "I can't… I can hardly hear you." She listened for a few seconds more, her brows furrowed. Then her eyes widened and her lips parted. "You're lying. You're…" She glanced at me furtively.

"What?" I asked, every nerve-ending in my body lit up. "What's she saying?"

Thea huffed a sigh and rolled her eyes. "I can't hear anything. Hold on." She covered her phone with her hand and said to me, "It's too loud in here. I'm going outside to let Delia bitch at me for a minute about the tattoos. I'll be right back."

"Thea…"

But she scooted out of the booth and out of the bar, her back straight and stiff.

I tugged at the label on my beer bottle watching the door. I couldn't see Thea, so I started a mental timer. Fifteen minutes. That was our agreement.

Thea returned just as I was ready to go find her. She speed-walked through the bar and slid into the booth breathlessly. Her eyes were bright and glassy.

"My sister, I swear…" She took a long pull from her White Russian, nearly draining it.

"What did she want?"

"Nothing," she said. "She's pissed about the tattoos. I knew she'd freak out."

"That's it?"

"That's it."

"I'm not about to be arrested, am I?"

She let out a short, loud laugh. "No, no, nothing like that. Just Delia being her Delia-self." She finished her drink and clanked the glass down. "Oh my God, I think I've got that post-tattoo endorphin rush they tell you about. Are you done with your beer? Let's blow this joint. We got more New York-ing to do."

She was already sliding back out of the booth but I caught her hand.

"Hey. Are you okay? What did Delia say to you?"

"It's nothing, I swear. Just… stuff about our parents. She's trying to make me feel guilty."

My phone rang from the inner pocket of my leather jacket. I fished it out. "It's her."

"Don't answer it." Thea's eyes were hard and intense; a look I'd never seen her wear before. "She wants to ruin this. Don't let her. Please."

The phone's ringing seemed loud even under the thrashing music.

Thea's gaze never wavered from mine. "I want this time with you,

Jimmy. I'm not ready to give it up."

Neither am I.

I shut off the phone and put it back in my pocket. "Just until tomorrow morning," I said. "Then we touch base enough to let her know you're okay. Like usual."

Thea's tight, tense expression broke up into a radiant smile. "Absolutely. I thought of where I want to go next," she said, practically vibrating in her seat. "To a club. Dancing. I need a fix of my techno-slash-EDM music."

I watched her for a moment, studying her.

Something is wrong. She looked almost terrified...

The thought floated in and out. I caught sight of her new tattoo.

Keep me safe.

It was my vow and it included keeping her happiness safe. Protecting her from Delia's attempts to tear it down.

"Okay," I said. "Let's hit it."

We took an Uber to a Korean barbecue restaurant on West 50th Street, near the piers on the Hudson. We ate a quick dinner, then crossed the street toward a massive, five-story dance club called FREQ.

"Night clubs aren't really your thing, are they?" Thea asked.

"Not so much," I said. "But I'll survive."

"You're so good to me," she said, sudden tears in her eyes. All during dinner she'd been on the edge of her seat, jumping at every noise. One second seeming on the verge of tears, then bursting out laughing.

"What's wrong," I asked.

She wiped her eyes. "Nothing, I'm just so... happy with you. And this trip has been so amazing. I hate that it's ending. I need to celebrate everything tonight. I need to dance. And drink. And then dance some more."

"Wait," I said, taking her hand. "Can you mix alcohol with Hazarin? I didn't think to ask in the bar, but are there side effects?"

"Oh, definitely not. Says so right on the label."

An itchy feeling came over me at her wild energy, along with the sudden urge to get her back to the hotel and...

And what? Watch TV? She wants to be out in the world, having a good time. Keeping it wild.

It was inked right into my skin—her promise to me. To stop holding back and second-guessing everything.

"You sure?" I said. "Swear to me there's no warning about alcohol on that label."

Thea turned to meet my gaze head on. "I swear there is no alcohol warning on that label. Why the hell would I jeopardize my memory?" A sudden smile twitched the corners of her mouth. "Don't worry, when we stumble back into the hotel tonight, I'll show you."

"It'll be too late by then," I said.

"Then you'll just have to trust me, Jimmy."

She was smiling but her eyes held the challenge. *Do you trust me to know what I want when no one has in years?*

"I trust you," I said.

Her shoulders relaxed and her gaze softened. "Thank you," she said, easing a breath. "Now let's have some serious fun."

We joined the line snaking around the corner of the club. Since it was relatively early, it moved fast. Once inside, Thea went straight to the bar and grabbed us two stools on the corner.

"We need shots," she declared. "Tequila."

"You haven't been drunk in more than two years," I reminded her. "Your tolerance is going to be shit."

"Which is why I'll only need one shot," she said with a grin. "Or two. Or three."

"Two, max," I said.

Her eyes flashed. "Are you telling me what to do now, too?"

"Babe, you weigh about a hundred pounds. I don't want you to get alcohol poisoning."

She smirked. "I weigh a lot more than a hundred pounds." She silenced my protest with a kiss. "Thank you for keeping me safe, but I can take care of myself too. I'll drink lots of water." Thea called to the bartender, "Tequila shots, sir."

"That's how you do it, honey," said a woman from the mixed group of young people next to us.

"Right?" Thea said. "If you're going to party, then par-tay."

Soon enough, Thea *was* the party. She had the bartender line up shots not only for us but our neighbors at the bar. I hesitated before taking mine.

"I'm keeping you wild, Jimmy," Thea said. "Don't give up on me."

I cocked my head at her choice of words, but in the end, she wanted this night, and I wanted to give it to her. We knocked back the shots in unison. The tequila went down smooth and I was suddenly hot all over. The dance music thumped so loudly, I could feel it in my pulse.

Another shot followed the first, and I tried to keep track, to make sure Thea wasn't overdoing it. Hell, *I* needed not to overdo it. But she slammed back a glass of water and then tugged on my hand.

"Come dance."

I shook my head. "I don't dance. It's just not in my DNA."

She pouted, then bounded off with her new friends. She danced with abandon, laughing, her eyes lit up and a thin sheen of sweat glistened over her skin.

More drinks followed, and the alcohol did what alcohol does—make bad shit feel a million miles away and consequences even further. I lost track of how many drinks were pressed on me while trying to keep track of Thea's. But as promised, she had a water glass in her hand more often than a cocktail and I relaxed. The enormous space was a pulsing box of light and sound. People talking, bodies dancing, flashing lights, and the pounding beat of one song after another.

The night began to break into pieces and time became a nebulous thing, stretching out and contracting. I felt as if I were underwater. Thea swam up like a mermaid with her long hair loose and flowing.

"Hey, baby." She put her arms around my neck and kissed me wetly, tasting of some sweet cocktail I couldn't remember her ordering.

Maybe it's the same as the one in your hand.

I looked down. A mai tai? The fuck. I didn't drink mai tais.

"I have to piss," I slurred. "Watch our stuff?"

"Anything for you," she said and plopped heavily onto one of the stools.

I slipped out of my jacket—why the fuck was I still wearing it? It was hot as hell in here. I stumbled through a morass of people to the bathroom and took a piss—mostly hitting the target. I washed my hands and peered blearily at the reflection in the mirror. There were two of me and I had to squint one eye to focus.

Time to call it.

I somehow found my way back through the crowd to Thea. "I'm drunk," I stated.

"Me too," she said, but her eyes looked clear. Or maybe it was the shifting lights.

"Let's go," I said.

A shadow seemed to cross her face before she smiled tipsily at me.

"One more dance," she shouted in my ear. "Please, Jimmy," she said. Begged. "I don't want this night to end."

"Thea…" But she was already gone, dancing to a song I put on my phone for her at Blue Ridge, a million years and a lifetime ago. "BOOM" by the Ambassadors. No, that wasn't right. There was an X in it. The X-Men. I chuckled then peered around for Thea.

She was a mirage of blue and gold on the dance floor that was full of dark, writhing bodies. Demons moving around her, intent on swallowing her up. I was drunk as shit but the fear found me anyway.

Something's not right and you're too wasted to figure it out, ya jackass.

What was wrong? I couldn't put my finger on it, my thoughts were drowning in booze. I dragged my jacket back on and batted at the pockets to make sure my wallet and phone were still there.

Wallet, yes. Phone was missing.

"Shit." I blearily searched the bar and the floor, nearly falling off the damn stool.

Thea returned.

"My phone is gone," I said.

"What?" she shouted. "I can't hear you."

"My phone…"

She kissed me hard. Sloppily. "I want to go now. Be alone with you."

"But my phone…"

She pressed her body to me, her breasts pushing out of her tank top. Her lips brushed my ear. "I need you to fuck me, Jimmy. Take me back to the hotel and fuck me hard."

"Sounds good," I mumbled. "Let's do that."

We stumbled into the street and into a cab. In the backseat, Thea was all over me. Wet kisses and groping hands that stroked my erection through my jeans. My ears were ringing after the loud of the club. I tried to kiss her back, but my hands kept sliding off her. At the hotel, I passed the driver some money and we pulled ourselves together to stagger past the front desk. In the elevator, Thea reached for me again, almost desperately. I could hardly stand.

Jesus, how much did I drink?

In our room, I made it to the bed and fell on my back. The room spun.

"I need you, Jimmy," Thea whispered, stretched out beside me, pleading. "I need you so bad."

"Wait…" I said, throwing my arm over my eyes. "I just need a minute. Fuck, I'm so wasted."

"Me too," Thea said, but her voice came from far away. "I'll get you some water."

"Yeah…" I said, and then the bed sucked me down, into oblivion.

When I opened my eyes again, the room was dark. No lights. My ears felt stuffed with cotton and my body weighed a thousand pounds. I reached my hand out, found empty bed. A soft sound near the window, like crying…

I got too drunk. I'm still too drunk.

I slipped back under.

When I came around again, the sun was slanting over my eyes, lancing straight into my brain. I lay on the bed in the exact same position I'd been last night. Completely clothed, down to my boots and jacket.

I muttered the morning-after declaration made by every single hungover person everywhere. "I am never drinking again."

The room was quiet. Empty. Thea was nowhere in sight. I sat up—too quickly—and nearly puked. Pain gripped my head in a vise.

"Thea?"

The bathroom door was wide open, as if bragging about how there was no Thea in it.

"Oh fuck."

My heart slammed against my chest, and then I did have to puke. I just made it to the bathroom, my head pounding with the strain of heaving, but I needed to sober the hell up and find her.

Jesus Christ, what happened last night?

My memory coughed up a mish-mash of scenes from the club— Thea dancing, shouted conversations, noise and light and too much damn alcohol.

How long have I been passed out on the goddamn bed? How long has she been out there, alone? God knows what happened to her…

The possibilities made me want to puke all over again.

You broke your promise. You promised to keep her safe. It's inked on her goddamn skin, and for what?

"N-N-Nothing."

My frantic gaze darted to the clock that showed a little after seven. A note sat beside it, folded in half, my name handwritten on it. I snatched it with shaking hands and devoured every line.

Jimmy,

Went for our morning coffee. (I think you're going to need it.) Be back in fifteen

xoxo

Thea

"Holy f-f-fucking shit." I sank on the bed, relief washing through me like a tidal wave. I let out a long, shaking breath, then sucked it back in to curse at myself. I was lucky. A second chance. She asked me to trust her. I should have trusted her.

I shivered in the room's air-conditioning. I'd broken out in a cold sweat that stunk of stale booze and fear. I stripped out of my clothes to take a fast shower, figuring Thea would be back by the time I got out.

She wasn't.

I stood in the silence of the room, a towel around my waist. Now the clock read 7:22 a.m. Fear started to creep back under my skin, and I reminded myself Thea wasn't the helpless person she'd been at Blue Ridge.

Call her. No big deal.

I dug in my jacket for my cell phone. Not there. Not in my jeans, either. A sliver of memory found me from last night. It'd gone missing at the bar.

Thea's backpack was at the foot of the bed.

Leave it. She'll be back soon. Trust her.

More memory flashes from last night. Thea's eyes alit with a euphoria that bordered on fear. The strange phone call with Delia. Crying in the middle of the night.

I clutched the towel around my waist and kneeled to dig through her bag. I found my phone at the bottom, shut off completely. I sat on the bed and powered it back up. Dozens of text messages popped up along with notifications of another dozen missed calls. Most from Delia, but also Rita, Alonzo, and Dr. Chen.

"What the fuck…?"

My heart stopped beating and then took off at a gallop. With shaking hands, I opened the string of text messages from Delia and read them one after another.

"N-N-No…"

I couldn't believe my eyes. Delia was fucking with me. Trying to ruin everything…

You're lying, Thea said during the call at the bar. Because she knew then. Delia told her and then Thea lied to me.

"*No,*" I barked. "This is b-b-bullshit."

Rage fueled by terror burned hot and fast. Delia *was* lying. She was a fucking liar and a thief trying to steal Thea from me.

And she somehow wrangled the Blue Ridge staff to go along with it?

My hand trembled as I hit the button on the first voicemail out of twenty, holding the phone to my ear as if it were a poisonous snake.

I listened to all of Delia's messages, which alternated between tearful begging and angry fear. Then the voicemails from Dr. Chen, cool and professional but laced with urgency. From Alonzo, his voice heavy with pain. And Rita. Fuck, Rita cried her message, and I nearly did too.

The phone fell slack in my hand. The blood drained from my face; the rage draining with it, leaving only the terror.

And a silent, empty room.

CHAPTER 33

Jim

The key slid into the door and Thea came in, balancing a tray of two coffees with cream and sugar packets piled between them.

"Oh, you're up," she said, then froze when she saw the phone in my hand.

God, she was so beautiful and alive and *right here.* And it was all going to end.

"I should've thrown both phones away," she whispered. "Or smashed them."

"And then what?" I asked. "Keep me drunk every night? Was that your plan?"

She stared back at me, defiant. "Maybe."

"You didn't smash the phones because you know what we have to do."

She moved quickly across the room to set the tray on the table by the window. "I don't have to do anything but go out into this amazing city and live my life."

I squeezed my eyes shut, mustering the will to try to survive this. "No, Thea."

She stiffened, her back to me, then slowly turned, arms crossed. "Delia called you?" Her voice struggled to stay strong and casual. "So what? Whatever she said, she's lying. She hates you so she's trying to ruin us."

"Dr. Chen called me too."

Thea flinched and my goddamn heart cracked.

"Seven of Dr. Milton's ten trial patients have had strokes," I said, hating every goddamn word. "Of those seven, two are nearly completely paralyzed, three are in a coma, and two are—"

"Stop," Thea said, hugging herself.

I swallowed the word down. "We have to go back."

"No."

"A stroke is not reversible, Thea. There is no medication for that."

"I'll take my chances."

"And if it kills you?" I cried. "The other two patients *died*. But if you stop taking the Hazarin now, there's a chance—"

"No. I'm not going back. I have time. I have a month's supply—"

"And then what? They won't give you more."

She won't make it a month.

Terror bloomed bright and glassy in Thea's eyes. "I'll worry about that later. I'm not giving up my time. I'm not. I won't."

"You can't take the Hazarin," I said, low and controlled. "It might kill you—"

"I don't care."

"I care!" The words reverberated around the room. "I f-f-fucking care."

We stared each other down, then her gaze darted to the bathroom where the Hazarin bottle sat beside the sink. As if a starting gun to a race went off, we took off for the bathroom at the same time. I was faster. I blocked the bathroom door and grabbed the meds off the sink.

"Give them to me," Thea said, pounding at my back. I turned, and she reached for the pills, grabbing at my arm. "Goddammit, Jim, give them…"

I held them in a vise grip and gently but firmly held her at arm's length. She tore out of my grasp and put her hand out, fingers trembling.

"Give them back."

"No."

A FIVE-MINUTE LIFE

"Jimmy, I swear to God…"

"What happens next, Thea?" I demanded, stalking out of the bathroom, forcing her to back up. "You keep taking it, and then what?"

"I have time. I get to live," she cried.

"Shit, Thea." I carved my hand through my hair. "We knew this was a risk—"

"Fuck you," she screamed and gave a rough shove to my chest. "Fuck you for saying that after everything we've had this week. After this time I've had, free from that prison."

"You're right," I said. "I'm sorry, but Jesus, Thea…"

"You have no idea what you're asking me to do."

"Neither do you," I cried, the frustration and anger raging back. "What are we going to do, Thea? Go *sight-seeing*? Be fucking *tourists*? Maybe let you get me wasted again so we can pretend everything is okay when it could explode at any fucking second?"

"Shut up." She shook her head, tears spilled over her eyes. "Just shut *up*."

"How about we go to the top of the Empire State Building so I can watch you collapse in my arms and die?"

"Shut up, Jimmy! Don't ruin my Empire State… Don't do this…"

The anger bled out of me, deepening into agony. "They'll make more medicine. Better medicine. They'll try again."

"No." She paced a small, frustrated circle in the center of the room. "No… No, I can't."

"And I can't watch you—"

"Watch me what? Fade away? Forget you? Go back to sleep? Five minutes, Jimmy," she cried, splaying her fingers out. "I get five minutes and nothing else. It's like living in a tiny little box and as soon as I start to climb out, I fall back in again. Except it's not even that clear. That would be *consciousness*. I don't have the luxury of consciousness. You're afraid of me dying? Without the meds, Jimmy…" She took a watery breath. "I'm already dead."

I shook my head slowly, my vision blurring. Emotions I'd never experienced swamped me. I could barely swallow them down.

She's not yours. She never was. Doris sneered. *You don't get to cry…*

"No…" I murmured, not knowing who I was answering.

"Yes," Thea cried. "I get a few minutes to build a life and then it's

267

torn down again, over and over. I can't begin to describe what a fucking nightmare it is. I already tried. I told you in those word chains. I *screamed* at you from those drawings."

I clenched my jaw. "I know."

"You don't know. I smiled and was so goddamn cheerful all the time, right? That's because all I had was a pitiful little flicker of hope. Hope for the things I knew were true: Mom and Dad were coming, and the doctors were working on my case. They were going to help me. That's all I had. For *two years*. Only Mom and Dad weren't coming, and the doctors had given up. Delia was going to let me rot in that prison."

"Not this time," I said. "Dr. Milton came close. He'll try again…"

"And how long will that take? Two more years? Two more years of me waking up again and again. Mid-shower. Chewing a bite of food." Her voice broke. "Or looking into your eyes and having the faintest suspicion that somewhere down deep, we mean something to each other. Like an itch I can never scratch. Not even an itch. An echo of a dream of an itch. A feeling I might've had once, but I can't grasp it. Can't *feel* it. I can't feel anything. Can you imagine having thoughts or feelings that only last long enough to know you don't get to keep them?" She shook her head, her body trembling. "I won't go back to that life. I'd rather die in your arms at the top of the Empire State Building."

The words hung in the air between us. The ground beneath my feet broke apart. Shattered. Everything we built was being ruined, along with everything we were going to build. All our future plans.

"You'll remember us," I said, faltering, grasping. "Like the music and your painting, you'll remember."

She shook her head, tears falling. "No," she whispered. "It's too hard."

"Don't give up on me, Thea," I said, moving toward her. "Isn't that what you asked me? N-N-Not to give up on you?"

"I know but… I can't, Jimmy."

I was in front of her now, reaching for her.

"I can't," she whispered.

"You can." I put my arms around her, my hand not holding the pill bottle slid into her hair. "God, Thea…"

She sank against me, her tears hot on my bare skin. She let me hold her for a few moments and then stiffened in my arms and shook her head.

"No. No, I won't do it. I won't go back into that tomb." She pushed me away and held out her hand again. "Give me the bottle, Jimmy."

"Jesus Christ."

"Please," she begged, her face crumpling. "Don't do this to me."

I hardened my heart against her pleas. The image of her convulsing, or falling to the ground, not breathing, eyes staring…

"It's not up to you," she said, reading my expression, her voice hardening too. "It's my choice. Mine."

"Thea…"

"You made such a huge deal about my choices and my consent and now you want to take it all back."

"This isn't consent."

"Isn't it? It's my life. Give me the bottle, James."

I couldn't do it. I couldn't hand over the poison and watch her swallow it down every morning until there were no mornings left.

Thea made a grab for it, but I snatched my hand away and blinked, momentarily confused as she grabbed her backpack at our feet instead.

"What are you doing?" I said. "Wait…"

She raced for the door, and I followed two steps behind. She wrenched it open and looked back, her voice breaking my heart. "Goodbye, Jimmy. I still have New York-ing to do."

Her hand whipped out suddenly. Again, I snatched the meds out of reach, but she'd gone for the towel on my waist instead, ripping it off and flinging it away.

"Fuck…"

I lunged as she slipped out and the heavy door clocked my elbow. Now pain piled on the rage and grief and terror. I slammed the door open with a ragged cry, but Thea was already halfway down the hallway and heading for the staircase. I'd never catch her. Wouldn't make it past the front desk bare-assed naked if I tried.

"*Fuck*," I raged and slammed the door shut, shaking the room. I hurled the bottle of Hazarin at the wall. It bounced off and rolled on the floor, whole and unfazed.

I yanked my clothes on, my shaking fingers tripping over buttons and tugging on boots that wouldn't fucking cooperate. Adrenaline surged in my veins as I jabbed the elevator buttons. Thea had sixteen flights to take on foot. I could make it. I could catch her.

"Come on," I seethed, jabbing the button again and again. Finally, it arrived and made an agonizingly slow journey down to the lobby. I spat another curse as it stopped on the tenth floor to let a guy on.

He took one look at my face and stepped back. "I'll get the next one."

In the lobby, my eyes darted around, begging for signs of Thea. I raced to the stairwell and threw open the door, hoping to hear her footsteps echoing down stairs. But for my shaking breaths, there was silence.

"Did a blond woman come past here?" I asked the guy at the front desk.

"I don't know, sir," he said, maddeningly calm. "Lots of people come past here."

I ran out the front door, searching up and down the sidewalks, across the street. No sign of Thea.

Back into the lobby, I watched the elevators and the stairwell. Minutes ticked by. Elevators opened and people got off. None of them Thea.

She's gone. You lost her. You failed. You don't get to cry...

I sank onto a chair in the hotel lobby, my head in my hands. It was too much. I felt too much. For Thea. For everything. Years and years of numbed feelings started to break free and well up in me; tried to spill over dams, break through walls. A deluge I was going to drown in if I didn't keep it back. But I was so goddamned tired of trying.

My shoulders rounded, my stomach clenched.

You don't get to cry. Not ever...

CHAPTER 34

Thea

I walked fast, keeping my head down to shield my crying eyes from passersby. With no plan or guide, I turned down one random street or another. They all looked the same now. The magic was seeping out of the city.

I glanced over my shoulder again and again, hoping Jimmy wasn't following me. Praying he was.

I sagged against a wall, pain flooding me until I could hardly see or breathe. I cried inside-out, sobbing until my stomach ached.

A woman passing by put her hand on my shoulder. "Tough day, honey?"

I nodded and forced a smile, wanting to collapse into her arms. "I'll be okay, thanks."

She gave me a final pat and moved on. I wiped my eyes and breathed until the tightness in my stomach loosened.

"What do I do now?"

Go back to Jimmy.

I'd run from sheer terror, not knowing what to do but to get away from the terrible reality, now that Jimmy knew. It hadn't felt real until he knew. My heart ached to be with him, but he'd make me go back to Blue Ridge. He promised to keep me safe. It was inked in my skin forever.

I can't go back.

My soul recoiled at the idea of returning to that airless, vast desert that was as wide as eternity and as small as a pin. But death—real, or the death of the amnesia—awaited me and I had to choose one.

Not yet.

I wandered into Central Park and sat on a bench.

I sat for hours, remembering. I recalled my entire life. As far back as I could go and all the way up to the accident, where memory leap-frogged from sudden blackness into the murky nightmare of two years at Blue Ridge. It arrived at the moment I woke up and took me through every moment since, in all their clarity and joy.

How could I go back?

Several times, I tried to muster the energy to get up and see another little piece of New York, but I stayed on that bench until morning gave way to afternoon. My stomach growled. My bladder complained.

I found a Starbucks and bought a doughnut. I threw it away after three bites. I used the restroom, then wandered like a sleepwalker. The pure joy and happiness of being here with Jimmy had been a fleeting dream, and my life in amnesia was the merciless reality, waiting for me to wake up.

I wandered until I looked up to see the monolith that towered over me. Some internal compass brought me to the Empire State Building at twilight. The sun's light was gold and turning to amber. The sky so blue it seemed like a piece of colored paper stretched above me.

I stepped inside the cool confines of the lobby and paid the admission to the Observation Deck. Along with a handful of tourists, I boarded an elevator that shot straight up to the eighty-sixth floor, making everyone's ears pop. The doors opened on the deck and the city lay spread beneath me.

An overwhelming tide of grief washed over me. This view was supposed to be the culmination of my dream and it was crumbling to ash with every breath I took. Every beat of my heart. Seconds ticking down to an oblivion of my choosing.

I gripped the railing as I stepped out of the center of the building and

272

went down to the ledge. A fence tipped with tall, menacing claws curved over the top to keep people from climbing up. Or jumping.

I pressed my face to the crisscrossing bars and stared out over Manhattan, shivering. It was cooler up here. Tears sprung to my eyes in frustration that I was too cold to have these last quiet moments in stillness. I had to keep moving.

I walked around the perimeter of the Observation Deck, arms crossed, hugging myself.

I rounded the corner and Jimmy was there.

He stood with his hands tucked into his jacket pockets, leaning against one curved corner of the deck and looking away from me. He was so ruggedly beautiful against the skyline, his eyes shadowed and his stubble dark. A strange warmth flooded through me and it took me a second to realize I was happy. Overjoyed. Brimming with it. Because of him.

I raised my fingers to make a pretend camera, and he looked over as I pressed the imaginary shutter.

I lowered my hands. "Hi."

He stood up straight, pulled his hands from his pockets as I crossed the distance between us.

"What were you doing just now?" he asked.

"On *The Office,* Pam told her Jim to take mental pictures of the best moments," I said, my voice already breaking. "Because everything goes by so fast."

Wordlessly, Jim wrapped me in his arms and enveloped me in his strong arms. He kissed my forehead, then pressed his cheek to mine while I gripped the lapels of his jacket with both hands, my face buried in his neck, safe in the warm darkness there.

"How long have you been here?"

"All day," he said gruffly.

"You've been waiting here for me all day?"

"I knew you'd come."

He kissed my temple, my cheek, and my lips before pulling away. His eyes were bloodshot and shadowed, the threat of tears in their brown depths. He reached into his jacket pocket and pulled out the bottle of Hazarin.

"This is yours," he said, pressing it into my hand.

I stared at the bottle, then at him. "You won't stop me from taking it?"

He shook his head, though it looked as if it cost him everything to do it. "It's your choice."

I smiled through my tears. "Not much of one, is it?"

"The fucking worst."

My eyes spilled over. "I'm so grateful for the time we had. When I saw you up here, waiting for me... It hit me how happy I've been with you."

"Me too, Thea," he said. "The best time."

I took his hand and put the bottle in his palm, curled his fingers around it. "I won't give up."

Jim made a sound deep in his chest and hauled me into his embrace. His sigh of relief expanded under my head and then turned into a ragged exhale.

"I hate this," he said, muffled. "I hate that I'm relieved you have to go back to that hell." He held me close, kissing my forehead, then his hands slipped to my cheeks, to hold my face. Tears shone in his eyes but he fought them back. "You're so brave," he whispered. "You're so fucking brave."

"I'm scared."

"I know. I'm going to be with you every day. Every day, Thea."

I shook my head. "I can't think about that right now. Not yet. I took the medication this morning. We still have tonight, at least. Let me have that before..."

Before I go away again.

He nodded, his thumbs brushing the tears that streamed down my cheeks.

"What do you want to do? Anything you want. Name it."

"I want to watch the sunset up here," I said. "I want to eat Italian food at a place that's dark and has little candles on the table. And I want you to sing for me. Will you do that?"

"Yeah, Thea," he said, hoarse and raw. "I will." He held up the pill bottle. "And these?"

I closed my eyes, inhaled deep. I breathed a prayer to those who came before me in Dr. Milton's study. Those who suffered and died so that I could make the right choice.

A FIVE-MINUTE LIFE

Please let it be the right choice.

I opened my eyes. "Throw them away."

Jimmy nodded and did as I asked, then came back to me. He slipped out of his jacket and wrapped it around my shoulders, then put his arms around me again, my back to his front, his chin resting on my shoulder. I held his arms and tried to capture the feel of him, his breath on my cheek and his strong body shielding me. Embedding his molecules into me. Indelible and unforgettable.

The sunset's last rays spilled between New York's buildings and the sky became bruised and beautiful.

I turned in Jimmy's arms and let my eyes fall closed. Inhale. Exhale. "I'm ready."

CHAPTER 35

Thea

We went back to the hotel so I could shower and change.

"What about Delia?" Jimmy asked.

"I can't talk to her yet," I said. "Would you mind calling her?"

"What do I tell her?"

"Tell her I took the meds today, but I won't take any more. We're going to have one more night here and head back tomorrow."

"Anything else?"

"No," I said. "Not yet."

I had plenty to say to my sister, but tonight was for Jimmy and me.

I showered and pulled on the pretty white sundress I bought with Rita at the mall. It was wrinkled from being smashed in the bottom of my backpack, but I'd hung it up in the bathroom when we checked in so the steam from our showers could smooth it.

"What do you think?" I asked.

Jim sat at the foot of the bed, phone in hand. His heavy gaze swept over me. "You're beautiful."

"I bought it for you. I told Rita I wanted to put it on just so you could rip it off me."

"Oh yeah?"

"She didn't tell you? Good. She kept the girl code."

Jimmy's smile faded. I stood between his knees and brushed my fingers through his hair. "We have tonight," I said. "So, let's really have it, okay?"

He nodded, and I kissed him softly, then headed back to the bathroom mirror to finish getting ready. "You talked to my sister?"

"She wants you back now. Even offered to pay for a flight."

"What did you tell her?"

"Thanks, but no thanks. She'll see you soon enough."

"Good answer."

I put on a little mascara and perfume and brushed my hair until it fell in soft waves over my shoulders. Jimmy was darkly handsome in black.

"I'm in white, you're in black," I said. "Like yin and yang."

"The brightest light..." Jimmy murmured, almost to himself. He took my face in his hands and kissed me deeply. I felt the grief in it. The goodbye.

Not yet.

"Come on," I said, forcing a smile. "We have more New York-ing to do."

We took a cab to an Italian bistro on the Upper East Side that was dark and had little candles on every table. The hostess seated us, and we opened the menus silently.

What does one order for their last meal?

For Jimmy's sake, I bit back the bad joke. The reality of my situation was sinking into him too. His expression was that of a man in chronic pain but putting on a brave face.

"Hey," I said, reaching across the table to take his hand. "Stay with me."

His brows furrowed. "How are you so okay right now?"

"I don't know, honestly," I said. "I freaked out this morning. And I probably have more freaking out to do, but right now is what we have. I have you and I'm happy."

"You deserve more than a few days," he said, his teeth gritted. "It's fucking... cruel."

"These last few days have been the best of my life. I would've learned about the Hazarin side effects whether I stayed at Blue Ridge or not. And if I'd stayed, I'd be going back to prison with zero memory of the outside world. But I left. And now I have this time in New York with you to carry me through. I have something to hold on to."

He nodded and did his best to carry on through dinner as if a huge mountain weren't about to drop on my head. I felt its shadow over me— it was coming, and it was going to hurt. But tonight, I wouldn't let the fear touch me.

After dinner, we strolled down Second Avenue and came to a bar with live music pouring out its open windows. A flyer on the window said it was open mic night.

"Let's get a drink here and listen to some music," I said. "And no, this isn't me passive-aggressively hinting you should sing in front of all these people, I swear. That's later in the hotel."

As he gazed over the bar, Jimmy's expression was unreadable. "You made me the better, stronger version of myself." He nodded his chin at the crowd. "They should know that. You deserve for them to know that."

"Are you serious?" I asked. "You're going to sing in front of all those people?"

"Don't cry *yet*," he said. "Wait until I make a complete ass of myself."

I laughed and wiped my eyes. "That's not going to happen."

"We'll see."

Jimmy put his name on the list and asked the guy if they had a house guitar he could borrow; his instrument was back at the hotel. The guy said they did, and we took a table near the side of the small stage. He nursed a beer, and I had a glass of red wine. Men and women got up and sang to the bar's sound system or used their own instruments.

"Jim Whelan," the MC announced finally. "Come on up."

Jimmy drained the last of his beer and got to his feet.

"I'm more nervous than you are," I said.

"Must be, since I'm not nervous at all," he said. "This is what's supposed to happen. Isn't it?"

"Yes, I think so. All of it."

He nodded and kissed me, then took the stage to a smattering of applause. The MC handed him a scratched up acoustic guitar. Jimmy looped the strap over his shoulder and adjusted the mic as if he'd done this a hundred times.

"Hey," he said. "I'm Jim. This song is for Thea Hughes—she's sitting right over there. She's the reason I'm sitting *here*. She's the reason for everything good in my life."

My tears came again, and I blinked them away quickly, not wanting to miss a single second of my Jimmy onstage in front of a crowd of people. Commanding their attention, gripping it in the palm of his hand with his simple dignity and honesty.

"We've been in the city the past five days," Jimmy said, "because it's where Thea always wanted to be. And I'm honored to be here with her. Honored she chose me..." He stopped, cleared his throat, and looked directly to me. "Thank you for keeping me wild. I love you, Thea. I hope you had the time of your life."

He strummed his guitar and began singing Green Day's "Good Riddance, Time of Your Life." My heart beat in my chest, filled with the love of a thousand lifetimes all crammed into one, all for Jimmy. Every single lyric written for us. This trip and what was coming after. To make the best of everything and not ask why because there was no why. Only now.

The room went absolutely silent and still. No one clinked a glass or so much as coughed while Jimmy's low, rough voice accompanied his expert playing. He filled every lyric with the depth of our experiences, singing as if he'd written the song himself.

When the last note dissipated, the crowd seemed to be holding its breath. I held mine. Then the applause came, slow at first and growing louder. A few whistles pierced the air, and he smiled.

"Thanks," he said into the mic, and turned to me, mouthing, *Thank you.*

He returned to the table, and I took his face in my hands and kissed him. We clung to each other and the audience cheered again. No doubt we looked to them like a happy couple in love with our whole lives ahead of us.

"Jimmy..." I whispered as he held me.

"I know." He huffed a steadying breath. "But hey, you said if I sang for you, you'd be naked by the second verse." He shook his head. "You're not even remotely naked."

A teary laugh burst out of me. "I see what you did there."

"I'm just trying to get us out of here before I fucking fall apart," he said. He took my hand and pressed it to his lips. "Let's go."

We grabbed a cab back to the hotel. In our room, Jimmy hung his jacket on the back of the chair and then I was in his arms. The city glittered outside the window, a thousand lights strewn over the darkness.

"Tonight was perfect," I said between Jimmy's deep kisses. "I can't believe you sang in front of an audience like that."

"I was singing for you."

"You told me you loved me."

He pulled away, his eyes beautifully dark and full. "I do. I'm in love with you, Thea, and have been for a long time… I just didn't know what it was." He stroked my cheek. "You don't have to say it back. I don't expect—"

"I know you don't," I said. "James Whelan, you don't expect anything for yourself. You just give and give… I love you for that. I love you for everything. All of you. I'm so in love with you, Jimmy."

He froze as my words sunk in. A muscle in his jaw ticked. He inhaled a shaky breath. Exhaled slowly.

"No one's ever said that to you before, have they?" I asked.

He tilted his chin up. "No."

They don't know who they had, right in front of them.

He took my face in his hands. "Don't cry for me, Thea," he said gruffly. "It was supposed to be you who said it first."

I stared, flooded by love for this man. "Yes," I whispered. "That's right. I love you." I kissed his mouth and kept my lips on his. "I love you, Jimmy. I love you so much. My warrior who never stopped fighting for me."

"I won't," he said. "I never will. I swear it."

I heard the future in his voice—the inevitable time when I was going away again. Sitting right in front of him and yet not all there.

"Stay with me," he said. He kissed me harder. "You're mine. You'll always be mine. I'll take care of you. Keep you safe."

I surrendered to him. To his mouth that captured mine, his tongue that swept through every corner. His gentle sucking pull taking me out of my thoughts and into him. Losing myself in his hands that roamed my skin and his body that pressed against me, hard and full of need.

We kissed until I had to come up for air, clinging to him as his mouth worked down my neck, biting softly. Memorizing me. Indulging in me and giving me everything at the same time because we had no way to know how much time I had left.

"Every inch of you," he said, undoing the delicate little laces at the top of my dress. "I'm going to put my mouth on every last inch of you."

"Yes…"

I tugged his shirt off just as he lifted my dress and we came together again, not frantic but deep. Needy. His hands slipped down my shoulders, down my sides to my waist where he gently turned me around. He held me close, my back to the warm skin of his chest. His mouth went to my neck, between my shoulder blades, sending heated shivers dancing across my skin.

"Oh my God…" I gasped, arching back as he unclasped my bra and let it drop.

His hands reached around to cup my breasts, to pinch and tease the nipples while he gave open-mouthed kisses across my back. I reached behind to stroke the erection straining against his jeans but he dropped to his knees, his kisses blazing a trail down my spine. He turned me around to face him, fingertips toying at the edges of my panties while his eyes worshipped me with a hungry, reverent gaze. He pressed his lips to the center of me, over the panties, and I cried out as he tongued the silk and sucked. Teasing. Wet and hot but not enough.

"Jesus…"

"All of you," he growled and tugged my panties down and tossed them aside. "Every inch…"

I sucked in a breath as he put his mouth on me, delving in deep immediately, his tongue working until I was dizzy and my legs weak.

My breath came short. "I can't…"

Never breaking his hold on me with his mouth, he gripped my hips and eased me down on the bed. He pressed my thighs apart, and I cried out louder at the intense thrust of his tongue and the maddening brush of his short beard over my most sensitive flesh.

Senseless words and mindless sounds fell out of me as he took me higher and higher. Every muscle pulled taut, back arched, as I climbed. My hands made fists of the bedsheets as Jimmy plunged into me, sucked and licked and nipped until I crashed over. Wave after wave shuddering through me, wracking my body with an orgasm I felt everywhere and left me boneless and breathless. My limbs trembling with aftershocks.

God, Jimmy," I gasped. "What are you doing to me?"

I reached for his shoulders to pull him up, but he moved slowly, taking his time, dragging his tongue over my skin and then biting the delicate skin beneath my navel. Slowly, his mouth journeyed up my body, between my breasts. He was over me now, his jeans rubbing against my nakedness, raw and hard. The first orgasm throbbing between my legs. I tilted my hips for more, writhing, as he took one nipple in his mouth.

"Please." My hands scraped his shoulder blades. "Oh God…"

His mouth took my other nipple, bit it to the point of pain and then sucked the ache. Up higher, he ventured up my neck, my chin, and finally my mouth.

"Thea." He kissed me deep and slow, braced over me. His hands sunk into my hair. "You're beautiful. So fucking beautiful."

"So are you," I said. "We take care of each other. Always."

He nodded, and I pushed him off of me to climb on top of him. My nakedness against the rough denim of his jeans. I kissed him softly, letting my hair fall around us to tickle his bare chest. I moved down his body, kissing the warm skin and then took his small nipple in my teeth and sucked. Jimmy made a sound deep in his chest and his hand gripped my hair.

I was memorizing him too. Every taste of skin, every sound, every movement of his body under mine, I took and kept. Locked them all away somewhere deep. The way he looked at me, his voice when he said my name, the emotion in his words when he told me he loved me.

He stripped out of his clothes and rolled me to my back again, his body wonderfully heavy over mine. I memorized that too—the weight of him as he slid inside me. He began to move, and I moved with him, our eyes locked, our kisses slowing down. His hands never left my face, forearms braced, his dark eyes holding mine.

"Stay with me, Thea," he whispered. "Please. Stay."

"I'm here," I whispered back, as the pleasure grew between our joined bodies. "I'm right here, Jimmy."

For now. But now was all we ever had.

I clutched him as the wave crashed again. Jimmy shuddered in my arms, his release spilling into me just as mine tapered.

A FIVE-MINUTE LIFE

We lay entangled for a long time, wrapped tight in each other, neither of us willing to let go.

CHAPTER 36

Thea

We'd spent the night bringing one another to the heights of pleasure again and again in the dark, desperate to keep the thoughts out. Now the morning was here, and the sharp light of day slanted across the sheets. Jimmy stirred and woke as I disentangled myself from him and slipped out of bed. He blinked at the clock. 9:23 a.m. Two and a half hours past the time I was supposed to take the Hazarin.

"Where are you going?" he asked.

"For our morning coffee," I said and reached for my discarded underwear and bra.

He sat up, rubbed his eyes. "Hold up. I'll go with you."

"I'm fine," I said, pulling his T-shirt over my head. I wanted to take his scent with me. "I'll be back in fifteen."

"Thea…"

"It's our last morning in New York," I said.

And one of the last times I might be able to do something simple on my own, like make a coffee run.

"Take your phone," he said. "Where are you going? Across the street?"

"Yep. I'll be right back."

"Fifteen minutes."

I grinned. "And then you'll send the warships to come get me?"

He didn't smile. "I love you."

"I love you, too."

Don't say goodbye to me yet.

I blew him a kiss at the door and headed out.

The day was already muggy and stifling, the sunlight ridiculously bright. But I inhaled it all in and wondered how much time I had before the slow slide back into oblivion began.

"Cheery thought," I muttered as I waited at the light to cross the street. "Don't go looking for it."

And maybe it won't find me. Maybe my neurons have gotten their shit together and don't need the Hazarin anymore.

I got in line at the bakery. The morning manager, Gregory, was behind the counter and he gave me a smile and a wave. I waved back, and I pulled my phone out and powered it up. A zillion phone calls and texts from Delia, Dr. Chen, and Rita awaited.

Bad idea.

I started to put the cell back in my shorts pocket when it chimed a text from Jimmy.

You OK?

Half a dozen smart-ass jokes came to me in response.

I'm great. I love you. <3 I typed instead. He'd never seen *I love you* written to him before. It was so much better than a dumb joke.

Love you, he sent back.

A smile split my face. *I'd* never had a man say that to me before. Out loud or in a text. I had a serious boyfriend in high school, but we parted as friends after graduation. A few hookups at art school but no one I loved. No one who loved me back. And now I loved a man more than I'd ever loved anyone or anything. The other half of my soul.

I looked at Jimmy's words, encased in a cheerful little blue bubble but crossed with the lightning bolts from my cracked screen.

Not whole. We're both a little cracked and imperfect, but I love us.

I took a mental snapshot of Jimmy's text and tucked my phone away.

"How are you today, sweetheart?" Gregory said when it was my turn to order. With his salt-and-pepper beard, he reminded me of my dad.

"What'll it be?"

"Two coffees. One black…"

"The other with, to quote you: a metric crap-ton of cream and sugar." Gregory beamed, then cocked his head. "You okay?"

"Yeah, fine. I'm just sad to leave. Today's our last day in New York." The words pummeled me in the heart.

"That's too bad," he said as he busied himself with my order. "But all good things come to an end, right?"

I swallowed and nodded. "I don't want to go back. I want a little more time."

Gregory didn't hear my whispered words or see me frantically blink the tears away. "Here you go." He handed me a tray with the cups of coffee lodged in the holders. "And here's some extra cream and sugar for you." He piled the packets between the cups.

I reached for the tray and he nodded his head at my arm.

"New tattoo?"

"Oh yeah," I said. "I got it today."

"This morning?" Gregory said, cocking his head. "Pretty early for tattoo guys to be up."

"Oh, no, I mean yesterday."

Was it yesterday? Or the day before?

"What's it say?" He peered over the counter to read it. "*Keep me safe.*"

"It's what Jimmy does."

"You look a little pale," Gregory said, frowning. "You sure you're okay?"

I nodded. "I should go."

"Well, it's been a pleasure, young lady," Gregory said. "Next time you're in town, make sure to pop in."

"I will."

"Thea?"

I blinked. "Yeah?"

Gregory shifted and glanced at the line waiting behind me. "I need to serve the next customer, honey," he said gently.

I glanced behind me, then at the tray of coffee in my hands, still outstretched over the counter. "Oh, right. Sorry. Bye."

Tears threatened again for Gregory suddenly pushing me out the door.

He's busy, that's all. And you're over-emotional.

I took the coffees outside, blinking hard at the sunlight that was relentlessly bright this morning. I went to the corner and hit the button to cross. The light was red, then turned green and a countdown of twenty seconds began to let pedestrians know how much time they had to cross.

"You waiting for a personal invite?" a man said, as he strode past me to cross the street.

I blinked. "What?"

The timer on the crosswalk was down to eight seconds. I hurried across and tried to calm my racing heart.

I lost twelve seconds?

"Not yet," I murmured to myself, sucking in a deep breath. "It can't be this fast."

I crossed the hotel lobby that was mercifully dark and cool. I rode up to the sixteenth floor. No problem. No lost time. Outside our hotel room door, I took a final, steadying breath and keyed inside.

"Here you go," I said, too loud and high-pitched.

I set the coffee tray down on the desk beside the window where Jimmy stood, wearing jeans and nothing else.

"What's wrong?" he asked.

"You mean my gaping at you standing at the window, looking incredibly ripped and manly?"

He crossed his arms, his mouth grim.

I sighed. "You're right. No bad jokes. I... I think I lost a few seconds. Twice. Once at the coffee shop and once crossing the street."

Jimmy's bare shoulders slumped, and his mouth parted, but he drew himself up quickly, mentally bracing himself.

"But I'm okay now," I said. "I need to call Delia. Let her know the plan."

I need to call her before I can't remember what I wanted to say to her.

"I'm going to shower," Jimmy said slowly. "Don't..."

"Don't wander out the door?" I smiled grimly. "I won't. It might've been my imagination. Go. Shower. I'll call my sister."

He nodded and went to the bathroom, probably to take the fastest shower in human existence. I sat on the bed and called Delia.

She answered after one ring. "How are you?"

"I'm okay," I said. "We need to talk."

"When are you coming back? James said it would be today. Are you driving now?"

"You need to rescind the conservatorship or power of attorney or whatever hold you have over me."

"We're not talking about that now. You need to come back. Be safe—"

"I'm safe with Jimmy," I said. "I'm coming back, but I swear to God, you cannot use your power to keep him away from Blue Ridge. Or wherever I end up. You cannot."

She sighed. "Thea, just come back and we'll talk about it."

"We'll talk now. I might not be around to talk to when I get back. Or maybe you'd prefer that?" I closed my eyes. "I'm sorry. I know you're only looking out for me."

"Has it started?" she asked, her voice gentle.

"I don't know. Maybe. Does Dr. Chen know how long I have before I... go back?" I put my hand to my forehead, willing myself not to fall apart yet.

"No," Delia said. "I asked her, but it's been a disaster in Sydney. She's trying to get as much info from Dr. Milton about the patients who survived."

"Keep me posted," I said. The water shut off in the bathroom. "We're heading out soon. But we're not racing back. We're going to stop and have lunch and take our time."

If I have time.

"Look, I think you need to go to a hospital. The patients who had strokes..."

"They were taking the Hazarin weeks ahead of me. I'm driving back with Jimmy and I'm not going to hear anything more about it. It's horrible enough that I'm losing..."

Myself. My consciousness. Everything I built with Jimmy...

"But I mean it," I added quickly, turning my back to the bathroom door. "If you care about me at all, you won't keep Jimmy away from me. I came here of my own free will. Do you hear me? *My own free will.* I love him."

The bathroom door opened, and Jimmy strode out in a towel. Relief so evident on his face, I guessed it was the last time he'd let me out of his sight.

"I gotta go," I said. "I'll call you from the road." I ended the call and tossed my phone on the bed.

"How'd it go?" Jimmy asked, drawing on a pair of boxer briefs.

"I'm afraid she's going to keep you away from me."

"Let her try." He yanked his jeans on.

"She can. You don't work at Blue Ridge anymore. She might ban you from visiting and I won't even know it. Or I will, but it'll be buried where no one can hear me."

Jimmy sat on the bed beside me. "I won't let that happen."

"You can't stop her—"

He kissed me. "I don't want you to worry about it."

I did worry. I knew my Antony would fight Delia for me. He'd fight too hard and she'd have him arrested.

"It's that damn conservatorship," I said. "If I knew she didn't have power over me, I'd feel a lot better about…"

Sliding back into oblivion?

I shuddered.

"There is a way we can take the power away from her," Jimmy said slowly. "I've been thinking about it a lot, actually."

"A coup? A sneak attack? Put eyedrops in her coffee?"

"We get married."

My eyes widened and my heart began to beat so loud, I could hardly hear myself.

"Married?"

"I don't expect… I mean, it's fast. I know that. But legally, she can't keep me from seeing you if I'm your husband."

My husband. Jim Whelan will be my husband. I'll be his wife.

"You'd do that for me?"

"Of course, I would. It doesn't have to be for real," he added quickly. "If you don't want it to be."

I glanced down at the flowered bedspread, tracing a line of a lily. "What if I want it to be?"

A soft inhale of his breath. An exhale. "Do you?"

I nodded and raised my eyes to his. "I think I do, Jimmy. I'm never going to love anyone like I love you. Ever. I know that in my heart. My soul. But you're right. It's so fast and—"

"Then it'll be real." His fingers stroked my cheek. "Because I want that too. I love you, Thea. I'll never love anyone else."

My face crumpled as I kissed him, bittersweet happiness flooding me, followed by reality.

He'd visit me every day. Disrupt his life. Maybe not go back to school.

"Wait, Jimmy, we shouldn't." I held his hand in mine. "It's not fair to you. It's not right to chain you to me like that. We have no idea how long it'll take before Milton makes a new drug. Years, maybe. Or never."

"I don't care how long it takes."

"I know you don't, but I want to be your wife, not your job. I want you to go back to school. I want you to pursue your dreams. I want you to be a speech therapist who does open mic nights on weekends. I want you to have friends you can talk to about me. I want you to have a place you can go on Thanksgiving. I want you to have a *life*."

Jimmy's voice was low and steady, his gaze strong.

"I will. I'm going to take care of you, and I'm going to go out and build a life so you have a place to come back to when they find a new drug. *When.* You're coming back, and I will be here the whole time, waiting and building. I'll never give up on you. I'll never leave you alone in the desert or sealed up in a tomb."

He kissed me urgently, then slid off the bed, to get down on one knee.

"Oh my God," I said. "You're really doing it, aren't you?"

He took my hands, a heartbreaking smile on his face.

"With no shirt on." I was sniffing and laughing now. "That's bribery."

His expression became intense, his dark eyes holding mine.

"Althea Hughes," he said, "will you m-m-marry me?"

His head bowed at hearing the stutter, and he murmured a curse. I lifted his chin in my palm.

"You stutter when it's important," I whispered, my eyes and heart full. "Yes, Jimmy. I'll marry you. Nothing will make me happier than to marry you." A watery laugh burst out of me. "I even have the white dress already."

Now Jimmy laughed, and we kissed again. Happiness defeated fear, and we lingered in the victory as long as we could, kissing and holding each other until it seemed the ticking clock in the room grew louder and louder.

I showered while Jimmy looked up the requirements for getting married in New York State on his phone. I was lacing up the front of my white sundress when I heard him mutter a curse.

"We can get the marriage license today, but there's a twenty-four-hour waiting period for the ceremony."

"Do we need a ceremony?"

"The officiant has to sign the license for it to be legal."

"Okay, so we wait one more day. It's not like I'm in a huge hurry to leave New York and I feel fine."

"You said you lost time at the coffee shop."

"But I haven't since." I moved to him. "Let's get the license and have one more night in the city. We'll drive back to Virginia as newlyweds."

Jimmy put his arms around me. "Delia is going to lose her shit."

"Yes, she is," I said with a laugh. "But after tomorrow, it won't matter what she thinks." I kissed his nose. "You make sure City Hall can take us tomorrow and I'll tell her the change in plans."

"Whatever you say," Jimmy said, kissing me back.

"Spoken like a true husband already."

I called Delia and, incredibly, my call went to voicemail.

Her wedding gift to us.

"Hi, Deel, it's me again. Change of plans. We're staying for one more day. I'm not taking the meds, I promise. I threw them away. But we want to do one more thing before we leave the city. We'll drive out of here tomorrow morning and be back late tomorrow night. Or maybe the morning after that, if it gets late and we need a motel."

Our road trip honeymoon.

"Please don't call me or Jimmy a million times. I'm fine. We'll keep you posted so you don't worry, just like we have been this *entire trip.* Okay?"

I started to end the call, but happiness coursed through my veins now.

"I love you. Bye."

"You didn't tell her the plan," Jimmy said, looking up from his own phone.

"She'll know soon enough. Ready?"

"Let's do it."

I wanted to save the dress for the ceremony, so I changed back into shorts and a tank. Jimmy held my hand, our fingers entwined, as we got in the elevator.

"I love you, baby," he said.

"I love you, too," I said and leaned my cheek on his arm. The elevator doors closed and then opened again immediately to reveal the hotel lobby. Like a magic trick.

I froze.

"You okay?" Jimmy asked.

My head nodded faintly. "Fine."

We crossed the lobby and into sunshine that seemed too bright. The heat wrapped around me too, and I broke out in a sweat. Jimmy let go of my hand to hail a taxi. I glanced around at the bustling corner; the cars driving past and the pedestrians striding toward their destinations. So much noise and color and searing sunlight. I put on my sunglasses, then reached for Jimmy's hand when he came back.

"It's so busy today—oh, God!"

My heart crashed in my chest; Jimmy's face had rearranged itself into blue eyes, a bigger nose, smaller chin... I dropped the stranger's hand and stepped back. "I'm so sorry. I thought you were someone else."

"No problem, lady."

My heart pounded as I turned a slow circle. I wasn't on the corner anymore but down the sidewalk, in the middle of the block.

"Thea!" I spun and Jimmy was hurrying toward me. "What the hell happened?"

"N-Nothing," I said. "I got confused. I'm okay now."

Jimmy rubbed his hand over his mouth, thinking. "I think we should go back."

"No, I'm fine. I'm okay, I promise."

"You're not fine."

"I am. It's really hot out today, that's all. And if we go back to Virginia without being married, Delia will keep you from me."

"Maybe not," he said. "We can talk to her. But I don't think—"

"That I'm of sound mind?" My hands made fists in frustration; my fingernails bit into my palms. "I can do this, Jimmy. Let's not waste any more time."

He hesitated and I could see the conflict warring behind his eyes. He finally nodded and we returned to the corner to grab the cab he'd flagged down. He kept his hand clasped tight to mine and didn't let go. I concentrated on keeping myself present, focusing on the city outside the windows, until the cab pulled over to the corner of Worth and Centre.

"Twenty-two fifty," the cabbie said.

I dug in my backpack. "Here, I've got cash."

"I got it," Jimmy said.

Suddenly I was standing on the sidewalk and he was reaching for my hand again.

"Oh God," I whispered.

"What is it? Fuck, another one?"

I sucked in a shaking breath. "Jimmy, I—"

My phone rang, and I hurried to fish it out of my bag so I wouldn't have to look at his anguished face.

It was Delia.

"What do you mean, you're staying one more day?" she demanded. "You can't stay in New York if you stopped taking the Hazarin. Dr. Chen said Milton's patients who stopped taking it started to regress almost immediately."

I stared out at the city, my hand trembling.

"God, Thea, I'm sorry," Delia said. "I'm so sorry. I don't want to scare you. I can't imagine how hard this is for you…"

Jimmy's brows were drawn, his face pale. "What's she saying?"

"What else did Dr. Chen tell you?" I managed into the phone.

"That you need to come back immediately." Delia's voice was soft now. "Or go to a hospital."

"Absolutely not," I said.

"You need to be in a safe, controlled environment as the Hazarin leaves your system. External stimuli could be too much for you. You need quiet and calm, not a seven-hour road trip in a car with that man."

"I just need a little more time."

I blinked.

"—then let us know where you are, and we can come and get you. Thea? Are you there?"

I missed what she said.

No, it's the phone. Not me. It's not working. It's breaking down and soon it won't work at all.

A muffled sob erupted out of me. Jimmy took the phone out of my shaking hand and wrapped his free arm around me.

"It's Jim," he said. "What's happening?"

I buried my face in his chest as he talked to Delia. I heard him ask if I needed a hospital, and in the next second, I was sitting on a bench with him outside the city offices.

"We're going back to the hotel," he said. "You'll be okay there so long as you stay quiet and calm. They're coming to help us."

"No," I cried. "We need to get married…"

"We can't," Jimmy said, his voice breaking. "Not like this. It's time to go back. Or to a hospital."

"*No*," I said. "No hospital. I'll scream and never stop if I have to spend the last hours or minutes of my waking life in a hospital."

"If anything happens to you, I'll never forgive myself."

I shook my head; the sobs tearing out of me now. "God, I'm so stupid. Why did I throw the pills away? Why? I should have married you first. I should have…"

"No," he said, his voice choked with tears. "You're not stupid. You're braver than anyone I've ever met. You did the right thing."

"It doesn't feel right." I clutched his jacket. "It's happening so fast. Why does it have to happen so fast?"

The terror was beginning to unravel me. I fought for breath as Jimmy began to sing. Low and wavering, his voice rumbled under my ear, "I Will Follow You Into the Dark" as I clung to him.

I concentrated on his voice as he gently got me to my feet, led me to the street corner and into another cab. He sang the entire time, his voice anchoring me to the present, and I clung to it like a drowning woman.

Once in our hotel room, Jimmy helped me take off my shoes and get under the covers. He drew the shades across the windows, then lay down beside me. I curled into him while he stroked my hair. His face was so impossibly beautiful, so full of love and care, and my heart broke that someday soon, when he looked at me like that, I might not know why.

You will. Down in your deepest self, you'll recognize his love for you.

"I love you," I told him, tears spilling across my nose and dampening the pillow. "I love you so much."

"I love you, too," he said, his eyes shining.

"You don't have enough to keep loving me. Only five minutes."

"That's all I need. That's all I ever needed."

He held me until sleep came. I fought it for as long as I could, terrified I'd wake up back in the prison. But exhaustion won out and when I woke again. I knew where I was. I knew *when* I was. Here. I was still here. The dark, quiet room seemed to keep the amnesia at bay, but I could feel the invisible vastness, infinite and claustrophobic at the same time, surrounding me. Suffocating me with emptiness.

Jimmy lay asleep on his back, one arm thrown over his eyes, his mouth drawn down. I wanted to wake him and kiss him and talk to him. Tell him everything. To get in a lifetime's worth of words and thoughts and life in one night. But I was fading away.

I slipped off the bed and went to the desk by the window. It was late afternoon, but with the shades drawn, it was dark. I clicked on the desk lamp, then looked to Jimmy. He slept on.

I took a pen and paper from the hotel stationery and began to write. Three times, I went away and came back to find my pen in midair or scraping an errant line on the paper. I pulled my focus as best as I could and when I was finished, I folded the page in half and crept back across the room, to the wall where Jimmy's guitar case leaned.

I kneeled down and…

Why am I on the floor in front of Jimmy's guitar?

A paper was in my hand, folded in half.

It came back to me in a rush and I grasped onto the consciousness with my entire being.

Stay. Please, stay.

Quietly, carefully, I set the guitar case on the floor and clicked open the little latches. I laid the note on the warm, pale wood of his guitar, shut the case, and set it back against the wall.

Jimmy rolled onto his side when I slipped back into bed. I lay face-to-face with him. My beautiful man. Peaceful in sleep.

My eyes were already falling shut. My thoughts breaking apart and I somehow knew they weren't coming back. I wasn't coming back. Not all of me. Not the way I had been.

"I love you, Jimmy," I whispered.
I leaned in and softly kissed him goodbye.

CHAPTER 37

Jim

A knock came at the door around five in the morning. I opened it to a crowd of people: a hotel security guard, two EMTs, Dr. Chen, and Rita Soto.

Chen went immediately to Thea, who was still asleep. Rita hugged me and I held on tight, happier to see her than I thought possible.

"I wasn't expecting to see you," I said.

"I wasn't expecting to still have a job," she said.

"Is Delia here?"

"She's waiting in Roanoke."

"Miss Hughes?" Dr. Chen said. "Hi. I'm sorry to wake you but—"

"Where's Jimmy?" Thea murmured, sitting up.

I rushed over, Rita following, and took her hand. "I'm right here, baby."

Thea's empty gaze darted between Rita and Dr. Chen. Then the light turned on in her eyes.

"Rita, what are you doing here?"

"Hi, honey." Rita hugged her over the bed.

"What's happening? Why is everyone here in New York?" She

looked at me. "Are we still in New York?"

Fuck, this is already too hard.

"Yeah, we are," I said.

Dr. Chen pulled a penlight from her pocket. "Thea, can I look in your eyes?"

"Why are they here?" Thea demanded with rising panic. "What's happening?"

"It's time to go back, honey," Rita said. "We're going to take care of you—"

"No, please," Thea cried. Her gaze swiveled to me. "I changed my mind. I can't do this. I don't want to go back. Please…" She clutched my shirt. "Please don't make me go back."

Tears stung my own eyes as I held her. "This isn't right," I said to Dr. Chen. "Can't you do something for her?"

"There's nothing else to do," she said, her voice low and heavy. "Not right now. She has to go back."

She has to go back. To Virginia and to that tiny prison.

Thea trembled in my arms, her hands clenching and unclenching my shirt. "Stay with me, Jimmy," she begged. "Please…"

"I won't leave you," I said. "I swear. Not for a second."

"If it makes things easier, I can sedate her," Dr. Chen said, with a nod at Rita.

"No," Thea cried, her hands releasing my shirt. "No. I'm not going back drugged up. I want whatever time is left." Now her tone turned strong and defiant. "Can we have a moment, please?"

She waited until everyone backed away, then put her forehead to mine, letting her hair fall to shield us.

"I'm so fucking scared, Jimmy."

"I know you are, and I hate it," I whispered. "I'd give anything to do this for you."

"Remember for me." Tears spilled down her cheeks and over my fingers, and then she pulled me to her, her voice tremulous. "Remember us… when I can't."

A FIVE-MINUTE LIFE

A hospital van idled in front of the hotel in the early hours as dawn started to break over the horizon. Clutching my hand, Thea walked to the van, stopping once as a blank spot hit. She'd had three more blanks as we packed our hotel room and made our way down.

Dr. Chen and Rita hovered close, but Thea refused to let them examine her in any way.

"It's almost over," she said dully, curling up against me in the van. "You can have me when I'm gone."

Rita shook her head as her eyes met mine. "I'm sorry," she whispered.

I nodded and held Thea tight to me and sang as the van pulled away from the hotel. I sang to Thea or hummed to her the entire ride, as her blank spots grew wider and deeper. Mercifully—and yet frighteningly—she slept for most of the drive.

"She's been sleeping a lot," I said to Dr. Chen. "Is that supposed to happen?"

"It's the Hazarin leaving her system. External stimuli become draining and make the onset of her amnesia more aggressive."

"Will there be another d-d-drug?" I asked, trying to keep my shit together. "Is M-M-Milton going to try again?"

Dr. Chen's expression didn't change, filling me with dread. "Things in Sydney are quite chaotic right now. It's unclear where Dr. Milton or his project's funding stand. However, his procedure is still a breakthrough in medical science and the entire neurological community is rallying around its potential. Obviously, it's the medication—the bonding agent—that requires more work. I think the chances of a new drug coming out are very good. I just can't say when."

Months. Years. Never.

I held Thea tighter.

We arrived at Roanoke Memorial Hospital around three that afternoon. Thea was groggy and sluggish as I carried her inside, refusing the gurney that was brought out. Dr. Chen and her staff directed me to a room, where I laid Thea on the bed.

Her eyes fluttered. "Jimmy?"

I brushed the hair from her face. "Shhh. Rest now, baby."

She fell back to sleep. "Now what happens?" I asked Dr. Chen.

"Now you leave."

Delia stood at the door, her eyes soft when they took in her sister on the bed but glinting coldly when she trained them on me. A man stood behind her—thin, hawkish nose, and with a gentleness that made Delia look even more rigid. Roger Nye, I guessed.

She and I stared each other down.

Inhale. Exhale.

"I want to be with her as much as possible," I said slowly. "Before she goes away again. And after—"

"I think you've *been with her* quite enough. You're done here."

My fists and jaw clenched. "That's not what she wants and you know it."

"Ms. Hughes," Rita said softly. "Don't do this. They're together."

Delia's jaw clenched. "I'll bet."

"I promised to visit her every day," I said. "That's partly why she agreed to stop taking the medication."

"She never would've risked her life over it in the first place, if you hadn't taken her away."

"She *wanted* to go," I said. "She would have gone without me—"

"Can we please take this conversation outside?" Dr. Chen said, ushering us into the hallway. I could hardly stand to leave Thea's side, but I had to make Delia understand without losing my shit or she'd ban me forever.

"Now let's have a friendly discussion," Roger said.

"She broke out of Blue Ridge with your help," Delia said, ignoring him. "She has a tattoo that she's not going to understand when the medication wears off."

"So fucking what?" I hissed. "She's a grown woman who can get a tattoo if she wants one." I sucked in a breath to fight for calm. "We kept in contact. We knew you were worried about her—"

"Don't tell me how I was feeling about my sister. You have no idea how much I love her."

"I love her too," I whisper-shouted. "You're not the only one who loves her, who would fucking die for her. Who wants to protect her—"

"Protect her? You took her away from the safety of medical professionals so you could sleep with her. You took advantage of what she *thought* she felt for you—a big, strong man willing to rescue her from her prison."

My fingers tore through my hair. "You're out of your goddamned mind. You never listened to her. You can't hear her. You never could. Or worse, you fucking could and *chose not to*."

Delia's eyes flared again, and a heavy anchor of dread sank to the bottom of my stomach. I'd fucked up.

"I've listened to you for the last time. Go. Get out of this hospital or I'll have you arrested."

Fuck me to fucking hell.

"Delia, wait. I'm sorry."

"Get. Out."

Two hospital security guards talking down the hallway looked up and grew curious. They started toward us from one direction, and then, like an ancient apparition, Alonzo Waters was at my side.

"Ms. Hughes," he said with a nod of greeting. "Jim. How we doing here, folks?"

"Everything okay?" one of the guards asked.

"We're fine," Roger said. "Aren't we? Let's all remain calm."

"I am perfectly calm," Delia said, never taking her eyes from me.

I glared right back. "I have to be there when she wakes up," I said, my stony voice cracking. "I promised her."

Delia tilted her chin. "That may be, but I'm here now. That's all she needs."

A tsunami of emotion raged in me, my limbs vibrated with it.

Alonzo put his hand on my arm. "Come on, Jim. Let's take a breather. It's been a tough day for all." He looked at Roger. "We'll take some time and regroup when everyone's had a chance to consider what's best for Miss Hughes, yes?"

Roger nodded, and his sympathetic expression kept me from flying into a rage and tearing down the goddamn walls of this place.

And then Delia gave me a parting glance. One I'd seen Doris wear a hundred times. A smug, triumphant look that said I was a fucking moron and she held all the cards and always would.

"I'm not going anywhere," I said. "I promised Thea I'd stay and I'm staying."

"You aren't," Delia said. "Security, please remove him. He's trespassing."

"Fuck you, Delia." I started for Thea's room.

"Now, Jim, hold on," Alonzo said.

"We need to stay calm," Roger put in.

"Get him out of here," Delia cried.

Security grabbed my arms and started dragging me back.

"Let go," I raged, struggling within their grip. "Get the fuck off of me."

"Hey, easy," Alonzo shouted.

All the raised voices became muted and distant as I fought to break free. To get to Thea at any cost. "I swore to her, Delia," I shouted. "Do n-n-not let her wake up alone. You better fucking not let her wake up alone."

I tore one arm free and jabbed my elbow into a guard's face.

"Okay, that's it." The other guard slammed me against the wall. Pain reverberated up my cheek. My arms were wrenched behind me, my shoulder sockets screaming, and then I was on the floor, a knee on my back, pinning me down. They slipped plastic ties around my wrists and hauled me to my feet.

Delia gave a final parting glare at the door of Thea's room.

I said nothing as the security guards dragged me down the hall. I had no words left. I was slammed into a chair in an office. Time slipped out from under me as voices talked around my head. All I could think was that I'd failed Thea. She was going to wake up and I wouldn't be there.

Eventually, someone hauled me to my feet, someone else shoved me out the front doors into the bright sunlight and muggy heat of a waning summer afternoon. It took a second to realize I was free.

"You okay?" Alonzo stood with my duffel bag and guitar case strapped over his shoulders. Rita must have taken them from the hospital van.

"No, I am not okay."

"Dumb question. Let me rephrase: you going to behave yourself now?"

I said nothing.

He knocked a cigarette from a battered pack and offered me one. I shook my head.

"I know nothing's okay right now," he said. "But at least you didn't get yourself arrested." He took a drag from his smoke.

I sank onto a nearby bench. He sat with me.

"I know this is killing you," he said, "but you have to go home now. Get some rest."

"I can't go home." My numbness started to crack. "I can't leave her, Alonzo."

"You have to, Jim. For now. We'll see what happens later."

"Thea doesn't have a later."

Our eyes met, and he sighed. "I know." He put his arm around me, pulling me into his embrace. I resisted at first then sagged against him.

"I got you, son," he said. "I got you."

I closed my eyes and let him carry what I couldn't, at least for a few minutes. After a time, I straightened, wiped my eyes on my shoulder. "My truck is in New York."

"I'll give you a lift."

He drove me to my house in Boones Mill and stayed. We drank a couple of beers and talked the hours away until the exhaustion started to drag at me.

"I'm going back to the hospital," he said, getting to his feet. "Keep your phone handy. If anything changes, I'll let you know."

"Thanks."

We shook hands and then he patted my cheek. "You're a good man, Jim. One of the best."

His words bounced off my failure. I'd broken my promise to Thea. Nothing was good in that.

Despite the fatigue, I lay awake, my nerves lit up. I kept my phone close, waiting, but no messages came. I got up and drank another beer.

Still nothing.

Go down there. Break in. Fight for her.

And get arrested for sure.

I needed to be close to Thea or I'd go fucking crazy. I started to open my guitar case but froze with my thumbs on the latches. I had no desire to play—it would hurt like a motherfucker to be accompanied by the memory of Thea watching as I sang at the open mic in New York, her eyes brilliant and full of love for me.

I picked it up anyway, because I had memories still—even if they stabbed me in the heart. Soon, Thea wouldn't have any. I owed it to her to feel them. To remember.

Remember us… when I can't.

I opened the case.

A piece of folded paper with my name lay on top of the guitar. I unfolded it with shaking hands. *The ArtHouse* was embossed across the top.

Dear Jimmy,

By the time you read this, I'll be gone.

Ha! I'm sorry, that's bad, right? But I'm scared shitless and you know I make bad jokes when I'm scared shitless. I'm scared because I will be gone. Not dead, but it feels that way. Nothingness. No thoughts.

Anyway, I didn't write this letter to talk about me. This is about you. I want you to know some things while I'm away. I want to put them on paper, in black and white, so they don't go anywhere. Like how I wrote my word chains—so my thoughts could stay somewhere when my memory wouldn't let me keep them for myself.

I see you, Jimmy. The real you. The loving, beautiful, honorable, sexy AF man you are. I know you think you haven't done much with your life but that's not true. You help people every day. You help the world even though the world hasn't been kind to you. You could've let your childhood make you bitter. You could've ruined yourself with drugs or alcohol, or become a violent, raging asshole. Because why not? No one gave you a reason not to. But you didn't. Your desire to help burns so strongly, it can't be put out. It's a spark in you that won't ever die. It's the kindness I saw in your eyes every time we met.

You helped people at Blue Ridge. And you helped me. You saved me.

304

A FIVE-MINUTE LIFE

You brought me back to life.

I'm petrified down to my soul to go back. But the only thing that makes it bearable is if I know you're out there, in the world, being what you were born to be, someone who helps kids that had it tough like you. I think if I know you're doing that, I could be happy in whatever way the amnesia lets me.

But no pressure, or anything. :-)

Okay, no more bad jokes. Read this letter and the next time you see me, tell me that you promise. That's all. I might ask what the heck you're talking about, but deep down, I'll know. Somehow, I'll know. And you know that I can know, in my own way. You were the only one who ever did.

I see you, Jimmy Whelan. And I love you. It makes going away again that much harder, but I'll take my love with me if you promise to take yours out into the world and share it with those kids. They need you. They're waiting for you.

And speaking of waiting, don't. Not for me. It's too much to ask. If they ever make another magic pill to wake me up and you're not there, I'll know, deep in the place beneath thought, you are doing what you were put on this earth to do.

I'll remember, and I'll be happy.

All my love to you, forever and always,
                    Thea

The letter crumpled in my fist as the tears spilled over. I tried to hold them back, but it was too much. Too much love for her, too much pain at the thought of what she faced so goddamn bravely. For the first time in ten years, I cried. For her. For me. For the kid who'd been shoved against a fence all his life. I'd been afraid if I faced that pain, I'd drown in it.

Doris and her fucking malevolent taunting were drowned instead.

When I was wrung out, a simple truth remained in the sodden debris: losing Thea was fucking agonizing, but it was better than never having her at all.

But I'm not giving up on her. Not fucking ever.

I grabbed my jacket off the hook and was halfway out the door before I realized I had no truck or motorcycle to get to Roanoke. I whipped out my phone to call an Uber, when it rang in my hand, Rita's name on the display.

"Jim?" she cried. "We need you here."

My heart dropped to my knees. "What's going on?"

"She woke up, and it's bad," Rita said. "She won't stop screaming."

My eyes fell shut. *God, baby. I'm too late.*

"You need to come right now, Jim."

"I'm on my way, but shit, Rita," I said, "Delia's going to have me arrested."

A muffled sound and then to my shock, Delia's tearful voice filled my ear.

"Jim," she whispered. "Please come."

CHAPTER 38

Jim

Alonzo was already on his way back to get me and pulled up to the curb in his old Toyota as I was struggling to get a signal to call an Uber. I climbed in and he drove faster than I expected a sixty-plus-year-old man to drive at night.

It was a twenty-seven-minute drive. We made it in fifteen.

"She's not great," Alonzo said on the way. "Be prepared for that."

We rushed into the hospital and Delia was there, her face half-buried in Roger's chest. She turned her tear-streaked face to me, and my heart plummeted.

I'm too late. She's had a stroke. She's gone.

Delia rose to her feet and calmly walked to me.

"What?" My throat went dry. "What's happened. Tell me…"

Even if it kills me…

"She's hysterical. Terrified. But she's fallen into an exhausted sleep."

My hands clenched even as the relief made my eyes fall shut. "I need to see her…"

"Not yet," Delia said. "Can we talk privately a moment? Roger, Mr. Waters, can you leave us, please?"

"Delia," I said in a low voice. "She's suffering."

She only sat and waited for me to do the same. I moved stiffly to the waiting area and sat in an orange chair across from her.

"I can't do this anymore," she said, a tearful whisper. As if it were a secret she was trying to keep from screaming out loud. "She's suffering and I can't do this anymore."

"Delia—"

"I can't put things back the way they were before the accident. I keep trying and trying. I just want her to be safe."

"So do I, Delia," I said. "And I want her to be happy."

Her face crumpled. "She had so much potential. She was going to be such an amazing artist…"

"She's still an amazing artist," I said. "She's everything she was before. She's not lost. She's still here."

Delia shook her head. "I can't do it anymore. The endless repetition. The questions. The smile on her face when inside she's screaming to get out? I can't stand the thought. It'll drive me crazy to see her like this."

"You don't have to," I said.

"She's my *sister,* of course, I have to."

"You don't," I said. "I'll come every day. She's my life. I'm not going to leave her, not ever. You can go, Delia, but only if you let me be with her. Isn't that why you called me back?"

This is my job interview.

Delia sniffed. "You won't leave her?"

"Never."

"You'll see her every day?"

"Every day."

Hope flared and died in her eyes. "No. You'll get bored. You're a young, handsome man. You'll need things from her she can't give so you'll find them somewhere else."

"I won't. I'll wait for her. However long it takes."

Delia's eyes filled again with a hope she didn't trust. "How do I know you're telling the truth?"

"Because I love her," I said.

No stutter. Speaking the purest truth of my heart to the enemy who'd tried to keep me from Thea, I knew I was free of it forever.

"I love her," I said again. "I will never stop loving her. To the day I die."

Delia stared at me and it seemed as if a shadow lifted from her. "I believe you," she whispered. She turned her glance away, her eyes spilling over, shame coloring her cheeks. "I can... I can get your job back..."

"I don't need it. I made a promise to her about that, too. And I intend to keep it."

She nodded. "I don't know what else to say. I'm so torn apart by guilt and yet so relieved."

"You took care of her for two years," I said. "You can step back. Live your life. That's what she wants for all of us."

She slowly got to her feet. "I'll tell them to let you visit as much as you want. I'll rescind my power of attorney and give it to you." She lifted her head. "I'm trusting you with her life."

"Thank you," I said, easing a low breath. "I'll guard it with mine."

A scream rippled down the hall then. "*Jimmy! Where is Jimmy? God, someone tell me where he is. Jimmy!*"

Thea had woken up. Alone.

"Go," Delia cried. "She needs you."

I was already out of my chair, racing toward her room, my chest caving in at the ragged pain in Thea's voice.

"Get away from me!" Thea screamed. "Fuck off. I don't want it. Where is Jimmy?"

A clattering crash as I entered. Thea knocked a tray to the ground, wrestling against a nurse with a syringe in her hand. All the while Rita tried to calm Thea's flailing arms.

"She doesn't want to be drugged," I barked at the nurse, then bent to take Thea in my arms. "Hey. Hey, I'm here. It's all right."

She looked up at me, full of suspicion.

"It's me," I said. "I'm here now."

Recognition dawned in her eyes and then she collapsed into sobs and clutched me. "It's happening. I can't hold on to anything. It's slipping away."

"I know," I said. "I know, baby."

"Come here," she pleaded.

As I climbed onto the narrow bed, the two nurses left the room, shutting the door softly behind.

Thea sobbed into my chest. My tears dampened her hair. I held her so tight, trying to keep her with me. She was in my arms and slipping away at the same time. And she *knew* it. She was sliding down a steep, unforgiving slope into the blackness of amnesia; desperately scrabbling for purchase, her fingers clutching my shirt.

"Thea," I whispered. "Listen to me. Are you listening?"

"Yes," she said in a faint voice. Sleep was taking her and when she woke up, the amnesia would too.

"I promise," I said, my voice cracking. "I promise."

She pulled away and her smile broke my goddamn heart. "You do?" Then her smile crumpled to confusion. "I wrote… something. Did I? I can't remember…?"

"It's okay, baby. You don't have to."

Her face relaxed into a smile of relief. She kissed me and I savored the taste of her tears and her soft lips before she laid her head down again. "I love you. Jimmy with the kind eyes."

I held her close, struggled to keep my sobs from shuddering through me.

"I love you, Thea," I said. "Sleep now. I'll see you tomorrow, okay? And every day after. I promise."

I blinked awake and the hospital room materialized around me. Thea lay in my arms. Morning light slanted over the bed.

Slowly she stirred and woke. Studied me for a second. Then her face lit up with recognition, heartbreakingly beautiful. "Jimmy."

"Hi, baby," I said, holding back the tears.

The words were barely out of my mouth when an absence seizure paralyzed her. She trembled a few moments, then blinked back into focus.

I saw her.

Beneath the confusion, beneath the amnesia, down in the clear blue depths of her eyes, I saw my Thea.

Her head cocked to the side and her smile faltered.

"How long has it been?"

EPILOGUE 1

Jim

Open mic night was crowded at Haven, as if all of Boones Mill had crammed into the small tavern that Saturday.

Maybe they have, I thought from behind the bar. *The town's small enough.*

Or maybe it was to keep warm. Winter was brutally cold this year, and weathermen said Christmas—a few weeks away—was going to be white.

I poured beers for a couple of regulars, Stan and Kevin. Two middle-aged guys who wore baseball caps and T-shirts no matter what the weather.

"Big night tonight," Kevin said. "You gonna play, Jim?"

"He sure as hell is," Laura said, sidling up to the bar with a tray full of empties. "Gotta give 'em what they want, right, Jim?" She gave me a wink.

I smiled. "We'll see."

"Oh, we will," Laura said. "Guess who's in charge of the playlist tonight?" She jerked two thumbs at herself. "This gal right here. Now I need two shots of Fireball, two Buds and a glass of water. The water's for you. Get your pipes ready."

The guys chuckled as Laura vanished into the crowd.

"Looks like you're playing," Stan said.

"Guess so," I said. "And here I thought this was a bartending gig."

It started out that way. I needed to work nights, and Haven's owner had just lost his best bartender and was desperate. I worked my way up from the shit gigs on Sunday thru Wednesday, to the more lucrative shifts on Thursday through Saturday. It was Laura who caught me singing Pearl Jam's "Black" while taking inventory one day. Despite the poor first impression I'd made on her all those months ago, she demanded I play at the next open mic.

And I'd been playing most open mic nights since.

Laura took the stage. "Heya! How y'all doing tonight? You ready for some music?"

A roll of enthusiastic applause and cheers.

"We're going to start things off with our own secret weapon, Haven's own, Jim Whelan!"

The crowd cheered louder, and Laura shot me an I-told-you-so look from across the room.

"You're up, Jimbo," Kevin said and leaned into Stan. "He's going to quit slinging booze to be a YouTube star, just wait."

"I'm racking up too many student loans to quit," I said. "I'll be working here until I'm sixty."

"Yeah, right." Stan tossed me a cocktail napkin. "Can I have your autograph?"

"Sign his boobs." Kevin laughed.

I chuckled and wiped my hands on a rag. I came from behind the bar to more applause. Laura had my guitar ready.

"Knock 'em dead," she said and left me alone on the stage.

"Hey, all, thanks for coming out," I said, taking a seat and adjusting the mic stand. "I'm going to play one song—"

Boos and catcalls.

"You want me to sing, or do you want to drink?"

They laughed and one guy called out, "When you put it that way…"

I smiled and settled into the guitar, letting my fingers feel the strings. The song I'd chosen wasn't easy.

"This one is from Mumford and Sons," I said. "It's called 'Beloved.'"

A FIVE-MINUTE LIFE

The crowd quieted down, and the room became still. The spotlight over me created a curtain of light. I was alone with Thea. Just her and me. I strummed the guitar and began to play.

For three and a half minutes, I sang to her, asked her to remember I was with her. And she was loved. Always.

The last note wavered and the crowd stayed still and hushed.

I leaned into the mic a final time. "That was for Thea."

Every person in that room lifted their glass or bottle. "For Thea!"

They all knew our story. When people spoke to me now, I talked back. Behind the bar, at the art supply store or just passing on the street. I was a voice in the world, not a mute observer watching from afar.

The crowd erupted into huge applause as I left the stage.

"Brilliant, Jim," Laura said in my ear. "Just beautiful."

I un-looped the guitar strap. "I'm glad because I'm nervous as hell."

"You? Nervous?"

"Not for this," I said and gestured to the crowd.

Laura's eyes widened. "Oh shit, is tomorrow the big day?"

"Day after."

"I knew it was coming up. So exciting and just in time for Christmas." She gave me a short hug. "I'm so happy for you, Jim. We all are."

"Thanks, Laura," I said. "It helps. It helps a lot."

Having someone—a lot of someones—on our side, even if Thea never knew it, had gotten me through many long days. But then again, if she'd taught me anything, it was you didn't have to know something was real in order to feel it.

The following morning, I drove over to Roanoke Speech, Language, and Learning Services. Jason Taylor was already in the therapy room, waiting for me. This was Sunday, so the room was empty. But the tenacious Jason wanted to put in as many hours of therapy as possible, and I needed as many practical hours as I could get for my clinical requirements at Roanoke University. So we made our own schedule.

"Where's your mom?" I said, shaking out of my coat and hat and taking a seat across from him.

Jason grabbed his iPad off the table and typed, *Getting coffee*

"Cool. You ready to start?"

He shook his head and looked away. His blond hair was neatly brushed, and he wore nice pants and a shirt. As if he'd come back from church. Jason was always neat and put together. He'd once told me it was so that no one could find some other reason to make fun of him.

I leaned over the table, arms folded. "What's up, buddy?"

He looked at me warily, then his ten-year-old fingers flew over the iPad with the agility of an adult who'd been typing his whole life.

Mom says this program is almost done

"That's true. My semester is almost over."

Jason's single mother qualified for this program between the speech center and the university. It allowed for free therapy by students, like me, who were still in training.

She said U won't be my therapist anymore.

His own arms crossed, bracing himself for my answer.

"Yeah, it's possible they'll assign someone else to you," I said. "Someone more qualified."

He shook his head and typed vigorously.

I don't want anyone else

I smiled gently. "Me neither, buddy. But I'm your starter-pack. You're doing so well, they want to level you up."

He shook his head slowly as he typed: *Not doing well*

"Yeah, you are, Jase. I promise. But tell you what, why don't we talk to your mom about meeting up once or twice a week anyway."

His eyes lit up. "Rrrrrrreally?"

"Sure, man," I said, my throat thick.

Jason was an only child. No friends. His disfluency was so severe, no one had the patience to talk to him. Except the assholes, naturally. It killed me to imagine this sweet, smart kid wandering the playground at school alone at every recess, just hoping to get through the day without being made to feel like shit. Never mind making a friend.

"Yeah," I said again. "We can keep working together or we can just hang out. You like basketball, right?"

He nodded.

"We'll shoot some hoops. If that's okay with your mom."

"If what's okay with me?"

A FIVE-MINUTE LIFE

Linda Taylor approached with two coffees and handed one to me. Jason started to type, but I reached over and stilled his hand.

"Tell her," I said gently. "Remember what we talked about last week?"

Jason reluctantly let go of his iPad because he trusted me. It had taken months to earn that trust, and I'd be goddamned if I let anything happen to it.

Jason made a deep inhale.

"Just let it flow on the breath," I said in a low voice. "Don't force it."

"Jim waaaaaaaaants to h-h-haaaaang out w-w-with mmmmmmmeee."

"My God," Linda said. "That sounded so good, baby!"

I beamed. "Great job, man."

Jason shrugged off the praise. He'd made huge strides, but it wasn't enough for him. He seized the iPad and typed: *Says we can play basketball sometimes*

"If they reassign him to a new therapist," I said to Linda. "Or even if they don't."

"You'd do that?" Linda's eyes filled as she sat beside her son.

"No brainer," I said, shooting a grin at Jason. "He's a great kid."

"Thank you," Linda said. "I know he is, but it's nice to hear from someone else. For both of us."

Then her eyes widened. "Wait... Tomorrow's the day, right?"

I nodded, my heartbeat taking off at the mention. "Yeah, it is." I looked to Jason. "We might have to cancel this week's appointment, buddy."

Jason rolled his eyes with a smirk and tapped his iPad: *Because of your GIRLFRIEND???*

"Look at that," I said turning the iPad to Linda. "I didn't teach him to be a smart-ass. Did you teach him to be a smart-ass?"

Linda gave her son a look, but Jase looked supremely proud of himself. He loved when I swore around him. It made him feel grown up.

"You'll let us know how it goes?" she said.

Perfectly. It has to go perfectly.

"I will," I said.

I finished the session with Jason, working with him on breathing and relaxation. Like mine, Jason's stutter was psychological, a result of his father's abuse. Linda escaped the marriage two years ago, but Jason's trauma remained. He struggled with elongation of vowel sounds and blocking of consonants. He had a long road ahead of him, but I knew he'd find his breakthrough. I couldn't give it to him, I could only tell him it was there.

In the parking lot, I gave him a hug and ruffled his hair. "Send me all your good mojo, okay. I'm nervous."

Slash, scared shitless.

"I h-h-hope she'll beeeeeee o-o-okay," he said.

"Thanks, Jase. I hope so too."

Linda gave me a wave and they drove off. I hurried to my truck and cranked up the heat, then drove to Blue Ridge Sanitarium.

"Hey, Jim," Melanie said from the front desk.

She'd replaced Jules awhile back when Mr. Webb was found wandering toward the security checkpoint. Jules had been on an illicit smoke break.

"Hey, Mel."

I signed in on the Visitor's Log clipboard. If I were to flip through the pages, my name would appear on every single one. For the last five hundred and forty-seven days.

Eighteen months.

Thea had been back in her prison for eighteen months. Tomorrow morning, Dr. Milton and Dr. Chen were going to try again to break her free.

They'd found the issue with Hazarin—an enzyme that caused blood clots, which led to stroke. The new drug—Laparin—had been tested for months and deemed safe, but there was no round of test subjects ahead of Thea this time. She'd be in the first group to trial it.

Because I had power of attorney over her healthcare decisions, it was up to me whether she took the new drug or not.

"Yes," I'd told Dr. Chen immediately, wondering how it was possible to feel incredible elation and heart-stopping fear at the exact same time. "Yes, give it to her. It's what she'd want."

Rounds of tests commenced. Thea's MRI and PET scans all came back clear. Dr. Milton flew in from Sydney and was ready to perform his procedure again, bonding the new drug and the stem cells. Erect a new bridge between Thea and her memories.

I was terrified but Thea was ready.

She's suffered enough.

Alonzo stood outside the door to the rec room, chatting with Anna and Rita.

"Hey," I said addressing the people I loved most, which I supposed made them my family.

"How you holding up?" Alonzo said. "One more day to get through. Lord, I'm too old for this kind of stress."

Rita gave me a hug. "It's going to work, and it's going to last," she said. "I can feel it."

I didn't let myself hope the way she did, out loud. If I let my hope out into the world, it might get beat up and come back mangled and bleeding. I kept it to myself, safe.

Anna pursed her lips. "Let's remain professional, please," she said, then smoothed her uniform that didn't need smoothing. "Though, honestly, I'm quite excited myself."

"Yeah, you look it," Alonzo said, giving me a wink. "*Bursting* with excitement."

"Oh, hush." Anna turned to me. "When are Ms. Delia and her husband expected to arrive?"

"In a few days," I said. "I wanted time alone with Thea after the procedure, no matter what happens."

"Good call," Rita said. "When Thea opens her eyes tomorrow morning, the first person she should see is you."

My chest tightened. "Goddammit, Rita."

"I know," she said, "but I'm just so happy. For both of you."

"Whatever happens," Alonzo said, "we're here for you. And her."

"Jesus, you too?" I said with a laugh choked with tears.

Alonzo blinked hard, laughing, before he slapped me on the back. "Christ, that's enough out of us. Go to your girl."

Thea stood at her easel, earbuds in, her jeans and bright yellow top smattered with paint despite the smock covering them. Hips swaying side to side, she hummed as she recreated a view of New York City from a high window; the lights strewn across the darkened cityscape like stars.

The view from our hotel room at the ArtHouse.

I moved close so Thea could see me from her peripheral vision.

"Jimmy…" She had enough time to smile and pull the earbuds from her ears before the absence seizure hit. I stood still until it passed, then she threw her arms around me.

"You're here," she said into my neck. "How long has it been?"

"Eighteen months," I said.

The script was altered slightly. Her prison had undergone slight improvements. As before, Thea remembered there'd been an accident, but now her parents' death was connected to the event. She knew they were gone and never slipped and asked when they were coming. She knew her sister lived far away and visited sometimes. She remembered Rita. She stopped saying she was an Egyptologist or etymologist. And she wasn't freaked out or confused about the tattoo on her arm. Rita had told me it somehow kept Thea grounded from being overwhelmed with sudden grief. That looking at it brought her relief. I kept mine hidden from Thea after that, so she wouldn't be confused and lose that peace.

The best gift of all was that I didn't need to wear a nametag or re-introduce myself. She remembered me. She remembered she loved me.

But *How long has it been?* stayed, and answering *sixteen… seventeen… eighteen months,* hurt like hell.

"Are the doctors working on my case?" she asked.

"They are," I said, and it was the truth. "In fact, they're going to try again."

She frowned. "Again?"

Eighteen months and I still made dumb mistakes. The word *again* had no meaning to Thea.

"They're going to perform a procedure on you," I said. "And give you some medicine to make you better."

I hated speaking to her like she was a child, but once, when a reset hit, I told her she wasn't coming awake for the first time, but she'd been awake and aware all her life. It spun her into a loop of panic and hysterics. Her amnesia was like staring into a hall of mirrors, her reflection multiplying itself by infinity with no way out, and I'd stupidly tried to tell her the door was right in front of her.

I never tried to explain it again.

But Dr. Milton's procedure *was* the door out, and I never stopped telling Thea about it. Again and again, every day—every five minutes—for the last two weeks. Since Milton called Dr. Chen with the news.

"It'll make me better?" she asked.

"Yeah, baby, it will."

It has to.

She hugged me tight, as happy to hear it as she was every other time. She didn't need to know the details about the procedure, only that it was coming. Thea was still in there, and she knew, down deep, that "being better" meant freedom.

"When is this procedure?" she asked. "Soon?"

When, soon, and *tomorrow morning* were all tricky words that had no real meaning for her either, but I told her the truth. "Tomorrow morning."

"Should I be scared?"

"No," I said. *Leave that to me.* "Everything's going to work out how it should."

Thea smiled and kissed me again. A peck on the lips was all I let her do. It didn't feel right to kiss her deeply. If a reset hit in the middle, she'd be terrified. I never wanted our kissing to be tainted by fear.

"I love this," I said, nodding at her painting. "It's fucking incredible."

"Thanks. I've never been to New York City, so I'm not sure where this image is coming from. But it's with me. Always. I've probably seen pictures of it."

I smiled. "Probably."

"Is Delia coming?"

"Not today," I said. "But she'll be here soon. You want to get some fresh air?"

Rita brought Thea her winter coat—a colorful wool coat Thea said was "fuchsia." A reset hit. She suffered an absence seizure, and then she threw her arms around my neck.

"Jimmy, you're here. How long has it been?"

We started over from the top. The time, the questions, until we arrived back to where we left off.

"Want to go for a walk?" I asked.

"I'd love to."

She linked her arm in mine and we strolled along the grounds, having our same conversation, over and over, every five minutes. I told her again the doctors were going to help her, and she was radiant under the heavy, gray sky. Her cheeks turned pink with cold and snowflakes drifted into her hair as the first snow of the season began.

"It's so beautiful," Thea said, holding her hand out to catch the flakes.

I looked down at her. "So beautiful."

My heart ached at the déjà vu—Thea looked like this at last year's first snow. She caught the flakes on her fingers and said how beautiful it was.

She's still smiling. Despite day after day of that prison, she has hope. She always has.

"I love you," I said, pulling her to me.

"I love you too. Jimmy with the kind eyes."

She rested her cheek on my shoulder and watched the snow come down.

"The doctors are going to give you a procedure, Thea," I said, my cheek against her hair. "They think it's going to make you better."

Excitement rippled through her. "Will it?"

I closed my eyes. "I hope so, baby."

She was quiet for a moment, then asked, "Will you be there?"

I lifted my head. She'd never asked me that before. "Yes. When you wake up, I'll be right there. I promise."

She cocked her head at me, a funny smile on her lips.

"What's that look for?" I asked, brushing a lock of hair from her cheek.

"I've heard you say that before. That you promise," she said. "I remember."

I stared. "You do?"

She nodded, her eyes impossibly blue, and her smile serene. "It was in a dream."

"Oh." My shoulders fell. *A dream. Not memory.*

But for Thea—trapped in the amnesia—a dream was the only memory she had.

She brushed her fingertips over my chin. "The best dream I ever had. You and I were together, and we were happy."

I smiled and held her close. "We were," I murmured into her hair.

A FIVE-MINUTE LIFE

"We are."

No matter what happens tomorrow, we were happy.
We had the time of our lives.

EPILOGUE II

Thea

I open my eyes for the first time…

"I cannot believe this is real," I said. "It's a dream and I'm going to wake up at any second."

"I can believe it," Jimmy said, slipping his arms around my middle and kissing my neck. "You're a genius. You deserve this."

I held the arms holding me and stared around the darkened gallery. It took up an entire wing at the Richmond Museum of Modern Art and was devoted solely to my exhibit. It opened tonight with a gala party thrown by the curator. Art critics called my paintings, "an extraordinary visual journey through the life of the world's second-worst case of amnesia."

Recovered case of amnesia.

I'd been on Dr. Milton's Laparin for the last ten years, and aside from one difficult side-effect, I'd stay on it for the rest of my life. It kept me *in* my life.

"Are you ready?" Jimmy asked. "They're opening soon."

"I want a few more seconds alone with you."

"That works for me. You look stunning." He bent to kiss my collarbone, across the scar there. "Was this dress expensive?"

"Why do you ask? Don't you want your wife to look pretty on her big night?"

"Just determining how careful I have to be when I tear it off you later."

I leaned into his mouth along my neck. "You always know exactly what to say to turn me into a puddle at your feet. And the tuxedo isn't fair. Excessive, really."

I'd hardly grown used to how handsome he was in the suits he wore to work meetings. But a tux?

Have mercy on my ovaries...

I grazed my fingers through his hair, admiring my confident, brilliant husband. Jim Whelan, SLP. He'd gotten his degree as a speech-language pathologist and now, at thirty-five years old, he ran his own practice in Roanoke. Every day, he helped children who'd been like him find their voice again.

My love for him deepened to something I hadn't thought possible. My Jimmy, who never left my side during eighteen months of post-Hazarin amnesia. Through every hardship since... and every unimaginable joy.

"I'm so proud you're my husband," I said. "I'm the luckiest woman in the world."

He gave a small, confused smile. "Are you okay? I mean, I know this is a lot," he said, glancing around the space, "but for the last few days you've been a little..."

"Emotionally all over the place?"

He pretended to think. "Yes."

I laughed. "I'm just happy. It's not every day a gal gets everything she could ever want."

He smiled and kissed me. "I know the feeling."

"Jimmy..." Inhale. Exhale. "I'm—"

"Daddy!"

Our two-year-old son, Jack, ran full speed at us in his little suit. Jim bent to scoop him up. I watched my husband hold our son—setting him securely on his hip, his arm holding him protectively, and my heart was full. Overflowing.

"Hey, little man," Jimmy said. "How'd you escape?"

"With my help, as usual. I tried to contain him, but he's done with us," Rita said. She slowed her steps for Alonzo, beside her with his cane he used for the arthritis in his knees. "He wanted Mommy and Daddy."

"He's a troublemaker, that Jack," Alonzo said. "Just like his father."

"There's quite a crowd in the lobby," Rita said. Ten years had added a few lines around her smile. "This is so exciting, Thea. It feels like a movie premiere."

"You look lovely, my dear," Alonzo said, kissing my cheek. "Your art is going to blow them away. Though some of us knew that a long time ago."

"Mama," Jack said, reaching for a lock of my hair.

"Doesn't Mommy look pretty?" Jim asked.

Jack bobbed his head. "Preee."

I took his little fingers and kissed them. "Love you, baby boy."

Decreased fertility was Laparin's lone side-effect, but a big one. It took two and a half years of IVF treatments to give us a viable embryo, which gave us Jack Whelan. The spitting image of his father—sturdy, strong nose, broad mouth, and dark hair. But his eyes were blue, like mine. Rita said he'd grow up to be a lady-killer, but I knew with a father like Jim, he'd grow up to be an honorable man who treated women with the same respect and consideration Jim showed me since the moment we met.

An assistant from the museum hurried over. "Ms. Whelan? They're ready to open now and Ms. Takamura wants to introduce you to some people."

Eme Takamura was my agent. She'd made it her life's mission to find unknown artists with unique histories and give them a showcase for their talents. Jimmy and I took a trip to Carnegie-Melon to view the stunning glasswork of one of her former clients, a young man who'd passed away shortly after creating his masterpiece.

"He had something real to say about life," Eme had told me. "I feel the same when I look at your paintings."

That was all it took to know I could trust her with my work.

And now the night had arrived. I heaved a breath.

"Well?" I asked the small group. "I guess this is it. Give Mommy a kiss, Jack?"

Jack put his wet little mouth on my cheek. Jim leaned over and kissed me too.

"I love you," I said, lingering in his kiss.

"I love you so much," he said. "God, baby, so much." He grinned. "I've been shot with cupid's sparrow."

I laughed and put my hand over my heart. During my eighteen months of amnesia, Jim had watched all nine seasons of *The Office*. Four times.

"Go," he said. "They're waiting for you to knock 'em dead."

Eme and I gave a guided tour of the exhibit to a group of art aficionados, critics, dealers, and press. Around us, the general public perused at their leisure while attendants circulated with little trays of champagne and hors d'oeuvres.

"This first room is called 'Desert Spring,'" Eme said. "The artist ready to bloom into her craft."

I leaned into Eme. "Bloom into my craft?"

"Just go with it," she murmured back.

"Desert Spring" featured my work from art school—the pyramids and desert scenes, the Nile and the Sphinx.

Eme led us into the next area, called "Scream." The drawings of Egypt now scratched out of word chains. My cries for help. There weren't many—only those Jimmy and Dr. Chen had saved in the weeks before the first stem cell procedure.

I overheard murmurs of awe and muffled talk as the group craned their necks to read the chains of tiny, precise script. I cocked my head to read one.

Carried buried bury born torn mourn moan loan alone lone lonely lonely lonely

My skin broke out in gooseflesh. It'd been so lonely in the amnesia, but those days were harder to remember and fading away with every passing moment with Jimmy and Jack.

"Next, we have 'Turning Point,'" Eme said.

Only one painting was displayed here: the ruined canvas of New York City. A bouquet of skyscrapers sprouting out of Central Park and black swaths of paint slapped across the blue sky.

I shivered again and said a silent prayer for anyone else who'd suffered assault or abuse or bullying—little boys on playgrounds or women trapped in their own beds—who felt they didn't have a voice left.

I see you, I thought and knew Jimmy did too. He'd made it his life's purpose to give kids their voices back.

"Thea?"

I blinked out of my thoughts.

Then came "Transition." Here were the Jackson Pollock-like paintings from after the first procedure. A different kind of cry for help lay in the composition. To be free to experience the world and all its colors. Not be contained to a single canvas.

A dimly lit alcove housed the paintings I made after I went back into the amnesia. All the paintings of New York at night as seen from the Arthouse Hotel. A few other canvases showing Times Square in geometric planes of color. Abstract, like photographic flares.

"This," Eme said dramatically, "is called 'Dreamscape.'"

I grinned. "Subtle."

"Shh, they love it."

Finally, the last room, brightly lit and the most colorful, was hung with the paintings I made after the second procedure. My best work from the last ten years. No more vast deserts or cityscapes, these canvases were all scenes from our little home in Boones Mill.

Jimmy on a Saturday morning, sleeping with our infant son on his chest. The two of them with their mouths open in identical expressions.

Our living room coffee table cluttered with Jack's toys and my sketches.

Jimmy's guitar in the corner of a room, the light streaming in from the window. Always with sunlight pouring in from every window.

The tour concluded, and the group murmured and perused and snapped photos.

"Do you hear that?" Eme said. "That's the sound of your art reaching them and making them want it to reach even further. Well done, my dear. Not that I'm surprised. I have an eye for these things."

"Thank you, Eme. For everything."

She beamed and took two flutes of champagne off a passing tray. "Cheers, darling." We clinked glasses, and she took a sip. "Now go find your people while I talk business with mine."

I took my glass and rejoined Jimmy, still holding Jack, who stood talking with Delia and Roger.

I'd long since forgiven my sister. Jimmy took a little bit longer, but he'd come around. Still, the residual guilt was etched into the lines of Delia's face. Evident in her tentative approach and the stiff peck on my cheek.

"It's incredible," she said. "I'm so proud of you. And I know Mom and Dad would be too."

"Thanks, Deel," I said. "I think so too. Roger, thanks for coming."

"Wouldn't miss it," he said, a little absently.

"How's the business in Vancouver?"

He didn't answer. He turned in a small circle, hands in his pockets, staring at the paintings.

"Roger, honey," Delia said mildly. "My sister asked you a question."

"Hm? Oh. Sorry, I'm just... It's mesmerizing. Just... incredible. The evolution of it... It's as if different people painted them at the different stages, yet it's entirely unified."

"Wow, Roger." I pecked him on the cheek and whispered, "Thank you so much."

"It's all true. Your work is—"

"I meant for making my sister happy." I itched to joke that it was a Herculean task, but I was too full of happiness myself to make bad jokes.

"Jack's getting so big," Delia said. By choice, she'd never had children of her own, but I sometimes wondered if she regretted it. Especially when she was looking at Jack with such longing.

"Here." I handed Jimmy my champagne and lifted Jack out of his arms to pass him to Delia. "Would you and Roger watch this little bugger? I need to talk to my handsome husband for a sec."

Delia bounced Jack on her hip. "You want to see Mommy's paintings? Come on. Uncle Roger and I will show you our favorites."

She put Jack down and held his hand as they walked toward the "Transition" display. Only a few steps, then Jack was reaching arms up to Roger, wanting to be carried again.

"We made him," I said to Jimmy.

"Yeah, we did," Jim said. "He's a little miracle."

I nodded, my heart crashing against my chest. "Our life has been filled with miracles."

"It has." Jimmy tried to hand me the champagne. "To you, baby.

They love it, don't they?"

"They do. But I don't want the booze." I sucked in a breath. "Or, moreover, I can't have it."

"Why not?" he asked and then stared, his eyes widening.

I nodded, tears springing to my eyes that I could finally say the words. "I'm pregnant."

He still didn't move. "What?"

I bit back a laugh at his dumbfounded expression. "I'm going to have another baby."

Jimmy's brows came together, the struggle of having Jack passing behind his eyes. The glass in his hand shook, and I took it and set it down before he dropped it.

"How…?" He swallowed. "How did that happen?"

"Well, when a man and a woman love each other very much, the man—you, in this case—puts his enormous penis inside the woman—"

Jimmy shook his head, caught halfway between laughter and shock. "Wait, wait, wait. Stop. Go back. Say it again."

"I'm pregnant, honey."

"But *how*? And you can skip the X-rated biology lesson."

"I don't know how," I said. "They said it was next to impossible."

"*Next to* impossible."

"That probably wasn't the official medical diagnosis, but yes… Not impossible."

He stared. "I just… I can't believe it."

"Me neither. Although, now that I think about it… Remember that afternoon you came home from work? Jack was napping, and you stormed into the house with hardly a word and took me right then and there against the kitchen counter?" Pleasant shivers danced all over me. "God, just thinking about it…"

"I remember…" Jim said. "One of my better afternoons."

"The best, it turns out."

Jimmy's brows furrowed, and he held my gaze intently, no more jokes. "You're really pregnant?"

"Eight weeks. Are you happy?"

"I'm somewhere beyond happy. But…"

"I know. I'm scared too. But I have a feeling, down deep, she's going to be okay."

"She?"

"I think so," I said. "I think I'm having your baby girl."

Jim stared a moment longer, then pulled me to him, holding me with his strong arms. An embrace that never failed to tell me I was protected, safe, and loved. So much love.

"God, Thea," he whispered against my hair.

I pulled away and held his strong jaw in my hand. "You gave my life back to me. Everything I have is because of you."

"I can say the same, Thea. You gave me my life back when I'd stopped living it."

He kissed me softly, and I leaned my head on his shoulder as we watched our son horse around with my sister—the last of my real family, who I'd love forever, no matter what. Because it felt better to rebuild bridges than it did to watch them burn.

Jimmy slipped his arms around me, his hand sliding over my belly.

"Love you," he breathed into me. "So much."

"Love you too," I said, giving it back. "So much."

I was infused with it, so much love for my Jimmy and this life he and I had built, five minutes at a time.

THE END

AUTHOR'S NOTE

The science of amnesia in this book is the result of my research of the condition itself, as well as extensive study of the current world's worst case. I have taken first-hand accounts of what his life is like and applied it to Thea Hughes in order to be as accurate as possible. But I have also taken liberties of the imagination to craft a fictional story. Therefore, the brain science of amnesia is as accurate as can be for a lay person such as myself, while Thea's five-minute reality, the medical procedures, and medicine featured in this book are entirely a work of fiction, as is Blue Ridge Sanitarium, which should not be viewed as the standard of care at any facility in Virginia or elsewhere. This book is a marriage of reality and fantasy and should not be taken as absolute medical truth, even though I endeavored to make it feel as real as possible. In short, I'm not a neurosurgeon, though I sometimes play one on TV. ;)

ACKNOWLEDGEMENTS

This book would not exist without the time, love, and support of a great many amazing people.

To my incredible beta team: Robin Hill, Joy Kriebel-Sadowski, Johanna Louise Weightman, Grey Ditto, Desiree Ketchum, Joanne Ragona, Terri Potts (*The Office*, *GoT*, and Jonathan are for you) and Shannon Mummey. Your feedback has been invaluable, and I love and appreciate you all so much.

To my author loves, who are always there with their support, love, midnight texts, and unvarnished opinions—Kate Stewart and Kennedy Ryan; I love you both so much. Thank you. #UDunite #TeamHeavy #curbside

To my tech team, Melissa Panio-Petersen for being everything and everyone to me, always.
Suanne Laqueur for being the editor of every author's dreams, and the friend of a thousand lifetimes.
Robin Hill for all the reasons and a hundred more I haven't thought of yet. Love you so much.

Angela Shockley, formatter extraordinaire who puts up with my crazy schedule and makes my books look pretty on the inside and sacrifices her time and sleep to do it. Love you.

Marla Selkow Esposito for her eagle eyes and who also accommodated me with grace and professionalism. You're stuck with me now forever, lady!

Grey Ditto for fixing some major medical boo-boos (though any lingering boo-boos are mine) and for being my on-call nurse out of the endless generosity of her heart. Love you.

To the readers and bloggers of this community—you ARE this community, and I would not be able to do what I do if not for you. Thank you for being there—in our fictional worlds and outside of them, with so much support and love. You are so appreciated in all that you do.

And to my husband whose belief in me is unwavering. He is the reason I keep writing, even still. I love you, honey.

Thank you all and much love.

SNEAK PEEK

Someday, Someday
A brand-new M/M emotional standalone, coming Fall 2019
Add to Goodreads TBR here:
https://www.goodreads.com/book/show/41450826-someday-someday

MORE FROM EMMA SCOTT

Bring Down the Stars (Beautiful Hearts Book 1)
*I was not expecting to feel so lost. So emotional. So desperately in love
with EVERYONE AND EVERYTHING about this novel." -Angie &
Jessica's Dreamy Reads*

Amazon: https://amzn.to/2Mra71M

Long Live the Beautiful Hearts (Beautiful Hearts Book 2)
*"***INFINITE STARS*** BEAUTIFUL. EXQUISITE. LITERARY
PERFECTION!!" --Patty Belongs to....Top Goodreads Reviewer*

Amazon: https://amzn.to/2pWynLv

In Harmony
"I am irrevocably in love with IN HARMONY." —**Katy Regnery,**
New York Times **Bestselling Author**
"Told through Shakespeare's masterful Hamlet in the era of #metoo, In
Harmony is a deeply moving and brutally honest story of survival after
shattering, of life after feeling dead inside. If you've ever been a victim

of abuse or assault, this book speaks directly to you. This is a 6 star and LIFETIME READ!!!--**Karen, Bookalicious Babes Blog**

Amazon: http://amzn.to/2DyByBK

Forever Right Now
You're a tornado, Darlene. I'm swept up.

"Forever Right Now is full of heart and soul--rarely does a book impact me like this one did. Emma Scott has a new forever fan in me." --*New York Times* bestselling author of *Archer's Voice,* **Mia Sheridan**

Amazon: http://amzn.to/2gA9ktr

How to Save a Life (Dreamcatcher #1)
Let's do something really crazy and trust each other.

"You're in for a roller coaster of emotions and a story that will grip you from the beginning to the very end. This is a MUST READ..."— **Book Boyfriend Blog**

Amazon: http://amzn.to/2pMgygR
Audible: http://amzn.to/2r20z0R

Full Tilt
I would love you forever, if I only had the chance…

"Full of life, love and glorious feels."—**New York Daily News, Top Ten Hottest Reads of 2016**

Amazon: http://amzn.to/2o1aK1o
Audible: http://amzn.to/2o8A7ST

All In (Full Tilt #2)
Love has no limits…

"A masterpiece!" –**AC Book Blog**

Amazon: http://amzn.to/2cBvM26
Audible: http://amzn.to/2nUprDQ

Never miss a new release or sale!

Subscribe to Emma's super cute, non-spammy newsletter:
http://bit.ly/2nTGLf6
Follow me on Bookbub: http://bit.ly/2EooYS8
Follow me on Goodreads: http://bit.ly/1Oxcuqn
Follow me on Amazon: http://amzn.to/2FilFA3